OOSTERBEEK

by

Laurence Power

Bloomington, IN  Milton Keynes, UK

AuthorHouse™
1663 Liberty Drive, Suite 200
Bloomington, IN 47403
www.authorhouse.com
Phone: 1-800-839-8640

AuthorHouse™ *UK Ltd.*
500 Avebury Boulevard
Central Milton Keynes, MK9 2BE
www.authorhouse.co.uk
Phone: 08001974150

© 2006 Laurence Power. All rights reserved.

No part of this book may be reproduced, stored in a retrieval system, or transmitted by any means without the written permission of the author.

First published by AuthorHouse 7/5/2006

ISBN: 1-4259-2786-6 (sc)

Printed in the United States of America
Bloomington, Indiana

This book is printed on acid-free paper.

For three little ladies
Lauren, Liz and Lea

Chapter One

Mam put down her sewing. She gave each of us, in turn, a severe look over her reading glasses.

"Your father hasn't come home so I want quiet from the lot of you!"

"Where is he?" I asked.

"I don't want to hear one word from any of the three of you when he does come."

She emptied a jar of buttons on to the tabletop and selected one to match the others on Dad's Sunday jacket. She always had buttons that matched.

"I'm hungry," said Gerrit.

We ignored him. Dad was into one of his prolonged silent spells. His longest was four days during the previous year, when Grandfather took ill and had to be rushed to hospital. Dad didn't say a word until Grandfather had passed away, then he talked non-stop for days, until the funeral was over. Currently he hadn't spoken for five days. Mam was worried too but wasn't telling us why. I guessed that it was the same as what every adult was worried about then, but I obeyed her order for silence.

"I'm hungry," Gerrit said again.

Gerrit's belly was always his biggest concern. Though only six years old, his obsession with food was usually the family joke, but not this evening. We never sat down for our evening meal without Dad. You could set the clock by my parents. Every evening we would sit down to the table to the sound of the Hilversum pips. Hilversum was where all radio broadcasts came from. In the hall the cuckoo clock chimed at exactly the same time.

"It's after seven now," Antje said.

"I know the time, Antje love," Mam said.

She never spoke crossly to Antje, partly because of Antje's poor health, which was rarely less than desperate.

The knob on the side door rattled, every head turned with a grateful sigh of relief.

"It's only me. I've come to milk my goats and collect the eggs."

Nana Nellie had arrived. For reasons known only to her, my father's mother took to calling them 'my goats' since Grandfather Frank had died. She came round every evening to milk the animals, and take the milk for cheese-making. She dressed like every grandmother back then, black from the neck down with a long skirt to within inches of her ankles. Her fine lace collars were for Saturday trips into the city and her Sunday church visits. Jaunty, vividly coloured hats were her only concession to fashion trends. She lived just a five-minute walk away in a flat over Huizens' Ladies Wear.

"Not home yet," she said, more a statement than a question.

"No."

"What's the latest?"

"You know as much as I do," my mother said.

"Everyone has a different story, Corrie. The news can't be good."

"We'll wait and see."

We heard another rattle at the side door. At last Dad was home with his bicycle. As he entered, Mam gave us another warning look. One glance at his grim face told us that nothing had changed since morning. Without a word, he sat at the table. Antje and I glanced at each other.

"Have you eaten a thing today?" Mam asked him.

He shook his head.

The clock was striking eight as Mam placed his overcooked meal on the table. Dad took a few forkfuls of runner beans before suddenly dropping his fork on his plate, then cupping his face to his hands. We looked at each other in disbelief. Mam put her arms round his shoulders. He turned his head towards her and let out a high-pitched groan. This was most unlike my father. Even when Grandfather died he held on to lead the prayers at Saint Elizabeth Hospital though he was overwrought for a moment. Nana Nellie made the sign of the cross and looked away.

"What is it, Wim?" Mam asked.

"Tonight."

"Maybe it's just another rumour?"

"Tonight," Dad said again more firmly.

"How can you be so certain?"

"We have it from a Dutch woman whose daughter is married to a German officer."

"Oh."

"Holland will be invaded tonight."

"God save us," said Nana Nellie. "The Prime Minister is to speak on radio at nine o'clock."

"De Geer won't be convinced until we have Nazi troops strutting along every street in Holland."

Dad was speaking the language of despair. Antje, Gerrit and I listened, but could say nothing. War was something our young minds were unable to come to terms with. It was Mam that broke the silence.

"What will happen?"

His face now looked forlorn.

"Who knows? Bombs, air raids, we'll have dead people on our streets, here in Oosterbeek. Holland will be no more. We'll be like the Poles."

He faced away from the table, tears returning.

"We survived the Big War. We'll survive this one too," said Nana Nellie quietly.

"We could have German soldiers in Arnhem as soon as tomorrow."

"Have we any chance of holding out?" Mam asked.

"With our bare hands?"

Dad was determined to see no false light.

"Other countries might come to help save us."

"What other countries? They have armies along our borders, twelve kilometres away. What's to stop them? They can pound us from inside Germany for days, or roll over us whenever they want to. They can cross the Rhine and be in Arnhem in a few hours."

"Holland has done nothing to Germany. We've been neutral since September," my mother said but sounded unconvincing.

"So?"

"Hitler said our borders were safe," Nana Nellie said. "He won't go back on his word."

"Ask the Poles about Hitler's word. Ask the Norwegians."

There was real bitterness in his voice. Antje put her arms round his neck and hugged him.

"Do you know what date Saturday is, Daddy?"

"Saturday? Is it the eleventh?"

"Besides that?"

"Tell me."

"My First Communion. You'll come, Daddy?"

"Do you think anyone would keep me from the First Communion of the bravest girl in Holland? Bombs might stop me, but not Germans. We'll be there, all of us, Antje."

He gave a shadow of a smile, and somehow his promise to Antje seemed to blot out all the bad news. Everyone wished her well, none more so than Dad. Antje, younger than me and older than Gerrit, was two years older than the other first communicants because of her lost time at school. Her moment had finally arrived. From birth she had brushed with death so many times. No one had expected her to survive till now but she had.

"Any luck in borrowing a camera for Saturday?" Mam asked.

"Yes. Henk de Groot will lend me his."

The de Groots lived two doors from us. Marie was Antje's classmate. Her brother Theo and I were the same age and in the same school class, but we weren't close.

"Won't he need his camera? His Marie is receiving her First Holy Communion too." Mam said.

"All military leave has been cancelled. He wants me to take pictures of his family."

"I'll buy film for you," said Nana Nellie.

"Are you sure you can afford it?" Mam asked, innocently.

There was an amused exchange of glances. Since Grandfather's death, Nana Nellie's reputation for stinginess had grown so much that it vied with Gerrit's obsession with food as the family joke.

"When it's for Antje."

Antje showed off her spotlessly white Communion dress and veil. The dress hung down loosely over her and accentuated how skinny she was. She was like a scarecrow.

"It's lovely, Antje," Gerrit said.

That Gerrit noticed was the ultimate accolade for Antje. As we were admiring her, I caught sight of Mr. Heemskerk and his wife passing our window to call on us. That meant only one thing, confirmation of Dad's news. Mr. Heemskerk would never drop in for a casual chat. He had been Grandfather's closest friend, though Mr. Heemskerk was a man of substantial means. He was considered rich as he owned several cargo vessels, one very large one on the Waal and a number of smaller ones on other waterways, mainly the Rhine. Dad's father had been more than another pilot of cargo vessels, for years he had been Mr. Heemskerk's right-hand man. Whenever Mr. Heemskerk had a problem, not infrequent in the transport business, he would turn to Grandfather. Nana Nellie once told me that their friendship had been sealed when my parents named me Cornelis, after Mr. Heemskerk.

I reached the front door first.

"How is the boy named after me?" It was his usual greeting.

"I'm fine, Mr. Heemskerk."

They had presents for Antje. Mrs. Heemskerk brought a beautiful bouquet of lilies and strongly scented carnations while Mr. Heemskerk brought a necklace in a beribboned box. Both belonged to the Dutch Reformed Church but were well aware of the significance of First Communion, especially for Antje. My parents would become excited whenever the couple arrived. This had nothing to do with their generosity or wealth, rather with the closeness and respect that existed between the elderly couple and my grandparents.

"You know?" he asked.

"Tonight," said Dad grimly.

"Our only hope is that it's over quickly. Trying to stop them would be a shameful waste of young lives. It's hard for a Dutchman to say this, but surrender is our only hope."

Mr. Heemskerk became emotional, and his wife reached out to comfort him. Though now in his seventies, he still had masses of wavy hair, snow-white and well groomed, and his rugged appearance never seemed to change with his advancing years.

"If Hitler had no intention of keeping his word, why did he promise?"

Nellie came from an era when one never made a statement of intent without following it through. Though Hitler was to show infinitely more sinister character flaws, that he should state something in public and not keep to his word said enough about the man.

"That's why we're going to have war, Nellie," Mr. Heemskerk replied.

Hitler's war dominated our conversation, but we would soon learn that what we regarded as Hitler's war would become our war. As our visitors were leaving, Mrs. Heemskerk turned to Mam.

"After church service on Saturday, you are all to come to our house for breakfast."

"We can't."

"You have no say, Corrie. It's all been arranged by Nana Nellie and me."

"But we're having Wim's brother Paul and Mrs. de Groot and their children here."

"Paul Baumann is always welcome and de Groots too. We'll be proud to have a soldier in the Dutch army if he is not called up."

"He already has been! All leave has been cancelled," Dad said.

As with other merchant princes in Oosterbeek, Mr. Heemskerk lived in a large three-storied house in its own grounds on a cobbled road between the Utrecht Road and the Rhine. His home was not much more than a kilometre away, but a world apart from theirs. Going to their house was no ordinary treat. Both Mr. Heemskerk and his wife loved the local woods and would regularly stroll there, arm in arm, at any hour. Their home had housemaids in starched aprons and their long mahogany table was big enough to seat twenty. Seascapes dominated the magnificently framed paintings on the walls. A large garden to the rear had an ornate fountain surrounded by flowerbeds, a lily pond and a surfeit of shrubs and ornamental trees.

"First Communion breakfast at Heemskerk's, Antje, how about that?" Dad said.

"I'll never be happier again in my whole life."

With several operations behind her and more to come, no one begrudged Antje her moment. That night falling asleep was hard. Antje and I shared the attic bedroom, mainly because she was afraid to sleep on her own, whilst Gerrit could and would sleep anywhere. I heard her tossing and turning. Our Prime Minister had told us on the radio to sleep easy in our beds, but I had visions of German tanks plundering our beloved Holland, smashing everything. I thought of Henk de Groot on call-up, having to obey orders to fight and wondering what dangers he would have to face.

I must have dozed off because when I awoke, I found Antje in my bed gripping my hand firmly. I was her protector. At birth, Antje had encountered major hip problems that plagued her young life, she was three by the time she was able to walk, but even then she walked with a waddle. The many operations helped. Her waddle grew less noticeable, though she would limp whenever she overdid things or became very excited. Antje had operations for tonsils, for appendicitis and for a throat abscess that nearly choked her. She had lost sight in her left eye from measles complications when she was five and her shaded-out lens was a constant reminder.

"I'm afraid, Nelis," she whispered.

"What of?"

"The noise."

"What noise?"

"Can't you hear it?"

I listened. Only then did I hear the drone gradually growing louder. I bolted upright.

"Aeroplanes."

I heard movement in Dad and Mam's room. The noise grew louder. Sirens screamed from the direction of Arnhem, less than four kilometres away. We jumped out of bed, Antje pulling on her bathrobe, and ran to the window. Dozens of people were already on the street looking at the sky. Others had collected a short distance from our house. The noise became deafening. We rushed downstairs and joined those already on the road. There was a heady spill of emotion as people knocked into each other, trying to see what was happening. Neighbours who had only ever exchanged hellos were talking non-stop. The barking of dogs added to the commotion. The peculiar old lady, Eliza Till, was talking to others for the first time in years. Her cats followed her, upset by the noise.

"No longer rumours," Dad said.

He had to shout to be heard.

"They are on their way to bomb England," someone said.

"Over Holland is the shortest route," said another voice in the darkness.

OOSTERBEEK

Bombs dropped on London were bombs not dropped on Holland. Antje gripped my hand tightly. Dad put his hand on my shoulder. "I'm glad we don't live in Amsterdam or Rotterdam tonight."

"After centuries of freedom and tolerance, everything we stand for is falling apart."

Mr. Brouwers, with his goatee beard and long hair, was speaking. He played the organ at St. Bernulphus, the Catholic Church on the Utrecht Road out of Arnhem. He would be the organist for the First Communion Mass on Saturday.

"How long can we hold out?"

"By morning they'll be pouring over the Rhine Bridge in Arnhem."

"Will they come this way?"

"Yes. They're bound to take the main route to Utrecht and Rotterdam."

As we moved into the early hours of Saturday, 11 May 1940, during Holland's final hours of freedom, in the racket of squadrons of aeroplanes flying to war above us, people debated soberly how we were about to lose our freedom. We felt powerless. We had yet to see a tank or lorry, let alone a single German soldier! But something that every person living in Holland had, until then taken for granted, suddenly dissolved in the time it took that first squadron to fly over. Our power and will, that which had made us the proud people of a free and civilised nation, had seeped away. Within days the freedom we had assumed as our birthright and by which we lived would be crushed and we could do nothing. My father was right to be worried.

Chapter Two

That Saturday we were up early. The cherry trees were blooming a light shade of pink along our road and on the Weverstraat. Johann van Veen's big black horse clip-clopped on the cobbles with a heavily laden milk cart behind. Mr. van Veen poured milk into enamel jugs on every doorstep. He lived five kilometres away and always wore a straw hat and clogs. His horse left plentiful manure piles on our road, which some householders collected for their flower boxes. The annual colourful floral display in Oosterbeek was largely due to the regular output of the milkman's horse and was noted locally as being one of nature's wonders.

"We should go now. The church will be packed," my father said.

"We've well over an hour yet," Mam replied.

"Listen!"

We did. Even from within the house, the constant hum of motorised vehicles on the move was heard. The German army had crossed the Rhine Bridge in Arnhem and was moving within a short distance of our house, along the road heading west towards Utrecht and Rotterdam.

"We could have difficulty crossing the road to the church," said Dad.

My mother was very close to panic at that moment.

"If the German army is on the Utrecht Road, we can't let the children anywhere close. We can't let them out of the house."

"We've no choice if you want Antje to receive her First Communion?"

"I'll receive First Communion. After that, I don't care what happens," said Antje.

"What a day for this to happen!"

"It's Antje's day." Dad was firm.

Other families were already on the Weverstraat on the way to the church. The noise of the army on the move grew louder as we drew closer. I was scared.

As we were leaving, Dad's brother, Oom Paul, arrived on a bicycle, his hair wild and untidy. His tie was crooked, his shoes unpolished. He wore his laid-back, easy smile. Nana Nellie looked at her watch. Oom Paul noticed.

"You took your time," said Nana.

"Did nobody tell you the German army has arrived?"

He bent to hug Antje. It was only a matter of time before Oom Paul and Nana would argue. No excuse was necessary for an argument as theirs was a constant battle of wills. He worked at a garden nursery nearby. He was a happy bachelor, although we hoped he and the lovely Catherine Haan would name a day soon. Mam reckoned Oom Paul's refusal to name the day was just another way of annoying his mother.

Antje made a point of walking in the centre of the road, her limp obvious. Dad wanted to carry her but she wasn't having that.

"Carry me on the way back, Dad. I'll walk up."

Mam was sporting a straw hat with a wide brim and orange ribbon, while Nana wore a black hat with an outsized cluster of handmade flowers, all orange. She oozed defiance.

Our joy in Antje as we walked to St. Bernulphus' quickly turned sour. Arriving on the road to Utrecht, we could see as well as hear the vast cavalcade of vehicles. Tank after tank, troop carrier after troop carrier and gun carriage after gun carriage passed in a non-stop and urgent turning of wheels and unstoppable movement. Young men on tanks looked at us, expressionless, with no hint of softness in any of their fresh faces. These were the men of the New Order, the vanguard of Hitler's occupation of Holland. Their swastika flags blew in the breeze, rubbing salt into our wounds. If they expected opposition, they seemed unconcerned. I was a few days past my eleventh birthday, too young to know or imagine what war and occupation meant. Dad's face was a mask of disgust that our neighbour could steamroller all over our land and devour our freedom was unbearable. He had been right, the Germans were on our streets sooner than anyone could have imagined.

St. Bernulphus was on the other side of the Utrecht Road. The church stood high on the landscape. At the time its steeple was a landmark with so few buildings on that side of Oosterbeek other than farmhouses and farm buildings.

We waited for a break in the flow of German troops to cross to the other side.

"We may have to wait for days. Armies don't stop for civilians," said Dad.

"They don't give a damn," Oom Paul said.

"We're helpless."

"They won't stop. We might not get across."

It was an appalling situation. To the Germans, we were civilians coming to look at an army on the move. Almost an hour went by.

"What if we drive four or five horses across the road?" someone said.

"With a hearse?"

"Get horses killed and maybe the driver."

"They won't stop."

"Hey look! There's a gap between two lorries."

"What the hell!" cried Dad as Nana Nellie and another elderly woman walked to the middle of the road and held up their hands before a troop carrier.

"Holy God, she'll be run down. Stop her."

"They're crazy."

"They'll get killed."

Suddenly the troop carrier pulled to one side and slowed to a crawl. The vehicles coming behind in the flow slowed as well. Nana and the other woman turned and waved us across. Dad grabbed Antje and carried her. We made it to the other side. A man ran to Nana and shook her hand.

"I don't believe what I've just seen," Dad said.

Oom Paul was angry at Nana. "She's mad. There's the proof. You stepped in front of the German army. You're one crazy woman."

"We'd waited long enough."

My parents lifted their eyes to heaven. Nana and the woman walked ahead, heads held high. I felt a glow inside at what they had done.

Dad was right as the church was nearly full when we arrived. I don't know how so many had managed to cross in time for Mass. Crossing back later would be a problem but for now we could attend to the day's main business. The church interior dazzled with colour and floral scents. Tulips, lilies and camellias adorned the altar, while small floral bouquets tied with orange ribbons were laid to the aisle-side ends of every pew. By the time Mass had started, the church was fuller than I had ever seen it. This was a statement that we Dutch would do whatever we wanted in our country. If we wanted to go to church, we would go. Mr. Brouwers played the organ loudly and defiantly to drown the noise of German tanks and transport vehicles still rolling west.

St. Bernulphus did not have a modern high altar then, the ornate high altar at the very top had marble-topped communion rails between it and the rows of pews. My heart jumped when Father Bruggeman came down the centre aisle and beckoned me to join the other Mass-servers, a gesture to have me there for Antje. In a moment I was in the sacristy with the other altar boys, donning a well-laundered surplice and soutane. Father Bruggeman, a pleasant man, seemed particularly serious as he robed. When he was ready he looked at the clock. Thanks to Hitler, Mass was more than one hour late. We followed the priest to the altar. The Mass was said, as always, in Latin.

The first communicants were at the front, the girls on the left, the boys on the right. The side aisles were packed. Mr. Brouwers softened his playing when the new communicants made their way slowly to the altar. As Communion was distributed, I walked ahead of the priest holding the paten. I remember and cherish to this day the magnitude of the moment and the emotion I felt when the priest laid the Communion Host on Antje's tongue. My frail little sister had endured against the heaviest odds and had bravely fought her own personal war since birth. Her expression and look of serenity spoke volumes. As a family, we were closer than most because of Antje's regular scrapes with death. When others developed a cold, Antje caught pneumonia, when others caught measles, so did Antje but she also lost sight in one eye at the same time.

Father Bruggeman faced the congregation. I sat to the side with the other altar boys. I was expecting something very different from the sermon he had delivered on the peaceful day when I had received my first communion, four years before. There was tense, nervous coughing in the church.

"Our words today are for the children. Our first word to you is welcome, children. I'll say it again. Welcome, children. This is your day. Welcome to God's army. If you are to join any army, the best army to join is God's. Why is that, children? Why is God's army the best army? Because God's is the one army that will never be defeated. Never. It may appear that God is on the losing side, but you know the words 'Thy will be done' and who it was who said them. Who said those words? Right you are, children. Mary, the mother of Jesus, said them. When the angel Gabriel told her she would bear a child who would be named Jesus, she said 'Thy will be done'. Remember. Thy will be done. That's the will of God that Mary was talking about. Jesus said 'He that eats my flesh and drinks of my blood shall have life everlasting.' How about that, boys and girls? You're in an army now, God's army. You're Christians, soldiers of Christ with the kiss of Jesus on your brows. God laid down rules for His followers. He gave those rules to Moses on Mount Sinai. Moses gave them to us. These rules are called? That's it, the Ten Commandments, the rules God gave by which man should live. One day each one of us will be called to judgment. God will ask: 'Did you obey my Commandments? Did you love your neighbour? ' When God tells us to love your neighbour he doesn't say love *some* of our neighbours. Love all your neighbours, even those who are hard to love. Obey the Commandments and know what it says in the Lord's Prayer... thy will be done. God will say, 'Come to me. A Christian with full and absolute faith in God and in his only begotten son, Jesus, shall have life everlasting."

The priest turned to the altar. I had been expecting more, as was everyone else, but that was it. Nothing about what was going on in Rotterdam, nothing about our queen, or about our lost freedom. Then out of the blue Mr. Brouwers did something extraordinary, which none of us had heard him do before. He played "Wilhelmus," the Dutch anthem, on the church organ. In a flash everyone was standing, young and old, even elderly women who rarely stood, if ever. Backs straightened, chests pushed forward. The Church of St. Bernulphus thundered as every voice sung out clear and strong through all fifteen verses.

I will never feel as proud again as I felt at that moment. Even now, sixty years later, I still get goose-pimples when I think of the magic of that moment. That day we cried and laughed at the same time, and hugged each other fiercely. Dignified gentlemen rushed from their seats to get to the gallery, but in St. Bernulphus the stairs to the gallery are narrow and spiral, so there was a jam of eager people, all trying to pump Mr. Brouwers' hand. How he coaxed music from such an old an organ was a miracle in its own right.

When Mass ended we gathered outside for family photographs and talk, ignoring the endless roll of German wheels and tracks. That day was important for all the families who had a child taking First Communion. Mrs. de Groot, there with her daughter Marie, appeared desperately sad. Never very cheerful and now with the uncertainty of her husband's call-up, she now seemed to relish letting everyone else see her misery. There are fewer tasks more difficult than trying to jolly up someone who wants to be miserable, and after a while Mam stopped trying.

"I'm sorry for her, but even if Henk were here, she'd be in a sulk," said Nana.

"I'm disappointed Father Bruggeman said nothing about the invasion." said Oom Paul, waiting for Nana Nellie to react.

"He preached the word of God. That's what priests are supposed to do."

Mam nudged us to keep moving. Dad kept a close eye on Nana. He could not allow her to tempt fate a second time. Again we faced a long wait to get to the other the road. We waited and waited. Many signalled to the passing convoy that a large group wanted to cross, but it neither stopped nor slowed.

"I hope Mr. Heemskerk knows what's happening," said Dad.

"They don't see us."

We waved and pushed on to the road, cursing Germany and Germans loudly. Father Bruggeman's words were already wearing thin.

"We could be here for days."

"The Nazis won't stop until all of them have passed."

Frustration turned to anger. Mrs. de Groot's face grew more sorrowful.

"Look, a gap!" Oom Paul shouted. He held out his hand to his mother.

"Not a chance. You'll get run down."

We flailed our hands in the air and signalled as one. No gap. The invaders kept coming. We craned our necks for a break big enough for us to sprint across. And we waited.

In the distance a tank slowed and pulled to one side, black smoke puffing from its exhaust. It was the half-chance we needed.

"Let's run for it."

Together we rushed across, Dad carrying Antje. We couldn't get away from the Utrecht Road fast enough.

We were two hours late and very hungry when we reached Mr. Heemskerk's house. Everything was set up in their garden to the rear, among the tulips and apple blossoms. Theo de Groot and I went straight for the food. Theo, as quiet as his sister Marie was extrovert, couldn't conceal his delight. I had eaten at Heemskerk's a few times, but never like this.

Inevitably the discussion turned to events in Amsterdam and Rotterdam. Every so often Mr. Heemskerk went inside with Dad and Oom Paul to listen to the radio, returning each time with ever-gloomier faces.

"Amsterdam is being hammered."

"It's the same in Rotterdam."

"They're attacking the bridge at Moerdijk."

"How could they have got troops to Moerdijk so fast?"

"Airborne troops, it says on the radio."

"Airborne? What do you mean?"

"Men jumping out of airplanes using parachutes."

"Imagine. Is there no way to stop something like that?"

"By flooding the countryside."

"If they've taken Moerdijk, it's all over," Mr. Heemskerk said. "We know that if Fortress Holland is cracked, our major card will be gone."

Mr. Heemskerk knew all about such things. Could one bridge make such a difference to the country's defences? It was over one and a half kilometres long.

"There are Dutch people helping these gangsters," Oom Paul said.

"Traitors to Holland you mean." Mr. Heemskerk's face reddened as he spoke.

Mrs. Heemskerk and Nana talked non-stop. Nana told her about what Mr. Brouwers had done in the church and this solemn woman punched the air. She made Nana retell it over and over again.

"Will you look on that face of misery on Mrs. de Groot," said Oom Paul.

"What do you expect? Her husband may be in danger," replied Mam.

"I'd rather fight Germans than come home to a face like that."

"That's a nasty thing to say. Henk de Groot is fighting for Holland and all you can do is to make smart remarks."

Oom Paul had a point. Mrs. Heemskerk made allowances but Mrs. de Groot made no effort to show gratitude for their hospitality.

That weekend Dad listened to every news bulletin. Three days into the invasion, I heard him let out a loud roar. Nana Nellie was with us when he did.

"The bitch!"

"Wim, your language in front of the children!" Mam said.

"How could she, the bloody bitch!"

"Who're you calling a bitch?"

"Our Queen. She's gone to England. She's not going to Zeeland. How can she walk away from Holland now?"

"She's looking after her own skin like everyone else. What did you expect?"

"That's a terrible thing to say about her majesty," Nana said.

"She's not going to Zeeland. She has abandoned her own people."

"She has done the right thing. How could her majesty help us if the Nazis take her prisoner? With her in England, part of Holland is free. I'm glad she's gone. Now Dutch people from all round the world will rally round her. Wait and see."

Nana Nellie made sense, but Dad would not see it her way.

"We have neither a queen nor a government when we need them most, nobody can stop Hitler now."

"I'll pray to St. Thérèse of Lisieux. Hitler's day will pass, our queen will return."

Whenever Nana called on St. Thérèse, she was determined not to lose the argument. Many times I'd heard the story of how Nana and two of her friends had, when they were young, taken their bicycles on a train to Belgium and cycled the rest of the way to Lisieux in France on a pilgrimage to the town of the mystic nun. We would listen to it, eyes to heaven, over and over again. In Nana's presence you could criticise the Pope, the Queen and the Prime Minister but St Thérèse, now dead for over forty years, was beyond criticism. It couldn't be done. Even Oom Paul wouldn't dare.

"Say a prayer to St. Thérèse that we'll get some good news soon," Dad said.

"There was no bad news until that wireless came. Now bad news is all we ever get."

"When good news comes, it will be on the wireless too. The wireless only carries the news, it doesn't make it."

"It carries bad news."

Dad yawned, ran his fingers through his hair, stretched back on to the couch and slept for what seemed to me the first time in days.

Chapter Three

"We're going to Breda," Oom Paul announced.

"Who is?" asked Mam.

"All of us."

"How? You know how far Breda is?"

"By car?"

"Of course."

"Next Sunday. Catherine's troupe has made it to the festival finals."

"Where are we going to get a motor? From the Germans?"

"An old Renault on loan. It'll be tight, but we'll manage."

"Who else is coming?"

"Just us and Catherine."

"Seven is too many. You take the kids and Catherine. We'll stay," said Mam, as practical as Oom Paul was impractical.

"We'll all fit. When are we ever going to have a car again for a whole day?"

In a land of a million bicycles, a ride in a motor was a great treat. Other than one short trip in Mr. Heemskerk's car to St. Elizabeth Hospital in Arnhem the day Grandfather died, I had never been on a long car trip. Mam worried about the lack of space, but as Sunday drew closer, she too wanted to travel.

That Sunday we rose at an impossible hour. Mam had made up a picnic for the day. Oom Paul sounded the horn when he arrived with Catherine Haan.

Mam, Catherine, Antje and I crammed into the rear, while Gerrit sat on Dad's lap in front with Oom Paul. Catherine carried her dance costume and shoes in a cardboard box. This meant that the crush of legs in the rear seat was worse than I could have imagined. It was a beautiful June morning and we started out in high spirits.

"How are you all back there?" Dad asked.

"Squashed."

"You could be worse. You could be in France."

This was enough to get them going on the war, Oom Paul leading the way.

"Can you imagine millions of people heading out of Paris on to the roads?"

"Six million," Dad corrected. "The entire population bolted."

"How can roads cope with six million? How can those with children cope?"

"We've been lucky," said Catherine Haan.

Catherine worked in Arnhem and kept us informed of everything going on there.

"We held out in Holland for five days," Oom Paul said.

"We don't know how many were killed in Rotterdam. It could be thousands. They bombed civilians, flattened thousands of houses. They continued bombing the city even when they knew the country had surrendered."

Still in shock over what had happened, Dad could not bring himself to say the word "German" without qualifying it as 'inhumane' or 'barbaric'.

After a lapse in conversation Antje giggled. She was sitting on Catherine's lap and I sensed the pair was up to something.

"Oom Paul, when are you going to get married?"

"Is that Antje? I was wondering if we had left you behind you were so quiet. Is my favourite niece comfortable back there?"

"I'm your only niece. When are you going to get married?"

"Aren't you the mischievous one? That was some day we had at your First Communion. You looked great. You were beautiful. We were all proud of you."

"When are you going to get married, Oom Paul?"

"I've no idea. I have a problem with getting married."

"What problem, Oom Paul?"

"Women are away too smart for a simple fellow like me."

"Simple?"

"I'm not too bright."

"Everyone knows that."

"Antje!" my mother said.

Antje gave a high-pitched happy laugh that spread throughout the car.

"How could I marry someone silly enough to marry a man too simple for his own good?"

"You are simple."

Antje laughed again, pleased with her own wit.

"Quiet back there, mischief-maker," said Dad.

The drive to Breda seemed endless with field after field of cows grazing in long grass. I had never known there were so many cows in the world, let alone in Holland. Those cheeses had to come from somewhere. We eventually arrived, stiff and sore. The festival was outdoors, with groups from all over Holland participating. Breda was thronged and everyone was wearing their brightest colours for the occasion, orange dominated. There was a heady sense of celebration in the air that day as if a strong message was being sent to the Germans: your armies may occupy our country but we're still Dutch, we'll carry on as before, we'll dress in our costumes, we'll sing our songs, we'll dance our dances and we'll go to church if we feel like it.

But thinking of the inhumanity and all the suffering that lay ahead, I can only cringe at how tragically naïve we were during that first summer of occupation.

Catherine took the box with her dance costume and shoes with her and left to join her troupe. We pushed our way close to the platform. The performers gave us a mix of choral singing and dancing. Loud applause followed each group as they left the stage. Sweat poured from us as the merciless afternoon sun beat down.

"Ladies and gentlemen, Group Number Twelve from Arnhem, led by Miss Catherine Haan. Please welcome Troupe van Lombok."

We prepared to applaud their entrance.

"Call again Troupe van Lombok."

No sign of Catherine. We waited. What was wrong? The conductor calmly looked to the wings. Nothing. A murmur ran through the spectators. This was not like Catherine or the troupe she had painstakingly coached. Something was wrong.

"Call again Troupe van Lombok."

Faces grew redder, and perspiring judges exchanged glances. Some of them wanted to get on with the next group. Dad lifted Antje high on his shoulders so she could see behind the wings.

"They're coming," she said.

As she spoke Catherine led in her troupe but they seemed panicky as they sang their first number. Catherine looked stunning, but nervous.

"Something's wrong," said Oom Paul. "I'll go round and see."

The troupe curtsied as they finished their song and then quickly took their positions for a very lively dance number. Some seconds into the dance part, a girl of about twelve stumbled, an outstretched arm stopped her fall, but it didn't look good. The judges noticed. Then a girl in pigtails collapsed. Oom Paul and another man rushed forward to lift her. She fell again, heavily this time. Oom Paul and the other man carried her off. The judges' faces left no doubt about how they regarded the performance. The troupe carried on but just then there was another audible gasp as another girl stumbled and passed out. Once again Oom Paul and the other man rushed in.

"What the hell!" Dad exclaimed.

Catherine beckoned frantically to her troupe to keep dancing. As they resumed, another dancer fell. Oom Paul and the other man rushed onstage once again. Catherine signalled to the conductor to continue playing. The girl in pigtails returned to link up with the others but collapsed again, this time with a thud.

Something odd was happening. When the fourth girl collapsed there was no longer any doubt. Something was amiss but, suddenly, the crowd began to cheer. Within seconds there was a frenzy of excitement, onlookers were seeing more than just another troupe, here was raw courage made flesh. The young girls may have been beaten, but they were willing to carry on, no matter what. In that moment those young girls represented how every man and woman of Holland felt, down but not out. People wept tears of joy. The crowd was wild for one fierce moment.

We knew as the troupe made their final bow that marks were irrelevant. Onlookers cheered and clapped. One of the judges, resplendent in dark blazer and rows of shiny buttons, came forward and kissed Catherine on the cheek. Dad elbowed his way out to where the air was fresher and we pushed after him. Oom Paul joined us, sweating heavily.

"What's going on?" asked Dad.

"I'm waiting to find out. Something, wasn't it?"

"Hey, there's Catherine," shouted Antje.

Catherine went down on one knee to greet her. Oom Paul ran to Catherine and lifted her up.

"Catherine Haan, I'm the proudest man in Holland. You're going to marry me."

"Put me down, Paul Baumann."

"When we set the date."

"You'll let me fall. Put me down."

"We'll go to Mussel's Jewellers to buy the ring. Say yes and I'll put you down. Say it."

"Let me back on my feet, you big brute."

"Say you'll marry me."

"Yes, Paul Baumann, I'll marry you."

Mam and Antje hugged her. And so in a moment of euphoria Oom Paul's life altered.

"What was wrong with all of you?" he asked Catherine.

"The Germans took their car."

"What?"

"Some German's car broke down. They stopped our dancers and took their car. The dancers waited for three hours in the sun before another car stopped. When one finally did, it already had two people in it. They have had nothing to eat or drink, they just rushed onstage as soon as they arrived, without warming up, or stretching, or water."

"How are they now?"

"They'll be fine."

"We're proud of you," said Mam.

On the way home, Mam and Antje teased Oom Paul.

"You'll go straight to heaven Catherine. Are you sure you've thought this thing through?" Mam said.

"He forced you. You still have your own free will," said Antje.

"My engagement stands. A girl could go a lifetime without a moment like this."

Her eyes were those of a woman in love. The journey homeward to Oosterbeek was much easier.

The euphoria from our happy day in Breda was short-lived. Within a week we were in shock from an occurrence that rocked our family to the foundations. It began with a simple outing where Antje, Gerrit and I were walking through the woods close to where we lived. Antje was hanging behind a bit more than usual.

"Wait for me, Nelis," she said.

"She's lazy," Gerrit said.

"Come on," I shouted.

I waited. She stopped. It was most unlike her to go into a sulk.

"We can't leave her there," I said, more to myself than to Gerrit.

"We'll never get to the pond," replied Gerrit.

He wanted to go without Antje with no thought to what Mam and Dad would say if we left our sickly sister alone in the woods. I had no choice. She stood with one hand against a tree, the other over her eyes.

"What's the matter, Antje?"

"Hold my hand, Nelis."

"Okay. Come on."

"Thanks."

"What's wrong with you?"

"It's dark."

"It's the middle of the day."

"It's very dark, Nelis. Don't leave me here in the dark."

She tightened her grip. She stumbled a few times as we continued to the pond in the clearing.

"Sit on the seat," I said.

"The seat? Where?"

It was then that I realised something was seriously wrong. Gerrit was too busy chasing frogs to notice. I sat Antje down. She wouldn't let go of my hand.

"What's up?"

"I can't see," she answered, and began to cry. I felt real pain in my gut.

"What can't you see?"

"I see only shadows. There's a black cloud over my good eye. I can't see clearly."

I didn't wait any longer. Gerrit was annoyed.

"She'll always be a nuisance."

"Shut up, Gerrit."

"She should get new glasses."

"Did you hear that? Gerrit thinks you should change your glasses."

"It's very dark," Antje complained.

Within an hour we were on our way into Arnhem, Mam with Antje on the carrier saddle of her bicycle with me cycling alongside.

We headed to Dr. Russmann's rooms on Hoogstraat. We climbed two flights of stairs and sat waiting on hard chairs in a small and musty room. There was one person ahead of us, an old woman, dressed entirely in black, the two parts of her spectacles held together by a soiled strip of sticking plaster. She snorted loudly from a snuffbox. Her craggy face bespoke a life of hardship and endless toil. She chuckled to herself after a moment, and then smiled at us.

Dr. Russmann had a lean face and a neatly trimmed, snow-white beard that made him look old. His rimless spectacles were perched on the end of his nose.

"Who have we here?" he asked, as he led Mam and Antje into his private room.

Waiting was hard. I had a pain in my heart. I was sure that the longer they stayed with Dr. Russmann, the better things would be. Finally, I heard movement from inside. One look at Mam's deathly pale face was enough. Dr. Russmann came with them.

"I'll arrange it right away, Mrs. Baumann."

It was not a time to ask questions. I held Antje's hand as we walked down to the street. Young German soldiers, bronzed and fit, marched briskly past. They were now a common sight in the heart of Arnhem. We didn't give them a second glance. We had to get home to Oosterbeek. Cycling out from Arnhem was harder because it was uphill for much of the way. We walked when the incline got too much for Mam. Nobody said a word.

When we got to Oosterbeek, my mother decided we should go to Nana Nellie's flat to break the news. I reckoned she wouldn't go there first unless Antje needed extra consolation.

When Nana came to the door, she put her arms around Antje. Somehow she had sensed it was serious and had known that Antje would need her sympathy.

"My good eye, Nana, its going."

Antje's voice was emotionless. Nana and Mam exchanged glances, Nana's trademark smile froze. More suffering, more pain for Antje.

"Dr. Russmann is getting a specialist from Utrecht to examine her."

"Oh?" Nana said.

"Say a prayer to St. Thérèse," said Mam.

"I'll pray to her that our Antje is given the strength to cope."

If telling the news to Nana Nellie was tough, telling my father was tougher still. He assumed for himself every pain and hardship visited on Antje.

"I'd like a glass of water," she said.

Soon Antje was blind. The following week the specialist from Utrecht examined her. His diagnosis was similar to that of Dr. Russmann. Antje would be blind for the rest of her life. She was just nine years old.

"I'll need a walking stick," she said.

Antje came to terms with her handicap more quickly and bravely than any of us. She rode her tiny bicycle, fell off, got on and fell off again. She made us laugh by talking about who she had crashed into each day. She could make her way up to Nana's flat and get back on her own. My sister dealt with her situation better than we could have imagined, but her handicap was a heavy burden. My father tried to figure out what was the best for her. He would not discuss the situation with my mother, who coped much faster with hard facts.

"If times were normal, we'd get you into a school for the blind," he said.

"No, Dad," cried Antje. She ran to Mam.

"Wim, how could you?"

"We can't give her special training. You would be well educated, Antje."

"I don't want to leave home. No, no, no."

"We want what's best for you. All of us will help you."

"I'm not going to any school."

"Not until things settle."

He back-pedalled a little when he saw Antje's reaction but never abandoned his notion completely.

Then things did seem to settle. By the end of June the French and Belgian armies had collapsed and meekly surrendered to the Nazis, everyone said the war was more or less over. There was talk of full freedom of worship and social justice. Germans speaking in frightful Dutch were regularly on radio discussing racial affinity between the Dutch and Germans. It seemed only a matter of time before the British would also see the light like every other nation, and peace and progress would be restored to every corner of Europe.

"What's racial affinity?" I asked Dad one day.

"Racial what?"

"Affinity. They keep talking about it on the radio."

"The Nazis tell us we're their blood brothers."

"You cannot send Antje away, Dad."

I was eleven. If I had opinions, I wasn't supposed to express them even if I was the oldest.

"I won't go to a special school. I won't go. I won't," cried Antje.

"I want her to stay too." Gerrit protested.

His was the least valued opinion, but tension levels rose considerably at his outburst. Nana Nellie stopped talking to Dad. She came and milked 'her' goats and collected eggs, but she had no word for Dad. When the container for the poultry feed went low she gave a written note to Mam to pass on. Dad had expressed an honest idea on the best way to ensure that Antje's handicap did not hinder her education, and now he was as good as an outcast in his own house.

"Nothing is the same any more. Our Queen gone, our Government too, German soldiers strut our streets. My own mother won't talk to me. A man can do nothing right," he said to Mr. Heemskerk one day.

"You're suffering from one serious condition, Wim."

"What's that?"

"Angst. Snap out of it."

"How?"

"You were wrong to suggest sending that child away. Losing the sight of her second eye is a major trauma. Now more than ever, she needs her family. You cannot put her through the ordeal of leaving home as well."

Dad was unaware of my presence. I wanted to see if he would act on Mr. Heemskerk's advice. With Mr. Heemskerk, there was no easy route.

Nana Nellie was with us when Dad said he had something to say. She remained still without a word or glance for him.

"Who's the black sheep in this house?" he said. "My ideas for Antje's education were wrong. I wasn't thinking straight after the shock. We'll forget about special schools."

"I'm glad about that," Mam said.

"However…"

"No." Several voices came at once.

"Each of us must pull our weight. Antje should get an education so we must all help."

The gloom lifted like a cloud on a hot summer's morning. Antje's smile of happiness said enough. Nana winked at Mam, victory in the face of male stubbornness. I saw Dad in a new light. He had been wrong he knew it and was man enough to admit it.

Marie de Groot, Antje's friend, was prepared to help. Every day she breezed in and took Antje through the woods or to any place she wanted to go. Marie helped her to brush her long dark hair. Antje found this hair brushing hilarious and said so after Marie had left. For Marie, the novelty of helping out lasted all of two weeks. She stopped calling. Marie was Marie, she would always please herself. No one needed to tell Antje why Marie had stopped calling. Antje's blindness was too much for her. Antje was going to need help every day for the rest of her life.

As we came to terms with the situation so did Antje. With her fingers she could tell whether a garment was clean and ironed or needed laundering. Mam put different types of covers on jars, and Antje knew which jar contained tea, coffee, or baking powder. Soon she could make her way round the kitchen as well as Mam. Two girls from her class, Ursula Boom and Cora Koeman, called regularly and, unlike Marie, would continue to visit. I couldn't go near our bedroom because it became their hideout. Ursula Boom's father owned a bicycle repair shop. Every day the girls would find ways of getting Mr. Boom to repair the daily damage visited on Antje's bicycle free of charge.

Life went on as June and July eased gently into August. Oom Paul and Catherine made plans for their wedding. Antje showed us the great courage housed in her frail body. Henk de Groot returned home. The instructions to Henk and to all Dutch soldiers from their German masters were direct: go home, settle down and behave. Mrs. de Groot still looked gloomy as she was upset that the only films now showing in the cinema were German propaganda. Peace was more or less at hand.

Chapter Four

I heard the rapping of the doorknocker. It was after seven. Mam had left the house with Antje and Gerrit to call on Nana, who had fallen while tending the goats and was nursing a bruised knee. I was in the kitchen doing my school homework, my father pottering around the house.

The knocker sounded again insistently. I heard Dad in the hallway and looked up from my homework to see if the caller was one of my school friends.

"You know me, Mr. Baumann?" The man had a distinctive accent.

"You're that Frenchman with the restaurant in Arnhem?"

"Oui, I am French. Since I come in Holland I am Dutch. Maybe now I am German. I don't know. I'm Luc Gauthier. Please call me Luc."

"Hello Luc. I'm Wim."

"Do you know Mrs. Beatrice Visser?" the man said gesturing to his companion.

"You're the lady with the dress shop?"

"That's me."

"Ah, Beatrice, he knows you. You are famous, no?" The Frenchman laughed.

"Can I help you?"

"May we speak with you in private?"

"Come in. My wife and children are out."

Dad took the visitors into the living room. The hatch between the dining room and the kitchen was ajar, and I was curious. I was able to hear most of the conversation.

"Take a seat, Luc. You too, Mrs. Visser. There's a bottle of French liqueur in the house."

"Non, non, merci. We'll come to the point. We need you."

"Me?"

"You do house repairs and carpentry?"

"Yes. Here in Oosterbeek. I avoid the city if I can."

"But you are a carpenter by trade? You work on houses?" Mrs. Visser persisted.

"Yes."

"We need you," said Luc Gauthier.

"We?"

"The Resistance."

There followed a prolonged silence.

"The Resistance? In Holland?"

The surprise in Dad's voice was palpable. The word meant nothing to me.

"We must build a Resistance in Oosterbeek and in the other suburbs of Arnhem."

Luc Gauthier spoke with conviction and passion. So did Dad.

"You want me to fight the Nazis? The Danes and the Norwegians held out for no more than a few hours. Our own army held out for five days. In one month your French army was destroyed. Our soldiers were told go home and be good children. The Nazis are running the show. Didn't anyone tell you?"

Dad's anger rose as he spoke.

"We know all that."

"But you want me to take on the Germans?"

"We're not looking for soldiers. We need tradesmen, skilled people."

"What can a tradesman do?"

"Carpenters can save lives."

"Where are the corpses? I haven't seen a single corpse in Arnhem or in Oosterbeek. The war's over. There is no war."

Dad was still on the boil.

"You think so? Chamberlain is gone. Churchill is no Chamberlain. The British won't give in. If the war is not over we must be prepared."

"Prepared? I'm a tradesman."

"We need hiding places that will not be found in thorough searches. In other countries fugitives hide in forests, in valleys, in mountains. Where are our forests or valleys? What woods we have can be combed inside out in a few hours. We need hiding places. In Holland our choices are limited. We hide in the ground or in buildings."

There was a silence.

"Who are you talking about? There's not a shot being fired. The Germans are buying Dutch goods left, right and centre. Your restaurant is probably busier than ever."

"Oui."

"Then let things be."

"The Nazis won't let things be. Before Hitler invaded Poland, we said it would never happen. I was in Cologne on Krystal Nacht."

"Oh! Bad?"

"It was bad, my friend. I vomited up my guts that night. A piece of my soul died and Cologne was nothing compared to Berlin and Frankfurt. Not many understand what evil runs in Germany. Your pride was offended but you don't understand what's happening in Germany. You don't really know the Nazis."

Luc Gauthier spoke his mind. I could hear faint approval from Mrs. Visser when the Frenchman spoke.

"Can you tell me why we Dutch don't understand it and a Frenchman does?"

"It is not because I am French that I understand. It is because you are Dutch that you do *not* understand. Tolerant people assume that others are tolerant. When was the last time a politician was assassinated in Holland? When was Holland last at war? I was born in France but call myself Dutch. I chose a Dutchwoman as my wife. I make my life here. My children are Hollanders. Christians respect other Christians, you respect Jews, respect those of no church. You tolerate communists. You allow Mussert to promote his fascism. It is because you do not comprehend hatred that you do not comprehend fascism. I come to Holland. Now Hitler comes too. I am afraid for my family, and for Holland. Excuse me, but now I am French, I am talking too much."

"I think the war is over. It's finished."

The woman's voice cut into the conversation. I could just see her left shoulder in a dark green cardigan.

"We hope you're right, Wim. Do you know that the Nazis have arrested hundreds of communists in Amsterdam. Jews there are petrified."

"Because they're communists or because they're Jews?"

"No communist arrested has been released. There are no charges, no trials. They take people in broad daylight."

Luc's voice became passionate. He must have sensed that Dad was wavering.

"Those who say the war is over should tell the people of Amsterdam."

Mrs. Visser was as earnest as Mr. Gauthier.

"Give me time to talk to my wife. I want Holland the way it used to be."

"Please, do not discuss this with your wife, Wim."

As the Frenchman finished speaking, Mrs. Visser cut in again. "Take no risks."

"What are you talking about? You said you wanted a tradesman."

"Holland needs you. We need hundreds of hiding places for people on the run. We live in a police state. Knowledge is dangerous."

"Who's to say they won't torture women or children? They're Nazis."

I waited for Dad to speak.

"Forget it. I'm not about to put my family at risk."

The visit was as good as over. Dad's voice was calm now with not a hint of aggression. I heard the others stand to go.

"If that's your decision, we respect it. Before you dismiss our request completely, we'd like if you gave it some more thought."

"Not really."

"How would it be if the one needing a place to hide was a friend or relation, if his life was in danger? That might be you."

This silence was longer. I held my breath.

"I won't expose my wife or my children to danger. Count me out."

I was proud of my father then. I heard the visitors move to the hall door.

"We respect your decision, Wim. One question and then we'll go in peace."

"Of course."

"If Mr. Brouwers needed a place to hide, what would you do?"

"Mr. Brouwers? Why would he want to hide?"

"He plays our national anthem during Mass. He's playing with fire."

"Mr. Brouwers is in danger?"

"Wim, what would you do? He's knocking on your front door begging you…, what do you do? Do you let him in?"

"Of course. He's my mother's friend. He's our neighbour. He's our church."

"Where would you put him?"

"Why, somewhere…," Dad stopped.

In that moment the argument was over and Dad had lost it.

"May we call again?" Mrs. Visser said.

"Call after seven. I don't want any of my family around."

"Friday evening?"

"Fine."

I resumed my study pose, half-expecting Dad to come in. I was certain he would do the right thing. It was hard to imagine Mr.

Brouwers being arrested for playing 'Wilhelmus.' Mr. Gauthier had to be wrong.

Friday came. I made a point of visiting Nana. Her knee was still swollen, so her leg was resting on a stool.

"How are my goats?" was her greeting. I had offered to milk them and told Mam I would take the milk round to Nana's house. I wanted to remain behind when she left with the others to see Nana.

My ploy worked. After evening wash-up they all left. Dad was in the back garden. Someone knocked at the door and he answered it. I heard the visitors enter, and opened the hatch door slightly, heart pounding.

"Mon ami, you have considered?"

"It is better to be prepared."

"I agree."

"I will do my duty for Holland, on one condition."

"Oui?"

"That I am asked to make hiding places. Nothing more."

"Of course."

"I'm a tradesman. I won't carry a gun or a grenade."

"Welcome, my friend. That's what we want you to say."

"Can you can start right away?" asked Mrs. Visser.

"I can begin tomorrow."

"Magnifique. Maybe now I'll drink that French liqueur. I salute you, Wim Baumann. Not every man decides to save the lives of his fellow citizens."

I listened as they toasted their fledgling efforts to thwart the occupier. Luc Gauthier's understanding was that we were already occupied, with worse to come.

"We cannot turn a blind eye to their inhumanity," he said.

"I'm hoping for peace, not war," Dad said.

"The decision will not be ours."

"Luc, shouldn't we tell Wim more?" Mrs. Visser asked.

"Oh?"

"There is more. We want you to form a cell with four or maybe five, here in Oosterbeek. Your choice is critical: no family members or close relatives. We need electricians, printers, engine drivers, pilots, and telephone technicians. We need people with knowledge or skills. We need false documents, passports, rail and ferry tickets. The person you select must be someone who can rely on you absolutely and whom you trust with your life."

"Why do you need a cell?"

"*We* need a cell. If someone in Oosterbeek is in trouble and you can't help at that moment, you must have someone to fall back on."

"I'm with you."

Dad was now calm and collected. He had made his decision.

"We'll arrange for you to see two hiding places."

"Two?"

"We have more. We'll show you two for now. Everything is on a need-to-know basis. Take no risks. This applies to each and every one of us."

They left. I was glad Luc Gauthier had stressed that no family members would be used. If Mam or Oom Paul were in any way involved, I would worry indeed.

In the following days Dad was at ease. Gone was the gloom of May and June. Nana sent word that she wanted to see me and that it was urgent. What concerned her surprised me.

"I'm worried about Eliza Till. She passes this way to Koeman's grocery every day, but hasn't for four days now. Look in on her, Nelis."

"Yes, Nana."

I knocked several times on the front door of Eliza Till's house, but got no reply. A stern woman emerged from next door to see what the noise was about.

"Go round to the back. She's stuck in there with all her cats."

I went around and knocked. No reply. I looked through a small window but saw nothing through the layer of dirt and dust. I went to another window. Several cats came to the window, tails high, teeth bared. Something wasn't right. Then the woman from next door joined me.

"What do you want with her?"

"She hasn't been seen for days."

"Are you sure?"

"My grandmother asked me. Her cats look scary."

"They always look scary. How she affords to feed them?"

"Do you think she's okay?"

"I've no idea. I hate cats. I never go in there."

I checked the rear door and found it unlocked. It opened into a very badly lit hallway with several piles of old stored newspapers. There was a door to the right. I knocked. No reply.

"I'm not going near those cats," the woman said and left immediately.

I pressed down the handle of the inside door and pushed. The door creaked. As it opened several cats came running out, and I was hit by an unbearable smell. I saw Eliza Till face down on the floor, surrounded by deposits of cat manure. I backed out quickly, feeling ill. Some of the cats bared their teeth, as if setting to attack me. I ran out.

Dad came with me when I returned the next time. By now the neighbours were gathering. Dad put his fingers to his nose and entered by the rear door. He opened every window as quickly as possible.

"She's been dead for days."

The shock of the event wore off slowly. Despite her swollen knee, Nana insisted on attending the funeral. She was more or less recovered, although she used a stick for support. She made a point of telling everyone that it was she that had first missed the old woman and that 'it was my grandson Cornelis who found the body'. Eliza Till's cats had not gone hungry during the days before Nana noticed her absence.

Days later, a nephew of the dead woman, Arnold Till, called on us. He wanted my father to do some work on the house. Intense and ill at ease, with horn-rimmed glasses, he was never still for a moment. With him was his son Jan, who was my age. While Dad and Mr. Till were discussing the work, Jan and I walked through the woods.

"We're moving out here when the house is finished. I'm dying to be near the woods, the freedom is incredible."

"How many of you are there? That house is small."

"Me and my father."

"Where's your mother?"

"Dead."

Somewhere in the awkward silence that followed, a solid friendship developed between us. Little did we know then to where it would lead.

Dad made the house habitable, and in October Arnold Till and Jan moved out from Arnhem and I now had a friend living nearby.

That October was eventful. Catherine Haan walked up the long aisle at St. Bernulphus as Mr. Brouwers' strong flourish on the old organ threatened to deafen us. Catherine was wearing a creamy yellow wedding dress to match her flaxen hair and looked stunning. Antje and Ursula Boom walked ahead of the bride, each carrying a bouquet.

Oom Paul was wearing a charcoal grey suit and, for Oom Paul, looked neat and spruced up for his big day. Mam noticed too.

"That's the thing about weddings even the untidy can look well."

The wedding reception was held at the Schoonoord Hotel, a short journey on foot from the church. We walked to there in noisy groups, drawing plenty of attention from passers by. On the way Nana Nellie introduced me to relatives I never knew I had, a granduncle from Zwolle, and cousins from all over Gelderland.

It was heartening to see Antje recognise voices of people she had known before she went blind. Wherever she went, Ursula Boom was close. Gerrit extracted money from members of Catherine's family, quiet poultry farmers from across the Rhine and then gorged himself on the food. I had been detailed to keep an eye on him, but fell down on the job.

"Gerrit is showing off."

He was long past being funny. I hoped for Mam's support in giving him a thump.

"I've never set eyes on the little rat before today," she said laughing.

"Oom Paul is putting him up to it."

I didn't matter. Gerrit was the hit, Antje the centre of sympathy. I was the spoilsport. Dad made the speech while Gerrit continued showing off. He had on a man's black top hat, two sizes too large. Dad looked serious as he stood to deliver his welcoming speech. He would keep it simple, so I wasn't worried.

"To the Haan family and to their friends, to our own family and to friends, we say welcome. This is a good day, one we've longed for but thought would never come. We have lived under a dark cloud for some time now. We salute the efforts of the many good and earnest people to bring this tragic affair to a peaceful end."

Oom Paul was puzzled.

"Up to now all efforts to create a lasting peace have failed. Today I have good news. The conflict has ended. We have peace. We say a special thanks … we do more, we salute the one person who has made peace possible. Raise your glasses please and salute the former Catherine Haan, now our beautiful bride, Mrs. Catherine Baumann, for bringing peace and ending the great conflict of our time. Ladies and gentlemen, the long battle between my mother Nellie and my brother Paul is over."

Everyone laughed. Oom Paul spluttered with two jets of red wine exploding from his nostrils. He rose from his chair and went to Nana. They embraced, and when they separated she was in tears.

"That's the first time I've seen that tough tough old bird cry," said Mr. Heemskerk.

"Cornelis Heemskerk, how dare you speak like that about dear Nellie?" his wife said. Her husband winked at me.

The reception was wonderful, a smile of delight remained on Oom Paul's face. Mam pretended not to know who Gerrit was, eight-year-old Ursula Boom looked after Antje perfectly, and the bride continued to draw hugs and congratulations. Mam kissed Dad to show her pride in his performance. It was a good day.

Chapter Five

"The Germans got it right," Mr. Heemskerk said at Christmas.

This brought a puzzled look to Dad's face. He was not about to give the Germans credit for anything.

"How?"

"Between guns and butter, they chose guns. With their guns, they've now got our butter," said Mr. Heemskerk.

This was our first Christmas of occupation. The buzz was like other years, perhaps better. Shops did a roaring trade selling Christmas goods that were not available in Germany. Shopkeepers rubbed their hands with glee because they could sell German-made goods back to Germans. The prevailing joke was how to tell the English spy, he was the one without a parcel. Everywhere noisy Germans staggered under loads of gifts. Some were friendly, but the majority looked down on us.

Jan and I collected holly in the woods. Jan insisted I keep what he had gathered. He began to call to our house often and Mam welcomed him. He had a two-hour spell to fill in between end of school and his father coming home from work. He would let himself in our side door, dump his schoolbag and sit.

On Christmas Eve, St. Bernulphus was in semi-darkness and crammed with Mass- goers. Antje and I sat on either side of Dad.

Mam was home with Gerrit, finishing her preparations for Christmas dinner. Nana Nellie was in the gallery, proudly singing in the choir.

At midnight the church was in darkness except for two candles that cast faint, disembodied shadows into the body of the church. Mr. Brouwers played softly on the organ, adding to the sense of joy and relaxation. We were tightly packed into our pews, secure from the problems of the world outside.

As Mass progressed, lights came on, first near the altar, then in the nave. By Communion time, the church seemed to glow softly with the spirit of Christmas. Father Bruggeman and two young priests distributed Communion to people coming up the church in two lines. The choir sang "Silent Night". The side aisles were crowded as communicants returned to their seats. There was a moment of silence, the only sounds were those of shuffling feet. Suddenly, a woman's voice filled the church. This extraordinary voice sang "Adeste Fideles" with such purity and resonance that all hearts skipped a beat. Every cough was stilled, every sniffle silenced in wonder.

Heads turned to the gallery. Who was she? Where was she from? No one could say.

Then came "O Holy Night" followed by "Panis Angelicus." Dad nudged me to stop looking round. In one glance I had seen the singer, tall and elegant with blonde hair under a pillbox hat. She looked like a city person, from Amsterdam or Utrecht. What was such an elegant lady doing in Oosterbeek? Wealthy people came to Oosterbeek in the late summer and autumn, not in wintertime.

After Mass I waited for Nana Nellie. If anyone knew, she would. She had been in the gallery and had to have seen this spellbinder close up.

"Don't ask me, Cornelis. I've no idea," she said.

The rumour mill was working hard when Nana, Oom Paul and Tante Catherine joined us for Christmas dinner. Nobody had any idea. We all agreed that the lady could sing like no singer that we'd ever heard before.

It was not until Dad and Mam paid a visit to Mr. Heemskerk later that day that the first hard information came our way. New people had moved into the large white house a few doors from them. The new owner's wife was an opera singer, she had to be the one who sang in our church. If so, this was the best of news. She was not a Christmas visitor, but was now living among us.

Within a few days Dad knew more.

"She's Mrs. Beatrice Becker, wife of Herr Rudolf Becker of Munich. The Becker family runs an international wine business," Mr. Heemskerk said.

"Why Oosterbeek?" asked Mam.

"They've bought the big house near Heemskerk's. They're wealthy."

"Is she Dutch or German?"

"Dutch. From Amsterdam."

Over the weeks that followed, we searched for additional information. Gradually, the accepted version was that she had gone to Berlin as a young woman to have her voice trained. While there, she had met with Rudolf Becker and married him. She had worked her way up to leading roles in Wagnerian operas, fashionable again after Hitler's rise to power. The woman was beautiful. However she had a dark sideas her husband was known to be a personal friend of Von Ribbontrop, Germany's Foreign Minister.

"That despicable thug," said Mr. Heemskerk. "Time will tell on that woman."

From then on Frau Becker became known only as "that woman". Before long we would focus all our rage on "that woman" for the dreadful events that were about to occur elsewhere in Holland.

I remember well the muttered outrage. In the last week of February 1941, news spread that Anton Mussert's fascists and others had attacked individual Jews and Jewish businesses in Rotterdam and Amsterdam. News headlines screamed of attacks on shops and offices, an orgy of looting and violence in north Amsterdam, with German police looking on. White-faced grown-ups whispered of how these hooligans were following the pattern of violence already established by Nazi stormtroopers in Germany, of how elderly Jewish men were forced to scrub pavements before being clubbed to the ground and have their beards cut off, of how onlookers could not believe what they were witnessing.

We heard there was widespread fighting on the streets of Amsterdam, when the communist party called for a work stoppage in the city. Late at night, behind the blackout curtains, murmurings of how the communists were the only cohesive group to make a stand, despite their lack of support, reached me as I lay in the dark. No group in Germany had dared defy the Nazis since 1933, were the fervent whispers. We got news that the Germans had arrested four hundred Jewish men, and that the communists were no longer alone. That winter, as we children played in the snow and on the ice, Amsterdam was frozen in a citywide strike when tram drivers, rail workers and others refused to work. The docks, usually a hive of activity, lay idle.

The Germans recognised the defiance for what it was, an anti-Nazi strike of opposition to occupation. It was time for a lesson. The Dutch would have to learn that opposition to Hitler's iron rule would not be tolerated.

Through his sources, almost certainly Mr. Heemskerk, Dad learned the Germans had heavy weaponry, tanks and large numbers of armed police. The people of Amsterdam had to be taught a lesson. It was a hard one. Workers who refused to return to work were shot to death, seven in Amsterdam. Hundreds were rounded up and Jews were sent to a concentration camp. A tram driver who refused to drive his engine had a revolver held to his forehead. 'Drive this tram or you're one dead Dutchman' was the order. He refused and was shot dead in his driver's seat. Dad heard that the bullet left a small hole between his eyes but a much larger one to the back of his head, his brains scattered over the roof of the tram engine. The strike did not just collapse, it was crushed within a few days. The sense of outrage at German brutality lasted longer.

OOSTERBEEK

The significance of what happened eventually sank in, slowly but but ever so surely. We needed time to adjust to a new morality for which we were unprepared, and the rage that followed the strike is hard to describe. Even in Oosterbeek, hours from Amsterdam, the mood was vicious.

"Fucking animals," Oom Paul snarled.

We looked at each other in astonishment. Strong language was simply never allowed in our house.

"Use your foul language outside, Paul, not in here," Dad said.

"Do you know what they're doing in Amsterdam? They're killing people in the street!"

"You cannot use foul language in this house." Mam was shocked.

"Paul, you should leave," said Nana Nellie.

"Is that how you take the killing of Dutch people on the street?"

Choked by his outrage, Oom Paul ran out of words. The silence was painful. Antje spoke.

"Why do we argue while others bury their dead? Only Hitler wins."

The wisdom was from Antje. Oom Paul walked over to where she was sitting.

"Antje love, you've more sense than the likes of me. I'm sorry. Am I forgiven?"

"I forgive you," said Antje and hugged him, laughing, and all tension dissipated.

The killings in Amsterdam marked a point of no return for Holland. The tolerable relationship that had existed for nine months was gone forever. The Germans had crossed a line. We resigned ourselves to the fact that Nazis were uncivilised barbarians.

Long after Oom Paul had left the house to return to his own home, Mr. Heemskerk stayed on to chat with my parents and Nana. I listened as they spoke.

"When Mussert's street thugs did their worst, they made bitter enemies of ninety per cent of the Dutch people," Mr. Heemskerk said grimly.

"We're defenceless," Dad said.

Mr. Heemskerk produced a newspaper and laid it on the table. He removed the pipe from his mouth as he looked at Dad.

"Take a look at this, Wim."

"What is it?"

"See who's surrounded by SS generals in the front-page photo?"

"Who?"

"It's that lady who sings in your church. It's Frau Beatrice Becker."

She was surrounded by smiling SS generals after a concert performance of some kind in Amsterdam. The SS men sported their distinctive insignia and trademark arrogant smiles. We were lost for words.

"How can she do that with God's gift?" Nana asked.

"She's a stinking corrupt Nazi bitch," Mam said.

"Corrie, how could you?" Nana was totally aghast at my mother's language.

"That's what she is, a Nazi!"

We passionately loathed Frau Becker. When she offered to sing in St. Bernulphus for Easter Sunday Mass, Mr. Brouwers expressed his feelings loudly enough for everyone in the church to hear."It's either 'that woman' or me."

Mrs. Becker turned and left both the choir and the church. That Easter morning Mr. Brouwers played the organ like a man possessed.

"If she's friendly with the SS, Mr. Brouwers should be more careful," Mam said.

That was precisely what Luc Gauthier had said to Dad. He had nicknamed her 'Frau Erica," a name that had stuck. She stopped attending Mass in St. Bernulphus, although on weekdays she was seen praying quietly in a front pew. Whenever we saw her now, she was ensconced as a back seat passenger in a well-polished Horsch Auto Union four-door convertible. On fine days the hood was down, her blonde hair blowing in the breeze. Singing Wagner for Nazi bigwigs obviously paid well. She gave no hint that she cared. On rare occasions she walked through the woods with her husband, a tall unsmiling man with a fedora hat. They had two German shepherd dogs, beautiful animals, but not to be messed with. As far as we were concerned, Rudolf Becker was a Nazi. Friends of Von Ribbontrop had to be.

The smashing of the strike in Amsterdam taught us a hard lesson. For the first time I was conscious of being fearful. Fear is useful when dealing with the unpredictable. It is an early warning system that tells you the most important thing is to stay alive. Fear tells you that you cannot fight injustice by using rage and fury as weapons, that if you are unarmed, you're no match for the armed police of a new order. Swallowing these facts was hard, but swallow them we had to and did. Anti-Nazi demonstrations died there and then. The Resistance went underground. We would have to fight the Nazis with subterfuge and subversion, methods alien to our nature. We would have to operate behind closed doors, at night, Dutchmen and women, united in a common goal of thwarting our ruthless enemy in situations where no guidelines existed, where neither rules nor morality counted.

Worse news came within days of the street killings in Amsterdam. I was at Mr. Heemskerk's house one Saturday afternoon in early March where my father was fixing leaking gutters. Mrs. Heemskerk invited us in for coffee. The look on Mr. Heemskerk's craggy face told us that something serious was afoot.

"What is it?" Dad said.

"More executions."

"Who?"

"A teacher and fourteen other prisoners in Amsterdam. Shot at dawn. No trial."

"For what?"

"They don't need reasons. They took the men to the prison yard and shot them."

"It's a battle to the death now. One of us has to destroy the other."

As they were talking, Mr. Heemskerk's elegant daughter Juliana and her husband entered the kitchen. The conversation died instantly, and greetings and lots of small talk were exchanged.

That evening I felt I knew the identity of one member of Dad's cell. Nothing was said or hinted at, rather it was things that were not said. The sense of reliance on each other's good faith was total. Mr. Heemskerk radiated gravitas. He had business contacts and his cargo vessels moved daily through the waterways of Holland. If indeed he was a cell member, Dad had chosen wisely. A tug or a cargo vessel is a good way of moving a fugitive to safety.

Chapter Six

There was a persistent rapping on the door. I answered it. Jan's father, Arnold, stood there. Jan was with Antje and Mam in the kitchen.

"Is your mother here?"

"Come in, Mr. Till."

He looked haunted. By now Jan and I were close friends, we would inevitably squabble but be friends again the next day. Jan would display rare flashes of temper, but with Gerrit in the house, exasperation was normal. Mam saw fit to overlook Jan's moods but never tolerated such behaviour from Gerrit or me. Antje never threw tantrums despite having more frustrations than any of us.

"Sorry to bother you, Mrs. Baumann. Shortly after we moved here, a friend gave me chickens to rear."

"Chickens?"

"Ten chickens. They're in the bicycle shed. I wonder if they're ready to kill."

"How old are they?"

"Twenty weeks."

"Some of them could be."

"I don't know how to kill a chicken."

"Gerrit, tell Mr. Till how to kill a chicken."

"With an axe. Chop its head off."

Arnold Till gulped. "Oh?"

"That's how you kill a chicken." My mother smiled.

"Is there anyone I can ask to do it?"

"I will," Gerrit offered instantly.

"No, you won't," Antje cried.

"My brother-in-law Paul will do it. He'll be here this evening."

"Thank you. Once I see the first one killed, I'll manage."

"Will your have your brother-in-law call?"

"Pick the plumpest chicken and bring it to our shed."

Mr. Till looked at Mam, bewildered. The idea of killing his own chickens revolted him. He had not yet adjusted to the brutal realities of life in our corner of Holland.

"I'll kill the chicken," said Gerrit.

"No, you won't." Mam was adamant, "Paul will cope," she said with a wry smile.

Within minutes Arnold Till was back holding a squawking white-feathered bird. Gerrit took the bird, pulled one wing under the other and laid the chicken on the ground.

"What does that do?" asked Mr. Till.

"It stops the bird from running away."

"Please tell your uncle I'm grateful. Once he's shown me how, I'll kill the rest."

"You couldn't kill a spider," Gerrit taunted.

Gerrit seemed to be amusing himself at Mr. Till's expense, but it was really directed at me. He resented my friendship with Jan.

The chicken was put in our bicycle shed and Jan went home. When Oom Paul arrived, Jan came back to observe the craft of chicken-killing at first hand. Gerrit ran to tell Oom Paul of the serious commitment made on his behalf.

"Lead me straight to this dangerous bird," said Oom Paul.

Gerrit, Jan and I followed him. When we got to the shed, the outside hatch was closed. Oom Paul pulled it and entered the shed. He was back out immediately.

"Who's the funny one?"

"What's up?"

"No chicken there."

We looked at each other, confused. We had seen the chicken being put in the shed. No one could have stolen it. Gerrit went in to the shed but came right back out.

"Nothing."

Just then the chicken ran past us being chased by a dog. We tried to catch it but broke left or right whenever anyone was close enough to grab it . We examined the fuel shed, the bird could not have escaped through the walls or the floor.

Oom Paul stated the obvious. "Someone let it out."

"Who?"

The question went unanswered. Gerrit was blamed first, then me, then Jan. I knew I hadn't done it and I was sure that Jan hadn't either. Gerrit had to be the culprit, but for once he wasn't caving in.

Slowly, it appeared he couldn't have had anything to do with the bird's escape. My parents were enjoying the whole affair.

"Just catch him. I'll come round tomorrow evening to do the job," Oom Paul said.

The following morning I caught the chicken after Jan and Gerrit had trapped it in a corner and we put the bird into the fuel shed again. We awaited the arrival of Oom Paul, then followed him to the shed.

"Holy Jerusalem," shouted Oom Paul.

"What?"

"Gone again."

"But the door was shut."

"Someone let it out."

"Who?"

We were back to where we had been the previous evening, only this time more of the neighbours joined in the hunt. Mr. and Mrs. van Gaal were among the onlookers.

"Why don't we tell the rest of the bloody world?" Oom Paul said.

Dad and Mam were bent over with laughter. Dad or Mam? Impossible.

This time the bird was recaptured in the de Groot's garden. It would have been simple for Henk to bring the bird to our house, but nothing was simple with Henk Till anymore.

"We caught it. It's ours," said Mrs. de Groot.

"It belongs to Mr. Till. He left in to our house to have it killed," I said.

"Why doesn't he kill his own chicken?"

"He's from Arnhem."

"So?"

"He's never killed a chicken."

"Nobody is that ignorant."

Mam thought the whole thing too ridiculous.

"I'm not getting into rows with Mrs. de Groot or with anyone else over a chicken."

Someone was guilty. When I realised finally who it was, I could have kicked myself for not tumbling to it earlier. I reviewed my list of suspects to eliminate them one by one. Expand the list. Who was omitted? Nana Nellie and Antje. Eliminate Nana, she hadn't been around on either day. That left Antje.

I asked her casually, "Who do you blame for the chicken?"

"Whoever it was, he never planned on Henk de Groot having it for his dinner."

"You said 'he', you're sure it was a he?"

"How can I be sure about anything when I can't see a thing?"

I played dirty by staying quiet. Antje couldn't see me and her tiny pinched face was the picture of innocence.

"What?" she said at last.

"What do you mean 'what'?"

"Am I a suspect?"

"No."

"I thought when you went quiet on me...."

"I know who it was."

"Tell me, Nelis. I'm dying to know."

"Why did you do it, Antje?"

"Oh Nelis, you're right. You're not going to tell on me, are you?"
"Well now."
"Nelis, you can't."
"Why not?"
"Because…because."
"Why?"
"I didn't want to see the chicken's head being chopped off. It would be blind. Don't tell anyone." She began to cry.
"You know Gerrit is still the number one suspect."
"He always is."

I had no way of knowing it then, but we were coming to a time when Antje would never fail to atonish us.

Chapter Seven

After Easter we put "that woman" out of our minds. Whenever we spotted her speeding by in her roadster we would pretend not to notice.

Oosterbeek was transformed, as it was every summer. Everywhere bloomed, beech, oak and lime trees were covered with rustling leaves, colourful butterflies winged silently and bees hummed about their business in bright warm sunshine. Jan and I cycled and hiked around the countryside, resting whenever we got tired. We would lay our heads in the long deep grass, hear insects chirping, birds singing and cargo vessels chugging up and down the Rhine.

We were into the second summer of occupation. Dad never had a moment to himself. Each evening he cycled off with his bag of tools. I knew what he was doing, even if no one else did.

Mam surprised us one Sunday.

"We're going on a trip."

"Where?"

"To a restaurant in Arnhem."

"Us?" piped Gerrit.

"When?"

"We're going now."

Before we set out, Dad called me aside.

"Do you know the way into Arnhem?"

"Yes."

Dad did not elaborate any further. Arnhem, on the Rhine was a hard enough place to get lost in.

"Keep your eyes peeled today. You may have to go into Arnhem regularly."

"I won't get lost."

"Don't tell anybody, not even your mother. Nobody."

"Okay."

"Do you understand what I mean when I say 'nobody'?"

"Yes."

"I'll fill you in when I need to."

We arrived on a busy street just off Utrechtstraat, near the centre of Arnhem, parking our bicycles outside Luc's Café. A large, swarthy man emerged to greet us. It was Luc. Mam had no idea who he was. He gave each of us a Gallic embrace, and Mam got a formal kiss on both cheeks. Luc Gauthier was a bigger man than I had expected, and a few years older than Dad.

"Welcome to Chez Luc. Entrez."

The dimly lit restaurant was simple. The oak beams in the ceiling were stained with centuries of smoke and the walls were bare except for one faded print of a large fish on a hook. A black stove gave off a heat that matched the warmth of the welcome. There were no concessions to the fashions of the time, not a tablecloth was in sight. A middle-aged waitress smiled at us as we entered, but her smile looked forced. Mrs. Visser? In the poor light, she looked older than I had expected.

"Sit near the heat. Mrs. Visser will take your order. I'll be in the kitchen."

How come a woman like Mrs. Visser, a dressmaker was working as a waitress?

"The soup is a meal in itself. I suggest smaller helpings for the children," she said. Gerrit was about to interrupt but a look from Mam silenced him.

The street door opened, and a party of six men entered. Mrs. Visser sat them at an adjoining table. They were Germans. The enemy was sitting at a table next to us! They were not in uniform but their appearance said 'army men' and well above the rank of privates.

Antje had insisted on sitting beside me. The Germans were noisy as they ordered, then settled into quiet conversation. Gerrit's couldn't tear his eyes away, and neither could I.

"Concentrate on what's before you. Let others do the same," Dad said.

Mrs. Visser flitted about the Germans. She brought two bottles of Riesling and large jugs of water to their table. Occasionally she said words in German, then asked how her pronunciation was. They laughed at her efforts. She laughed her silly laugh with them. This couldn't be the woman who had coaxed Dad into the Resistance? She was pathetic, prepared to laugh with and for everyone in view. In my opinion, she wasn't the sort of person to rely on in the underground.

The main course at Chez Luc was an experience. For our family, eating out meant a picnic in the back garden with a charcoal grill or in the long grass on the bank of the Neder Rhine in summertime. This was our first visit to a restaurant. Six decades later I can still savour Luc's roast pork steak and applesauce. Privately I hoped that the Germans would order something other than the pork, I didn't want to share this experience with barbarians. Antje nudged my knee.

Gerrit was silent, too busy clearing his plate. Mrs. Visser was hovering between our table and the Germans, trying out her pronunciations and laughing her predictable hee-haw. She spent more time with them than with us. Mam commented on it but Dad's look silenced her.

Antje nudged me under the table again.

"What?"

"Later," she whispered.

Luc came from his kitchen to our table, his face deadly serious. As he approached, the tantalizing smell of baking bread wafted in our direction. I wanted more and our next meal in a restaurant could be years away.

"Pardon. I have only one dessert. I am so ashamed. Can you imagine, just one dessert for a table with five persons. Moi, a Frenchman? Alors."

"Don't worry about dessert, Mr. Gauthier. We've had a lovely meal," Mam said.

"There is no excuse. "What do you want me to do? Bring the one that I have?"

"Really, we're fine," my mother said again.

"Let the children have it, Luc," Dad said.

Luc returned to his kitchen and came back with a huge baker's tin full of apple tart, fresh from the oven, with a lovely brown crust on it. The aroma was wonderful. There was enough for ten.

"I have only one dessert for five people. Madame Baumann, will you please serve. Manage as best you can."

He enjoyed his joke, Gerrit's eyes lit up. Mrs. Visser arrived with custard.

"Cloves and all. Delicious," said Mam.

The Germans smiled at the goings-on at our table. I concentrated on finishing off the last scrumptious morsels. Mrs. Visser danced attendance on the Germans.

Antje nudged me again. Whatever she had picked up would have to wait. Luc brought liqueurs to Mam and Dad. We laughed. Mam never touched alcohol. Dad whispered in her ear and she sipped. Dad wanted to stay until the Germans had left.

When Luc arrived with the bill, Mam handed it to Dad.

"Time to pay the man and go home, folks," Dad said.

The Germans left. Mrs. Visser continued to fawn over them until they had departed.

"The bill, please," Luc said.

He took it from Dad's hand before Dad could stop him, and tore it into shreds.

"I want to pay."

"I am well paid with the company of your family. The bill was for the benefit of Les Boches."

"Can I show you the lavatory?" Mrs. Visser asked Mam.

Her face had changed, it was different now. Gone was the fawning look, the dizzy smile. She now looked very serious indeed.

Mrs. Visser led Mam and Antje to the rear of the restaurant. Gerrit followed. Luc sat beside me.

"You and I are going to see more of each other, Nelis," he said.

"Mr. Gauthier wants a regular supply of cheese. You'll find your way around?" Dad asked.

"Of course."

I was more than proud to play my part for Holland. Soon Mam, Antje and Gerrit joined us again, and I made to go to the lavatory. On my way, Mrs. Visser grabbed my hand.

"You and I are to meet regularly. Walk by me if we should meet on the street. Give no indication you know me. I won't know you. Do you understand?"

She was as hard as nails now, stern to the point of rudeness.

"Yes, Ma'am."

"What do you understand?"

"I won't recognise you. You won't look at me."

"Do you know why?"

"No, Ma'am."

"Arnhem is full of spies and dangerous people."

I didn't like Mrs. Visser. She had fawned on the Germans, yet spoke to me as if I were a traitor of some kind. In bed that night I learned more about her. Antje was about to amaze me once again.

"You know why she was drooling over those Germans?"

"She was disgusting."

"She was brilliant."

"What?"

"She was taking in everything they said."

"She doesn't speak German?"

"That's what you think, Nelis?"

"Well, yes."

"Why do you think I nudged you?"

"What was that about?"

"She *is* German. She was spying on the Germans."

"Mrs. Visser?"

It added up. She had transformed from a simpering idiot to a hard woman in an instant. She was in the Resistance and was a close friend of Luc Gauthier. If Antje was right, then Mrs. Visser was indeed some performer.

Bang, bang, bang. The knocking was unusually loud.

"Get the front door, Nelis, before whoever it is breaks it down," Mam said.

Henk de Groot pushed past me into the hallway. He was never polite, but was not usually so ill-mannered.

"Where's your father?"

"Out back."

He smelled of alcohol. His shirt was hanging out and his normally short and tidy blond hair was tousled. He was unshaven.

I led him to where Dad was planting cabbages. I picked up a hoe, to help.

"I want advice, Wim. I don't know what to do."

"What can I do, Henk?"

"They want me to join the police."

"Who?"

"The authorities."

"The police? Are you sure?"

"Why not?"

"Where would you be trained?"

"Schalkhaar. They're looking for ex-soldiers to train men like me."

"Schalkhaar! Rauter's police! God in heaven, Henk, you want to join Rauter's police?"

We had heard about Rauter. We could not but have heard of him. Rauter was one of Hitler's people, his deputy in charge of security to Seyss-Inquart, the Nazis Reich Commissar in Holland. Rauter had control of the police and had used his powers to strike terror into the population at large. He was a man to be feared and feared he was.

"You know about the killings in Amsterdam last February?"

"What about them?"

"You know whose name was linked to those killings?"

"Who's to know that?"

"If you want to join..."

"They're looking for ex-army men as recruits."

"They want Dutch soldiers to do their dirty work for them."

"Since when did police work become dirty?"

"Since the Nazis came. Who shot those people in Amsterdam, Henk? Who transports people to Germany?"

My father, no diplomat, gave his honest opinion. Henk did not doubt his feelings. He rubbed his stubble and was about to say something when Dad spoke again.

"You know the sort of people they are."

"I should have known. Soldiers like me are not wanted while others look down their noses at me. I fix bicycles at Boom's on Saturdays. I need a real job, Wim."

"We all need work, Henk. How the hell would you feel if you were one of Rauter's policemen with orders to tear someone's house apart, perhaps a house full of children. Would you tear my house apart, or Koeman's or Till's, or anyone else's house? Would you treat women like they did in Amsterdam?"

"I can work in Germany if I volunteer. It's here I need a job, not in Germany."

"You wanted my opinion, Henk. Dutch people shouldn't do the Nazis' dirty work for them. Do you think your training will be for police work?"

"What do you mean?"

"They'll train you to be a Nazi."

Henk turned purple with rage in an instant. Dad had hit a raw nerve.

"I should have known. Big shot Wim Baumann, the mighty patriot. He gets an invitation to sit at the table of Bigshot Heemskerk, so he sees fit to tell everyone else."

"Henk, you asked me…"

"A man wants to do the right thing by his family and gets called a Nazi by a shit who never lifted a finger for Holland."

"Calm down, Henk."

"I'll never be a Nazi, but you'll always be a shit."

"You'd better leave."

"Glad to escape the strong smell of shit."

Henk stormed off, his rage rising as he did so. Dad shrugged.

"Can you imagine Henk as a policeman?"

"Why are people being taken to Germany, Dad?"

"That's a big question, son."

We fell silent and finished planting the cabbages. We were interrupted by Mrs. de Groot, with Mam, in pursuit, trying to calm her. Henk's wife had fire in her eyes.

"You're too good for the likes of us, I suppose."

"Mrs. de Groot, don't say anything that…"

"Those with several jobs never pass a day's work on to those prepared to work. Don't tell me you don't know what I'm talking about. I've seen you with your box of tools several evenings, even Sundays, but is Henk ever asked to help? Soldiers aren't wanted any more. You don't want to give work to a man who fought for his country. To hell with you, Baumann, and with your bitchy wife and your pathetic misery of a daughter who shouldn't be let loose. My husband will join if he wants to join. We won't ask for approval and certainly not from a shit like you."

She turned and left. Mam looked at Dad, astonished.

"What's going on?"

"Henk wants to join Rauter's police. He asked my opinion."

"Did you hear what she said about our Antje?"

"Calm down now, Corrie. Say nothing."

That big blow-up with our neighbours was the evening's main topic of discussion. Mam surprised the rest of us with her understanding attitude.

"They're struggling, Wim. They have been for ages."

"I know."

"They haven't got two guilders to their name."

"But Rauter's police?"

"Maybe he should join. He would have information that could be useful if…."

Dad signalled at Mam to shush. They both got flustered. Gerrit was too busy eating to pick up on anything, but Antje was on full alert. I pretended not to notice. It was then that I knew that my mother had to be another member of my father's underground cell.

It worried me that both my parents were involved in the Resistance. I had reason to be more wary than ever. As Luc Gauthier had said, information in a police state can be more than serious, it can be deadly. The slogan on the streets was ears open and mouth shut. Now I can say with pride that my parents stood up for Holland when it mattered.

I was in my bedroom a few days later when Mam cycled to back our house, the contents of the reed basket on the carrier mysteriously covered with her cardigan. She went upstairs to the main bedroom and then quickly went downstairs again to prepare the evening meal. Curiosity got the better of me. I was in her room in a flash, and quickly found two rolls of wallpaper under the bed. The following day the two rolls were gone. Another hideaway was being prepared.

Chapter Eight

It was high summer. The weather was as balmy and enjoyable as it could be. We had time to enjoy ourselves and we did, but only up to a point. After the bust-up with de Groots, we were into a period of nothing happening. During the occupation we needed good news regularly. Whenever the news was bad Dad would go silent. This was more often the case. When the news was good it brought sustenance with it, it spread like wildfire, and being first with it was always a bit exciting.

No one living in Holland on 22 June 1941 can forget the day. It was a Sunday. Nana was with us. Dad, listening to the radio, shouted suddenly.

"Quiet everyone."

"What is it, Wim?"

"The Germans have invaded the Soviet Union!"

"Never!" Mam and Nana said together.

"The British are no longer on their own. This changes everything."

He got up from his seat and slapped his thigh.

"Russia is a long way from here," said Mam.

"Exactly. Russia is a long way, thousands of miles away. How can Germany occupy a country the size of Russia?"

Dad's excitement was contagious, and we ran to share the news. The sense of liberation and exuberance of that lovely June day is hard to describe. Bells pealed from every church in Oosterbeek and Arnhem to proclaim the news, it was carnival time on the streets. It seemed more official when Mr. and Mrs. Heemskerk arrived, his craggy face wearing a broad smile. Mrs. Heemskerk was bareheaded. They had left their house the instant they heard. From Mr. Heemskerk I would learn what this news meant.

"The sheer scale of that part of the world, it's an enormous place. Holland could fit there fifty times over and that's before you get to the Urals. It swallowed up Napoleon's army. It was the beginning of his downfall. Hitler has learned nothing from history and he has taken on the Russian winter as well. This is no ordinary mistake. Wim, mark my words, this has to be the mistake of the century."

"I agree," said Dad.

We sat around a table in our garden, Nana's goats tethered alongside. Neighbours were flitting in and out.

"Corrie, bring glasses and a corkscrew."

"Look who's here," cried Gerrit, as Oom Paul and Tante Catherine arrived with bottles of wine. Oom Paul's face beamed happiness. Mam, Antje and Catherine disappeared to the kitchen, the rest sat discussing the news. In a corner Nana and Mrs. Heemskerk were talking about flowers and shrubs. I sat beside Oom Paul.

"Churchill will smoke a cigar today," he said.

"More than one," said Dad.

"I salute the British."

"Amen to that. Hitler's given them a break."

Jan Till and his father arrived just as food was being served. Oom Paul saw them first.

"It's a great day, folks. There's a rumour that Arnold Till was seen smiling."

Everybody laughed and looked at Mr. Till.

"It's all right, Arnold, it's only a rumour," said Oom Paul.

Mr. Till smiled, the first time I had seen him do so. Jan beckoned me to go to the woods and join the celebrations there, but I wanted to hear what Mr. Heemskerk had to say.

As night fell and all the wine was drunk, Mr. Heemskerk grew more serious.

"Hitler has to fight on two fronts now, that's great news, but it'll mean big trouble too. They'll need fresh supplies of everything..., equipment, transport, weapons, ammunition and food. They'll have to make Holland their breadbasket. Hitler will fail, but there's a long way to go. A long way..."

"You could be right," said Dad.

"The Germans will need more workers. We could be made an easy touch. It's possible that our young men could be forced to work for them."

"You're joking," said Oom Paul.

"We're dealing with the Nazis."

Good news in war was always a double-edged sword and it also brought its own problems, whereas the bad news never had a silver lining. But that June day in 1941 was still memorable.

"Where are we going, Mam?" Gerrit asked one day as we were preparing to go out.

"No place special," Mam said.

"Why am I being scrubbed?"

"Gerrit, your ears are filthy."

"I know where we're going," said Antje.

"You do, do you?" Mam said.

"To the nursing home. Oom Paul and Tante Catherine have a new baby."

Mam's head jerked. Right again, Antje.

"Enjoy the day. Nelis, be careful with Gerrit on that bicycle," Dad said. He wasn't coming with us.

Antje was right about the new baby. Tante Catherine sat up in bed, smiling as she showed us Cora Theresa, her new daughter. Theresa? Was this in deference to Nana? The gesture was a small one because the baby's first name was Cora.

She cried when Gerrit held her.

"Here," he said, handing the infant to me.

I took her in my arms. She continued to cry.

"Let me hold Cora," Antje said. Tante Catherine's face showed her concern when I handed Cora over but she needn't have worried.

"I can't see you, Cora, but I can tell you're beautiful. You're my pet."

The baby stopped crying. Mam and Tante Catherine giggled.

"What?"

"Nothing, Antje. You look so happy."

"Cora and I are going to be friends."

Antje would not be separated from the new baby. Gerrit and I tired of the endless chatter and left the room. We wandered outside, tossing pebbles and counting birds, and wondered what more the adults could have to say to each other.

By the time we got back home it was after eight in the evening. Antje repeatedly told Dad how beautiful the baby was. Dad yawned, he seemed exhausted.

When I awoke, bright sunlight was pouring through the window. Antje was sitting on the side of the bed in her nightgown.

"Awake at last," she said.

"What is it?"

"You tell me, Nelis. What's going on?"

"What do you mean?"

"What do you see? Please tell me you see something unusual."

I was perplexed. Antje and I occupied the attic room, of which two walls followed the slanted contours of the roof. There was space for two beds, a dressing table with a mirror, a small table between our two beds and a wardrobe in one corner. Hanging on one wall was a framed picture of red and white speckled cows grazing on a riverbank, with a windmill in the background. Everything looked exactly the same to me, but Antje was right.

"What am I looking for?"

"Something has changed. I counted the steps from my bed to the wardrobe in the corner. Last night it was only three steps. Our room is smaller than it was yesterday."

I looked again. She had noticed something I had missed.

"You're right! The room is smaller."

"That explains yesterday."

"What about yesterday?"

"Where were Oom Paul and Dad? Remember how long we spent in the nursing home? Why didn't we come straight home?"

"I don't know."

"They wanted us away yesterday to change our room. There's a step less today."

"Maybe your bed has been moved."

"I've checked. It hasn't."

"How could you notice when I didn't?"

"You were too tired. I smell wallpaper glue. Why would they do something like this?"

It was a straight question. I hesitated a second too long before answering.

"You know something, Nelis?"

"Let me see if it sounds hollow."

"Why would they change our room?"

"Maybe it's some sort of hiding place."

"A hiding place?"

"If it's a hiding place, it's got to have a door."

"Find it."

I searched. There had to be an entry of some kind. I got on my knees. I lay on my back. I probed with my fingers.

"Have you found it?"

"Nothing."

"How many entrances can there be into a bedroom?"

"Four."

"Wrong. Six. Four walls, a floor and a roof. We know the four walls are out, that only leaves the floor or the roof."

"And the floor is out because we're over Mam and Dad's room."

"That's it! Through the attic," said Antje.

There was a small square opening from the landing into the attic. I had never been up there, but Dad had gone up during the hard frost to check the lagging on the water pipes. I was certain Antje had found the answer. She stayed sitting on the edge of her bed. I looked at her in a different light. I went to the attic to check on what she suspected.

"What did you find?" she said.

"Not a lot. You need a ladder to get into the attic. They've put a flap behind the water tank, with steps down from it. But I'm not sure it's the entrance."

"Did you get into the room?"

"I did. There are shelves stacked with tins of food and blankets. It's the perfect hiding place. You could search the house with a toothcomb and still not find it."

"Could there be another entrance from this room?"

"There has to be from where we are. I know there is, but I can't see it."

"Is it dark?"

"I found a light switch."

"We can't tell Gerrit."

"Definitely not."

"Why has Dad built a secret room?"

"He may have to hide someone."

"You know things, Nelis, but you're not telling me."

"Nobody knows that I know anything."

"You do know something?"

"I've heard odd bits of talk. Anyway I've promised not to tell."

"Promised who?"

"I can't say."

"What do they want to hide in it, Nelis?"

"Maybe people on the run. I'm not sure."

"From the Germans? It's our duty to help them."

We shared a secret and kept it from Nana, from Gerrit, from our neighbours. I looked at Antje. She seemed so skinny and delicate. She was also pretty extraordinary.

My heart raced with the danger and excitement of it all. Dad's hidey place was up and running. On the streets everything looked calm.

"We'll wait for our first visitor," said Antje.

She walked to the false wall and tapped on it.

"Sounds solid."

"A hollow sound would be a giveaway."

"They'll find nobody here except you and me."

All we needed now was to keep our nerve.

Chapter Nine

Mr. Heemskerk was right about the second front. The German army was deep into the Soviet Union. The further east it went, the emptier shops in Holland became.

"I can't buy a bar of soap any more," Mam complained.

She lost her temper with Mr. Koeman when he was out of stock. With each passing day Mr. Koeman became more frustrated.

"Look after your friends and neighbours," Mam told him.

"I have no friends." He looked so weary.

Mam was always unfair to Mr. Koeman, who was trying his best in volatile times. He was forever arguing with customers.

"It's not worth it any more, Mrs. Baumann. Dealing with stamps and ration cards takes all my time. The harder I work the more abuse I get."

"Keep me with enough tea and soap and I'll be nice to you."

"I can't give you any more tea, Mrs. Baumann."

"What am I supposed to do without tea?"

"Use the same leaves again."

Mam looked at him as if he had two heads. He was round, though not as stout as his wife, Wilma, and he panted. His jolly wife stopped being jolly. Her ready smile vanished. She would wait, with fat hands on fat hips, for someone to get out of line. I was there when Mam asked for more tea and got better than she expected.

"He only sells tea, he doesn't grow the stuff" Mrs. Koeman said. "He'd sell more if he had any. Why don't you try elsewhere, Mrs. Baumann?"

"That's exactly what I'll do. I'll take my ration-books with me."

"Good. That's if anyone will have you."

Mam stalked out, with me in pursuit.

"A big mistake, that," Dad said when Mam gave him a blow-by-blow account.

"I don't have to put up with abuse from Wilma Koeman!"

"The Koemans are good people. You can't pour from an empty bucket."

That same week I went back to Koeman's with my mother. She had baked a homemade pear tart as a peace offering. I had to run to keep up with her.

"I owe you an apology, Mrs. Koeman. I had no idea of the pressures you're both under. Can you forgive me?"

"Old friends…, yes. That's nice of you. You won't be the last to crawl back."

"Oh? I made a lovely pear tart for you, but seeing as I'm crawling…"

"Right now I'd kill for a bit of your tart, Mrs. Baumann. Apology accepted."

They burst out laughing, Mrs. Koeman her former jolly self again. Her husband remained deadly serious. The two women were convulsed. As Mr. Koeman looked increasingly perplexed, the more they laughed. Mr. Koeman sat on a sack of flour. They stopped laughing, and inside a minute we were upstairs in the Koeman kitchen with Mrs. Koeman cutting the tart. Determined to stay fat, she gave herself the largest helping.

"I'd better leave the rest aside for my serious husband when he comes up."

"If only we had more sugar…" Mam said.

"When we say we haven't got it, we haven't got it. People don't believe us. We have no bags hidden away. If the sugar doesn't come in, we can't sell it."

Though the evening of the first Sunday of December was chillingly cold, we danced and ran on the street in a skelter of excitement, telling people the latest bit of good news. Although we were eager to be the first to deliver the news we also had to appear to know what we were talking about and had to wait while Dad slowly put away his tools and went to wash his hands. "Father" we implored but he wouldn't be rushed as he weighed up the significance of this development.

I ran to the street with my newfound knowledge, delighted to find I was breaking the story.

"The Japanese have attacked Pearl Harbor," I shouted.

"Where?" I got the same response from every house.

Nobody had heard of Pearl Harbor, or knew where it was. I asked Dad.

"In the Pacific. That's what they said on the BBC World Service," he answered.

Pearl Harbor was at the other side of the world. This was all he could tell me about the precise location of the now-famous harbour. Of Mr. Heemskerk, there was no sign. Perhaps an attack on a naval base on a small island in the Pacific wasn't that important. If it were, Mr. Heemskerk and his wife would have been down to our house by now.

"He'll come," Dad said, certain this latest attack was a major event in the war.

"When the Americans entered the First World War, the Germans got too stretched. After that, it was only a matter of time."

"But Pearl Harbor is between Japan and the United States. It has nothing to do with the Germans," Mam said.

"We'll see."

The next few days grew colder. Mr. Heemskerk still didn't come. The excitement of Pearl Harbor was a one-day wonder. We had finished our evening meal on the Thursday when the door knocker sounded. Mr. Heemskerk stood there, the look on his face saying that all was right with the world. His severe, unsmiling wife was at his side, wearing the faintest hint of a smile.

"He's gone and done it," said Mr. Heemskerk, taking a seat near the coal fire.

Nobody said a word for ages. Mr. Heemskerk kept us waiting. He enjoyed being dramatic when the news was big. Dad spoke first. "Who has?"

"Hitler has declared war on the United States of America when he doesn't have to. Now the world knows he's a madman."

"On the United States!"

"It's on the radio."

"On the United States?" Dad repeated and followed with a high-pitched whistle.

When we thought the news couldn't get any better, Nana arrived.

"Nobody should have a radio," Dad said. "All the bad news we get from it."

"What's happened now?" Nana said, walking into Dad's little trap.

"Hitler has gone and declared war on the United States of America."

Nana stood between me and the light. Her head jerked towards Dad.

"Never."

"Tell her, Mr. Heemskerk."

We hugged each other, celebrating Hitler's lunacy.

"Should we hold on to that radio, or throw it out? What do you say, Nana?"

"It's time it gave us some good news, after all the bad stuff."

As always, the good news was a double-edged sword. Later Mr. Heemskerk made certain points.

"The Japanese have burned their bridges now. They'll go on a rampage."

"Will that affect us?"

OOSTERBEEK

"Yes, Corrie. The first great cartographer, Mercator, came from the Low Countries. He helped us to use the sea better than anyone else. If we cannot put a canoe to sea here in Holland, how can we protect our merchant navy thousands of miles away? The Japanese are certain to take the Dutch East Indies."

"But our situation isn't any worse than it was," said Dad.

"How do we replace what our merchant navy brings from the East Indies to Holland?"

"We can't. But Hitler's goose is cooked."

"When it comes to sourcing supplies, we leave the rest of the world standing. If you don't have the vessels, you don't have the food. That means hunger."

Dad nodded. Now we understood. In matters of shipping and cargo, Mr. Heemskerk was not just an expert, he was the rich man. This was his world.

"We don't mind going hungry for a while if it that means Hitler is finished."

"If that takes too long, we could be vulnerable to severe shortages."

Dad's face darkened. It was unlike Mr. Heemskerk to raise a false alarm. The possibility of hunger in Holland was unthinkable. No one doubted but that our Dutch farmers were the best in the world. Food shortages maybe, but hunger...It couldn't happen, not in Holland. Never.

Two other events occurred in December 1941. The first was in Mr. Koeman's shop in the Koningstraat. A housewife berated Mr. Koeman for having only brown flour with too much bran in it. She demanded white flour for her Christmas cooking. Why couldn't Mr. Koeman understand such a simple request? As she was speaking, Mr. Koeman fell forward on his counter and collapsed. The doctor arrived minutes later, but he was too late. Our grocer had died of a heart attack before anyone could help him.

"No man should have to endure what that man had to put up with," said Dad.

"Am I glad I apologised to him and his wife," Mam said. "I was so unfair to him. I feel so bad."

"It's hard to say no to old friends every day."

Then a greater shock occurred. On the Saturday before Christmas, a police car drove into our road, its siren at full blast and almost deafening us. Tyres screeched as it came to a halt two doors from us, in front of de Groot's house. We watched in stunned silence as a man emerged from the vehicle with a cold smile on his face. He was wearing a green uniform. Henk de Groot, our neighbour was now one of Rauter's Green Police.

Chapter Ten

Late January 1942 brought a sharp cold spell. These were nothing new, but now we could no longer do the things we had done in other cold spells. We couldn't buy woollen clothes for grown-ups because none were available.

"The Germans commandeer everything for Russia," Mr. van Auken at the man's shop told Mam. She tried other shops in Arnhem but everywhere it was the same.

The ponds and streets froze. When the school heating system broke down, my mother kept us home for three days. By day we skated on the street and at night wrapped ourselves in woollen blankets. I made only one delivery of Nana's goats' cheese to Mr. Gauthier during this cold spell. I had stuffed short written messages in the hollow of the handlebars of my bicycle as I cycled past groups of hard-faced Germans. The messages were coded and meant nothing to me, but I was pleased to be involved. I wore gloves Mam had knitted for me, but the ice-cold wind cut through my clothes.

"I can't buy wool any more. From now on we throw nothing out," Mam decided one evening.

"Nothing?" Dad gave me a wry look.

"Nothing. We keep everything."

"Children, this is your mother, Mrs. Baumann talking. This woman could have thrown out any one of you as babies, were it not for me. When she tidies, everything goes. When any of my tools go missing, the first place I look is the dust bin."

"Laugh all you like, Wim, but we need to hold on to everything."

There was a timid knock on the front door.

"Who's calling on a freezing night like this?"

I answered the door. It was Jan Till's father.

"Jan's not here, Mr. Till. He went home an hour ago."

"It's your parents I want to see."

I led him in to the kitchen. He seemed intensely frightened.

"I'm sorry to burst in like this, but I have to talk."

"Take a seat, Mr. Till," Dad said. "Sit here beside Nelis."

"I need help, Mr. Baumann. You've been such good friends since we came here."

"If we can help, we will."

"It's my son Jan. I don't know where to turn."

"What's the matter with Jan, Mr. Till?" Mam asked.

"I'm going to be arrested soon. I'm in trouble."

"What sort of trouble?"

"I may be shot. I need someone to look after Jan."

Dad whistled through his teeth."How do you mean, shot?"

"If they arrest me, they'll shoot me."

"What's happening, Arnold?"

"I'm being blackmailed, I can't hold out."

"By whom?"

"A woman I work with."

"How?"

"I was an activist for the Communist Party at one time. This woman knows. Her husband is a black marketeer."

Dad's face didn't register any change. I knew he hated communism, as did Mam, and most of our friends.

"What do they want?"

"Contracts. There's a public works contract coming up. They want it or they'll tell."

"Are you still active?"

"Not since my wife died four years ago. If they tell, I'm dead. The Germans raided my brother's house in Amsterdam. They took him to Germany. Jan doesn't know."

"Can you call this woman's bluff?" my father asked.

"I know that's the right thing to do. The Public Works Department has set procedures for contracts. Contracts go to reputable firms. I'm dealing with frightful people. I'm scared."

Dad's face clouded. Antje never moved a muscle, taking in everything. Mam looked at Mr. Till's trembling left hand.

"What are your choices?" my father asked.

"The few looked good at first but then. How long would I last in Germany? I could 'dive' but I have to provide for Jan. This woman is relentless."

Diving was a new word now in common usage, used when someone had to drop out of sight to protect others, or their own life. Mr. Till was much too intense for diving.

"If we can't look after other's children, we don't deserve our own," Mam said. She looked to Dad. Antje smiled.

"This is Jan's house for as long as necessary."

Mr. Till buried his face in his hands, crying.

"I'll never be able to repay you. Never. He'll be no bother, I promise."

"He lives here half his time as it is. Jan's always welcome," Mam said.

"I have to be honest with you, Mrs. Baumann. I may not be alive next week."

"Go into hiding," Dad suggested. "Can you not give them a small contract to save yourself?"

"I cannot give blackmailers control of water quality and public health in Arnhem, Mr. Baumann. I won't put lives at risk."

"Can she be scared off?"

"Not her husband or the others."

"Have you other family?"

"My late wife's sister lives in Amsterdam. Her husband is Jewish. They have five children. I can't bring any of my troubles to her doorstep. I have a sister who dived when my brother was taken. I have no idea where she is."

"Consider Jan taken care of," said Dad.

"Why don't you dive, Mr. Till?" asked Mam.

"Tomorrow's Saturday. I'll work tomorrow and decide after that."

"Don't risk it. We might be able to do something for you."

"There's something I want you to have. My late wife's piano is yours now."

"Wonderful," said Antje before Mam could object. "I'd love to play."

"That'll be easy. Mrs. Rimmer is a bossy teacher, but she's the best. My late wife thought the world of her. She lives off Koningstraat."

"Don't go to work tomorrow," Dad pleaded.

"I'll be all right for tomorrow. I'll collect my personal things."

"Send a medical note."

"I'll finish up tomorrow."

"Come and see me when you get back."

Antje tilted her head very slightly. So did Mam.

The piano arrived the following afternoon. After a lot of huffing and puffing, Mr. Till's two helpers managed to get it into our sitting room.

"When can I get Mrs. Rimmer?" asked Antje. "Today?"

"When she's available."

"Everything okay today, Mr. Till?" Mam asked.

Mr. Till's expression did not change but he shrugged, uncertain about his situation, not wishing his helpers to hear anything. As he left, Antje was already trying out the piano. Her excitement was infectious.

As darkness approached that afternoon, we heard a noise that was soon to become familiar, the urgent two-tone siren of a police vehicle. That sound would eventually cause a shiver of panic in every citizen, law-abiding or otherwise. For us it was sound of occupation, for many a tocsin of death.

We listened to the horn's strident urgency, the car was nearing. It halted outside Arnold Till's home. We watched with other neighbours as two Green Policemen ran into the house, and before anyone could react, they came back out, frogmarching Mr. Till to the car. He was in his shirtsleeves, helpless, and made no attempt to resist. One policeman threw him roughly into the car, which sped off. Arrest, Nazi style. A brown-laced shoe was lying on the road.

Mam and I rushed into Till's house. Jan, deathly pale and crying, was in the kitchen, where I had found Miss Eliza Till dead among her cats.

"You'll be safe with us, Jan," Mam assured him.

"Where are they taking my father?"

"We don't know, Jan. Stay with us until he returns."

"Why have they taken him away?"

"Strange things are happening in Holland," Mam said.

As we walked to our house, Jan handed a letter to my mother.

"Dad told me to give this to Mr. Baumann if anything happened."

Jan was quiet. I could only guess how he was feeling. We did our best to make him welcome, but he was confused. His pale face showed only incomprehension. Antje rubbed his hair and laid her head on his shoulder.

"You're safe here, Jan," she said.

Dad was shocked when he heard of the arrest. Injustice was one thing, but his sense of powerlessness was worse. He pursed his lips as he read the letter and then handed it to Mam. They exchanged glances.

"Do you know what's in this letter, Jan?" Dad asked.

"No, Mr. Baumann."

"Your father wants me to let your house until he comes back. He wants a proper legal agreement in place immediately."

"He's not coming back soon then?"

"We don't know. He knows you're with us while he's away."

The letting of Arnold Till's house was much easier than Dad had expected. When he told Oom Paul, my uncle's face lit up.

"Catherine and I want to move in from Renkum. It's perfect."

Dad was surprised. "Why would you want to move away from your work?"

"I'm going into business."

"What sort of business?"

"Killing poultry."

Oom Paul had been in business before, and had lost money. He had persuaded Grandfather to put up some of his nest-egg and it was probable that much of the constant warfare between Oom Paul and Nana arose from that failed venture. Her nest-egg was considerably smaller than it might have been if her son had been more astute.

Dad's face betrayed his concern.

"The business is up and running. Catherine's brother Ruud has bought a poultry place in Arnhem and wants me immediately. Till's house is perfect. And there's another good reason to get involved," Oom Paul added seriously.

Dad's voice was suspicious. "What?"

"It's the food business. Young men are being threatened with having to work in Germany. Anyone working in food production is exempt."

"You said you were killing poultry."

"I can work in production. I take the ferry to Driel every few days and help Catherine's father on the farm."

And so Oom Paul and Tante Catherine, along with baby Cora, came to live near us. Dad insisted that they sign a document at a notary's office.

Arnold Till's instructions were carried out, but only in the nick of time. On the day Dad and I helped Oom Paul haul his furniture and other belongings from their rented home farther out from Oosterbeek, three men arrived in a car. One of them was carrying a large bunch of keys and replacement locks. They looked like city toughs. One had a pockmarked face and hair slicked closely to one side. He also had tools hanging from a belt round his waist.

"What the hell do you think you're doing?" the fellow with keys barked.

"Helping the new tenant to move in," Dad said.

"Forget it, mister. We're taking over this house so you take your pieces of rubbish furniture back to wherever you brought it from."

Oom Paul emerged from our house. Dad signalled for him to stay calm.

"Who the hell are you?" asked the pockmarked one.

"I've a valid rent agreement, signed in a notary's office. I also have a spade, which I'm ready to use it. Who are you?"

"We have an agreement with the current owner of this house. Anything you have means nothing. Shift your stuff, shift yourself and these clods you have with you and don't be seen in these parts again."

Smoke was rising from Oom Paul. Dad kept calm.

"It's simple. We have signed instructions from Mr. Till to let this house on his behalf, a valid agreement, signed and dated. Come to the notary's office and take the matter up with Mr. Hedman."

The intruders seemed uncertain. They looked at each other. The one with the keys and locks turned to Dad.

"You guys should be careful. You're crossing serious people."

Chapter Eleven

"I'll make an exception, Mrs. Baumann. I wouldn't do this for anyone else."

"That's kind of you, Mrs. Rimmer."

"It's a challenge, Mrs. Baumann, not a kindness. I've never taught a blind student before. You pay me when I call. I'll apply the same criteria that I apply to every other student. If she's not good enough, I'll tell you. You must accept my judgement, which will be final."

Mrs. Rimmer wore the same faded, ill-fitting fur coat summer and winter. She was a small, peevish-faced woman who wore flat-heeled shoes that were too large and a black hat with worn-out feathers. Despite her odd appearance, she was able to intimidate my mother in her own home. Mrs. Rimmer wasted no time in laying down her ground rules. The house had to revolve around her, no meals were to be served during the lesson, there was to be no radio, no talking, no noise. Privately I hoped Antje would be unable to play the piano and spare us these visits. If Antje couldn't read music when she could see, how could she succeed now that she was blind?

"I presume you'll tell us whether or not Antje should spend more time on the piano," Mam said one Sunday.

Antje was playing in the sitting room while I helped Mam to dry the dishes. Mrs. Rimmer removed her glasses, placed them on the piano and stared hard at Mam.

"Mrs. Baumann, don't you know?"

"Know what?"

"Your daughter is no ordinary student."

"We know she's blind. But...-"

"But nothing, Mrs. Baumann. If I had seen no progress after the first month, I would have told you, but your child intrigued me. Others might have called it a day. I saw that something special."

"You mean she can play?"

"The gods have had their sport with your daughter, with her size, her limp, her blindness. Mrs. Baumann, what they have given your daughter is a gift."

"Does Antje know?"

"She knows. She thinks that it was God that brought a piano into this house when it was never in your minds to buy one?"

"That's great news?" Mam was wavering.

If Antje was half as good as her teacher said, it meant we were stuck with Mrs. Rimmer.

There was a pay-off when Antje played the piano. Even I, with no great ear for music, liked listening, especially when she played soft melodies. She had the ability to create a mood, to make you listen. Her face was rapt and serene when she played.

"She's a beginner, Mrs. Baumann," said Mrs. Rimmer one day. "She needs time. She can't read music. She has to play by ear, practise more, but when I play a piece for her she plays it back, note for note, correctly. If I give her a false note, she gives me back the note I've played. Incredible."

"That's great."

"She'll have to play piano at my house."

"What's wrong with this piano?"

"An ordinary piano is for ordinary pupils, Mrs. Baumann. Your piano is a limiting factor. I want a student worthy of my piano. I'm glad I've met your daughter, Mrs. Baumann. To be as good as she can be, she'll have to go to a teacher who is better than me. When the war ends, we must find her the very best. Her talent deserves it."

"She's ten and she's blind. She's going nowhere for a long time."

"As I said, Mrs. Baumann, that's down the road."

Mrs. Rimmer never let anyone else have the last word.

"She makes me feel guilty even in my own house," Mam said to Dad that evening. Oom Paul was present.

"We'll put up with her, for Antje's sake," my father said.

"We'll take her down a peg." Oom Paul said. "When is she coming next?"

"Keep out of this, Paul," Dad said. "Your bright ideas always backfire."

"What are you talking about?"

"Let it be, Paul."

The following Sunday Oom Paul, Tante Catherine and baby Cora came to our house for lunch, along with Jan Till and Mrs. Rimmer.

"I've bought bottles of fruit juice, Corrie," Oom Paul said.

"I don't take alcohol. It's a principle with me," Mrs. Rimmer said primly.

"For the kids, Mrs. Rimmer," he assured her.

Tante Catherine said. "It's raspberry flavour."

"I like raspberry. I'll have a glass." Mrs. Rimmer decided. Mam poured for everyone. Mrs. Rimmer graced the head of the table.

"Did you hear the sirens last night?" my mother asked.

"They go all the time. I worry more with each day that passes."

"What was the big commotion last night?" Oom Paul asked. "It went on for hours."

"Frau Erica was entertaining her Nazi bigwigs in Benedorpseweg. You should have seen the cars."

"Did you see the Maybach?" asked Oom Paul.

"A Maybach here on Weverstraat?" Dad said.

"Honest. A Zeppelin, the most expensive car in the world."

"Von Ribbontrop himself. Holy God but...." He stopped and looked at Mam.

"It must have been some party," she said.

"The Tafelberg Hotel did the catering. There's never rationing when Frau Erica splashes out."

Dad knew what went on there. I guessed Mr. Heemskerk was his source.

"She can keep her tasty morsels and her champagne," said Mam. "The rest of us can't buy a bar of soap or a kilo of sugar."

Mrs. Rimmer giggled. We all looked at her. I wasn't sure if I had heard right and I didn't seem to be the only one. However, Mrs. Rimmer was serious again and was concentrating on the conversation, which swung back to Frau Becker.

"The black market is a disgrace, three prices for everything," Oom Paul said. "You can't buy tyres, no matter what the price."

"That only affects those who can afford cars," Mam said.

"No, Corrie, bicycle tyres. I'm on the rim, but I can't buy a bicycle tyre."

Another giggle. This time there was no doubt, we definitely heard her. Mrs. Rimmer put her bony hand to her mouth, and hiccupped. Dad glanced at Oom Paul.

Mrs. Rimmer giggled again.

Oom Paul was a picture of innocence. Mrs. Rimmer reddened. Gerrit's mouth sagged.

"This fruit juice with the....tee hee...more, please?"

"I'll open a fresh bottle," said Oom Paul.

"I'll taste it first," Dad said, rising.

Mrs. Rimmer tittered again, and put her hand to her mouth.

"Why are you laughing, Mrs. Rimmer?" Antje asked.

"Me, laughing? I'm not...I'm not...hee hee, hee hee." Mrs. Rimmer couldn't help it.

All stared at Oom Paul. Innocent or not, he was being blamed.

"It's fruit juice, Wim, believe me," he said.

"It's from my father. There's no alcohol in it," said Tante Catherine.

Mrs. Rimmer was the only one drunk. She stood up and walked awkwardly to the sitting room, sat at the piano and began to play. Occasionally she tittered but she didn't look round, although we were right behind her. She played, slowly and softly at first. She increased to a faster tempo, bony fingers moving on shiny keys, in a world of her own. This small woman could make music. We stood in silence, scarcely daring to breathe as tears rolled down her cheeks. In that moment she was both pathetic and wonderful. We knew that, musically, Antje was in good hands.

Mrs. Rimmer didn't arrive for her next session. Antje was distraught. Mam went to Mrs. Rimmer's apartment and was back within an hour.

"She won't come. Antje has to go to her house."

"If that's what it takes," Dad said.

"I'll see how wonderful her piano is," said Antje eagerly.

We couldn't have known the consequences of that simple decision in the summer of 1942. Two years had passed since the trauma of invasion. What everyday miseries we had to endure were nothing compared to what was about to befall one section of the Dutch population. Unknown to the general population, the Nazis had already made decisions regarding the Jews of Holland. As summer began, they put their plans in motion. No one knew what was about to be initiated under our noses. Even if we had known, we could have done nothing. My father's hiding places were going to be used regularly.

We lived in a twilight world of events we couldn't quite be sure of. Jan and I went swimming, we cycled and ran through the woods. One day, as a family, we visited the farm of Mr. Haan, Tante Catherine's father, across the Rhine, near Driel.

Oom Paul craved excitement. He was about to create some excitement of his own. We were in a field where some black and white cows were grazing lazily in the sun. A small canal created a boundary between two fields of pasture.

"Jump, Oom Paul," Gerrit urged.

"Paul Baumann, don't you dare try jumping that canal," Tante Catherine said.

"It's only four metres wide. Hold my shoes, Gerrit," said Oom Paul.

I assumed he was just teasing Tante Catherine.

"Say nothing and he'll do nothing. Tell him not to jump and he'll jump," said Mam. "He's one headstrong man."

"He'll make a fool of himself in front of the children."

"Let him jump. A good wetting will teach him," my father said.

Oom Paul removed his jumper and stepped back. As we shouted "don't do it, don't do it" he ran for the canal and cleared it easily.

"Don't do it, Paul, don't do it," he mimicked from the other side, grinning.

"He won't make it back," said Antje quietly. Dad looked at her in surprise.

"What did you say, Antje?"

"Oom Paul won't make it back."

How could she say that when she had no idea how wide the canal was? She didn't see the wide margin he had cleared on the first jump.

"Stand back folks, here I come," Oom Paul shouted, and began his run.

We watched his take-off, feet raised high before landing dead in the centre of the canal, his face puzzled as he splashed below the water. He thrashed his way to the bank, and when he emerged, black slime was running down his face and body.

"What happened?" Paul asked.

We laughed so hard. Dad pounded the ground with his fist. Even Tante Catherine laughed so much she had to hold her hands to her side to ease the pain. Gerrit laughed a high-pitched whinny and my sides ached at Oom Paul's bewilderment.

"How did you know he wouldn't make it back, Antje?" Mam said.

"The ground on the far side is soft. His take-off for the jump back was soft."

Oom Paul's mouth opened wider. Could Antje really hear something so faintly muted? Mr. Haan turned and looked at Antje, smiling.

"She's right. That's pure black polder on the far side."

"Antje, you're a wonder," Mam said.

Mam and Tante Catherine teased Oom Paul relentlessly, and Mr. Haan fixed him up with clothes that smelled of chicken manure.

"Don't do it, Paul," said Mam when Oom Paul offered to pay the ferryman.

That set the rest of us into fresh fits of laughter.

"This is funny to you all?"

"Don't die before me, Paul. Life would be too dull without you," said Mam.

When we got home that evening, there was a letter for my father, marked urgent. He opened it immediately, and his face grew serious. Mam noticed, as did I.

"What is it, Wim?"

"Father Bruggeman wants to see me."

There had never been any letters from Father Bruggeman or indeed from any priest. Dad left for the presbytery right away, and was back within an hour.

"What was all that about?" Mam asked.

"I have to get a job."

"What's he talking about?"

"Dutch workers are to be deported. Those in non-essential work will be taken to Germany by force."

"How does Father Bruggeman know?"

"He begged me not to ask him questions."

"What kind of a job is he talking about?"

"Farm labourer."

"You? He's joking."

"Those involved in food production are exempt."

"Do as Father Bruggeman says, Mr. Baumann," said Jan Till.

"What farmer would want to hire you? You're a city man, Wim."

"I'll cycle six kilometres every morning. I'll be home on Sundays."

"And if you don't take it?"

"Take it, Mr. Baumann, please," Jan pleaded.

"It boils down to a choice between working somewhere in Germany, or on a farm in Holland. I start early and I finish early in my own country."

"Who can live on farm labourer's wages?" Mam asked.

"Father Bruggeman left me in no doubt about the job."

Antje posed a curious question.

"Why you, Dad?"

"What?"

"Why did Father Bruggeman send for you, Dad, and not someone else?"

"When I have the answer to that one, I'll tell you, Antje."

Not long after that Antje went silent for days, just like Dad sometimes did. We took turns to get her to talk, but it was a waste of effort. A few nights later I awoke to find her sitting on her bed, crying. She grabbed for me when I went close to her.

"What's wrong, Antje?"

"Oh, Nelis."

"What is it?"

"I have terrible dreams."

"You're okay now. You're awake."

"I'm scared, Nelis. It's the same dream every night. I'm on a lorry. It's crowded. I can't breathe…I can't…oh Nelis."

"It's only a dream, Antje."

"The lorry was sinking. People with badges. I couldn't turn. I couldn't get my breath. That's what frightens me, being unable to breathe."

She trembled and put her hands in mine. It was a dream, I said. She kept saying that it had been so real. She eventually went back to sleep and I thought that was the end of it.

Three days later Oom Paul came in by the side door, greatly excited. He had some major but ominous news.

"Who do you think I saw in Arnhem today?"

"Tell us, Paul."

"Mr. Mussel, the jeweller. Catherine and I bought our wedding ring from him. He was wearing a badge with the letter J on it. So was his wife."

"She had a badge?"

"It's the law. Every Jew has to wear a badge."

Antje rose and went into the sitting room.

I stayed up late, hoping that she'd be asleep when I went to bed. Not a chance.

"I keep seeing people wearing badges in my dreams, Nelis. I was in a lorry with other people. We were sinking."

Days passed and soon Antje was back to normal.

This was around the time of Gerrit's First Communion, a rerun of Antje's, with Nana excited, Mam getting everything in order, Dad promising to attend the Communion Mass no matter what. Father Bruggeman gave his usual First Communion homily.

This time around, there was Tante Catherine and Baby Cora, and Jan came to Mass with us. He had never been inside a church before. We were guests of Mr. and Mrs. Heemskerk for First Communion breakfast, but without Mrs. de Groot or her family.

Any mention of the Green Police or of Mr. Rauter in the presence of Mr. Heemskerk was not permitted. Otherwise it was an enjoyable day. This was Gerrit's day.

The reality of what was going on outside shocked us. Until then we had discussed rumours as casually as the weather, but now the rumours had a chilling menace. It was common knowledge that life for Jews was becoming more difficult with each passing week. They were dismissed from official jobs and forced to quit business activities. They could not run shops or sell goods except to fellow Jews, and were barred from public parks, public transport and other places in an avalanche of repressive measures. We knew things, *bad things*, to be fact but hoped that nothing worse would happen. All of our hopes and wishes died in that summer of 1942.

"They're trapped. With those badges they are in a prison. They might as well have surrounded them with walls," Mr. Heemskerk said quietly to my father. I kept close. Mr. Heemskerk was aware that I regularly carried messages to Luc Gauthier.

"What if we all wear badges?" Dad suggested.

"They tried that in Amsterdam and were arrested on the spot. I don't understand it."

"Me neither."

"Pushing people off buses and trains? Their children can't attend public schools any longer? I have no answers, Wim."

"They're not even allowed to ride bicycles."

It was a dismal conversation. Mr. Heemskerk's forecast after Pearl Harbor, that the Japanese would take Dutch East Indies, had proved correct. Now Dad and Mr. Heemskerk were both profoundly worried.

The Nazis did not deal with individual Jews but instead ordered them to set up their own Jewish Council. The Jews walked headlong into the trap, with Jews obeying orders and doing the Nazis dirty work for them. The real blow came in June when the Jewish Council was told that all Jews were to be transported to Germany to help with the war effort. The Jewish Council would have a useful role to play. They were to get their people to obey all instructions.

"Preposterous," said Dad. "What use are old people in a workforce?"

"It seems they want every last Jew out of Holland."

One Sunday, from the pulpit, Father Bruggeman read a pastoral letter from Archbishop de Jong. The Archbishop came straight to the point: "A Catholic who wishes to receive the Sacraments cannot and must not take part in manhunts for citizens of this country. A Catholic cannot receive Holy Eucharist if he assists in deportation of Jews or of veterans threatened by reinternment. Loss of job or livelihood as a policeman or a civil servant is not a valid excuse for a Catholic to obey an immoral order. The only cases were where an immoral order may be obeyed is when one's life is threatened, or when one's family may be sent to a concentration camp."

Archbishop de Jong's letter was directed at people like Henk de Groot and the thousands who served in the Green Police. I accompanied my father to Mr. Heemskerk's house that afternoon. Dad told him of the very direct message from Catholic pulpits.

"I had hoped for better from the churches. These last threats have caused our people to back off," said Mr. Heemskerk.

"Churches have hard choices to make. If they protest, the Nazis threaten to deport all converted Jews. If they don't, they fail the Jews, they fail all citizens."

"Nazis are Nazis. They'll deport all Jews, converted or otherwise, sooner or later. Church leaders should make a stand, today, tomorrow, every day. Deporting old people from their homes is barbarism."

On my next trip to Chez Luc in Arnhem, I saw people wearing Star of David badges. Others passed them by. The public's acceptance posed the question. "What of it?" Master's orders. What can we do? NOTHING was the answer. Stay alive, see nothing and say nothing.

"Mon Dieu, Cornelis," Luc Gauthier said. "Terrible. Mrs. Visser has to wear a badge. She's hysterical."

"Mrs. Visser?"

"Jewish. She came from Germany when the Germans announced their race laws."

"She's German?"

"Oui. From Aachen."

Antje had been right. I was reasonably smart, but not as smart as my blind sister.

"I'm forbidden to employ her. She cannot run her dress shop, or work here. Do you know what is happening, Cornelis?"

Laurence Power

Mr. Gauthier spoke to me as an adult. He assumed that whatever he said to me I would relay back to my father. I felt that silence was best in this instance.

"The Jews will panic. They are not being deported for work. How can elderly people with walking sticks work? What do they want with children and old people?"

"I don't know, Mr. Gauthier."

"When there are no logical answers, I worry, Nelis."

The round-ups came to Arnhem, as to all the cities and larger towns. For the first few days it was matter of-fact. Then, as Mr. Gauthier had foretold, consternation spread like wildfire among Jewish people. Some walked obediently from their homes to where they had been instructed to present themselves. Others, in desperation, sought places to hide. A safe place, any place. For how long? It might be possible to hide a Jew or a whole family for a night or two, but hiding Jews was dangerous. Other problems arose. What about ration books? As food got scarcer, ration books became a necessity.

"No ration cards means that your own family eats less," said Oom Paul. "Your house is torn to bits, you could be deported. I'll take risks for myself, but not for Catherine or Cora. I won't put my family in danger."

We adapted to the constantly changing situation, easily adjusting to Dad's new job. He left the house each morning before the family awoke. In the first few weeks he was home early in the evenings, then gradually later and later. My mother said nothing. Money became scarcer, food dearer. Worn clothes were tolerable, but a boot or shoe that let in water was a real problem.

One sweltering hot Friday afternoon in August I was walking with Antje to Mrs. Rimmer's house. On the way back I met Jan, along with a few other boys. We played a five-a-side football game, after which Jan and I returned to the house. Gerrit was alone. This was unusual unless Mam had gone up the road to talk to Tante Catherine.

"Where's Mam?"

"Koeman's shop. She got a message."

Gerrit wasn't alarmed, but I got a sinking feeling. Jan stayed behind while I ran to Koeman's, on Koningstraat. Mrs. Koeman's placid face changed as soon as she saw me. Since her husband had died, a man called Roy Keeter was running her shop. She whispered to him and then came round the counter to me.

"Do you know where your father is, Nelis?"

"No, Mrs. Koeman."

"Oh God."

"Where's Mam?"

"There's a problem, Cornelis. She's trying to sort things out."

"What problem?"

"They came for Mrs. Rimmer, and they took your sister."

"Who came?"

"The Green Police. Mrs. Rimmer is Jewish. They took her, and her mother, and Antje. Your mother has gone to Arnhem to see what she can do."

"Mrs. Rimmer was not wearing a badge."

"The Germans have files. Not wearing the badge hasn't saved her."

Antje arrested! I had to do something, but couldn't think what.

I ran from Koeman's shop to Mrs. Rimmer's apartment. I banged on the door. A woman outside looked at me.

"She's gone. They took her and the old lady and that little blind girl."

"How long ago?"

"Two hours."

It had to be a mistake. I went home to tell Gerrit and Jan. A shadow crossed Jan's face, just like the one I had seen the day they took his father. Mam returned at six, having been to two police centres to make enquiries. They were able to tell her nothing.

"They told me to calm down, it was just a mistake. If she's not Jewish, she won't be deported."

By now Mr. and Mrs. Van Gaal, Mrs. Koeman and other neighbours had gathered with Oom Paul and Tante Catherine. Mam and I called on the de Groots.

Mrs. de Groot was surprised to see us. She had grown flabby of late, now her face was puffed out and sullen.

"What do you want?"

"Is your husband here?"

"My husband is on official police business."

"Antje is missing. The police took her this afternoon."

"Antje?"

"She was with Mrs. Rimmer when they were taken."

"If she stuck with her own, she wouldn't be in trouble."

"Your husband might know something, Mrs. de Groot."

"I don't think so." She closed the door.

That was my first encounter with a truly venomous person.

Dad went white when he heard about Antje. His voice broke for a fraction of a second.

"It's time to call on real friends," he said.

He departed immediately on his bicycle, leaving us with friends and neighbours. I remembered Antje's dream, of being among people on a lorry with J badges that she had dreamed it before anyone saw Jews wearing badges on the street and something that she herself had could certainly never have seen. I couldn't bring myself to tell Mam.

Nana Nellie was hysterical. Tante Catherine worked hard to calm her. At midnight Dad returned. The look on his face was heartbreaking.

"They took Mrs. Rimmer, and her husband and children, her husband's brother, and his wife and children as well. Their oldest boy was at school when they called. The Germans came back later in the evening for him and also carried off Dr. Russmann"But what about Antje?"

"An SD man at police headquarters asked if I was aware that there's a war on. I said I was aware that there's a war on defenceless civilians taking place. He told me to calm down, once the Jew problem is out of the way, things will be back to normal. I can't tell you where our Antje is. I don't know. I have alerted friends. We'll know as soon as there's news."

Nana became hysterical again. Mam wept, long heart-wrenching sobs, which grew louder the more she tried to compose herself in front of us. Jan sat beside her. I panicked. Antje's dream of being on a lorry, gasping for breath, haunted me. Now the weather was steaming hot and humid. There had been several heavy cloudbursts during the night.

We slept in broken snatches, interspersed with bouts of panic, all the time feeling that Antje was beyond our help.

Mr. Heemskerk came the following morning to assure Dad that he knew people in high places who would help. He and Dad devised a strategy to make the authorities aware of their mistake, that Antje was not Jewish, she was a piano student in the house of a Jewish woman.

Our concern for Antje clouded our concern for Mrs. Rimmer and her family. We wanted Antje back.

The hours passed, neighbours gathered. We were afraid for her. What could a ten-year-old blind girl do in Germany? I went to pray at the church. Nana Nellie was there, lighting candles and saying prayers to St. Thérèse. I returned home. Gerrit sat on the doorstep, head in his hands, making me feel even worse.

We had no appetite. It was a painful, draining, endless day. If someone would only tell us something, anything at all, we would have been more at ease.

News finally came from an unexpected quarter. The now familiar siren of a police car rang across the town. It grew louder and came closer. We rushed outside. Henk de Groot in his green uniform emerged businesslike from the car. He opened the rear door and reached back into the car. It was then we caught a glimpse of Antje.

"You're home, Antje," said de Groot.

He walked towards us, holding her. Mam nearly ran me down in her rush to reach her.

"It's your Mama, darling, your Mama. "

"Oh, Mama."

Antje reached for her, then they were hugging and kissing, then Mam handed Antje to Dad. He put his strong carpenter's arms round her. We ignored Henk.

"Where was she?" Tante Catherine asked.

"She'll tell you herself," de Groot said.

He returned to the car, none of us thinking to thank him in the emotion of the moment. Dad carried Antje into the house, put her on the couch and a finger to his lips. Mam pulled a rug over Antje, and she was asleep in a moment.

She slept for ages. Our rampant curiosity was put on hold. She slept all that afternoon and night. We tried to stay awake but dozed off, one by one. It was morning when I awoke. Antje slept on. When she finally awoke at midday, she became distressed.

"You're home, love, you're safe," Mam reassured her.

"Where's Dad?"

"I'm here," he said reaching out to stroke her hair.

"And Nelis?"

"Here."

"And Gerrit?"

We wanted Gerrit to say 'I'm here', but he began to cry.

"And Jan?"

"Here, Antje," Jan said, delighted to be included in the family roll call.

Oom Paul and his family arrived and we all sat round waiting on Antje.

"I'm hungry."

Lunchtime was strange that day. Even Oom Paul was silent. Antje's intake amazed us.

"Antje love, please tell us what happened," Mam said quietly.

It was quiet when Antje began to talk.

"I was playing the piano when an impatient knock came. Mrs. Rimmer told me to keep playing. I heard loud voices telling us to collect one case and come immediately. Mrs. Rimmer asked where we were going. They shouted 'raus, raus'. Mrs. Rimmer said I was not her family, then I heard her scream. Mrs. Rimmer's mother was there. She's lame. She has a walking stick. A man shouted loudly in German. One who spoke Dutch said it was best to come quietly, there was a van waiting outside. Mrs. Rimmer said she wanted to stay. They gave us no time, one moment I was playing scales, the next I was thrown into a van. There were others there already, on the floor. A woman was crying for her children. The van moved off. We drove towards Arnhem and turned off right, then left. I could hear traffic, men and women talking. Someone said we were in a courtyard, with policemen standing guard. We waited in the van. A man lifted me into a lorry. The lorry was full... everyone standing... and in the crush I got separated from Mrs. Rimmer. A man behind me shouted in Dutch to lift the tailboard. The crush got worse when the lorry moved forward. I couldn't move. Every time someone fainted, there were shouts. The smell was awful. People were being sick and doing other things. Mrs. Rimmer called my name. I vomited and a woman beside me screamed. My feet were wet with puke and pee. It started raining, and the noise on the canvas drowned our screams. The lorry stalled until the rain ended. Water was pouring in. I heard a cow bawling so I knew we were in the country. My feet were so wet. I knew if I lay down once I wouldn't get up. They said that it was dark outside, that the lorry would travel all night. We heard a tractor moving in the opposite direction. The lorry went faster. The screaming stopped. Some slipped to the floor. I was so tired. We ignored the smell and vomit. Suddenly the lorry stopped and everyone pitched forward. A man said it had gone off the road. It listed to one side. People screamed that they were choking. We couldn't move in any direction because the front was lower. I heard shouting. The loudest voices were German. There was panic. Two men were arguing, a German and a Dutchman. Women were screaming that their children were suffocating. I tried to hold on to something. A fat woman was between me and the side of the lorry. I wanted air. I didn't know how long I could bear the crush.

Someone lifted me up so I could breathe again. The screaming to the front was terrible, because the lorry was sinking lower. I heard water splashing. A man shouted that we'd all drown. "Don't do it, don't do it" voices said. Someone was trying to climb over and get out. I heard bursts of gunfire. Then silence. I heard a man scream that his child had drowned. A man's voice from outside said, 'they'll all drown if we don't get them off.' He was arguing with a German. I heard a cutting noise through canvas. Someone held me by the waist and handed me to a man who spoke Dutch. I stood in water high up my legs. A German roared to put our hands in the air or he would shoot. I put my hands up. I could breathe again. The Germans shouted loudest. I prayed for a miracle. Children were crying. Every place was under water. I couldn't lie down. I kept my hands over my head and prayed. I knew men were pulling the lorry from the canal. I could hear more German voices. Then I heard Mr. de Groot ordering people to keep their hands up and I knew God had heard my prayer. I called his name. Shut up, the others said. Just shut up. I kept calling Mr. de Groot. They kept telling me to shut up. 'Who's calling me?' His voice was beside me. 'I'm Antje Baumann', I said. He said 'Holy Christ' out loud, twice. The Germans and Dutch argued again. Mr. de Groot took me to a car and told me to wait until they could get the lorry back on the road. Another man roared at him to get a move on and to stop talking to a little Jewish bitch. I think he meant me. They shouted again when they got the lorry back on the road. There were more screams. Mrs. Rimmer's voice came from beside me. 'Antje, save me, Antje!' Imagine that someone could ask me for help. Me!

Mr. de Groot and another man who spoke Dutch were sitting in the front. Mr. de Groot drove me to a house where a woman dried me with a towel and gave me dry clothes. Mr. de Groot said he'd got a call to deal with a traffic accident, which was all he knew. Mrs. Rimmer and her mother are gone. I know that. That's all I have to say. Nobody is to ask me another word on this ever again."

She clasped her hands across her front. Mam cried while Dad wiped tears from his face. Oom Paul put one hand to his forehead and groped for Tante Catherine's hand with the other, trembling with emotion. "I'll know what I'll do from now on," he said.

"I've this month's sugar. I'll make a cake for Henk," Mam said.

"So he can help the Nazis load children like cattle on to lorrys," said Oom Paul.

"Antje is alive because of him." My mother replied. She was angry.

"The Germans have traitors like de Groot to do their dirty work."

Dad raised his hand to avert their argument.

"With many bad things being done, we should welcome a good deed, no matter who does it."

Mam baked the largest apple tart possible in her cooking tin. My parents went to de Groots' house with their peace offering, the apple tart and a full bar of soap wrapped in newspaper. They were back in minutes.

"What happened?" I asked.

"Henk wasn't there. She took what we offered and shut her door in our faces."

It didn't matter. Antje was back, and she was safe. Over six decades later I still have no explanation for her dreams or premonitions. I have related them as she spoke of them.

Chapter Twelve

"Are you awake, Nelis?"

"Who is it?"

"Shhhhh."

"What is it, Dad?"

"Will you sleep in Gerrit's bed?"

"What's up?"

"Shhhhh, don't wake Antje. We want your bed for your cousins."

"Cousins?"

"Greta and Walter Verbeek from Utrecht. They'll be gone in the morning."

"Okay."

I went downstairs to Gerrit's bed. I hadn't known of cousins called Greta and Walter in Utrecht. I got into bed and then heard movement outside the bedroom door. My 'cousins' were on their way upstairs to my bed.

Dad had already left for work when I came down the next morning. Mam was busy with breakfast. Gerrit and Jan followed soon after.

"Sleep well, boys?" Mam asked casually.

"Yes, Mrs. Baumann," Jan replied.

"I had a scary dream. I dreamt a big animal, a horse or something, was in my bed. I thought this horse was going to roll over on top of me," Jan said.

"A horse in your bed! That was a scary dream."

"It was a nightmare, Mam. I was afraid."

Gerrit was solemn. Jan looked at me. He knew something unusual had happened.

"What happened to the milk and butter?" Gerrit asked.

"We'll get more when Koeman's open shop."

Neither Mam nor Dad said anything more about cousins from Utrecht. Ears open, mouth shut was the motto.

A new set of "cousins" regularly stayed overnight. I never met or even saw our late-night visitors, or asked questions.

"Was Oom Paul here last night?" Gerrit asked one morning.

"No. Why?"

"We've a savage in the house. There was plenty of bread there last night."

Mam was able to hide her reaction, no matter what was said. Antje was the one to bring the secret of our night-time visitors into the open. She continued to play the piano without her teacher. A lazy girl from the other side of Arnhem, called Jean Thijssen, came to help at Mam's request. Antje assured Mam she knew much more about playing the piano than her new teacher and Miss Thijssen didn't fancy the long cycle to Oosterbeek to teach a blind child. The day she left Antje said something unexpected.

"Miss Thijssen's perfume is the same as some of our late-night callers."

"What late-night callers?" Gerrit asked.

"They haven't told you, Gerrit?"

"Antje, what are you talking about?" asked Mam.

"The children who sleep in Nelis's bed, the adults who hide in the hideout in our bedroom, the ones who leave no bread in the house when they leave. We don't speak of them. I'm the only one here who has been arrested, but you don't trust me. I hear voices in my room. I smell bread being baked at two in the morning. I have four senses left that work and work very well, you know."

"You know about that, Antje?" asked Dad.

OOSTERBEEK

"Nelis and I have known since you and Oom Paul built the hidey place in our room. What I don't know is how they get in there. We haven't found the entrance."

Dad looked at Mam. It was time to come clean.

"We don't know what's right any more. We help people who need help, Jews mostly. What we do know is that most of them have been picked up and sent to the refugee camp in Westerbork before they're taken out of Holland by trains. Don't ask me where to, or why. They're not the only ones. Old people are being deported. The Jews are nearly all gone. Those who have not been picked up are in hiding. We don't know who it is who sends them to us. We hold them for one night. When they leave we give them an address in the country. Then they're on their own, beyond any help from us. The Greens or the SD can pick them up at any time. We follow our instructions."

"A baby cried in our room the other night."

"Her mother took her in the morning, we gave them an address. That's all we know."

We sat in silence. Dad was shocked that Antje and I knew so much.

"Is that why we have no bread some mornings?" asked Gerrit.

"How do they get into the hiding place?" Antje wanted to know.

"The middle of the three clothes hooks in your bedroom, push hard upwards on that and a flap door opens in."

"I never heard that baby crying," I said to Antje.

"You were in Gerrit's bed that night."

"My bed?"

"Only an odd night," said Mam.

"He's the horse?"

The following night I was reading when Mam brought Antje to bed. Immediately she sniffed something I had missed.

"We have visitors," she said casually.

"Is there someone below?"

"Someone is hiding in there."

"But I haven't seen or heard anyone."

"Our visitor is someone silly enough to use strong perfume. You can't smell it?"

"There's nobody here."

"Why not open up and see for yourself?"

"We might scare them."

"You said there's nobody here."

"I didn't see anyone arrive."

"Knock gently. If there is anyone there, they'll know we're not Germans. Germans never knock gently. Come on, Nelis."

I was as keen as Antje. I knocked. There was no reply. I knocked again, louder this time. Still there was no reply.

"There's nobody there," I said, "I told you."

"Press the coat hook upwards like Dad said," Antje whispered.

When I pushed the hook I felt something give, but nothing happened. I pressed against the panel just below the hook. It opened inwards, just like a bedroom door on hinges. It was a low narrow opening, the darkness barely relieved by my bedroom light. The perfume Antje had picked up hit me instantly. We did indeed have visitors.

A dim electric light was switched on within the hiding place, and I saw the outlines of three people, a man, a woman and a baby. That moment is etched forever in my memory. I was a witness to terror in its purest form. The woman's eyes were bulging, her mouth hanging on the verge of a scream, not sure whether she was safe with friends or was already in the grasp of her deadly enemies. Her black hair was wet with cold sweat.

"You can sleep in my bed, if you like," Antje said.

"We're going first thing in the morning," said the man. He had about him an air of resignation with no fight left.

"You shouldn't wear perfume," Antje suggested.

"We go in the morning. We don't want to cause problems."

"Can we get you anything?"

"Your parents are great people," said the woman. "We need passports."

"No, Margreet. These people have taken us in for the night. We cannot impose further on them."

"We're for the lorrys if we don't get new passports."

"I'll ask my father."

Dad became angry when I went downstairs and even angrier when I asked him if he could get forged passports for his the couple.

"Nelis, they come under certain conditions which they have accepted. We have to stay alive too. Tell them bluntly. Don't argue."

"We cannot help you with passports," I told them when I returned upstairs.

Both the man and woman exuded a naked fear. No passports. In the distance I heard the faint but scary hee-haw sound of a police car siren.

"We're being raided," said Antje.

"What did you say? What are you talking about?" I asked.

"We're going to be raided tonight."

"How can you say something awful like that? That siren is up on the Utrecht Road."

"We'll see," Antje said. "Switch off your light."

I dismissed her prophecy, but soon I was to be proven wrong. The sirens halted outside our house. As I sat up in bed my heart was pounding. We were about to experience our first raid from either the SD or the Green Police with Jews in hiding behind the wall. Fists pounded on our front door. The fear I had at that moment became a physical thing as if some giant thing had a grip on my body.

Dad ran to answer. Our guests were back in hiding. Antje pretended to be asleep while I sat upright in my bed in darkness. The reputation of the SD and the Green Police with their transport lorrys and deportation centres was terrifying. Fugitives hiding in a secret place in our bedroom added to the panic of that night.

I heard loud Dutch voices barking orders to search the room.

"Look in every wardrobe, search all outhouses for hiding places. Comb the place. Tear it apart if you have to."

The door to our bedroom burst inwards, lights went on. Men in uniform that rustled and holding guns, stood there, making huge shadows on the walls. They dragged bedclothes off, pulled drawers from the dressing table, letting the contents scatter across the floor. Antje asked, "What's up?" appearing to waken from her sleep. I told them she was blind. A blond policeman searched behind the curtains, Antje's bed was turned upside down and then mine. They shone a torch on each wall, first at the front windows, then the door towards the hiding place. I gripped Antje's hand. "What's happening Nelis?" she asked. The men probed, tapping walls, searching for a door or an opening, eyeing the carpet, pulling up and ripping the tarpaulin, searching for loose boards, but there was nothing to see. The room was a shambles. They moved to the next one and found the manhole flap to the roof. A policeman got a chair to stand on, pushed up the flap, was hoisted by another and the torch changed hands. The voices of two people carried through the walls, "Water tank, nothing else up here, no room up here. None I tell you". "Well check the water tank". "I already have". "Check it again, nothing I tell you, help me down, take the torch first, hurry."

There was another knock at the front door, I heard Dad say "What do *you* want, de Groot?" Then Henk's voice, apologising, but the other Greens wouldn't listen to him. Then another voice called out.

"Hey, who's in charge here? What in hell's going on?"

"Keep out of it, de Groot, this is not your affair, we have information."

"Fuck your information. This is a quiet place..."

"Shut your face, de Groot. Go home to your slob of a wife."

"There are no Jews here, I live two doors away."

"Who gives a fuck about Jews? Offices have been raided, ration cards are missing."

"You're off your rocker. He works on a farm."

"De Groot, when we want to hear from you we'll ask you. Get to hell out of here right now. Where's de Boer?"

I heard Dad say, "I'm not de Boer. My name is Baumann, this is my house."

"Well where is fucking de Boer?"

"I don't know any de Boer."

"If you're lying we'll be back and we'll tear this place apart. Do you hear me?"

"Yes sir, but there's no de Boer here."

"Some fucking clown in Hoogstraat is going to pay for this mess."

"Who's going to tidy my house?"

"You want me to send my mother round to do it for you? It's your fucking problem. Get out, de Groot. Come on fellows. Somebody is going to pay."

Car doors banged, they drove off. That was our first raid of the war. Mam, holding Gerrit's hand, was as white as a sheet. Jan stood close to her, trembling. Antje held tightly to my arm, breathless, like me.

"We'll tidy up. Everyone, get going right now," Dad said. That immediately focused our minds and helped prevent us feeling sorry for ourselves. We started sorting out the chaos. There was another knock at the door. I opened it. Henk de Groot stood there.

"Tell your parents I'm sorry. They had wrong information. It happens all the time."

"Okay, Mr. de Groot."

Everyone was still too shocked to comment on Henk de Groot's apology. No one slept that night.

At daybreak Dad tiptoed into our bedroom. He pressed the coat hook and pushed the narrow door inwards. The couple emerged, badly shaken, the woman carrying the sleeping child. Antje had been right, the woman's perfume pinpointed her presence. Then they were out of our house and into the morning, back into the lethal world for Jews that was Holland in that autumn of 1942.

Chapter Thirteen

Jan Till and I tossed a ball to each other. We'd been told to stay close to home. Raids by the Green Police were routine. Although we wanted to give the impression that we were fully absorbed in our game, we were on constant alert for strangers. Conversations resounded with words like collaborators, informers and spies. I reported every stranger I saw on our street. Imaginations ran riot what with couriers with dispatches, spies with information, British spies, German spies and Dutch collaborators. We watched and knew a lot, but we said little.

"A visitor," said Jan. "Behind you on a bicycle."

We kept throwing the ball. A stout woman dismounted beside me.

"Where does Mrs. Baumann live?" she gasped, perspiring heavily.

"My mother?"

"Maybe your grandmother. Mrs. Nellie Baumann?"

"She's in the house."

"Tell her Armin Kessel's daughter wants to talk to her."

Nana was helping Mam in the kitchen when I entered.

"A woman wants to see you, Nana. She says she's the daughter of Armin Kessel."

Nana's expression changed instantly and she rushed outside to hug the woman. The daughter of Armin Kessel, Marlene was her name, had to be German. Why was Nana hugging her? Who was Armin Kessel?

"Can you come with me to Wageningen," Nana said to me.

"When?"

"Now."

It was a long journey by bicycle, but Nana's stamina amazed me. We pushed Marlene Kessel where the ground rose. The nearer we got to Wageningen, the slower the woman cycled. When she finally pulled left off the main road I sighed with relief. We were in a quiet suburb, not unlike Oosterbeek, although with fewer woods.

We were introduced to Dirk van Beek, Marlene's husband. Even though his wife had a German name, this was a Dutch house, and very orange. A framed and serious portrait of the Queen hung in the hallway, below the national flag. He even joked about being one of the van Beeks from Oosterbeek. I felt a bit easier about his wife.

"How is he?" Nana asked.

"He is hanging in there. He'll die happy when he sees you."

Even in bed, Armin Kessel was a giant of a man. He was propped up on a pile of pillows in the dimly lit room when we entered.

"Nellie Baumann is here Daddy. She cycled from Oosterbeek with her grandson."

The sick man's hand groped eagerly for Nana's hand. She leaned over and kissed him on the forehead. Both shed tears, no words were spoken. Kessel groped for my hand and squeezed.

"Your grandson?"

"My grandson, Armin. His name is Cornelis."

I watched a flood of emotions flicker across the craggy lines of his bearded face. He attempted to speak but choked. Nana kept holding his left hand and smiling at him. She was content to wait.

"Talk when you're ready, Armin. Don't upset yourself."

He must have been a powerful man in his day. I guessed that he was now in the final hours of his life. Nana massaged his hands, smiling warmly at him. With a handkerchief she wiped away the tears flowing down his bony cheeks. He grew calmer.

"I'm sorry, Nellie."

"Stop that now, Armin Kessel."

"I'm sorry, Nellie. That's why I sent for you."

"You've nothing to be sorry for, Armin."

"I'm filled with shame every hour of every day."

"It's not our dear friend Armin Kessel doing these awful things."

"I was a proud German. I am dying of shame, the shame of watching good men being betrayed by criminals and thugs. All those killings, oh Nellie, it's bad. I wanted to be buried in Rhineland, close by the river. Now I want to be buried in Holland beside my true friends, beside that boy's grandfather."

He cried again. Nana held his hand, smiled and waited.

"I want to be buried beside a man like Frank Baumann. That second time ... Gott im Himmel, only one man in the world."

The old man wanted so badly to talk.

"I don't want to be buried in Germany. Will your family object to me lying in the same graveyard? I'm not German any more."

"Frank would like that," Nana said. She turned to me. "How do you feel if Herr Kessel is buried alongside your Grandfather?"

Two hours before I hadn't heard of Armin Kessel, but I had heard comments about Grandfather being fearless and of an old German attending his funeral. I had a vague recollection of stories about Grandfather saving someone's life. Mr. Heemskerk had more regard for Grandfather than for any other man alive.

"What is the second time that Mr. Kessel is talking about?"

Armin Kessel turned and for the first time looked directly at me. He had steely grey eyes in a craggy face.

"Be proud to be grandson of Frank Baumann," he said.

"Yes sir."

"You tell him, Nellie. Tell him everything."

His breathing rattled. Nana held his hand and smiled at him, then looked at me. She turned to look at Herr Kessel's daughter, and relaxed her grip. Calmly Nana laid her hands on his forehead and pulled down his eyelids.

"A good man," she said.

"He always spoke of you after that time…always," Marlene van Beek said.

Nana turned to me, more serious than I had ever seen her.

"Nelis, you've heard the dying wish of a good man. It would mean so much to his family to have that wish honoured".

It was my first time seeing a man die and I was unprepared. I was a thirteen-year-old Dutch boy with a deep loathing for all Germans. Seeing Armin Kessel as a man filled with shame for the horrors visited on our country by his countrymen was a jolt. I had to make a decision based on one dead man, not a nation of living people throbbing with hatred and inhumanity.

I wanted my dilemma to go away. Nana rescued me.

"You want to discuss it with your Dad first. Is that it?"

I nodded. I felt Dad should know about the request.

"Then you have nothing to worry about. Your Dad knows about the friendship between your Grandfather and Herr Kessel."

"Okay."

Mrs. van Beek shook my hand formally. She had made me feel like an adult. Nana smiled. After a meal and chat about the life of Armin Kessel, Nana and I began the long cycle back to Oosterbeek. For half an hour we travelled in silence. She liked to cycle in front but after a while she allowed me catch up. "I'm glad you met Armin."

"What did he mean about Grandfather and the second time?"

"We'll walk a bit, Nelis."

We dismounted and walked. The evening sun was on our backs.

"Before your Grandfather and I met, he worked on fishing vessels on the North Sea. There were no radios then, nor weather forecasts, nor lifejackets. Boats were unsafe in a squall. Too many men drowned who shouldn't have. The only rescue service was the bravery of crewmen, and the captain's skill. One day Armin got tossed overboard in a gale. Your Grandfather fastened a rope around his body and jumped in to save him. When they got him ashore, Armin was rushed to hospital with a severe head injury. It looked as if he might die, so your Grandfather volunteered to carry the news to the girl Armin was engaged to marry. He travelled to Den Haag. She travelled back to Den Helder to see her fiancé. That was over forty years ago, when travel was much slower. When she got there, Armin was in really bad shape. Your Grandfather offered to stay with her until Armin woke up. Over those few days a love affair developed between the pair."

We continued walking.

"There were terrible rows when Armin rejoined his boat. Armin and your grandfather fought over everything, over Germany and Holland, over duty rosters, over who did what. They fought over…over the girl. Finally they were put on separate boats to keep them apart. They fought in bars when they met. One week, when the boat Armin worked on was in for repairs, he was sent to a larger boat with your Grandfather. They wouldn't talk. There was freezing fog that night, the sort of weather that fishermen dread. Every boat in the North Sea headed for port. Another fishing boat hit them broadside on, and Armin was washed overboard. It was freezing, and nothing could be seen. A man overboard was a man dead. Armin Kessel knew his time was up. Nobody jumps into freezing cold water in a black fog. But one man did. A sailor fastened a rope to his body and jumped into the water and rescued him. It was the same man who had pulled Armin Kessel from the sea the first time. That's what he meant by saying your Grandfather jumped the second time."

"What happened?"

"Armin met another girl, Mette. Your Grandfather and I were guests at their wedding. Men of the sea have respect for each other, always, even though they fight. Your Grandfather would be proud of what you did today. I'm proud of you."

Later that week Armin Kessel was laid to rest in the plainest of coffins, close to Grandfather's grave. Mrs. van Beek, her husband, their two girls and other family members came to our house after the funeral. The significance of the event became obvious when Mr.

Heemskerk and his wife arrived and greeted Marlene van Beek like a long-lost daughter. Mourners huddled in small groups, speaking in muted tones. Nana kept referring to me as 'my grandson Cornelis' and spoke of my decision regarding Armin Kessel's burial place, much to my discomfort and Jan's delight. Little did I realise then what my decision then was to mean in time.

The war grew noisier. Allied bomber planes flew east over Arnhem to bomb cities in the Ruhr and other parts of Germany, mostly at night. It was sobering, knowing that the noise in the skies meant that bombs were dropping on other people's houses to kill those inside. Even so, I had no sense of concern or remorse for these bombings. Public round-ups and civilian executions were now commonplace. Razzias or lightning raids to lift people off the street in broad daylight occurred in every city and those arrested were shipped to Germany as slave labour. Jews who were still at large were demented with fear, hiding in garrets and cellars. Those who helped them put their own lives at risk. It seemed that every last residue of hope was steadily draining away.

Mr. Heemskerk called one November night. By now I could read faces like a book, even his. He wasn't smiling but instead had the look of someone who knew something the rest of us didn't. He sat and lit his pipe. We waited.

"They've done it," he said.

Mam became still, Dad waited in silence. Mr. Heemskerk was nothing if not dramatic.

"Who?" Mam finally asked.

"The British."

Mr. Heemskerk held down a block of hard tobacco with his left hand while he pared off thin slices and worked them loose in his palm. He slowly refilled his pipe and pulled out a box of matches. He paused before lighting a match. "The British have just won a major military victory over the Nazis in North Africa."

Mr. Heemskerk lit another match, sending sweet-smelling tobacco smoke towards the ceiling.

"The German Afrika Corps has been beaten in a major battle. It looks like thousands upon thousands of them have been taken prisoners; lands that the Germans had conquered have been taken back from them. This is big."

Hope. Each day brought fresh news, bad news meant bad days, hope draining away, good news meant good days, hope reborn. Mr. Heemskerk was back within a few weeks, his pipe in one hand again, a block of tobacco and knife in the other. This time he passed on some news he had picked up on the BBC World Service that he thought might be important. Soviet soldiers defending the city of Stalingrad had broken out to launch a counterattack and had encircled a whole army.

Mr. Heemskerk was in no doubt that an army marooned in the Russian at the height of a Russian winter could be very significant indeed.

"Have a cup of tea, Mr. Heemskerk," Mam said. It was considered polite to say 'not now, thank you', because the cup of tea accepted today was the cup foregone tomorrow. "Don't worry about tea," Dad said, "I've a bottle of French liqueur." He was still trying to lay off the same liqueur Luc Gaulthier had tasted two years before.

"Good idea," said Mr. Heemskerk.

They toasted the coming year, an end to the war, a return to normality. If we had known then that we were only at the halfway stage of the occupation, we might not have been able to carry on. God does right by us when we are denied seeing into the future. Compared to the people of Poland, the Soviet Union and others, we in Holland had seen nothing yet. We had to learn that the Nazis were one form of menace while they were winning and their horizons were expanding but another entirely when their empire was in danger of shrinking. Nazism was about to be revealed to us in all its starkness.

Chapter Fourteen

One Saturday morning in May 1943 I cycled to Arnhem to deliver dispatches to Luc Gauthier. I had my packets of Nana's strong-smelling goat's cheese in the front basket, along with six fresh eggs in an enamel jug. Mam thought that if any of the shells cracked, Luc could still use them in a dish. More importantly, Mam would get paid. The dispatches I carried were stuffed into my bicycle handlebars.

As I neared the city centre, I saw what looked like a major commotion ahead. People were running, women were screaming. I got out of there as fast as I could, going to Luc's place around the corner. It was better to get the dispatches I was carrying to Luc than to keep them stuffed in the handlebars. As I walked in, Mr. Gauthier grabbed me roughly by the hand.

"Razzia. Haul in your bicycle."

A razzia was a lightning search and snatch operation. No longer looking for certain suspects, Jews or black marketeers, the Nazis were taking civilians of working age and forcing them to work for long hours with no pay in munitions factories in Germany. Shoppers and shop assistants in Arnhem were easy targets. Able-bodied men going to work were seized and tossed on to lorrys. Within hours they would be part of an assembly line, producing the tools of war to use against our allies. Albert Speer, Hitler's armaments minister, bragged that German munitions production had increased every month since the 1941 summer invasion of the Soviet Union, small wonder when the workforce was recruited through snatch and grab operations. In the minds of Seyss-Inquart and Albert Speer, the rules of war in the matter of civilians had no currency. Slavery had come to Holland and our people had been relegated to the status of serfs.

"Don't put your head outside the door for anything," Luc said.

His temples were greying and he looked more worried than ever. We peered through the café window. A young woman in her early twenties across the street was looking in our direction. She wore a knitted scarf on her head. She had that look I knew well, the look of prolonged fear. Glancing to each side, she walked quickly to Chez Luc and pushed the door. She looked at me briefly and then saw Luc. Relief crossed her face as she whispered urgently in his ear. Luc pursed his lips at what she had told him. He went to the café door and turned the "closed" sign and locked up. He told her to sit, trying to get his head around some problem.

Suddenly another woman was standing at the café door banging with her fist. Luc rose to open it.

"It's house to house. The razzia is house to house," the woman shouted.

We saw people running in all directions away from the city centre in great haste.

"They've blocked it off at the top end," I heard another woman's voice cry out.

Old and young were running for their lives. In their panic, they bumped into one another. Men lost their hats but didn't stop, women's shoes slipped off but they continued running on bare feet. Children were being dragged so fast their feet barely touched the ground. Dogs slunk round corners, sensing the fear and tension. Young men banged frantically at doors trying to get in and through to the next street. One man in overalls used a bicycle pump to smash through a window, then jumped through the broken glass from the street. Another man lifted the street cover of a sewer and lowered himself down, pulling the cover back into position as he disappeared. Horses and carts were abandoned.

OOSTERBEEK

I watched as soldiers chased down two young men who were beating frantically for entry on a shop door, but their banging was futile. One surrendered, the other dodged and resisted strongly until a soldier clubbed him on the side of the head with his rifle butt. He staggered and then fell to the ground, blood spurting from his mouth. Another soldier kicked him in the face, grabbed him by his collar and dragged him along the pavement.

Soldiers emerged from a bicycle shop behind two men, one of whom was in greasy overalls, the other with his shirtsleeves rolled up, both with their hands in the air. These were more able-bodied slaves for Speer's industrial production line. "Quick, in here," said Luc Gauthier. I turned and saw him push a corner table to one side and lift a trapdoor.

The young woman did not need to be told twice. She curled up inside the small underground store. Space was very tight beyond the trapdoor.

"You too, Nelis."

I got in quickly and nestled up alongside her. Luc closed the trap door over us. We lay beside one another in total darkness. The space was so small that her elbows were sticking into my body. She shushed me. We didn't dare move. I sensed the warmth of her body, but her breath smelled faintly unpleasant. She was trembling. I was afraid for her, for myself and for Luc overhead. Was this how Antje had felt when she was taken in the lorry? Was this woman Jewish? Why was Luc so concerned? Questions were running through my head but I knew I had to stay still and silent.

German voices were directly over us. It sounded as though Luc could speak German. One German sounded so very close, he must have been standing directly above us. I heard Luc say, 'General Harzer won't like it if he has no place to dine the next time he's in Arnhem.' There was a short laugh, then shuffling feet. I felt the woman's sigh of relief. Ja, ja, *guten tag, auf wiedersehen, au revoir, mes amis.* I heard the trampling of heavy-booted feet, then the café door opening. Luc was in no hurry to let us out of our hiding place. We waited. I needed to pee. Open up Luc, I thought, we have to be safe now. When the trap door finally opened, the fresh air was like a sea breeze. I got out first. Luc helped the young woman out. She was deathly pale.

"The razzia is over. Things will be back to normal soon," he said.

"Did they take many?"

"Oui. Nelis, this is Anna. We have a problem. You can help, but it's dangerous."

"How?"

"A boy in short pants may get away with what has to be done. An adult has no chance."

"What do I have to do?"

"See that horse and wagon across the street?"

"Yes."

The sturdy wagon had high sides with a tailboard, the sort used by market gardeners to bring their vegetables and potatoes to the market.

"Sit on the wagon and follow Anna." He turned to the woman. "Lead Nelis to where you want him to go."

"What do I have to do, Mr. Gauthier?"

"Follow Anna."

"That's it?"

"Are you ready?"

"Yes Mr. Gauthier," I said.

Luc stayed grim. "May God go with you, my son."

Before I moved off Luc put out his hand, I thought he wanted to shake mine, but he pointed to the handlebars of my bicycle. He was looking for the dispatches I carried. Good thinking, I thought.

Anna pushed my bicycle on to the street and turned right. I climbed on to the wagon and took the reins. The horse made no move. There was a short stick on the floor of the wagon, which was empty except for a few jute sacks that smelled of onions. One touch of the stick to the animal's rump got it moving. I had never driven a horse before.

I was now a thief, having taken the property of another person without his consent. I followed Anna who cycled slowly ahead of me. We passed soldiers and Green Police. I kept my eyes fixed between the street and Anna's back. When she turned a corner, I followed. She went straight on, and then left. I was in an unfamiliar part of town, with narrower streets. The horse slowed down. Children were shouting and playing football on the pavement. I kept Anna in sight. The doors of most of these houses were peeling, there were many broken gutters. This was a poorer part of the Arnhem, a far cry from the more affluent and wooded suburb of Oosterbeek.

Anna went to a faded red door, gave it three quick knocks and then continued walking. First she nodded and then gave me a quick hand signal to stop at that door. I reined the horse in and dismounted. The door of the house opened a few inches inwards.

"Quick," said a female voice from inside. "Leave the horse to us."

A woman with a serious face and untidy hair beckoned me up one flight of stairs, then another. On the second floor landing was an old storage cupboard. She opened the door where I saw a number of shelves stacked with hand tools and household goods. She pulled a short piece of metal bar and tapped lightly three times on the rear. We waited. Then she stood back from the cupboard and the whole thing opened out towards me. I saw more stairs going upwards. A grey-haired man with a very grim face was there. He beckoned to me to follow him. I did, and was hit with such a strong, obnoxious stench I could barely breathe. The higher up I went, the worse it became.

I followed the man into a room. Here there was no escaping the sickening odour. Eight people, three elderly, two middle-aged and two young men and a young woman, surrounded me. One woman was sitting on a couch. For a moment I thought I recognised her but quickly realised that I didn't. I guessed that they were Jews in hiding, terrified hostages to fortune.

"We couldn't hold out for even another day," the grey-haired man said. "Follow me."

"God's blessing on you, whoever you are," said an elderly white-bearded man.

We entered a room off that one. The roof window was wide open to let in fresh air. The smell in there was almost more than I could bear. A corpse was laid out on a bed, a snow-white old woman with pinched lips pulled over her partly shut mouth. Her rigid body was tightly wrapped in an attempt to contain the smell. Her skin was like parchment, with flakes of dark peel across her forehead. She was skin and bone, and must have been dead for days.

"We beg you to bury this woman in a grave. Do not dump her body in a wood or river. She reared eight of us."

The old man cried and the others mostly stood speechless. The young woman stepped forward and touched his arm gently. 'It's all right, Papa,' she said.

I had to bury a decaying corpse someplace safe from ravening dogs.

"Go, son, don't delay," said another of the elderly ladies.

"It is very dangerous to the rest of us."

"Baumann. You're young Baumann. You're Wim's son. I know this boy," the woman on the couch said.

She looked familiar. She stood up. Who was she?

"I fed you in Chez Luc" she said.

"Mrs. Visser?"

Luc Gauthier said she had been taken away in a lorry. She had gone grey within a year, and looked ten years older. Her appearance shocked me.

"Her name was Hepsibah. Bury her deep in the earth away from dogs, Nelis."

"I'll do my best, Mrs. Visser."

The stench of decaying flesh was barely tolerable. I had to carry the corpse downstairs on my own. I hoped I would be strong enough to lift her. There were no last farewells, no intimate or final touches. Every single person in that room was at breaking point.

A waterproof sheet was wrapped around the body. I put my right arm under the dead woman's shoulders and my left arm under the hips. The corpse was rigid, and lighter that I had expected. I was glad my stomach was empty.

I moved downstairs, through the storage cupboard, which was pulled shut as soon as I cleared it. They couldn't get me out of the house fast enough. Their fear of capture was matched with the stench of decomposition. The lady who had let me into the house opened the front door. I lifted the corpse into the wagon that was hitched outside. I found my bicycle lying on the floor of the wagon, no doubt left there by Anna. In the open air the stench was still terrible, but more bearable. I took the reins and urged the horse to move. Children were still shouting and playing football. A young man was walking ahead. When I got to the end of the street, he nodded left.

I got hopelessly lost in that part of Arnhem. I felt my only chance was to head back to the centre of the City and work out my way after that, even though there were still street checks after the razzia. I needed a spade for my task. I finally spotted a familiar landmark, the Church of Saint Eusebio.

I drove through the very heart of Arnhem towards Oosterbeek, the reckless act of a terrified fourteen-year-old. I knew a safe place in the woods to bury a corpse and that I could use a spade from our garden shed. If Jan was home, he would help me dig. To reach Oosterbeek, I had to avoid being seen by the owner of the horse and wagon, and not be stopped and arrested by either Germans or the Green Police.

The first roadblock was outside St. Elizabeth Hospital. When two German soldiers raised their arms to stop me I calmed down. I jerked the reins, standing upright in the wagon. The horse responded as I intended, moving awkwardly to one side rather than halting. One of the Germans had to jump out of the way. The other saw his colleague's discomfort, looked at the horse and wagon, then glanced at me. He waved me on. I was thankful for my choice of clothing that day. Luc was right, a kid in short pants could get through road checks more easily.

I carried on. One kilometre farther on and I encountered another roadblock, even tighter this time and operated by the Greens. My earlier calm deserted me. I felt certain that the Greens would not let me pass.

"Halt."

I tried the same quick jerk to the reins and stood up in the wagon. A thickset Green Policeman grabbed the horse by the bridle.

"What are you carrying?" As he spoke he moved closer to the wagon.

"A bicycle, sir. The gears are not working."

He gave me a suspicious look and walked around to the side of the wagon. He looked me directly in the eye. He had to have smelled the stench emanating from the body.

"What have we under the sacks?"

"A body, sir," I said. "A dead body."

No matter how many times down the years I told myself I was bluffing, the truth is I was petrified with fear. Cold sweat trickled down my back.

"A body. Whose?"

"Granny's."

He pulled one of the sacks aside and there, right beneath his gaze, was the corpse's head with snow-white hair. He recoiled instantly from the stench and looked from the corpse to me, then back to the corpse, disgusted. Silence. My throat had gone totally dry. He looked round to see if his colleague was watching, then his jaw went slack as he waved me on.

I was drained. Two roadblocks encountered, both cleared. My hands were sweating and I needed to pee urgently. I drove towards Oosterbeek, and when I arrived, headed left into Weverstraat, towards our road. Jan saw me.

"Bring two spades," I told him.

"What's the awful smell?"

"Get the spades, Jan."

I drove on, hoping he would follow. When he caught up with me, he climbed aboard the wagon, grimacing at the smell, but didn't ask questions. I guided the horse towards the woods off Hoofdlaan.

"I've got to bury this corpse."

"I know a place with good cover. Leave the body there, take the wagon towards Benedendorpsweg and tie it up, then come back here and we'll bury it," said Jan.

"Right."

Jan showed me the ideal spot. Beneath some lime trees there was laurel and other hedging, spindly but adequate. Jan nodded and we carried the body from the wagon and concealed it under the ground cover. I handed Jan the spades and continued down the lane. I tied the horse to a post near a water trough and urinated against a tree, then returned to set about our grim business.

Digging in the back garden was one thing but digging into virgin earth with the roots of big trees coming from all directions was another matter. We piled the excavated earth to one side. Every time I stuck the spade into the earth, I hit a thick root.

"Company," Jan muttered under his breath.

Above me, Henk de Groot's son Theo stood on the mound of freshly dug clay, within two metres of us. My heart sank. The corpse was under the ground cover but the smell alone would give us away, and no explanation was possible.

But Jan held his nerve.

"Burying a corpse?"

"Two corpses. Some dogs that were hit by a car last weekend. They smell."

"Whose dogs?"

"Someone out from the city maybe."

"Oh, Christ, the smell. Phew, let me outta here."

Theo left. We resumed work right away, not daring to speak or stop. When we had dug about a metre deep, we pulled the corpse from its hiding place. The smell rose with the movement. We laid the rigid mortal remains of an old Jewish woman named Hepsibah at the bottom of a grave beneath a large tree. We pushed freshly dug clay over her body and pounded it down as tightly as we could. Both corpse and the stink vanished as loose earth filled the grave.

In silence I said the Lord's Prayer for the soul Hepsibah, while Jan looked into the distance. We picked up the spades and headed back to Hoofdlaan.

"That was fast thinking, Jan. But why *two* dogs?"

"Any fool could see the grave was too large for just one dog. Theo may be a policeman's son, but he'll never make a detective."

Jan headed back to the house. I returned to collect the horse and wagon, which I felt I had a duty to return to the rightful owner. I headed towards the city via the lower road, between the Utrecht Road and the Rhine.

By now I thought I was beyond surprise but I was wrong. On Benedendorpsweg I saw 'Frau Erica' Becker walking towards me, several paces ahead of her husband. She had two brown cats with black-tipped ears on a leash. Behind came her husband with two German shepherds, also leashed. I had never seen cats on a leash before.

I didn't acknowledge them as they passed. This couple enjoyed their privileged life while ordinary men and women were being rounded up on the streets of Arnhem for enslavement in Germany, and Mrs. Visser and the others in that stinking apartment lived in a state of permanent terror. I had seen pain in the face of the young woman with whom I had hidden under the trap door. My loathing for Frau Erica intensified. How could a privileged Dutch woman behave like that?

I met just one roadblock on my return journey, and this time two young German soldiers searched the wagon thoroughly. All they found was a bicycle and a few jute sacks, but the stench still lingered. They caught it, but waved me on in sullen silence.

There was more in store. As I dismounted from the wagon near Chez Luc, I was grabbed from behind and slapped violently across the face. The owner of the horse and wagon had big bushy eyebrows, and lifted me by the neck of my pullover so that my feet were off the ground. It happened so fast, I was rendered powerless and scared.

He slapped me on the face again. People gathered around, gazing at me with hostility. A young lad of my own age was with my tormentor.

"Easy on there, Pim."

It was a voice that I knew. It was Luc Gauthier.

"No, Luc. This thief took my horse and wagon."

The crowd got bigger. Luc walked up to the man Pim and whispered in his ear. The man turned to me for a moment and then looked back at Luc.

"Him?"

"Him."

Luc nodded and then said something else into the man's ear, and the man loosened his grip. He removed his cap and held it in his left hand. With his right hand he saluted me formally. He turned to the boy beside him.

"Give this lad the price of a meal at Luc's place."

"Yes, Dad," the boy answered.

"I'll look after him," said Luc, and led me inside.

"Roadblocks?"

"Two on the way out, one on the way back."

"Afraid?"

"Yes."

"Stay afraid and stay alive."

Luc's demeanour had changed. He was now a man who had left the morning's burden behind.

"I make no apology, Nelis. The razzia made it possible. Burying that old Jewish lady was important. It reminds us that some of us are still human beings. I'm proud to know both you and your father."

It was near eight o'clock when I got home, tired, but with a full belly. Mam asked no questions. Neither did Dad. Later, Antje spoke very quietly to me.

"When nobody says a single word I know that something has happened. You're in the thick of something. Nobody said anything about the smell from your clothes, so I won't ask either."

"Good."

"Do just one thing."

"What?"

"Stay alive. I get so scared. Stay alive for my sake. Please, Nelis. Are you listening?"

"I'm listening."

I wanted to stay alive too, for my own sake, but that summer of 1943 I was slowly coming to terms with the fact that life in Holland was no longer simple.

Theo de Groot walked past the front of our house two days later. Whatever respect I had for any member of that family it was for Theo.

"Follow me," he said in a whispered voice and not looking in my direction.

He continued walking. His unkempt mother stood at her front door, wiping her hands on her apron and staring after us. As soon as she went back inside the house I dropped my garden spade and strolled after Theo. Every so often he looked behind. When he got to the trees, he threw his leg over a small earth bank and disappeared into the woods. I followed.

"What is it?"

"You're in danger."

"Who is?"

"You. Your family."

"Danger of what?"

"Ask no questions. Just believe what I tell you, Nelis."

"How do you know?"

"No questions."

"Tell me."

"If strangers leave your house at odd times in the morning, do people notice?"

"Your father?"

"Leave it at what I said."

"What does your father know that puts us in danger?"

"Forget my father. People are watching and are not blind. Strangers go to your house late at night and leave early in the morning."

"Friends call. So what?"

"Deny it all you want, Nelis, but stop taking stupid risks."

"What are you talking about?"

"Do you think I was fooled by that ridiculous story of dead dogs?"

"Who's watching us? Who could report us?"

He looked away.

"Your sister?"

He gave a very brief laugh. Clearly he thought the question ridiculous.

"Your mother?"

Theo jerked his head. This time he didn't laugh. Neither of us spoke. He continued walking through the wood. I stood rooted to the ground, and eventually walked home in shock.

I told Dad. He went quiet, pondering on what I had told him.

"At least one person in that family has a spark of decency."

Oom Paul arrived as we were speaking. The war was getting him down. He was no longer the carefree extrovert who laughed at everything life threw at him. Only the day before Mam had teased Tante Catherine by asking her what was she doing to her husband to turn him into such a sourpuss.

"It's the war," she had replied. "Before, the Germans kept records and they paid regularly for everything they bought. Now they take what they want, they keep no records or make no payments. There is nothing he can do."

"I need a favour," Oom Paul said to Dad. "Two of our best workers were lifted in Saturday's razzia. We might not see them again for a long time."

"What do you want me to do?"

"I've got a husband and wife couple coming from near Nijmegen to replace them. They will need a place to sleep for a few nights until they can sort out accommodation in Arnhem."

Dad's first reaction to such requests was usually a nod, but now he hesitated, looking at me before he spoke.

"Have they genuine identity papers?"

"I wouldn't ask you otherwise."

"I'll check their papers before I let either of them inside the door."

"What is this all of a sudden?"

"We're living in Holland, Paul. That's what."

"You're right Wim. Saturday's razzia was the worst yet. They took Philip Leaden. He lent me his car a few times, now his wife is in hospital having their fifth child and I was the one sent to tell her. She asked me how she was going to buy food without money. What could I say to her?"

The couple from Nijmegen arrived as we were going to bed. Dad scrutinised their identity papers and made up a bed for them on the settee. The man towered over his tiny wife. They thanked Mam for accommodating them at such short notice. The woman gave her a small bag of tea in gratitude. Mam accepted it silently.

We put out the lights, expecting to sleep. It was Antje who first heard the police siren in the distance. She called to me and we both sat up in our beds.

"A raid," she said.

Suddenly there was uproar, with everything happening at once. Car doors were banging again and again, the doorknocker was being pounded, lights were going on, dogs were barking. Dad rushed downstairs, calling, "What's up? What's up?"

"We ask the questions, where are they?"

"Where are who?"

"Papers, papers, papers, produce your papers, your identity cards this instant, this is a house search, everyone downstairs, everyone downstairs right now, now, now."

Antje and I ran downstairs together. Green Police were running past us, two, three, four, five of them at least. Gerrit and Jan came out together from their room.

"Cover yourself, Gerrit, wake up," Mam called to him. She was crying as she was coming down the stairs. I wanted her to stop crying.

"Hands up, you, everyone in here, you in the bathrobe, in here, search the house top to bottom. If any one moves, blow the fucking heads off all of them. Yes, women too, shoot the fucking lot of them if any one of them disobeys."

"Do as you're told." Dad Said. "Everyone do exactly as you're told."

"Keep your fucking hands up!"

Dad's hands shot up again. "I can't show you my papers unless I can lower my hands."

"Who are these people Frank and Betsy van Dyke?"

"We're staying..."

"Shut your fucking mouth."

"Let him talk, let him explain."

"They work in a poultry killing place in Arnhem with my brother, they're from Nijmegen. They're staying one night, maybe two, until they get accommodation sorted."

"Show me your papers right now."

"They're in my coat pocket."

"Get your papers. The woman gets her head blown off if you make a wrong move."

Three, four men came rushing down the stairs.

"Anything?"

"Nothing, sir."

"No Jews, nobody sir, we searched it clean."

"Where are the Jews?"

"We've no Jews here, and all our papers are in order for everyone one of us."

"Search the floor, pull up the carpet, they've got Jews hidden somewhere."

"No Jews, we've no Jews."

"We'll get the Jews. When we do you'll wish you never saw a Jew in your life."

The leader pulled Gerrit by the arm and put a revolver to his head.

"You've got ten seconds, from now, to tell us where you have the Jews hidden."

"We've no Jews, I swear to God."

"Nine seconds, eight, seven, I blow his head when I finish counting."

Gerrit's eyes were bulging and I saw a puddle of urine appear underneath him. "Six seconds, five, four..."

"We've no Jews, I swear before God!"

Gerrit looks at Dad, his jaws slack, lips trembling. He was terrified.

"Three seconds, two, you've one second left before I blow his head off."

One of the four Germans shouts at the leader. "We've searched sir, there's nothing up there."

He's crying, actually crying, his round Tuetonic face is young, he is distraught.

"Please, sir, don't shoot the boy, there's nothing up there, no Jews, nothing, just bedrooms."

The leader looks at his other men.

"Nothing sir, nobody."

"You sure?"

"Certain sir, nothing."

He removed the point of the revolver from Gerrit's head and pointed it at Dad.

"Listen to me and listen well, one single Jew in this house *ever* and you're all dead. Come on, let's get going." Doors banging again, car doors opening, then banging shut again, engines revving and driving off. We looked at each other, Antje holding on to me for which I was glad. Her tight grip had helped to control my shaking. Mam rushed to Gerrit and hugged him. Frank van Dyke consoled his wife, who was rigid with fear. My father suddenly snapped himself together.

"Let us tidy up right now."

We went to work immediately. We picked up chairs, collected drawers, refilled them, returned to our rooms and tidied them.

Restoring order as quickly as possible was good, it gave nobody time to think. We said nothing. We would not talk again that night. Gerrit was alive though he could have been shot in front of us. We were in shock, Mrs. Van Dyke wept, Antje wouldn't let go of my hand and Mam held on to Gerrit.

The following day was a jumble of emotions. Everything else in our lives paled beside the evilness of such an outrage, and the wickedness of whoever had reported us to the police. Our visitors' papers had been in order. A traitor's call to the police or a formal piece of paper casually thrown away could spell instant death.

The shock of the second raid was far greater than the first. Mam went silent. When Nana Nellie came round she had lost her natural bounce, saying little. Gerrit clung to Mam for several days.

But Jan surprised the rest of us by carrying on as if little had happened. He was the epitome of calm under stress, his courage matchless. Only now did we appreciate the depth of his trauma when his father was taken.

"We're being watched," said Antje the evening after as we were eating.

"Who is?" asked Mam.

"They came expecting to find Jews, but found the van Dykes with papers in order. Whoever reported us lives close by. Five policemen came in two cars, expecting arrests. With all the assassinations going on now, I reckon Henk is too scared. His wife is stupid, but she's not weak. She has a grudge. We have a dangerous neighbour."

"Antje!" began Mam.

"We're in danger, Mam."

Dad and I exchanged glances. She had somehow worked out in her head exactly what Theo had cautioned me about just before the raid. Antje's reasoning powers were more than formidable.

The assassinations she had referred to were regular occurrences in 1943. Those who collaborated with the enemy were targeted, and the outrage at killings, a certainty a year earlier, was now more muted. There was no sympathy for those who did Hitler's dirty work. But

Laurence Power

whenever a known collaborator was assassinated, there was usually a counter-reprisal by the Green Police or the SD. It was one thing to eliminate someone who was prepared to betray a compatriot, but doing it now had to be weighed against the murder of innocent civilians. The cycle of violence notched upwards into a cycle of reprisal killings.

Collaborators came from all walks of life. A Dutch army general took two bullets in his body and a former Minister for Agriculture was shot dead in his kitchen. In Nijmegen and Utrecht, high-ranking policemen were assassinated. Several farmers openly sympathetic to the National Socialist Bund were killed and their houses burned. The shock of sudden and violent death lasted for only a matter of minutes now.

The Germans responded in kind and in the way they knew best, with mass arrests and executions. It was an unequal battle. But now Germans had a new situation, they had to think of their personal security.

New Year, 1943, was a bad one for the Germans. In spring Mr. Heemskerk's prophesy made months earlier about Russian winters came to pass when most destructive battle in this or any other war was fought in the frozen rubble of Stalingrad. Mr. Heemskerk remarked that the Germans hadn't just lost a battle, they'd lost a whole army of men to an enemy that was now suffused with feelings of invincibility and revenge. That September, news came from Italy that Mussolini had been deposed and imprisoned. Meanwhile, the British made successful raids on the Eder and Mohne dams, causing havoc to industrial production in the Ruhr. We heard that there were enormous casualties suffered in Hamburg as Allied bombers pulverised the city. Europe was in a state of total war, one that carried no concern for the lives of civilians.

Mr. Heemskerk had a sixth sense about how events would turn out. A few weeks before the May razzia in Arnhem, he called unexpectedly, late one evening. Dad asked me to stick around to hear what Mr. Heemskerk had to say.

He began by filling his pipe. "The Germans are either the stupidest or the smartest people on the face of the earth."

"What makes you say that?" my father asked.

"They've signed a new order that all Dutch army personnel are to be reinterned."

"Army personnel reinterned?"

"Maybe they want to ship these men to Germany and use them as cheap labour."

He was right. Within twenty-four hours, news of the order emptied factories all over the country. Dairy farmers stopped delivering milk to dairies and when people couldn't get milk major riots followed that spread throughout towns and cities. Even sedate Oosterbeek showed its anger with protest placards at all intersections. Arnhem shut down. Mass arrests of strikers and protesters followed, trials took place as fast and efficiently as the Nazis could organise them. The verdicts were as predictable as the parade of prosecution witnesses. Execution teams aimed and fired. Five hundred, a thousand, perhaps even more were rumoured to have been shot. Many shops in Arnhem stayed shut. Chaos reigned. Death was in the air.

At the height of the pandemonium, the Germans added to the rage. A new regulation ordered that all men between the ages of eighteen and thirty-five register for work in Germany. Oom Paul was crestfallen. He could be called up at any time and shipped out to Germany. He came to Dad for advice.

"You're exempt. You're in the food business," Dad tried to reassure him.

"I'm killing chickens, not producing them. Anyone can be shipped now."

"Leave it with me."

"What can you do?"

"I said, leave it with me."

Dad could do something but wouldn't say what.

"How about Catherine's brother? Is he okay?"

"I think so."

"If he has any worries, come back to me."

"Okay."

"Bring us a chicken ready for roasting next Sunday."

"If I can get one past the roadblocks, consider it done."

Oom Paul kept his word in part. Instead of a chicken, he supplied a plump goose, all stuffed and ready to roast. Tante Catherine came too, with Baby Cora.

So too did Nana Nellie. Her hair was going whiter by the day. She was ageing rapidly and was thin as a whip. She drooled at the prospect of roasted goose.

"To what do we owe this good fortune?"

"To Herr Hitler, who made a law that your son Paul doesn't like, so someone finds ways around his problem and your generous son rewards us with the biggest, fattest goose in Arnhem if not in the whole of Holland," Mam said.

Dad looked at me wryly and smiled, knowing Nana wouldn't give Hitler any credit.

"I can't bring myself to say thanks to that demon from the sewers of hell. Thank you, Paul. Now and again I dream about a roast goose like we used to have."

"With stuffing and roast potatoes."

"And vegetables and sauce."

"Stop driving us crazy," Mam said.

Even the baby was affected by the aroma of roasting goose. She bawled incessantly. My mother refused adamantly to take the bird from the oven until it was cooked to her satisfaction.

"Connie, you won't have a gramme of waste. I could kill for this," Nana declared.

"Don't nobody talk of killing. Too many executions close to home," Oom Paul said.

The war was never more than a casual remark away. A few mouthfuls of succulent goose and the baby stopped crying and beamed happily at everyone. Nana was right. When we were finished the goose was reduced to bones, not a morsel going to waste.

"Expect the next goose at Christmas," said Oom Paul, and smiled the first time in ages.

After our guests left I asked Dad why Oom Paul was so happy all of a sudden.

"He's got a new birth certificate. He's officially three years older, with a document to prove it."

"But the Nazis, haven't they've got all the files?"

"They had all the files. The more desperate things get, the more inventive our civil servants become. They're more afraid than the rest of us of being shipped to Germany."

"Is the underground growing?"

"You cannot imagine what's happening. Those civil servants who kept methodical files have now become master forgers. The Germans are becoming more confused by the day. Every move they make is undone even before the notices go up. Once we put our minds to it, we Dutch can be as disorderly as the best of them."

Though Dad was extremely careful when speaking to Nana and Oom Paul he was frank with me, keeping me informed and up to date. Rauter kept hitting us with more new orders shortly after the May rash of strikes and execution of workers and protesters. The owners of all radio sets had to hand them in to police stations. After the initial predictable outrage and abuse, Mam saw her opportunity. She collected every old worn-out radio and gramophone piece she could find and handed them in, with request for a receipt. She wasn't alone. Within a week the police ran out of space to hold all the radios surrendered. We held on to our Phillips battery set, but we had to hide it in the secret closet we had used to conceal Jews on the run. Listening to a radio was still a serious risk, but one most were prepared to take. Through our clandestine listening, we learned about the Russian big advances in the Ukraine, the Allied bombardment of German cities, the sinking of the *Scharnhorst,* the slow and systematic destruction of the German u-boats in the Atlantic, and the latest assassinations. That radio was more than a link with the world outside, it was the link to our ultimate dream of freedom from occupation and terror.

A gentleman's war was long out of the question. There could be no sympathy for Dutch citizens who openly collaborated with such an enemy, a perverse and violent force of nature that operated at a level where civilized people could not travel. There could be no sympathy for Dutch citizens who sustained that enemy, or helped them in any way. We shed no tears for any assassinated collaborators.

As the violent year of 1943 wound down to our fourth Christmas of occupation, the food situation worsened. The bread was disgusting and what was now being sold as jam was nothing more than a reddish liquid, which contained neither sugar nor pectin. However, hope springs eternal, and 1944 could only be better, we said. Everyone now spoke of an invasion from the west, where the Allies would launch a massive assault to smash the Nazi stranglehold. We were to be rid of Hitler and the Germans, Rauter and Seyss-Inquart and their SD and Green Police. The anticipation was heady.

We nourished our fantasies, drawing on our capacity to ignore our experiences, and forgot that every time something good happens, something bad happens. While the invasion from the west was taking place and we were rejoicing at events in Belgium and France, things would work out differently in Holland. Everything that had happened before was nothing to what was now in store. For the people in Arnhem and Oosterbeek the war was to explode on us, and when it was all over our lives would be forever changed. The war came to us, to our city, to our suburb, to our street, to our house. We saw it close up. 1944 was a year we would never forget.

Chapter Fifteen

Gerrit was walking with a severe limp. When I asked him about it he snapped at me saying that I should leave him alone. I mentioned the matter to Mam but she muttered something about not bothering her now, and did nothing. This was unlike Mam, especially when it was her pet who was involved. I would have said something to Dad, but he left the house so early each morning and got home late at night I didn't get the chance.

When I mentioned Gerrit's limp to Antje, once again she astonished me.

"Gerrit has been lame ever since Mam and Dad stopped talking."

"What are you saying? Since when have Mam and Dad not been talking?"

"They haven't spoken a word to each other in two weeks."

"Rubbish."

"Can you tell me the last time Dad had a hot meal put in front of him?"

"He's away so early in the morning…"

"And home late at night. Why do you think that he gets home so late?"

"He helps other people."

"They're not speaking. Gerrit doesn't understand it so he goes lame." There was no point in arguing with Antje, she seemed so sure, but how could she know if she was blind? That our parents weren't talking was hard to absorb, so I started looking for signs and hoped Antje was wrong. She wasn't. When Dad was around the following Sunday, I noticed the pained silences around meals being cooked and served up. Perhaps it had to do with the war, Mam was angry with Dad because of the risks he was taking. The de Groots lived two doors away, Henk de Groot was an unpredictable slob, while his wife was vengeful and bitter. They were collaborating with the enemy. There was no doubt about that, the same as 'Frau Erica' and her Nazi husband, Rudolf Becker. With such dangerous neighbours, it was no wonder people were on edge.

I wondered if I should do something about Mam and Dad, but Antje was against it.

"Let them sort it out. Something will happen."

Something did happen. Mr. Brouwers went missing. We no longer had a church organist. A missing person in Oosterbeek was no longer news. Some dived and went into hiding, others moved out quietly. No questions were asked. But with Mr. Brouwers, we were worried. He was a heavyset man, not an ideal candidate for diving. We discussed it at dinner. Dad said nothing. Nana and Mr. Brouwers were old friends. She was in the choir at St. Bernulphus and he and Nana occasionally drank coffee together.

"He's such a nice man," she said. "I wonder if I'll ever see him again."

"Of course you will, Nana!" Mam said. "He's playing a fine organ somewhere."

Father Bruggeman made his usual announcements at Mass the following Sunday but said nothing about Mr. Brouwers' disappearance. Antje thought this most unusual.

"Dad says nothing. Our priest says nothing. Those who know say nothing."

Within days I learned from Luc Gauthier that a churchgoer had reported Mr. Brouwers for some musical transgression. Mr. Brouwers had done the smart thing, he didn't hang around for a late night snatch. His silent flight left us without an organist.

Oom Paul came up with a likely suspect "Who would recognise rare pieces of music?"

"Who?" Mam asked.

"Frau Erica Becker, your one with the two cats on a leash."

"She doesn't go to Mass in Oosterbeek."

"Sometimes she sits in the church during the week."

She was my usual and favourite suspect, though not Antje's. "The only thing we have against that woman is her husband."

"She's married to a friend of Herr Von Ribbontrop who is an evil man. She sings for the SS in Amsterdam," Oom Paul argued.

"I think someone entirely different is responsible for Mr. Brouwers' disappearance."

"Who?"

"Closer to home. I'll say no more," Antje said.

"We all know Frau Erica is well versed in music?"

"Why would an opera singer report him and why now? A true lover of music would sit and listen to the organ being played as well as Mr. Brouwers plays it."

Oom Paul was not about to let up on his theory, "Mr. Brouwers said he wouldn't play the organ if she sang in the choir."

"She could have reported him any time over the years but she didn't." Antje argued.

"We know the sort of woman she is."

"Who tipped off Mr. Brouwers to dive?"

"We don't know."

Antje was not about to give in. "Mr. Brouwers was reported by a collaborator, who lives nearby and who doesn't know the first thing about music. I think that her husband tipped off Mr. Brouwers."

Oom Paul laughed. Dad remained silent, happy to let Antje and Oom Paul argue it out. Mam was talking again.

"Why would the husband of the collaborator tip off Mr. Brouwers?" asked Oom Paul.

"A policeman is the first with information."

The expression on Dad's face closed the subject of Mr. Brouwers' disappearance. He wanted to discuss the impending invasion from the west. Where might the first landings take place? Everything hinged on the invasion.

"It has to be in France," Mam said, over and over.

"Why fight across half of France when they could get a thousand kilometres closer to Berlin by landing in Holland? What do you think, Wim?" Oom Paul asked.

"It'll be bloody. If the Allies get a toehold then it'll be all over for the Nazis."

Dad was right. April and Easter came, but no invasion. Life went on. Night after night Allied planes flew noisily over us to bomb German cities and The Ruhr.

The weather softened, the days lengthened, the summer blossomed, but there was no invasion. We were into June. Everyone was restless for the big strike, it couldn't come soon enough. The forced evacuation of Dutch civilians continued, as did the razzias and deportations, the random executions, the fear and the terror.

Dad didn't return home on the first weekend of June. On Sunday Antje moved downstairs to sleep with Mam. Nobody commented.

The next morning my history teacher, Ronald Thijssen, was standing at the school entrance as I approached. He nodded to a youngish woman with dark hair, a plain round face and a sensible look. She beckoned to me.

"Where's your bicycle?"

"At home. It's on the rim."

"There's a bicycle in the porch of St. Bernulphus. Take it. Then follow me."

I asked no questions. It seemed at times that every young woman on a bicycle was a courier carrying dispatches or orders, a silent and relentless army of information gatherers and disseminators. The young woman cycled to the Utrecht Road. I followed on foot and found the bicycle. The saddle was low and loose, the chain slack, the handlebar grips and tyres worn but then every bicycle, and indeed everything else in Holland, was like that.

The woman reappeared below the steps on the road. I followed her from a safe distance. She slowed down as we passed St. Elizabeth Hospital.

"Keep me in sight at all times," she said.

We entered the centre of Arnhem. Soon we were near Musis Sacrum, the concert hall. Plenty of people were going about their business. The woman parked her bicycle and pushed her way through the oak door of a large building. I followed and climbed two flights of stairs, then came to in a large room, with about twenty people inside. I was easily the youngest person there.

As I entered, two men approached me, one looking like a preacher, the other youngish, with a sad expression. The first one handed me a bible and both shook my hand. There was a blackboard to the front with New Testament references on it. What was I doing at a bible meeting? The young man with the sad face stepped forward.

"Ladies and gentlemen, Pastor Braak will say the opening prayer."

Pastor Braak said a brief prayer and asked God to attend on our deliberations and to alert to us to any immediate dangers. The other man then resumed control.

"It's been a bad weekend. One man was assassinated and another is in prison. We ask for your prayers for them. Another man, one of The Strong Ones has dived. We cannot use those channels for now. But we must stay on track. With or without us, the landings will happen. We have urgent matters to deal with. Doctor Numan wants to go first."

A bald-headed man with high cheekbones stepped forward. His cheeks were bluish, but otherwise he looked hardy and wiry. The downward curve of his mouth signalled more bad news.

"Last night I failed to deliver a young woman of her baby. There's nothing more damned serious for a doctor than losing a mother during childbirth. It's always hard, even if it happens only once every few years. In the past month I've seen it happen four times. Four young mothers have died in childbirth in four weeks, all of them under twenty years of age. The root cause is prolonged malnourishment. We have an added problem to cope with now. Resistance to tuberculosis has fallen dramatically. The disease is rampant, it's killing whole families. We have to concentrate now on those mothers due to give birth in the coming weeks. Food is scarce but in the poorer parts of Arnhem, Christ Almighty, it's bloody awful. The last time I saw rickets was forty years ago, in Haarlem. I've seen several cases of it here in Arnhem in recent weeks. You can live on bread and lard only for so long. We medics called tuberculosis the disease of poverty but now it's a death sentence. There wasn't a morsel in that house last night. What chance has that woman's baby? More mothers will die. Don't ask me what we can do. I don't know. People are starving. We need food. We need it urgently."

The silence that followed was painful. An elderly man stood upright and then spoke.

"Are The Strong Ones totally out of business?"

Everyone waited for an answer.

"Not at all. Some got away. The Gestapo is taking the city apart looking for them. One of them is represented here."

A man of Dad's age stood to speak.

"The ration books aren't the problem any more. There's no food when the coupons are presented. Doctor Numan is not exaggerating, the hunger is real. If young mothers die today, children die tomorrow. Everything is about food."

Nobody wanted to speak, yet they had to respond. If there was no response it meant that there was little or no hope.

"Our other doctor has something to say," said the chairman.

I watched as the second doctor rose to speak. He was young, baby-faced, perhaps in his mid twenties, with a worried look. His dark grey suit hung loosely over his thin body.

"The Strong Ones have done remarkable work in getting ration books. The most important thing now is money. The SD are corrupt, the Greens are a disgrace. Cold cash is what counts. We have to have cash to bribe officials. It's our only way."

"Correct. That's what the Strong Ones should work on."

"Taking money by force is not something we can all approve," Pastor Braak said. There was such a murmur of disagreement that the pastor looked uncertain. He sat down.

The door opened, another man entered. He was stocky, with a short neck and his hair sleeked back. He had a cocky, arrogant air about him. He looked a military type to me. As he went to sit his eyes locked with mine.

"Whose bright idea was this?" he said, curtly.

"What idea, Harry?"

"What idea? To bring a kid to this meeting! I've told all of you about Eisendorfer, but none of you will listen. You people don't ever listen. How long do you think that this kid could hold out if Eisendorfer ever got his big hands on that chin? Seconds, that's how long. Whose idea was it?"

The man acting as chairman spoke in calm, measured tones.

"I am responsible Harry. One group has done incredible work in gathering information over the past three years. I wanted you to meet another member of that group. This kid has passed roadblocks when an adult couldn't have, he has undertaken a dangerous mission in the middle of a razzia. He is old enough to take care of himself. His father is someone very special to us. I'll say no more."

"You brought him here to get a good look at him? Is that what you're telling me?"

The discussion had deviated from the food crisis.

"No, Harry, that's not it. We've had to shut down one channel of communication, but we can establish a new one. This kid will be an essential part of the new channel."

"Being smart on the street doesn't mean he's ready for any of the serious stuff. You have to level with him, you must tell him about Eisendorfer before he gets involved."

"You tell him, Harry. Be my guest."

Pastor Braak turned to his chairman.

"We're losing sight of why we're here. We mustn't get sidetracked. You've heard of what our doctor colleagues said about getting food into the poorer areas of Arnhem."

"The rich pay bribes and get things done. No money means no chance. The poor can't afford black market prices, they can't buy medicine or feed their children and their women are starving."

Harry reacted badly to this lecture.

"Let me have the kid, I'll tell him about Eisendorfer. I'll show him how not to be taken alive. I'll take him with me on my next job."

Pastor Braak jumped to on his feet.

"Absolutely not, Harry. Many here may well applaud your activities but this boy is not meant for any of that. His ability is to carry out duties that involve a capacity to obey orders and to keep silent. A boy in short pants with a steady nerve gets away with a lot."

There were murmurs of 'hear, hear.' Pastor Braak had the support of the meeting. Harry looked around, then at me.

"Have it your way, Pastor. Don't anybody dare say I didn't warn you."

I guessed then that my father was one of The Strong Ones. Perhaps that was why he and Mam had fallen out months before. Clearly being one of The Strong Ones carried considerable risk.

I also guessed Dad had dived on Saturday, two days before. He hadn't been back to the house that weekend. Something had gone wrong. Mam said nothing. She asked no questions and made no fuss. She almost certainly knew that Dad had dived. The meeting was over soon afterwards. Everyone was guarded and spoke only in the vaguest terms. As I was leaving, Pastor Braak took me aside.

"Call on your grandfather's friend tomorrow morning, Cornelis. He'll be expecting you. Walk to his house. Go early."

I nodded.

"Return to your class straight away now."

I did as he told me. I sat at the rear of the classroom with Ronald Thijssen teaching what it was that made Napoleon Bonaparte the most successful general in history. Napoleon's inevitable defeat in Russia ended his reputation of invincibility in battle. Mr. Thijssen looked around the classroom, allowing his words to sink in. We were free to draw conclusions. I was free to dream. The landings would happen soon, when they did Hitler's rule in Holland would be over, Dad could return again to his family. Those women who might otherwise die in childbirth could be saved once these events began.

D-Day: June 6 1944: one of the most feted days in history. While it is generally remembered for the events that occurred on the Normandy coast, with me it was different. Life in a war zone was always a series of shocks and unexpected events piled upon each other, some trivial, some important and some very personal. I remember that historic day more for the personal events of the day than for the history-making goings-on in France.

I left the house at the normal time that Tuesday morning, with my school satchel in hand. I had said nothing to my mother of the previous day's events. The weather was dry, if somewhat overcast. The first days of June had been poor, but that Tuesday morning was fresher than usual. Shortly before 9 a.m. I pressed the doorbell of Mr. Heemskerk's house. A maid in a starched apron, called Lisette, let me in.

Mr. Heemskerk had a serious frown on his face. "Nelis, come in to where I can have a good look at you."

He led me into a small conservatory off the spacious drawing room. I laid my satchel on the floor.

"This is what war does. A boy of your age should be learning other things. Blame me for your little journey yesterday morning. What have you learned?"

"Has my father dived, Mr. Heemskerk?"

"Your father is safe, Nelis. Assure your mother of that, please?"

"I will. From what was said yesterday..."

"The Greens were waiting for them. We're pretty sure we know who tipped them off. One was captured. He was still alive when the others made their escape. Your father is safe. Tell your mother."

"When is he coming back?"

"When the war is over, next month, next year, he'll be back. We don't know, Nelis."

"The man they captured? Was it Luc?"

"Not Luc. The man they took is married with young children. He will be tortured. They will make him talk and they will execute him. We've had to close down that channel entirely. Have you any idea what I'm talking about, Nelis?"

"Yes sir, I do. What about Dad's job on the farm"?

Mr. Heemskerk looked at me first and then laughed out loud.

"Your father never worked on a farm but he has done a fine job in not telling you that."

He was amused at my surprise. "You're so like your father, Nelis. You both have the rare capacity to do what has to be done. I was there when Luc Gauthier told your father how you collected that corpse. It wasn't the fact that you did what you did, or that you did it during a razzia, that amazed all of us. It was that you never saw fit to tell your father. Cornelis Baumann that was cool. Your father could not have been prouder of you. Nor could I."

I waited for him to continue.

"You're the man of the house now. You'll have to play a father's role."

"I won't be able to bring home money every week."

"Yes, you will."

"How?"

"Some consider your father's work is important enough to ensure that he takes home enough money for your mother to have no worries. Money will still come through."

"Who puts up the money, Mr. Heemskerk?"

"No names, Nelis. Some people of my church see fit to ensure that a good Dutchman is well taken care of. Nothing will change there until the occupation ends."

I heaved a deep breath. Many families went on the breadline as soon as their breadwinner dived or was lifted in a razzia.

"Thanks."

He waved away my thanks.

"You're going to earn money soon. You'll have to work for it. Is that a problem?"

"No, sir."

He looked round the corner of the conservatory to ensure nobody was listening.

"We are going to change your role. From now on we want you to gather information. You can get away with things that full-grown men can't. Am I making sense to you?"

I nodded.

"You are to work in the kitchen of the Hartenstein Hotel here in Oosterbeek. Don't look too surprised, Nelis. Wehrmacht Generals, Luftwaffe, SS, political advisers, they all turn up at the Hartenstein. We need a smart young lad in there as soon as ever possible. When the time comes, you will be instructed on the type of information required by your personal contact. The Nazis love their insignias, especially the SS. Knowing that some German general is dining in Oosterbeek means he's not on or even close to a battlefield in France. I put your name up for this. The hotel owner is agreeable. You feel up to it?"

I nodded vigorously. The sooner the Germans were beaten, the sooner Holland would be free and my father would be home with us again.

"Yes, Mr. Heemskerk. What do I do?"

"The day your school finishes for summer, come to me, before you go near the Hartenstein. I'll have your instructions. You'll make little or no money for yourself, but you can do a lot for Holland. We could have a long haul yet before this war is over."

"Most say that if the landings succeed the war will be over in no time."

"Everyone could be wrong, Nelis. The closer the Germans get pushed back to their own borders, the harder they'll fight. This worries me."

"I'm not sure I understand, sir."

"The Allies will have to cross the Rhine somewhere. The Rhine Bridge in Arnhem is very close to the German border. We hope for the best, Nelis, but prepare for the worst."

"Mr. Gauthier said that to me once, Mr. Heemskerk."

"Good advice. Luc is brave, but I worry for him. Some of the top-brass Nazi generals like his French cooking, but the SS is not very bothered about cuisine. Luc has used up many of his nine lives. Does the name Eisendorfer mean anything to you?"

"It was mentioned yesterday. People went quiet when his name came up."

"He is one man to fear above all others. He's Gestapo. I abhor assassinations of all kinds because getting into such matters makes us no better than Nazis, but he would be my one exception to this principle. The man is a cancer on humanity. If he shows up at Hartenstein Hotel, you'll have to move pretty fast."

"How will I know him?"

"I like that in you, Nelis. You're focused. Eisendorfer is easy to pick out. He's taller that any other man you'll ever see. He is considerably taller than two metres, he's huge. He has black hair slicked back and a long scar running from his left eye down a long lantern jaw to the side of his mouth. He is a scary man for another but very particular reason, his hands. The prisoners that talk are the lucky ones, they are taken to a yard and shot. Those that refuse to talk never again say anything. He grips his prisoner's chin in his huge hands and then he squeezes. He can crush a man's lower jaw into fragments. He always takes his time. If he encounters a lower jaw so tough he cannot crush it, he pushes the lower jaw up into the skull. His prisoner has no choice. Talk and be shot or don't talk and have your chin crushed. Even the Greens are scared of him, and they are a pretty bad lot. These are terrible days that such people have power of life and death. Terrible."

"I hope I never get to see him."

"Talk to your personal contact on what to do if you do see him."

"What do I say to my mother about the job in the Hartenstein?"

"Your mother won't ask questions Nelis. Earlier on I said you are to be the man of the house from now on. Do you know what I'm talking about?"

"Well."

"It looks as if you don't, Nelis. Your mother is expecting a baby."

I gasped. It was like a punch in the stomach. A baby? She can't be, not now. We're grown up, I'm fifteen. I'm nearly a man. There's a war on. There are food shortages. Dad is gone for goodness knows how long. How could she? How could they? I was speechless. Women are dying in childbirth. I tried to conceal my bewilderment.

"Accept this like a man and do the right thing by your mother."

I was still breathless. "What should I do, Mr. Heemskerk?"

"Take responsibility. Do what your father would do if he were at home. Look after the family. Ensure your mother gets enough good food, no matter how you get hold of it, that she gets rest, that she doesn't do things a woman in her condition shouldn't do. Your mother is a woman who copes well. If the landings go well, your father will be back. Take full responsibility until he returns."

Mr. Heemskerk did not give information or fatherly advice without direct orders. He looked me straight in the eye.

"Don't be shocked. It's the stuff of life.."

It became a monologue from then on, my mouth was open, my tongue dry. I couldn't have spoken even if I had wanted to. A knock at the drawing room door ended the awkwardness.

"Come in," Mr. Heemskerk shouted, a little louder than usual.

The maid Lisette entered the room. It was clear from her looks that she was excited about something.

"Madame wants you to come immediately, sir."

"What is it, Lisette?"

"It's the radio, sir."

Mr. Heemskerk quickly jumped up, belying his age. He beckoned me to follow him. In a moment we were in a small office, probably the only small room in the house. The domestic staff stood at the door, buzzing with excitement. They made way for Mr. Heemskerk.

I squeezed in after him. The illegal radio was on full blast. Mrs. Heemskerk held her head sideways and gave one of her rare smiles.

"This is the BBC World Service in London, we repeat, a message from the Supreme Headquarters of the Allied Expeditionary Forces in Europe. Allied Forces have gone ashore in Normandy. In combined air and naval attacks, the Allied Forces have gone ashore in Normandy. We repeat, the Allied Forces have gone ashore in Normandy."

The information given out was sparse, but the fact that it was the very correct BBC World Service made our hopes soar. Mr. Heemskerk tuned to a German station.

"Will you see what lies the Nazis are spinning about this?" he said to his wife.

We watched their faces. Mrs. Heemskerk nodded her head and moved her lips. Suddenly she put her hands around her husband.

"Something is happening. When the BBC and Germans broadcasts agree on something, it has to be big. The landings have begun. It's Normandy, in France."

The absence of hard information was a killer, but for now it was all we had to go on. Allied troops were back in Europe and landing in Normandy, that was enough. There were no shouts or cheers. We had waited for this day for over four years, we would have to wait a little longer.

Mr. Heemskerk looked about him.

"I am glad that no one is getting too carried away. That coast will be defended to the death. The Allies have to land all the weaponry necessary to supply the biggest army in history on a scrap of coastline. Expect a lot of fighting. Getting a tiny toehold in Normandy and winning back big stretches of territory are two different things. They'll crawl over the corpses of their own men before getting to Paris. It will be quite terrible."

Walking from Mr. Heemskerk's house to school, my head was a jumble of thoughts and emotions. My mother was expecting a new baby, my father was wanted and in hiding, I was about to start my first job and my role in the underground had changed, I knew about Eisendorfer, and now the Allied forces had landed in Normandy.

Yes, I remember D-Day, June 6 1944.

Chapter Sixteen

It was a terrible summer. While the Battle of Normandy raged unremittingly during June and July, as Mr. Heemskerk had prophesied, thousands of Allied soldiers died in France. At home food supplies dwindled further. My mother spoke of nothing else other than where the next meal was coming from.

My belly was full because I worked in the Hartenstein kitchen where the food was not too bad even though the pay was a pittance. I ate as much as my body would allow me while I was there so that I didn't use vital rations at home. I was learning plenty about the hotel business in a place that was well run despite the difficult circumstances.

Even in the Hartenstein, the growing scarcity of food was unmistakable. One day the chef took three of us to one side and told us that from now on potatoes would no longer be peeled. We were to wash them very well. This was immediately followed by a 'waste nothing' order, which meant that outside leaves of cabbage heads and all carrots, no matter how small, be used. Rhubarb leaves were to be cut less than a centimetre from the stem. Cut down on the big helpings, cut down on waste, cut down. It became a mantra.

Chores in a hotel kitchen were endless and repetitive. I checked deliveries in and signed for them. This gave me an opportunity to leave the kitchen and to observe the cars parked at the hotel. I committed nothing to paper. I had to memorise everything I saw. Messages written down could mean the difference between life and death. After one week I had a good idea of what was required of me. When I met up with my personal contact, it was no surprise to discover that it was my history teacher, Ronald Thijssen. He was ideal, he looked very much like a history teacher as opposed to a subversive. He said very little and lived an outwardly unexciting life close to Saint Elizabeth Hospital. He told me how to distinguish between Waffen SS and Wehrmacht. Initially both groups seemed the same, all Germans, the enemy. The SS had their deaths-head insignia on their caps, their uniforms and their cars. Only the very top brass of the Wehrmacht had insignia on their cars. Knowing the difference between the SS and the Wehrmacht was more important than I had realised.

Whenever officers, especially generals, were in the vicinity, the place crawled with sentries. The German treated their sentries so badly. They were made to stand to attention in the rain, sometimes for hours. Many of them had to stay on alert throughout the night, some must have slept standing up. A few of them, scared young men, would see me and nod as I was passing. I would nod back. We would sometimes exchange an odd word, but never enough to learn anything.

For me, the Hartenstein was an ideal workplace. Located just off the road to Utrecht, it was no more than a few minutes walk from the Tafelberg and Schoonoord Hotels. Merchant princes from Dutch East Indies and other exotic places had frequented it at one time. Now Nazi bigwigs were the clientele. It was less than a fifteen-minute walk from our home and I could run it in less than ten. It was a fine old-world building, with well-laid out grounds. To have a job, any job, in the Hartenstein, was a distinction.

I quickly developed a sense of what was important. Ronald Thijssen told me to watch out for anything and everything. Soon I would know what was important or not. One day I described the insignia of a Horsch Auto Union. He looked at me incredulously.

He whistled through his teeth, "Are you sure?"

"I'm sure."

"Great stuff, Nelis. Great stuff."

Mam's pregnancy worried me. She was getting larger by the day, while getting food through legal channels was getting tougher. She wanted no fuss, least of all from me. Gerrit went lame again once he became aware of the arrival of another baby, or so Antje said. I was slow to contradict her on anything any more, she seemed to have an inside track. She was thrilled about the prospect of a new baby. When I told her Mom's secret, she laughed for ages.

"Nelis, you're amazing. If I wanted to get through ten German roadblocks with fake ration books in my pockets, you're the one I'd want with me. But at home you hear nothing, you see nothing, you know nothing. You didn't even know Mam and Dad weren't talking last February. That's when I guessed."

She laughed again.

"How did you know?"

"Signals, Nelis. God is sending this baby for a reason. I know He is."

Antje's deep faith and trust in God was another source of amazement. Even with her shrunken body, blindness and poor health, it was steadfast. I envied her that.

"Have you felt Mam's tummy yet?"

"No, I haven't," I said. I didn't want to.

"It's only a baby bouncing about. She won't kill you."

"She?"

"It'll be a girl. Will you?"

"Will I what?"

"Touch Mam's tummy?"

"Stop talking like that."

She enjoyed my discomfort. Pregnancy was a taboo subject then, especially for a fifteen-year-old boy on the pregnancy of his own mother.

"So the Hero of the Resistance is scared of a little baby."

Antje had a wicked streak when she knew I was unable to share her joy. To me every day was a new embarrassment. Mam was getting huge and I couldn't look her straight in the face, I could hardly say three words to her in case she thought I was looking at her belly. Tante Catherine visited every day and the pair of them would talk in whispers for hours on end, like a pair of conspirators.

Eventually I tumbled to the whispering, Tante Catherine was pregnant as well. Two babies due in November. Fervently I prayed that the war would be over quickly, that Oom Paul would not have to dive or that Dad would get himself home soon. I could gather and pass on information, obtain fake ration books, source bicycles tyres and boots better than most, but I found my mother's pregnancy very difficult to deal with.

One day, shortly after I had started working at the Hartenstein Hotel, Antje switched the topic from babies to another matter.

"If you can work at Hartenstein, why can't Jan work at the Tafelberg Hotel?"

It was a good question, so good that I passed it on to Mr. Heemskerk at once.

"Is he cool, calm and collected?"

"Yes, sir."

"Is he discreet?"

"When I turned up with a dead corpse in a stolen cart he asked no questions. We buried the corpse, he told no one."

Mr. Heemskerk beamed and asked the final, most important question.

"Do you recommend him?"

"Absolutely, I do, Mr. Heemskerk."

"Have him go to Tafelberg. Does he know about Eisendorfer?"

"No, sir."

"Give him the facts before he makes up his mind. Eisendorfer spent a night there recently. Don't tell Jan who your contact is, nor that you and I talk together. I want to stay alive long enough to see Holland rid of every last Nazi and to fly the flag of Holland on my lawn again. If God calls me home after that, I'll be ready for Him."

And so Jan went to work in the Tafelberg kitchen. Jan, normally quiet and serious, didn't stop smiling for a week. The Tafelberg was smaller than the Hartenstein, but judging by what Jan said Nazis on the move provided plenty of business. We exchanged information and gossip every night. Mr. Thijssen referred to what I passed on to him as intelligence. I was delighted to be a channel to the underground, but I rarely knew if what I passed on was of value.

One night Jan Till shared something with me in strictest confidence.

"Something is happening with the Germans, Nelis. They are jittery as hell."

And little wonder. Allied troops had smashed their way out of Normandy and rolled on to Paris. When Paris and the rest of France were liberated, surely Belgium and Holland could not be far behind?

My mother got bigger and bigger. I prayed that with myself and Jan both eating as much as we could at the hotels that there was enough food to keep her healthy. She started wearing her hair loose, hanging down over her shoulders. I couldn't believe how long it was. It really suited her like that.

Tante Catherine also got bigger. She hummed *Old Tough One* over and over. Food became scarcer. Gerrit grumbled continuously. Antje said he wanted more attention. She felt Mam's tummy every day. As she was sharing Mam's bed, I reckoned she felt Mam's tummy in the daytime to embarrass me. She was very excited about the new life growing, and her joy became our strength. I was regarded as the man of the house now and I didn't want Mam to worry about a thing. I prayed that Oom Paul would stay close as he had seemed totally lost when Dad dived. Most of all I prayed for Dad's safe return.

Sugar? Rationed. Tea? Rationed. Butter? Rationed. Potatoes? Rationed. Flour? Getting coarser and scarcer. Jam? Sorry. Cocoa? Sorry. So sorry, lad. In Koeman's grocery, this was Roy Keeter's only response to every request. We would joke that when he greeted passers bye on the street, Mr. Keeter would say 'sorry' rather than 'good day.'

There were no written messages of any kind from my father, nor did we expect any. We got occasional oblique assurances that 'everyone' was fine. Mr. Heemskerk was getting uneasy about something. A few times he was on the verge of telling me what it was, but pulled back. Finally, one evening at the end of August, he spoke.

"Nelis, some men care so much for their families that they are prepared to take big chances. They just want to see their wives and children. We tell the wives that such visits are strictly forbidden. If a man is wanted by the Greens or Gestapo, he's not allowed anywhere near his home. We want the wives and the mothers to tell us that their men are not to come close until we give the signal. We won't take any chances. You understand?"

I did. Mam smiled when I told her. To me it seemed then that a pregnant woman smiles at everyone because she carries a secret. Mam was now enormous, but still she smiled her secret smile.

"Tell Mr. Heemskerk that I agree with his advice."

"Is there anything I can do for you, Mam?"

"Listen to Mr. Heemskerk."

Nana Nellie called to the house each evening to reassure Mam. She would pray to St. Thérèse of Lisieux every day, asking for a fine healthy baby. Besides her daily prayers, Nana milked the goats and made cheese from their milk. We eventually ate it, even though Antje hated the strong flavour. We also had eggs, though by now it was impossible to buy feed in sacks for the hens. The hens had to scratch for a living. They turned every bit of the green-grassed area in the back garden red. Without the feed, the number of eggs fell seriously. Nana had the idea of including eggshell fragments in leftovers fed to the hens. The egg count rose but only for a short while.

The first few days of September 1944 were indescribably exciting. After August, when the Nazis had lost Paris along with a huge chunk of France, in addition to Bulgaria and Romania, the BBC World Service announced that the Allies had crossed into Belgium. On the first Sunday of September, it was confirmed that the Allies were indeed deep into Belgium, and that Brussels had definitely fallen. The tense excitement of the times was transmitted through the radio announcer's voice, "Listen folks, listen to the Belgians, hundreds upon thousands of their citizens are on the streets cheering and waving on their liberators. Listen to them, listen to the noise, young men and girls are climbing on to the tanks as they roll slowly down through the streets. The streets are wedged tight with cheering crowds. Listen to that welcome for the soldiers!"

The next day it was Antwerp. "Yes, we can now confirm to our listeners that the Allies have arrived in Antwerp, they are in Belgium's greatest port city, it's very important, yes, we confirm Antwerp is now in allied hands, people are on the streets cheering in their thousands, free again."

Now allied troops and tanks were getting closer and closer to the Dutch border, if they hadn't already arrived there. Nobody walked to pass on the latest reports. We ran through the old village with the news, we skipped to tell others that German wives and children had been ordered to move to the east of Holland, to be close to the German border, just in case. From London, our Queen broadcast that the hour of liberation for Holland was at hand. German soldiers were moving across Holland from west to east, shredding documents as they retreated, packing their bags and going home. We ran with our hands in the air, until we could run no longer. We wanted to see the Germans go back the same way they had come in, in 1940. Most of all, we wanted to be as welcoming as, if not to outdo the French and the Belgian civilians welcome to the allied troops, by cheering them fervently as they marched through the streets of our towns and cities to free us of the terror, assassinations and hunger. Over four years previously we had stood on that very corner to cross the Utrecht Road to St. Bernulphus for Antje's First Communion. That day we had to wait for ages to cross the road. Now that would be impossible, there would be no break in the endless parade of the defeated.

Rumours became fact. Germans poured along Utrechtseweg on their way through Arnhem on their humiliating retreat to Germany. No longer were they a strutting army of arrogant young men riding on tanks bedecked with swastikas. Now, they were an army of stragglers, looking panicked and pathetic. With Gerrit and Jan, I watched as the road east to Arnhem had become choked up with every conveyance imaginable, trucks, buses, half-track vehicles, staff cars, BMR and Zundapp motorcycles with sidecars and machine guns, old pre-war rattle-bone civilian cars, farm carts, horses and bicycles. Swarms of dusty and war-weary soldiers rode on bicycles, some with tubes and tyres. Others cycled on the rims. Two massive farm horses pulled a hearse, complete with chrome fittings, two men rode astride each of the horses and the hearse was stuffed with exhausted German soldiers wearing the skull-and-crossbones insignia identification. I knew that this meant that even the SS were now on their way home.

Mostly they walked. Weary civilians pushed eastward, many with heads down. There were old men and women, pregnant women, women with children, the followers of Mussert, an endless cascade of distressed people for whom there could be no room to live among the rest of us now.

"Look, Nelis," Gerrit said, tugging at my sleeve, as he pointed to someone walking in the very middle of the road.

"What?"

"There."

It was Henk de Groot with his wife pushing a handcart piled high with suitcases. Marie walked with them, her head down. A short distance behind came Theo, looking bewildered. Was he going to Germany? Germany was welcome to his parents. I felt sorry for Theo, he had once alerted me to danger. I could do nothing for him now. The best place for him now had to be with his unsavoury parents.

The de Groots were not the only civilians on the march towards Germany. Others, collaborators, Nazi-appointed officials, traitors, black marketeers, Dutch and German Mussert followers, a rag-tag army of discredited people were walking. They received no pity from the rest of us. Sympathy, like food supplies, was scarce.

Two soldiers were riding on a horse that suddenly bolted. One fell off. The other didn't stop to help him. The one who fell off approached a civilian close to where we were standing. He offered to sell his rifle for some guilders. Women spat at him. He kept on walking. We watched him try to jump on the fender of an old Renault. Those already on the car tried to push him off, but he held on despite their shouts and abuse. He seemed determined to make it back to Germany.

A tractor passed with its trailer full of soldiers. The tractor halted. Two men jumped off and grabbed a man in a leather coat, ignoring the hissing from the sidewalk. It looked like an arrest. They took his leather coat and jumped back on to the trailer. The war was as good as over. The Germans had no fight left. This was a defeated army.

Fatigue made us return home. My mother wasn't there when we got back. Neither was Antje. What was going on? I ran up the road to see if Tante Catherine was home. She wasn't home either. Where was everyone?

"Maybe they're watching what we've been watching," Jan suggested.

"My mother would not get herself into a crowd like that," I said.

"I'm starving," said Gerrit.

Typical. It was Holland's most historic day and all Gerrit could feel was his hunger. Jan looked at me and the pair of us burst out laughing. On the kitchen table lay a note from my mother telling us that they had gone to Mr. Heemskerk's house. We cut thick slices of her homemade bread. Mam had hidden the meagre ration of butter so we had to make do with goat's cheese. We drank glasses of milk, knowing that it meant no milk for breakfast in the morning. So what? The Germans were going and good riddance to them. Let tomorrow take care of itself. Tomorrow the Orange flag will fly over Holland. Long live our Queen.

I went to Benedorpsweg to fetch Mam and Antje. There was a party going in the big house, as I should have guessed. Mr. and Mrs. Heemskerk, their two daughters and their husbands had rustled together all they could manage from every quarter and had thrown open their doors. Nana was chatting with Mrs. Heemskerk, the pair dressed in black, whispering confidences into each other's ears. Tante Catherine, Oom Paul, Mam and Antje were there, as were many other family friends. Oom Paul and Tante Catherine were leaving as I arrived, little Cora asleep in her father's arms.

As soon as he saw me, Mr. Heemskerk beckoned me into his conservatory. All smiles in front of the others, he abruptly grew serious when we were alone.

"What does it look like to you, Nelis?"

"It's over. The Germans are going home. It's the most incredible sight."

"We're short on hard facts. We're living on false rumours."

"False?"

"There are no British troops in Breda. The BBC World Service is giving out inaccurate information."

"Are you sure?" I had asked the question before I could stop myself.

Immediately I was embarrassed.

"We gather information. We check facts. The BBC World Service does not have its facts right."

I blushed. I was being dressed down for letting the day's excitement get in the way of duty.

"What's the main worry, Mr. Heemskerk?"

"Generals. German generals are too close to their own borders to repeat the mistakes they made in Normandy. The British generals worry me because the BBC hasn't made any mention of Walcheren Island and Bevelend Peninsula. I wonder if they know the importance of those places."

"Why are those places so important?"

"To get to the port area of Antwerp, every vessel has to travel more than eighty kilometres up the Schelde Estuary, a journey of several hours. If the Germans are controlling both sides, nothing travels. They hold the neck of the bottle. Antwerp Port is a great prize, but only if we control the estuary from each side. Without that, it's useless. They'll have to bring in supplies through ports much further away from Holland. General Montgomery's staff must know that much. If the estuary is all ours, the war in the west is over. If not, we have serious fighting ahead. Pray, Nelis, that the Allies have a grip on the neck of the bottle."

The absolute last thing I wanted to hear was that Mr. Heemskerk had reservations of any kind. However he knew more than anybody about supplies and shipping, and he had been right in every analysis and forecast he had made so far. I felt honoured that he had shared his knowledge and opinions with me.

"Will my father be back soon?"

"What's another week? Keep your eyes wide open. Don't rely on rumours. We want hard facts, Nelis. All of us have to stay on duty until the last of the enemy has left."

"Yes, Mr. Heemskerk."

Mad Tuesday wasn't over yet. It was dark as my mother, Antje, Nana and I left Mr. Heemskerk's house for home. We didn't worry about curfew that night. There was little light to see our way safely, but I knew it like the back of my hand.

As we walked together a figure suddenly loomed out of the darkness.

The figure staggered and fell against Nana. She screamed. Antje screamed too. We drew close together. I had my fists at the ready. Then silence. The figure was a man, groaning on the ground. Perhaps he was drunk after wild celebrations.

I leaned over him. If he was drunk there was no smell of liquor. His breathing was much laboured.

"Bitte? Bitte?"

I jumped in fright. It was a German. I moved away.

"Bitte? Bitte? Bitte?" He spoke as if in agony.

"Yes?"

"Bitte? Bitte."

"What is it, Nelis?" my mother said.

"He wants something."

"For God's sake, Nelis, come home. We should all be in bed by now."

"Hold on."

I leaned over the fallen man again.

"Bitte. Bitte."

"He's a German. Come on home."

Two new figures loomed in the darkness.

"Nelis. Is that you? Nana? Mam?" It was Gerrit's voice.

I told my mother, Antje and Nana to go home with Gerrit.

"I'll go to Mr. Heemskerk's house. He'll know what to do."

Moving into the dark I heard the pained voice call "Bitte, Bitte."

I explained the situation as best I could to a surprised Mr. Heemskerk.

"We'll go and take a look. We might learn something from him."

Lisette and another maid came with me to where I had left the man. He was trying to get to his feet when we got back to him. The two maids helped him to Mr. Heemskerk's house.

He gratefully accepted a glass of water. He wore private's uniform. Mr. Heemskerk sat the man down. His face was gaunt, his eyes sad and slightly wild. He looked around. He saw the house and Mr. Heemskerk in his bathrobe. The German was seriously ill.

"Help me write letter to my wife. Bitte." He spoke Dutch with some difficulty.

Mr. Heemskerk nodded to his wife and indicated that she should do the writing. She spoke German well.

"Eat something first. Then write your letter."

"I write first. Bitte." The German looked as if he might collapse again.

Trembling, he began to speak, mostly in German. As he spoke Mrs. Heemskerk translated for us as she wrote.

"To my wife, Katja Schmundt. She lives in the village of Holzkirchen, near München. Hello Katja. This is me, Ernst. It is over."

He paused for breath. We waited.

"I won't see you or Hans or Conrad again. I am sorry, Katja. I am trying to get home to you but it's too late for me."

His breath rattled.

"I have walked for several days. I tried to get on a truck from the coast but I'm not strong as the others. I am near Arnhem now and the Rhine. I am ill. I went to the doctor like you told me in your letter. He was busy. He said come back again. The pain in my chest never leaves me. When I think of you and the boys it stops me thinking of the pain and of the other bad things."

He stopped again and inhaled through his nose, making a slight whistling sound. He seemed happy that his words were being translated. I think it was because it gave him time to catch his breath and summon up extra energy.

"It is hard to breathe. I left my post without permission. There was no one to ask. I think the war is lost. I hope every day that it ends soon. I will not live long. I am so sad I will never see you again, my Katja. I wish I could say goodbye to you in person."

He paused again. Mr. Heemskerk and Lisette stood watching.

"Thanks, Katja, for the photograph. Hans has grown so tall. He is the man of the house. You can rely on Hans. He will be a good man. Many Germans were not good men. I know Hans will be a good man, Katja. Say good-bye to him for me. I am sorry I will never climb peaks with him."

His breathing eased for a moment. I looked at Mr. Heemskerk to see if there was something I should do. He shook his head. The German stopped panting.

"Conrad looks tall, like your brother Franz. Tell him that I am sorry. This war has stopped everything. I wanted to see Conrad grow up, like Hans. Conrad will drive a bus in Bavaria when he becomes a man, like I wanted to. Tell him he has to listen to you and to Hans. If he does…"

Tears of grief came. Mr. Heemskerk pursed his lips and nodded to his wife to indicate that she should help him finish off the letter. We waited for the German to regain control.

"Dutch people are good, they are not barbarians. Good-bye, Katja. I hope that I will have a priest with me so that I will die in peace. Pray for my soul, Katja. *Ich verabschiede mich, Katja, meine Liebe.* I love you always. Ernst."

He leaned back and put his head against the back of the high-backed chair, and sighed heavily. He seemed at peace.

"This man should be in hospital but all roads are clogged. Nelis you get home to your mother. We'll deal with this."

I did as Mr. Heemskerk ordered. It was approaching midnight on Tuesday, September 5, 1944, the day that has entered Dutch history *Dolle Dinsdag*, or Mad Tuesday.

A few days later Mr. Heemskerk sent word to me that I was to go to his house. I sensed it had to do with Ernst Schmundt. I was right.

"He died, Nelis. Our pastor spent time with him. They talked and prayed together. Our man got Father Bruggeman to come and he made his last confession to him here. He died peacefully."

"Will his wife get the letter?"

"Yes. Father Bruggeman told me something you should know."

"Yes?"

"All Catholic priests in parishes have instructions to leave the doors of their churches open after the Germans leave."

"Why, Mr. Heemskerk?"

"They are to be used as places of asylum for collaborators. I hope my church does the same. We've a whole lot of vengeful people out there. It will be dreadful if some of them take the law into their own hands. We Dutch must never become or act like the Nazis."

"Many want vengeance."

"Four years of barbarism is four years too many. Civilised people all over the country must stand up and be counted. You agree, Nelis?"

"I haven't given it any thought, Mr. Heemskerk."

"I received interesting information today. Remember what I said, about whoever controlled the Schelde Estuary controlled Antwerp? The German general in command there has pulled his troops across to Walcheren Island, across to South Beveland and on to the mainland under the very noses of the Allies. The Germans control one side of the

Schelde. There are more German troops now in the south of Holland. That worries me."

"That's information to send up the line, sir."

"Already done, Nelis. Can you to see to the burial of that soldier?"

"How, Mr. Heemskerk?"

"We cannot involve the Greens. The Germans will shoot us if they find the corpse of one of their own here. Dr. Koeman said he died of heart failure. You've already buried one corpse, Nelis. Bury the German."

Jan Till helped and again he asked no questions. We dug a grave in the late afternoon, and after dark we collected the body, wheeling it on Mr. Heemskerk's handcart to the burial spot. It was dark when we put reddish brown earth over the body of Ernst Schmundt, alongside the body of Hepsibah, the elderly Jewish woman. Without giving it any thought I brought Mr. Heemskerk's handcart back to our house when we had finished. I had no idea then of the vital role that sturdy handcart was about to play in our lives.

Dad did not come home that week either. Mr. Heemskerk was right. The panic among German troops eased, and the great exodus slowed to a crawl. Roadblocks were erected. Those attempting to pass were told they would be shot if they tried. The German reputation on such threats was too well known to ignore, so nobody did, and the panic march back to Germany was halted. Mr. Heemskerk surmised that some tough German general had calmed the situation. History books would give us the name of Field Marshall Gerd Von Runstedt, the man Hitler had dismissed in July for daring to suggest that it was time to end the war, but had then recalled him in September to restore order and take command in the west. The change among German troops was instant and obvious, military iron rule was back. Back too were the Green Police and Henk de Groot, in uniform, with the rest of his family. Mrs. De Groot, as sullen as ever, was back as well, a cigarette dangling from the corner of her mouth.

We gave up on our hopes for instant liberation. I sensed something odd happening around Arnhem, but mentioned my worries only to Jan.

Mr. Heemskerk and Ronald Thijssen became agitated over the course of a few days, and with good reason. I told them the Hartenstein was full of Waffen SS, and that Jan had told me it was the same at the Tafelberg. We saw truckloads of soldiers and German tanks arrive in the woods to the west of Oosterbeek to set up camp. We had confirmed reports that SS troops were located all round Arnhem. The Germans were taking over every hotel in Oosterbeek. Routes through the woods were declared off limits, there were road checks every one hundred metres. Jan said that all Dutch staff members at the Tafelberg Hotel, himself included, had been told to stay home until further notice. He also reported seeing new telephone cables being installed there. We guessed, correctly as things turned out, that the Tafelberg was being taken over to serve as a German command centre.

Rumours abounded. The Allies were about to launch an attack from the Belgian border, into the heart of Holland. The Germans knew of the Allies' plans and were lying in wait for them. Some high-ranking military persons had moved into the Tafelberg. Shops were getting unusual requests for special wines, caviar and smoked German meats. Fresh German troops were pouring into Holland from the east. Something was definitely brewing. Holland would be different to Belgium, there would be a big battle somewhere and it would be bloody. It won't be Arnhem, we were too far north, too far from the Belgian border.

The Dutch underground stepped up its surveillance operations. Ronald Thijssen, no longer the mild history teacher, barked orders.

"Go into the woods. List every tank you see. List any markings you see. Is the tank stripped down? Is it operational? Check all insignia. Find out exactly what's going on at the Tafelberg. Get some excuse to get close up. Check any cars and insignia you see. Don't report rumours. I want facts and only facts. Go to Doorwerth. Go to Renkum. Cover ground. Get off your backsides and get out and about."

"I've no bicycle, sir. No tyres."

"Steal one with good tyres."

There seemed to be solid substance to the rumours. Thousands of Germans troops were around Arnhem and Oosterbeek for a reason. These were tough, hardened soldiers. As their numbers on the ground increased, so did the numbers of underground members. Major risks were being taken. Dutchmen from other areas were openly seeking information from locals. Whose side are they on? Careful, Nelis and Jan. Say nothing, look innocent. Jan told me and me alone what he saw. In turn I told only Ronald Thijssen and Mr. Heemskerk.

One evening during the week following Mad Tuesday, Jan came home in a state of high excitement. I followed when he caught my eye and indicated to his bedroom. Mam noticed but pretended not to.

"Today a man asked me to walk past the Tafelberg with him. He knew my name and that I worked there. A sentry stopped us. The man was as cool as the breeze. 'We work at the petrol station up the street', he said. The sentry waved us on. He looked to the hotel grounds where cars were parked. Suddenly he said 'Lord Jesus' under his breath and then said in a whisper 'look at the front door'. I looked. I saw a German car with a chequerboard black, with red and white metal pennant. 'Keep walking,' he said. Besides being cool, this fellow could walk very fast. When we were out of sight of the sentries he spoke again.

"The insignia of an army group commander. Not many of those about."

The man had been right. I was soon to learn that there was only one German army group commander in this part of the world and that was Field Marshall Model. So the rumours that shops were being asked for supplies of fine wines, caviar and smoked German meats were true.

I couldn't keep this information from Mr. Heemskerk for very long.

"Are you sure? Here in Oosterbeek? We know that 9th SS *Panzer* Division 'Hohenstaufen' is spread out between here and Appeldoorn. This information is incredible. London must have this straight away."

My relationship with Mr. Heemskerk was unusual, to say the least. We would sit in his house, having long private uninterrupted discussions. He would clam up whenever either of his sons-in-law appeared. We spoke like old friends, yet he was more than sixty years my senior. He weighed everything he said, and I copied and honed this trait. He never asked me for the details of Ernst Schmundt's burial and I didn't see fit to mention it.

Ten days after Mad Tuesday, I was sitting with Mr. Heemskerk in his house.

"Pastor van Zenden from my church visited his doctor on Tuesday, Nelis," he said and waited for me to react. We out-stared each other. He liked testing me.

"The doctor's assistant sends you his regards. He also sends his warmest regards to your mother, your sister, your brother and to Jan. He is well himself."

"Good."

"He hopes to work closer to Oosterbeek in the near future."

"Good."

"He attracts more visitors than the doctor he works for."

"Good."

"Your mother is a great woman, Nelis."

Mr. Heemskerk had a reason for saying something so unexpected. I waited.

"Her husband is on a wanted list, she treats Jan as her own, she takes Antje's blindness in her stride, you're rarely at home, and much of what you do is dangerous. She knows about Eisendorfer. She's had several house raids that you have never told me about. She does things that you're not aware of. She's seven months pregnant. Does she complain? You're one lucky fellow, Nelis."

He was sending me a message of some kind. As I returned home that evening I had more than an uneasy feeling, I was fearful of something about to happen. There was no one I could carry my fears to other than Antje.

That night the Green Police made several noisy and violent raids on our road and all over Oosterbeek. Rauter's reign of terror was back, with the police and SD as brutal as ever. Ours was one of the first houses to be raided. Several policemen violently barged their way into our hallway, led by a clinical German holding a short stout baton in his gloved right hand. The invaders proceeded to pull things apart. They knocked over chairs and other furniture and tried to upend the stove. One of them, a flat-nosed brute, got angry when the stove refused to budge. The kitchen floor was strewn with broken crockery and clothes. They shouted at the tops of their voices. They swore at Mam who stayed sitting on a chair, her arms clasped around Antje. They must have known she was pregnant. Gerrit sat between Jan and me. My mother never moved a muscle nor showed emotion of any kind. When the German in gloves enquired in a low, menacing voice where her husband was, she gave what she thought was a good reply.

"You took him."

The fellow hesitated for a moment, surprised.

"What do you mean, Frau?"

"In the razzia. You took him to Germany. Is he safe?"

His baton caught her flush in the face. She screamed. I jumped to protect her. Her chair tumbled. Antje screamed. Mam and Antje were both under me. If more fists or rifle butts flew I would catch them, rather than my mother. Her arm was caught under her and she screamed for relief. Pain ripped through me as I took three hard blows to the small of my back in quick succession. One of the blows had to be from a rifle butt.

"Madame you are the wife of a terrorist so I will ask you questions. You will answer them. Where is your husband?"

"He's in Germany, sir."

"If Madame is lying to me, it is something Madame will not regret. A dead person cannot have regrets. The child you carry will never see its father. Holland has too many mothers carrying terrorist children. Be assured, Madame, I will not hesitate to apply a solution. Let's go."

The German who had struck my mother was unlike most other Nazis we had encountered. He was not a shouter. He spoke calmly. In other circumstances he was a man one might transact business with. For now his business was that of terror, of making people afraid and of terrorising them. If he felt there was information to be had he would get it. I dared not move a muscle until the raiders left. We gasped for breath. My right arm was across my mother's swollen tummy. I felt the baby kicking. She knew I did. With blood flowing from beside her right eye she gazed at me steadily for a long moment. She smiled a slow and knowing smile. If she was scared, and how she must have been, she never showed it. Mr. Heemskerk was right, she was some woman.

We got to our feet. Antje was trying to say something, but could only utter incoherent grunts. At times like this we could only imagine the fear she endured.

"The silences scare me more than the shouting," she said later. My mother hugged her again.

"If your Dad were here now, what's the first thing he would do?" Mam said.

"He'd want us to get busy setting things right again."

We had come off lightly. The home of the van Gaals was raided and their son Boudewijn arrested. It was a brutal affair. Boody, as we called him, was an advanced medical student who spent most of his waking hours at the St. Elizabeth Hospital. He was knocked unconscious from a blow with a rifle butt before being bundled into the police vehicle while his mother screamed. We heard her screams from our house. In another house two men were found with questionable identity papers. It was the same story, a rifle butt in the head, oblivion, arrest, screeching tyres, prison, after that who knows. Maybe Eisendorfer.

Mad Tuesday was now history. The SD and Green terror was back and more frightening than ever. The Greens needed the status quo. Holland free of Germans was the last thing these Dutch traitors needed. Summary justice was again the order of the day.

My mother's eye swelled up and turned to an ugly blue black. Tante Catherine, now as large as my mother, came round in the morning and applied zinc ointment and insisted Mam stay sitting while she helped Jan and I prepare our midday meal. She came again that evening, and again the following morning after Sunday Mass.

It was a noisy Sunday morning. Besides the usual aircraft flying over Arnhem, there were occasional loud explosions in the city, which we could hear from the house. Then a fast plane flew low over Oosterbeek, followed immediately by another. A fresh explosion sounded extremely close to the Oosterbeek Dutch Low Church. Bullets zinged, tiles splintered. It couldn't be the Allies. Unless allied pilots dropped their loads in Holland in error? In the end, when bombs are falling on you, it doesn't matter who drops them. Holland was again being bombed, but this time it was on our own city of Arnhem. Bullets were zinging in Oosterbeek. We were puzzled and seriously concerned.

The afternoon provided the first part of the answer. When it came it could not have been more dramatic. We were about to witness something quite extraordinary.

Chapter Seventeen

I had a modest but important task to attend to that afternoon. Reliable information was needed, now more than ever, if the Allies were to push up from the Belgian border into Holland. I was a small cog in a massive wheel and I was pleased and very proud to be of service. I had procured a bicycle with good tyres the day before. A Green dismounted outside van Beek's bakery that Saturday afternoon, and by the time he came out I was long gone with his bike. I satisfied my conscience by telling myself that he had almost certainly lifted it from someone local. With good tubes and tyres I could cover a lot of ground.

I could have headed in any number of directions. As fate would have it, I cycled west towards Heelsum. Only for the explosions in Arnhem and the machine-gun fire from aircraft flying over Oosterbeek, it was like any other September Sunday. I encountered the usual number of road checks, the more the better. It gave me time to take everything in, to check numbers, tanks, insignia and anything else that might come into sight. I had developed a knack of knocking off my bicycle chain just as I was braking to halt. Replacing the chain gave me plenty of time to observe the scene.

As I approached Heelsum I heard several explosions. They were too close for comfort. I changed my mind about going directly towards Wolfheze. Then the explosions came from other directions. As I slowed on my bicycle to turn I heard the noise of airplanes and also an unusual swishy noise. The noise level was growing louder by the moment. The air throbbed. What on earth? I dismounted and looked round. What I saw in that moment was, by any measure, incredible. For there, from a southwest direction, came a vast army in the sky, descending to earth by parachutes. There were so many men and their planes and gliders and parachutes up there that the sky was almost dark.

It truly was a miracle of organisation. The sky was filled with thousands of paratroopers with brilliantly coloured parachutes, floating down to earth. It looked like a magic carpet stretching all the way from where I was standing to Wolfheze and beyond. This wasn't forty of fifty men touching down on open ground, this was several thousand men jumping from planes and filling the sky. Some swung and bobbed in the air, others eased their way gently towards earth. Huge packs with bright red and brown chutes fell more rapidly than the paratroopers, smashing into the ground. Some were within a hundred metres of where I was standing.

Gliders were also landing, hundreds of them, some crashing into the ground, others coming down as smoothly as a feather. It was a wild scene, gliders slipping their towropes, some crashing hard into each other, some breaking into splinters before my eyes, men rolling and tumbling on to the ground, others hitting it at a breakneck pace. One man who was trying to unravel his parachute fell violently to the ground when a descending paratrooper crashed straight into him. The one who fell was helped to his feet and resumed his efforts to discard his parachute. The two laughed at each other.

My heart thundered. The world must know about this. These are not, nor cannot be German troops. These troops are coming from the southwest. If they're not German, then who the hell are they?

"They are British," an elderly couple, standing close by, said together excitedly.

British. The British are here, close to Arnhem. Eureka. There's a God in heaven after all. Thank you God for the British, thank you for these stubborn and hard-headed bastards for not surrendering when everyone else rolled over. In my own mind I welcomed them to Holland. If only Dad could have been here to see this miracle in the sky. Incredible. He would come home soon, he had to. This was the moment we had been waiting for, history in the making. The British were landing in Holland, honest to God, I was crying and couldn't stop, I felt I should be laughing and cheering because these incredible men coming from the sky were here to fight my battle, to liberate me, my country. I waved in frantic excitement. But they were not hanging about. I could see those paratroopers assembling jeeps and motorbikes and trailers from where I stood. The Allies are here. Thank you, God.

My mind worked faster than my legs. The British had come to bring the fight to the Nazis. Seyss-Inquart and Rauter would no longer have things all their own way, no longer can the SS squash us like insects or execute us at will, no longer can they take people in razzias, nor can they invade our homes and hit pregnant women and cart people away. Now they had a battle on their hands and not with unarmed civilians this time. British paratroopers were on their patch. The Germans would surely find them hard to beat, there were so many of them, all well-armed.

The heath was jammed with gliders, supplies and troops. I watched the paratroopers organise themselves and readying to move off. Four Jeeps rushed towards me. I could see and hear men shouting loudly in to radio sets, and I sensed frustration. One banged his helmet against the side of a jeep. His mate looked at him and shrugged. Men were screaming at each other. My English was not good at the time but I got the general gist.

"Is something wrong? Keep trying".

"Keep trying for Christ sake".

"What the hell do you think I'm doing? I'm trying my level best! Nothing, fucking nothing, from these radios, I'm not getting a damn thing, nothing..."

"Keep trying, keep trying."

They were close to me. I could almost touch them. A lot of extraordinary traffic was coming in my direction. I needed to get on the bike and out of the way, to give them room. They kept coming, dozens of revving jeeps pulling artillery pieces and four-wheeled carts loaded with guns and stores heading my way. They swung east for Arnhem, which meant they would have to go through Oosterbeek. I had to get out of there and return home with this information. I had to pass it on to somebody else, it could be important, there could be fighting in Oosterbeek. I needed to be with my family. I had to tell the people what I'd seen in case they didn't already know.

I became a madman. I panted and sweated and cycled like one. The Jeeps with their towed loads were revving noisily but had yet to gather speed. I got in front and pedalled on a mix of exhilaration and fear. I had a duty to report on this miracle from the sky. The glorious hour which all of Holland had been waiting for had arrived. Somehow the news had travelled faster than I could cycle. I saw two men climb on to a farmhouse rooftop and hoist an orange flag. It flapped and snapped in the sweet air of freedom. Hurray for the House of Orange, hurray for Holland. Sweat poured down my face, I tasted salt. I tasted freedom. My heart rose and fell. I saw small groups of German soldiers scurrying about, by now they knew too, they were either getting themselves out of harm's way or preparing to greet the liberating troops with mortar and machine-gun fire. Men would die on this road and soon. They had to. I didn't want to be one of them. I kept those pedals turning, ignoring drops of salty sweat and my drenched shirt. I was almost airborne on my way back.

I reached Oosterbeek and pandemonium. The Germans were in panic and evacuating the Hartenstein Hotel. Uniformed men were scuttling in every direction, horns hooting, officers shouting, cars and trucks revving, tyres burning. Traffic poured down from the Pieterbergseweg on to the Utrecht Road, they were also abandoning the Tafelberg. It was bedlam. This could be the bigger news. We knew from our intelligence that the Tafelberg was a major command centre with Field Marshall Model in residence. It was now being vacated, with everything on wheels heading east into Arnhem. There were too many German troops around, especially SS, who wouldn't give up without a fight to the death. While the brass was pulling out of the Hartenstein, others were wheeling equipment and guns into positions for action. They knew of the airborne landings, they could not but know by now. The road from Oosterbeek to Arnhem was blocked. It looked as if it might be a hard battle. Maybe. My instinct was to let them escape and take their fight elsewhere, preferably to the east over the German border. Sweat clouded my eyes and I gasped for breath. I passed through German sentries and troops. Only combatants made the casualty list. Civilians were of no concern. As underground Oosterbeek was preparing for an ecstatic celebration, something at the back of my head kept telling me to get home. Though this was surely the hour of our liberation, I couldn't help feeling anxious. Maybe I had talked too much with Mr. Heemskerk.

Mam was crying when I returned. Antje tugged my right arm and sank her face into my sweaty sleeve. Oom Paul and Tante Catherine were also there.'Tell us', Nelis, 'tell us', they urged. I told them about the landings and the number of troops on the way. I didn't mention the Germans rushing to take up positions. They were so excited. I let them enjoy it while it lasted.

We could taste freedom now. That much was for sure. The British were coming to push the Nazis back to Germany. The British must have known the situation on the ground, surely. They came in the clear knowledge that they faced a battle. And they wouldn't enter battle unless they were sure they would win, no matter what resistance the Nazis put up. There would be a battle. The only question left to answer was where?

Nana Nellie arrived, wearing an ostentatious hat that was dominated by a massive cluster of hand-stitched orange coloured flowers. For a woman who always wore black, the flourish of orange was a statement of overstatement.

"I'm scared. Men are coming down in parachutes in an area that is crowded with Germans. I'm scared. The battle could be here. I want to check my goats."

She checked them, the animals were fine, chewing the cud and unaware of human events unfolding so close at hand. She went to the hens.

"Only two eggs so far today. It's all the noise."

There was nothing she or any of us could do, other than keep a brave face, and let no one know how scared we felt. I was scared for my family and for Oosterbeek. What were those people doing with their flags, heading for the Utrecht Road? I prayed that if there was to be a battle it would be far away from here. It could be on the heath, or in the east of Arnhem, or in Germany. My ignorance of modern warfare was total, as it was with most Dutch people. At no time though was I naive enough to think there would be no fighting.

None of us knew then, though maybe we should have guessed, the main objective of those airborne troops was the bridge over the Rhine in Arnhem. Bridges over great rivers have always been an objective of military men in war. It is so much easier, faster and safer for an army to cross a river via a bridge on foot or in transport vehicles than in ferries or boats, with no protection from enemy fire. If the Bridge at Arnhem was the objective, why would the paratroopers land so far out from Arnhem? It made no sense. Did they not heed our intelligence reports? How could they have not known? The whole of Arnhem and Oosterbeek knew there were German troops in the area, many with tanks in the woods further west. If the British reconnaissance planes hadn't seen them, then surely the intelligence provided from the Dutch underground should have left no room for doubt. The British had to have known.

The British troops had a choice of three routes into Arnhem. The two main ones were the Ede-Arnhem road and the Utrecht-Arnhem road. By now I was certain that the Germans would have troops in position across these highways. The third route to Arnhem was the smaller road between our house and the Rhine, from Doorwerth via the Benedorpsweg, where Mr. Heemskerk lived. This road was quieter, and cobbled. It was a possibility. However, the most likely scenario was that the troops would use all three routes. Our home was bang in the middle, between two of them. We were in danger.

We could hear the noise of battle in the distance, of mortar and gunfire. Antje came outside and held my arm tightly.

"Why are you so worried, Nelis, when everyone else is celebrating?"

"Who's worried?"

"You are. What are you afraid of?"

"I wish I knew."

"What do you think?"

"The British are headed into Arnhem on either side of us. I don't see how we can avoid fighting around here."

"Should we move while we still have time?"

"We have no idea where trouble will strike. We'll stay put."

I didn't give enough thought to my reply. It's easy to be wise in retrospect, but of all the decisions I've ever made that was the worst and it still hurts. It has been explained to me that if the Allied generals had no idea what was about to happen in Arnhem and Oosterbeek, then I shouldn't have been so hard on myself. I was fifteen years old, what could I know? But I had seen enough to feel mighty uncomfortable. I ignored my sense of foreboding and made the wrong decision. You have to live with your mistakes.

By now there was heavy fighting at a few locations. We could hear the sound of continuous machine-gun fire. Loud explosions boomed from both east and west, the big guns were hard at work. I wished from the bottom of my heart that Dad was near. With each passing hour I knew that the fighting would come closer. Was I scared? Yes.

British troops arrived in Oosterbeek from the west in a long line, one by one and close together, marching briskly, to a frenzied welcome of cheering and flag-waving. We saw jeeps, a few at first, then some more. A little green car drove unsteadily all over the Utrecht Road, as if driven by a drunk. The driver, however, was alert and sober, he didn't look at us. Beside him was a serious-looking man, his face flushed as he tried to coax a response from his radio. The welcome from the sidewalk grew and grew as more arrived on the scene. Houses were bedecked with hastily stitched orange flags. I should have had my orange flag, but I didn't. Nobody, least of all the British, seemed concerned with the noise of battles being fought in the background.

The soldiers were heading east in exactly the opposite direction the Germans had taken in May 1940. We waved at those incredible men from the sky in their big yellow coats and helmets covered by nets full of green strips. Some were gazing ahead, bent on their mission, others smiled cheekily and waved back to us. They were so young and fresh-faced, and created a sense of confidence that spread to the crowd. We threw apples to them and cheered them again. They caught the apples as if they were jumping for footballs and smiled back. They had cameramen, in open-topped vehicles that were encouraging the young girls to kiss the soldiers enthusiastically, to press against them, give them a big embrace, to look as if they wanted to make love to them. Some of the soldiers laughed, others pushed on, their faces sombre. They still had four kilometres to march. They would be in Arnhem within the hour, unless they met resistance on the way. Unless…

The Germans were gone, they had moved eastward out of Oosterbeek. I made my way to the Pieterbergseweg and Utrechtseweg intersection. The place was jam-packed. I heard a groan and saw injured men lying on litters who were being carried by their comrades to a first–aid centre somewhere near the corner. I presumed that these were the first casualties but I wasn't sure. The bell at St. Bernulphus rang out, as did the bells in other churches in Oosterbeek.

We heard explosions and mortar fire in the distance, mainly to the north. Serious fighting was going on somewhere not too far away. The soldiers stayed marching, we continued shouting. We heard a loud bang, this time from the south. That made me anxious. It came from the secondary road, close to the Rhine, from between Mr. Heemskerk's place and Arnhem. Could it have been the Railway Bridge across the Rhine? Was there fighting there too? I kept my ears open for further noise from there, but it was hard to hear anything in the din.

The troops stopped coming. We waited, looking towards the Hartenstein Hotel. It was getting dark. It was time for me to get home and be with my family. The first of those Tommies who had marched past earlier should be well into Arnhem by now.

Antje sat beside me. She gripped my right arm firmly with both hands. I was in for the night, whether I liked it or not. She was totally scared but said little. Finally she fell asleep with her head on my lap. I carried her to Mam's bed. Mam yawned. Like me, she was exhausted. It had been some day. It was time to go to sleep, if I could. Large numbers of Allied troops had landed and were headed for Arnhem. Things could never be the same again in Holland.

Monday morning was eerie. Battle noises came from three directions. From the west came a constant thunder and boom, the thumping of heavy guns, almost certainly from the drop-zone on Renkum Heath, near Wolfheze. The non-stop noise from the north was a mix of machine-gun fire and a steady discharge of rockets. But it was from the east, from Arnhem, that the full measure of what was happening could be heard. Columns of black smoke spiralled upward to the sky from all over the city as heavy guns thundered non-stop in the crisp September air. The fresh young men who had marched past the day before must now be in the thick of whatever was going on. The thunder of heavy guns never let up.

Oosterbeek was in a battle zone. Mortars landed in several parts of the village, the smell of cordite was unmistakable. I decided to call on Mr. Heemskerk, for the benefit of his experience. Before I left for his house, Oom Paul and Tante Catherine arrived. Oom Paul hadn't gone to work in Arnhem the constant booming from there was enough to keep even the bravest away. He was unshaven, which for him was unusual.

"Everyone should stay indoors," he said.

"Oom Paul is right," Antje said. She was back to gripping my hand in both of hers.

"What have you heard?" I asked Oom Paul.

"The British are digging in all round, they're already in the Oosterbeek Low Church. They've turned several houses into first aid centres. I heard a British officer telling people on the Utrechtseweg to take in their flags because we're in a battle zone."

"Those whooshing noises, those are shells going into Arnhem over our heads," said Tante Catherine. "Houses near us have been hit. I'm scared."

"Are the bakeries open in all of this?" my mother asked.

"I'll go and see. We must buy bread and supplies. This will go on for a while," I said.

It was the excuse I needed to go to Mr. Heemskerk's house.

"Hurry back," my mother said, staring hard at me as I left.

Oom Paul couldn't sit still. "I'll come with you."

"One is enough," I told him.

"Nelis is right," said Tante Catherine. "You buy bread for all of us, Nelis."

"Come back soon," Antje pleaded as I was leaving the house.

Van Beek's bakery was open for business, and a larger queue than usual had formed. More than half were men and that in itself was unusual. The mood had changed from the day before. Scraps of news were being exchanged in whispers, every ear cocked.

"St. Elizabeth's is crammed to the rafters with casualties. It's bad."

"They've turned Tafelberg Hotel into a casualty station."

"And the Schoonoord."

"The British are all over the Hartenstein, they've taken prisoners. I saw them with my own eyes. They're using it as their headquarters."

"The Germans left the Tafelberg like a pigsty, they had to get out so fast."

"The Tommies have a lot of casualties," said a bearded man with a sailor's cap.

"Yesterday seems a long time ago," said another.

"Why would they make Hartenstein their headquarters? That's so stupid, so ridiculously stupid," said the man in the sailor's cap aggressively.

"What's stupid about that?" someone else said angrily. Others are equally angry. What a moment to criticise the decisions of the Allied officers?

"The right place to turn into a headquarters is the Westerbouwing Restaurant."

"Why the Westerbouwing?"

"Location. It looks right down on the ferry across the Rhine to Driel. Whoever holds the Westerbouwing controls all the approaches. It's the perfect bridgehead."

"The British know what they're doing."

"It doesn't matter. Monty will be here before the day is out. You'll see."

"Everything will change when Monty's men get here."

"Careful, the bread is hot, it is straight out of the oven," said Mrs. Van Beek.

"Will you be open in the afternoon?"

"We'll stay open while we can."

I bought loaves too hot to hold for Mam and Tante Catherine. The noise from three separate battles areas was unremitting as I made my way back. I prayed silently when rockets screamed over my head. One hit and it would all be over. I stayed close to buildings, using them for cover.

I stopped by Nana's apartment on the way back. She was calmer than I had expected, and she enquired again about her goats. She wanted to remain where she was, but I wouldn't have it. I insisted she come with me until things settled.

"What kept you?" asked my mother. She was annoyed with me.

"There was a long queue."

It was mid-afternoon by the time I knocked on Mr. Heemskerk's door.

"No school today, Nelis," he greeted me.

He smiled as usual as we sat down. Unlike the mood in van Beek's bakery, Mr. Heemskerk was unusually positive and upbeat.

"Montgomery means business. We'll be running Holland before the week is out."

"There are separate battles going on, Mr. Heemskerk. The smoke and the noise from Arnhem is something desperate. That non-stop artillery is frightening."

"Of course it's non-stop. The SS can't live with that sort of hammering."

"It may be the SS that are doing the firing."

"You've gone all serious on me, Nelis. General Montgomery is not going to send his troops here to have them slaughtered. Its Normandy all over again, he sends his airborne troops in first to take over specific targets, and follows up immediately with the main body of ground troops. He'll make another landing like yesterday and his land armies have already begun their move up from the Belgian border. Give it a day, maybe two."

"I'm not so sure, Mr. Heemskerk."

"He's not going to do anything rash."

"There's an SS division here."

"The Germans have two SS divisions here, as well as the division that was stationed down on Walcheren Island. They had many more divisions in position in Normandy, but they were smashed. Our Underground has supplied him with lots of information and he has made his decision. Cheer up, Nelis. Within days you'll be just another student sitting in your school classroom. You've buried your last body in the woods."

He laughed, and I couldn't help laughing with him. His high hopes lifted me. But even as we spoke we could hear more shells exploding in the distance.

"By the way, my pastor has visited his doctor again."

"Oh?"

"His assistant has moved up in the world".

"Oh?"

"He's now a hospital administrator."

"At St. Elizabeth?"

"Promotion has been rapid."

"Does my mother know?"

"Maybe we should leave it at that until after Monty arrives."

There's a sudden knock on the drawing room door. Lisette, the maid, entered, followed immediately by Luc Gauthier. He was perspiring and breathing very heavily.

"Luc Gauthier? How on earth did you get here, my dear friend?" cried Mr. Heemskerk. Luc shook my hand with unusual force. He was very tense.

"I took the ferry from Driel across the Rhine. That climb from the ferry up to here has me exhausted."

He was more than exhausted, he was seriously distraught.

"Get this man a strong drink, Lisette," said Mr. Heemskerk. "Whisky?"

"Oui, merci, double," Luc replied.

"What's the news from Arnhem?"

"Massacre, mon Dieu. It's a massacre."

Mr. Heemskerk and I exchanged glances, and held our breaths.

"I spent the morning building a roadblock to stop the Boches. Do you know what we used for sandbags? Huh? Do you want to know? Huh? Corpses. We used corpses we collected off the streets. That's what. Huh? We used the corpses of British and German soldiers and the corpses of Dutchmen and women and children. There is no shortage of corpses in Arnhem right now. We stacked them a metre high. We put the bodies with German uniforms on top of the barrier, but they kept coming. It is massacre. Alors. Disaster."

Luc was looking towards the door to see if the whisky was coming, and when it did he gulped it down, and placed the glass back on the tray as if to ask for more. Mr. Heemskerk nodded to Lisette.

"You cannot imagine what its like. Buildings collapse without warning, people are being buried alive. It is disaster. The shelling is something else."

"Have they British taken the Bridge?"

"No. They have a foothold on one side. The Germans hold the other side and they're attacking from two directions. It is a no-man's land. Buildings close to the bridge are being hammered. The old town is being torn to pieces, with shells going off everywhere. I couldn't continue piling corpses, I couldn't do it. I loaded up bodies with another man, he supplies me with vegetables, he used to. He took a fit of vomiting. Just as he was bending over to puke, his head came off, before my eyes, it came clean off. I dragged his torso to the pile to stop a German tank. I couldn't take any more. I ran out of there, back to my family. Everywhere it is the same, buildings crash on to the streets. My wife went hysterical. We left everything behind us. We went with a neighbour and his family through side streets and back streets until we got to the Rhine. God was with us. Our neighbour had a row boat moored on the riverbank. We rowed across, too many of us. Not many boats will cross the Rhine today, not near the city. We walked from the ferry into Driel. It's a different world over across. Everything is calm, you hear the noise, but it is not like Arnhem. Arnhem is hell. I left my wife in Driel with the children. The railway bridge over the Rhine is gone. You know that?"

"We heard the explosion that took it yesterday evening," said Mr. Heemskerk.

"I've got my family out of Arnhem, mon Dieu. The ferry from Driel is still running, I came here to tell you what it's like. Cornelis, How can anyone who's seen what I've seen ever be the same again. Mon Dieu."

He was unable continue. He looked towards the door again, desperate for the second whisky. When it arrived he gulped it down in one go.

"All those bodies, this is Normandy, piles of bodies, all of those dead people!"

"The Germans were pushed back at Normandy," Mr. Heemskerk said. "Montgomery will do the same here. He'll bring up as many men as it takes from the Belgian border."

"There will be no city left if the shelling continues. I'm scared. I saw terrible faces today, people were running to the wrong places, running into burning buildings which collapsed on them. They were blinded by smoke and kept tripping over dead bodies. Mon Dieu. It is all so terrible."

Luc's distress was affecting Mr. Heemskerk.

"We have to hold our nerves until General Montgomery gets here. He'll be here by Wednesday."

"There will be no Arnhem by Wednesday. The men on the bridge can't hold. I won't stay longer. I'll cross back to Driel while the ferry is still running."

Luc rose to leave. The feeling of cold fear that had lurked in my gut since the landings had returned, stronger than ever.

"Montgomery must get a move on," was all Mr. Heemskerk could say.

As Luc was departing I told Mr. Heemskerk I too had better go. He nodded, his face was grimmer now. Deliverance, if indeed that was what it was, coming at a price.

There was consternation at our house when I got home. Only moments before, a shell had hit the chimney at the corner of van Gaal's house, leaving a gaping hole in the roof. The entire chimney was blown off. My mother was out with Mrs. Van Gaal, consoling her. Their son Boody had recently been taken by the enemy. One of their upstairs bedrooms was filled with rubble and mortar. We could see to the sky where the roof had been. We could see inside one of their bedrooms. It brought home to us that if van Gaals' house could be hit by a shell, then so could every single house on the street.

I was in the van Gaals' kitchen when Henk de Groot's wife entered. Her fleshy face was flushed.

"Can I help?" she asked.

"You get out of our house right now," Mr. van Gaal said.

"I want to help after what's happened."

"Get out of here, you Nazi-loving bitch. Get yourself and your greedy family out of here before Hatchet Day. I won't be responsible for my actions. That's my personal promise to you," he said.

"I only came to help."

"Like you helped the night Boody was arrested. Like you helped have several houses raided. Get out of here while you're still alive. Your days here are numbered."

Mrs. de Groot was nothing if not brazen. She grabbed a broom as if to defend herself from attack, stuck out her jaw, her face redder than ever.

"We get blamed for everything around here. Just because my husband took a job..."

"We want no collaborators here. Get out or I'll hand you over to people who won't wait for Hatchet Day."

"It's because we're poor. Frau Erica walks her dogs and cats and her German husband through the woods and pinpoints anyone she doesn't like..."

"Get out," Mr. van Gaal shouted. I hadn't known the man was capable of such rage.

Mrs. De Groot backed away to the door and threw the broom down. In a moment she was gone. Mr. van Gaal went pale. He was so upset I thought he might be having a stroke. We were not the only ones with a low opinion of Mrs. De Groot. Through the shattered windows and damaged roof of van Gaals' house, the roar of battle was growing louder. Oosterbeek, our lovely village, was now a dangerous place to be. Luc's experience in Arnhem and his talk on piles of bodies had scared the daylights out of me.

Wednesday. We were deafened by the noise and battered and weary beyond belief. The war had come to Oosterbeek. We did not have the capacity to cope. The relentless bombardment began to feed our darkest fears. We'd had enough of the rumours and reports, the frustrating and endless wait for Monty's men. Where were they? His phantom army now had a name, Monty's Second Army. The men of the Second Army could call themselves whatever they liked, if only they would get here and bring relief.

We hadn't slept in two days. Mam's right eye was bloodshot, her face drawn, but she carried on working as best she could. Despite her size she looked frail, and trembled at every loud explosion. She pulled the curtains in an attempt to close out the noise, then opened them again. The electricity was gone so we needed the light from outside. She tidied relentlessly, even when there was nothing left to tidy. The strain was unbearable.

Antje gripped me and wouldn't let go. She was very frightened. Wherever I went, she stuck with me. Every time an explosion went off, she jumped and winced.

Nana went out every hour to check on 'her' goats and collect eggs. She complained the hens had stopped laying eggs. Gerrit didn't look at her. He had not spoken in a full twenty-four hour period. His silence was hard to take.

Jan was calm and never once complained. I caught him looking at me intently. He knew the score but didn't dare let on to anyone else. We were like caged rats. More and more houses close by were taking hits. When a shell blasts a house it is never seen, is never expected - poom. The house is gone and those inside are dead. If this was what it was like in Oosterbeek, what was it like in Arnhem? They had endured three days of continuous shelling and ferocious fighting. The Tommies had told us that their mates on the bridge had started out with supplies of food and water for two days, so by now they must have been out of both. For how much longer would we have to take it? Where was Monty? Why hadn't his army come?

The British soldiers astonished us. Their cheerfulness was amazing, the one bright spot in our precarious existence. They kept themselves busy and were organised. They shouted warnings to us to get cover. And they did odd things. I think they were telling each other jokes while they cleaned their rifles they certainly laughed a lot and at one stage a stocky fellow started to play on the harmonica they all started to whistle along in harmony. I didn't recognise the tune then but now I know it was 'Danny Boy' and every time I hear it now my mind instantly returns to that time when we sat innocently waiting on the sidelines of the battlefield. They slept in brief snatches, they joked and puffed cigarettes. But by now it was impossible to ignore their changing mood and sense of urgency. However, they persisted in keeping a bright side out, and dug in. More and more of them were injured or killed, they were incredibly brave as they ran with their injured into the bedlam outside.

"Can we kip here, missus?" a sallow-faced one asked. My mother, who had quite a bit of English, had no idea what he asking for. We laughed at his strange question. One of his colleagues rephrased it. Kip? Only the British could come up with a word like that.

"You've dug a huge hole in front of my house without my permission, and now you want my permission to sleep in it?" Mam said. She smiled a weary approval.

"Ta, missus. Can we have a fill of water please?"

"Of course."

A tall young man of no more than twenty, with fuzz for a moustache, downed the second glass of water in a gulp.

"Ta, luv. Our supplies ran out last night. We were to be relieved but there is no sign of those lazy buggers from the south. They'd better get 'ere soon, cos I'm dyin' for a puff. Can I have another glass, please?"

"Of course," Mam said, and turned to enter the house.

"No more water. It's gone," Gerrit cried, his voice trembling after his long silence.

My mother was shocked.

"First we have no electricity. Now we have no water! Is there anything else we can do for you boys?" she asked the soldiers.

"We need water, missus. Tell us where we can get some and we'll fetch it. Those lazy buggers pushing up from Belgium have plenty water but they're not 'ere, are they?"

Mother looked at me. Getting water in Oosterbeek on an ordinary day was very simple, but nothing was ordinary any more.

"Van Gaal's has an old pump to the rear. Try there," she said.

Jan and I, carrying a couple of glass bottles apiece, had to travel the sixty metres, a mere sprint, but not today. We crawled by the goats' shed to the rear of our house. There was some cover if we crawled behind the houses, none if we took the road. We climbed through the de Groots' back garden. If Mrs. de Groot were to come out and hurl abuse at us we'd have to let her, we needed water and we could live with her abuse. The Tommies needed water, they were suffering and losing too many men, they needed whatever help we could give them. We needed help ourselves. If de Groots saw us going through their garden they didn't react. We reached van Gaal's house. It was a shambles. The rear of their house was just a large pile of rubble.

"What on earth?" said Mr. van Gaal.

"We need water. Mam says you have an old pump here."

"That thing hasn't worked in years. Sorry, boys."

"Do you know anywhere close by?"

"I don't know anyone with a pump that works, but Koemans have a tank. The water is probably filthy."

"The Tommies are desperate for water. All of us are."

"Go back to your home boys. It's not safe even inside."

Jan and I exchanged glances. One of Jan's great qualities was his capacity to remain calm in a crisis, and we were in a crisis now.

"Koeman's orchard," Jan said.

"Apples. Of course. Mrs. Koeman can't refuse us."

She could and she did, not because she didn't want to help, but because every tree in her orchard, if not in Oosterbeek, was stripped clean. No water, no apples. The explosions were closer now, the unrelenting noise was driving people mad. Poom. Would it ever stop? For an hour? Even for just five minutes? It seemed our eardrums would burst. Poom.

Jan and I persisted. We crawled over and under fences, through several back gardens. Tommies saw us and cocked their rifles. They looked at us as though we were mad.

"Any water, mate?" a skinny young soldier with a blackened face asked.

There had to be water somewhere. We knocked at back doors, ignoring barking dogs. We weren't sure if the dogs were barking, so great was the noise. We ignored shouts to get out of gardens, it's for the Tommies, we said. The mention of Tommies brought calm, but got us no water.

"In the woods. The stream there, we could try it," Jan suggested.

"It's more dangerous there than here," I said.

"We have to find water, Nelis."

With our bellies flattened to the ground, we passed back by our own garden, working our way to the woods. I was terrified of getting killed, but water was paramount. My survival instinct was telling me go back, better thirsty than dead, there were lots of dead men up there, but the Tommies needed water. We should be trying to find a house with a cellar. Let the boys try, tomorrow could be worse, but I felt certain tomorrow would be worse. Again, my sense of hope and survival told me maybe not, maybe Monty would come, but reality kicked in, what was he waiting for, his boys had been fighting here for more than three days now, the Germans had been picking up the fresh supplies parachuted in, the woods were littered with corpses, Germans were all over the place, shouting and shooting on sight and driving British jeeps. We should be getting home.

Jan kept calm. "Crawl close to trees," he said, "I know a place with a lot of big trees, we can't go back without water."

"Okay, let's try," I said.

The whole thing was madness, machine-guns were spitting bullets, spraying them over our heads. My hands were sweating. Bullets were whipping into trees beside us.

"We've no chance."

"I've an idea," Jan said.

"What?"

"Drain the cistern in the airing cupboard."

Drain the cistern in the airing cupboard. Why didn't we think of that before? Huge branches were snapping and crashing all round us, but they gave us some cover. I lay flat on the ground, my face touching the earth, Jan lying close alongside. Bark and splinters flew. Felled branches, our temporary cover, were being shredded to a pulp. Without our cover both of us would have been long dead. We backed away on our bellies from the direction in which we came, centimetre by centimetre. I held my breath, my heart pounding in my chest. I dared not raise my head too high. We crawled backwards for hundreds of metres. Machine-gun fire came from nearby. I glanced sideways, my heart stopped. Five, no, six German soldiers were right beside us. Jesus Lord. Jan saw them too. We froze. Two to the front were crouching, the rest stood alert. One, wearing a peaked cap, was holding a revolver in his right hand, looking straight ahead. The others wore helmets and were holding rifles waist high. Maybe they didn't see us? They were using tree cover, and looked like a patrol. If even one of them glanced to his right we were dead. One did. I glimpsed a flash of blue eyes. He gasped and tried to say something, but no words came. What was he scared of? Us? There was more machine-gun fire. They dived to their left. Bullets whipped into wood, splinters filled the air. There was a short pause, and they rose slowly. The one with the peaked cap waved one hand, a revolver in the other, they moved forward. The soldier who had seen us didn't look around. They stood behind three big trees, and peered out, there was more machine-gun fire. Suddenly their bodies jerked and twisted, the soldiers let out high-pitched yelps, dropped and died. A leg twitched for a moment, then stopped. Jan didn't move. Neither did I. A German rifle lay on the ground. We waited. My heart was pounding hard. The one with the blue eyes had fallen across another, and a trickle of blood flowed from his nostril on to the soldier underneath. I dared not touch the rifle. I struggled to stay calm. I waited and then edged backwards, slowly, slowly. I kept my nose close to the earth, there was gunfire from the left, from British guns. British machine-guns killed too. I moved a few centimetres, all of my instinct screaming to me to get out of there. Jan was gesturing something. What? Holy God, there was a dip in the ground, but no water. I had to concentrate on breathing and not lifting my head. I kept my belly to the ground, nose in the clay, and backed away, metre by metre, through grass and weeds, through another metre. The dip ended. We were exposed again, but now we were near the road with smaller trees for cover. We crossed it, flat on our bellies, into the cover of shrubs, we were closer to home now, we were scratched and torn, and we had to make a run for it. We made it. We were home.

Mam cried when she saw us, Gerrit cried with her. Nana put her arms round Mam.

"Where's Antje?"

"In bed."

"How can she sleep in this noise?"

"I gave her sleeping pills. Did you find water?"

"We'll drain the cistern."

"Lord above. Water in the house and you two nearly get killed," cried Mam.

I was worried about Oom Paul, who had three days growth of beard and a wild look. He was laughing to himself. Tante Catherine saw me watching, and looked away. She held baby Cora close to her and stayed silent. Everything had been said a thousand times already. It was strange. Oom Paul didn't help drain the cistern. Nana found a bucket for us to hold the water.

Monty's Second Army hadn't come, we didn't know if the British held the north side of the bridge. What had happened to those men we had cheered on the Utrecht Road? Were they alive or dead?

Three loud explosions came in rapid succession, much too close. I ran out the back. I heard screams. Van Gaal's house had been hit again, now one side of the house was gone. The gable and part of sidewall was totally gone. The first floor hadn't fallen, not yet. The bed and wardrobe were in place, an upstairs bedroom door was hanging sideways, splintered. It was an eerie sight, with two walls gone. A dressing table was perched sideways, ready to tumble. Tiles were falling from the roof on to the bed. A dense cloud of dust was overhead.

"Nobody alive in there," said Jan.

We called out. Others called too. There were more direct hits. Rubble and debris flew in all directions. Bricks fell at our feet. We ducked. The rest of the house collapsed. It was terrifying. If van Gaal's home could be flattened so easily then so, too, could ours. We would all die. I remembered what someone shouted at me earlier, to go to a house with a cellar. Was this why the Tommies had dug holes and trenches in the ground? They served as gun pits as well as for cover.

"We must get to some place with a basement," said Jan, reading my mind.

"Yes."

Houses cannot stand against shells. Oosterbeek would soon be rubble. We didn't discuss Mr. and Mrs. van Gaal, they had to be dead. Nice people, good neighbours, but gone, buried in the rubble of their home. Digging them out was pointless. When or if their son Boody returned it will be a hard homecoming.

"We have to move," I said firmly.

"Definitely," Jan concurred.

Mother agreed. So did Tante Catherine. Oom Paul laughed. Did he not realise? Nana raised an urgent concern.

"Where can we go? The fighting is all round us."

"If van Gaal's house can be destroyed, so can ours."

"Where can we go, Nelis? We daren't put our heads outside the door."

"We must go to a safer place."

"I'm staying with my goats, Nelis."

We delayed moving. Fresh explosions rocked us. We were deafened, and were going nowhere for now. We had no electricity, but that didn't matter because we had nothing to cook. Mam produced a few jars of jam and chutney and a tin of beans.

An explosion rocked another house near us with a loud bang, like the one that hit van Gaal's house, only closer. I ran out the back door. The goat shed had been hit, virtually destroyed. Two goats, the old ones, were running around, terrified. I looked inside. There was a fire, the straw bedding was on fire. Hens flew through the air to escape the flames and smoke. Fortunately, there was little straw to burn. Jan helped me put out the fire. Why wasn't Oom Paul prepared to help?

"My goats. My goats," cried Nana.

"Two alive. Two dead," I told her.

"Can we skin them and take them with us?" Gerrit said.

"There's nothing left to skin."

Tante Catherine came from the house and took Nana inside. Jan went in and helped to calm Nana.

When I got inside Mam was berating Oom Paul. He was not arguing back, he was not resisting. This was not the Oom Paul the rest of us knew.

"You let Nelis and Jan do everything. Act like a man. What's wrong with you, Paul?"

He sat still, with his fists clenched tight. His face was blank He didn't register anything my mother said to him.

"He's gone deaf, Corrie," said Tante Catherine, "I'll look after him."

She grabbed his hand and took him into the sitting room. He went without resisting. Baby Cora cried and tried to follow them. Antje tugged at my sleeve.

"Can you bring Cora to me, Nelis?"

I lifted Cora and put her in Antje's lap, and Cora stopped crying. The bombardment and shelling continued. More houses were crumbling into rubble. We had to move but where to? Where was Monty? Where was the Second Army? Would it ever end? Nana took out a rosary beads and prayed aloud. We shouted the responses to drown the noise of battle. I was sure the bombardment could be heard in Utrecht, if not as far away as Amsterdam.

I tried to think clearly. Were we safer indoors or outside? We might end up like Mr. and Mrs. van Gaal. Indoors a stray shell can kill, but walls protected us from machine-gun fire. I had no answers, I knew nothing. Imprisoned as we were in a small house in the middle of a major battle, there was little we could do. One thing I did know though was that a wrong decision could be fatal. I felt responsible for the others. I had to make decisions using only the knowledge I had. Three days had passed, and still there was no sign of the Second Army. The heavy action was close to Oosterbeek, it was all round us. The British were being pushed out of Arnhem, but none of them was showing signs of giving up. Was it possible they still expected Monty's men to arrive? I snatched an hour of sleep. Jan and Gerrit watched me closely, waiting for me to decide.

"We stay for now. We'll move at the next lull."

"I can't leave my goats."

"You'll move with the rest of us."

"Oh, Nelis…I'm afraid."

"We're all afraid, Nana. Who around here has a cellar?"

"Mr. Heemskerk has a cellar."

"We might as well try to get to the moon."

"Kate van Renkum has a cellar. She has got a houseful of kids and a husband who has dived."

"We'll go to her," I decided.

"Kate's too brave for her own good. She probably has half the neighbourhood with her. It's a big solid house, but getting there…"

"We'll go before dawn. We'll run into the fighting whichever way we go."

Everyone was silent. Mam gave everyone half a cup of brackish water. It was horrible stuff. We listened, but there was no change. The battle was unremitting. It grew dark.

Chapter Eighteen

Dawn came. But no bird called it. There was no birdsong. It seemed that every bird had left us forever. Why should the birds of Oosterbeek linger when they could spread their wings and fly to where there were branches on the trees and where the only noise was that of other birds singing? Why would they want to stay with us, when all we could do was kill one another? The trees and their branches were by now shredded to a pulp so who could blame the birds for leaving?

I was no longer sure whether this was the morning of the fifth or sixth day of battle. I wasn't even sure what day of the week it was. We were in pain from the thirst but, at last, we were moving. If Monty was doing the same we were not aware, nobody told us anything any more. The previous twenty-four hours had been shattering. We left our house just in time. A shell smashed into our front door as we were walking out through the gate. The windows shattered in all directions. We didn't stop, we couldn't so we kept going. We didn't know if we would ever return or if even we would have anything to return to. Nana drove the rest of us crazy, saying she would only come if she could bring her ridiculous and infernal goats. She tethered the pair together with a short piece of rope. I thought it outrageous for her to arrive at someone's house looking for shelter with eight other people and to insist on bringing her two goats along too. Jan stopped me from losing my temper. Tante Catherine caught the sleeve of my jumper and told me that the goats were Nana's contact with reality, they were keeping her sane in the ghastly circumstances. I shut up as no one was listening to me, or to anyone else.

We saw uncountable bodies of soldiers and civilians as we crawled to Kate's van Renkum's house. The bodies of three Tommies lay in a gun pit, their helmeted heads and shoulders on show, the rest of them covered with freshly minced clay. We could see dried blood and fresh blood. Blood was still flowing from one soldier's head. I could see the hole where the bullet had entered. We walked past. I saw another soldier rolling in agony on the ground, his face black, his tunic on fire. He gasped for breath, blood spurting from his lips. He was dying and he knew it.

The houses along the way appeared empty and none had escaped damage. We were now outside the old village. A house close by was being used as a first-aid centre, and was clogged with wounded soldiers, as medical orderlies bravely ran through sniper fire, carrying in even more. Those heroic souls had paid a heavy price. How much longer could they carry on?

Oosterbeek was now being pulverised. It had become the centre of the heavy fighting. Artillery and mortar was coming from both north and west. The town as I had known it was destroyed, it was a blitzed landscape of rubble, with craters and shell holes, spent cartridges, burned-out jeeps and vehicles, collapsed trees and branches, flattened houses and houses half standing, of dust and chaos and corpses. This had been my town, my home, and it lay crumbled before my eyes. I had thought I knew something of war, but I realised then that I knew nothing, there is nothing to know, nothing to say, who lives, who dies. These things are all a matter of luck. We really were in a hellish situation. Kate van Renkum shook her head, her sleeves and apron covered with dried blood, her blonde hair covered in grime, her face fretful. Two small blond children kept a close grip on her skirt, their cardigans spattered with blood.

"We're an emergency First Aid here. We send those who can be helped to the Tafelberg Hotel for emergency operations. We've injured soldiers everywhere in the house, the attic, the bedrooms, our kitchen and the basement. We can't help you, Nellie. We've buried twenty-seven bodies right where you're standing since Tuesday. That's my front lawn, where I grow my flowers. You and I admired the roses when I had them. Go to a house with a cellar, Nellie. Go now."

"How can we get away?" I asked her.

"You can't, unless you can swim the Rhine, if you can get to the Rhine in the first place. Arnhem has being levelled, the Germans have taken full control of the bridge."

"What about the woods?" Jan asked.

"Germans are everywhere. There are bodies all over. Go to a house with a cellar."

"Any word on Monty?"

She shook her head."You'll have to excuse me. We have soldiers injured and dying here. God be with all of you."

Antje twitched in my arms. Tante Catherine put her arm round Mam's neck, smiling faintly. Tante Catherine's inner strength impressed me. Oom Paul, on the other hand, was in terrible condition. His teeth were chattering, he was deathly pale and had to be held by the hand. We headed towards the Utrecht Road. On the way we saw a three-storey house with part of its roof damaged. It had a cellar. A youngish woman came out of nowhere and dashed for the side door. Suddenly she spun around, making a short grunting noise. She fell down and died. A wife? A mother? Whose? Children? We dived for cover. Bullets pockmarked the front wall of the house as splinters of masonry flew and a channel was cut in the wall. I saw a small bank of earth thrown up by a shell. I dived behind it, carrying Antje with me, screaming at my mother to come. Bullets whizzed over our heads. We were showered with chips of flying masonry. I was hit on the right ear, it stung like hell. I felt blood flowing to my neck. Mother and Gerrit rolled in beside us. The side door of the house opened a little, then a little more, I watched it, hardly daring to breathe. When I saw a chance, I shouted at my mother to run for it. She did and made it inside the house. I thanked God for that. I told the others to stay down, not to move. Baby Cora screamed, I ran and grabbed her, then dived. Antje held out her arms for Cora. How did she know? Bullets seared into masonry, Nana's goats ran in terror. Nana ran after them. I knocked her to the ground with a flying tackle, and hauled her to our cover with her screaming at me, she was crazy with fear and anger. Jan and Gerrit held her down, almost sitting on her. Tante Catherine and Oom Paul lay flat. They had no cover, they would get hit, I tried to get her to roll over but she couldn't, she was too bulky. I pushed her and then tried to reach Oom Paul, but in his terror he was deaf to me and everyone else. Tante Catherine screamed at him to stay put, not to move.

"One more roll, Tante," I urged her.

"But Paul, why doesn't he answer?"

"He doesn't hear you," I told her.

"What's wrong, Oom Paul?" Gerrit whispered.

Machine-gun fire burst over our heads.

"Stay down! Don't move!" I cried.

There was a pause. I ran for Tante Catherine and dragged her along the ground, her clothes pulled up. The back of Oom Paul's head had drying blood on it. I finally got Tante Catherine into cover.

"Paul, my Paul, pull him in Nelis, he's injured," gasped Tante Catherine. What was wrong with Oom Paul? He couldn't be dead or could he? There was more firing from machine-guns as glass shattered, timbers splintered, and masonry flew off the wall. We were pinned down.

"Nelis, get my husband," Tante Catherine gasped.

"Not now, later."

"Pull him in Nelis. We can't leave him lying there."

"Later, Tante Catherine. You get in the house. Mam is inside, you follow her in. Go now. I'll take Cora, I promise."

I grabbed the child, she screamed for her mother, and one by one we got inside the house. Tante Catherine was oddly calm even though her husband was in the line of fire and injured. Oom Paul looked as if he had been shot. The basement of the house was packed. If a rocket hit the house we would have been buried alive in a mass grave.

Those already in the basement were as desperate as we were. "Have you water, any water, is there no water," came their cries.

"Keep your heads down, snipers are out there, they've picked off a six or seven upstairs already."

"Have you water? I want water."

My own mouth was so dry that I could hardly speak. I wondered at the futility of asking for water when you knew there was none. I asked whose house we were in, I was told Graaf's, Kobus Graaf, he was upstairs, injured. His wife was hysterical, desperately trying to get upstairs, but voices shouted at her telling her to stay where she was, there were too many injured people upstairs, there was no room, lie still. The stairway was packed tight with bodies, some alive, some dead. All begged for water.

Mother sat against a wall. She needed water. She really had to have some soon. I decided to try to get her a slug of some liquid at the first opportunity, but first I had to get to Oom Paul. I waited for my chance. Fresh bursts of machine-gun fire came from two separate places. Why were they firing on civilians? They must have known there were British Tommies upstairs. If they shelled us, we were doomed. Tante Catherine remained calm, her face covered in dust, her gaze firm. She started to say something but no words came, she looked away and then looked at me again.

"If there is a lull, Nelis, bring my husband in," she pleaded.

"Not now Tante Catherine. I'll go when there's another lull."

Nana? Where was Nana? She was beside me in deep shock and she wanted to pray for her son. Tante Catherine put her hand on my shoulder and looked me in the eyes.

"Do it when it's safe, Nelis. Don't leave him alone out there for too long." Her voice cracked for the first time.

"Jan, where's Jan, I'll need Jan with me." There was a sudden pause in the firing.

"Go now, Nelis, I'm right behind you," Jan said.

I dived for cover behind a mound of earth. Jan landed beside me. "Is he alive, Nelis?" "I don't know. He has blood at the back of his head and down his neck. Can you see him, he is beside that gun-pit."

A shell gouged a fresh hole in the ground, Jan and I got on our knees and dashed to where Oom Paul was lying. We pulled and rolled him and got him into the shell hole. He was breathing, trickling blood. Somehow we had to get him into the house. We lay gasping for breath, while above us bullets gave off eerie sounds as they flew over us. Then there was a moment of silence.

"Let's go," I said. Oom Paul was heavy as we pulled him from the shell hole, then the firing started again, and bullets were bouncing off the house.

"Keep your eyes covered," Jan shouted.

We made it to the door and then we were inside. I was desperate for water. Two men took Oom Paul, one said there was First Aid upstairs, and Tante Catherine went with them. I sat beside my mother.

"Go with Tante Catherine, Nelis. Is he badly hurt?"

"I don't know. He has blood coming from the back of his head."

"Get me water, Nelis."

"I'll try."

I was gasping. Antje had a death grip on my arm, someone was standing over me. It was Jan.

"Some water for you, Mrs. Baumann."

"Where?"

"Upstairs, very little."

"Thanks, Jan."

Mam drank first from a jug and then put the jug to Antje's mouth. Others asked to share. I took a gulp.

"What's it like upstairs?"

"Don't go up, they've got bodies, four bodies."

"Snipers. They're real bastards. Don't they have any regard for the Red Cross flag?"

"Christ in heaven, we're all casualties here."

Tante Catherine arrived from upstairs. She was calm.

"He's got a head would but he's conscious. He needs a doctor. There's nothing you can do. The British are treating him. Where did you get the water, Jan?"

"The water pipes."

Outside, the battle continued to rage. I prayed that if relief was on the way it would come now. Otherwise it would be too late, there would be no one left alive. Was death so bad, surely it could be no worse than this? Why worry about it? We were past worry now. I prayed the others not be taken with only me left alive, if they should die, then so should I.

How could our situation have deteriorated so fast? I was so tired. I needed water, and food. There was none. I needed sleep, but sleep was impossible. I needed a few precious seconds of peace, to forget the pain, forget what was happening, to wake up to silence, to birdsong, to ordinary things, to an absence of weariness.

Someone tried to sing an Old Dutch song, the older people knew it and joined in. Mam tried to sing a few lines, the singing faded. We hadn't been to the toilet in days, there was no water to flush the bowl. We had nothing to pass, we had not eaten since Monday, or was it Tuesday? It was several days ago, it was in another life. I was worried about Antje, her thin body needed food and water, but she wasn't complaining. Everyone had gone silent, why not the guns, the artillery? I swore at Monty and at his Army. His generals or somebody had fouled up because now we were like rats, delirious for water and we couldn't even surrender. Soldiers can surrender but not civilians. Those who went out were shot. In battle we don't count. Battle victors count dead soldiers, they do not count civilians.

A woman started banging her head against the wall behind her. No-one attempted to stop her. Her skull thudded against the plaster. A man with grey wispy hair took her hand but she still wouldn't stop, the noise seemed to intensify, blood flowed from her nose. A young girl put her arm round the woman's neck. She would not stop. Blood started to come from both her nostrils, the young girl started to cry and turned to the white-haired man, he removed his jacket and put it behind the woman. Thud, thud, thud. It went on and on.

Tante Catherine came downstairs. "Oom Paul is okay, he is all bandaged up and he'll live," she said. What a difference that one scrap of good news made. We could live off that bit of news for an hour, maybe two. It gave us hope that something would happen soon. It had to because we couldn't endure much more. We had to have water, even one cupful. I thought things couldn't get any worse. Every other time I had thought that, it had turned out that I was wrong. I wanted to be right this time, I said it, that things couldn't get worse, over and over. But they did. They were about to get an awful lot worse.

Two women were arguing. "It's Saturday." The other contradicted her. Some agreed with the first woman, others with the second. The women arguing were not alone in their confusion. The loss of sleep was taking its toll on all of us. Others argued with vehemence that it was only Friday, with one man insisting it was in fact Tuesday.

Is there a limit to the degree of weariness a person can experience? Figuring out an answer was too difficult. It was necessary to stop thinking, to switch off, to block out thought, to ignore the thirst, the splitting headache, the eardrums sore from the bombardment, to surrender, to wondering what the Germans would do to us if we surrendered.

It was a different kind of fighting now. Jan noticed too. It was no longer machine-gun fire and shells from afar. It was much closer now. Soon we could both hear and see why. Tanks, Tiger tanks, sixty-ton German monsters were moving in. These floating mammoths of mayhem uprooted the street foundations, shredding the pavements as they manoeuvred their vast weight along.

The woman banging her head against the wall had stopped. There was a frightening amount of blood around her neck and shoulders. She might have been dead, nobody cared. Death now seemed so inevitable that the precise timing of one's departure was of no consequence. As long as the finale was fast, we had done our suffering, our fasting and thirsting, we had had our sleep deprivation, we had been deafened by the noise, terrified by the explosions, we had inhaled the dust, we had drunk the communal despair. I prayed for a fast death. I didn't want us to be buried alive.

We waited for the end. I didn't think about food. I hadn't eaten in days, none of us had, but food was not a concern. Water was. It would have been nice to have one last drink of cold clear water, one last indulgence before meeting my Creator. So would sleep, to lie on a soft bed and crash out and drift into oblivion, to breathe deeply, perhaps to snore, without headaches, without earaches. I wondered if my eardrums had burst, people were saying things to me and nothing was registering, was I dead already, perhaps waiting for God to pass judgement, perhaps with so many dying all round, there was a queue to get into Heaven.

A man stood up. He looked familiar. It was the man I had seen on Monday, in van Beek's bakery, with the sailor's cap. He was the man with the strong opinions. That was last Monday, that was one million years ago. He had a week's growth of grey and black beard and he was much thinner. He removed his cap and held it tightly. He hit the wall hard with it, over and over. Nobody said anything. He continued to hit the wall. I could hear a faint noise when he made contact, my hearing was not totally damaged. I could still hear the constant noise from outside. The military battle was a fight to the death.

There was a loud explosion close by. Nobody jumped. Was everyone stone deaf? I remember thinking I should be patient that my turn would come, that a Tiger tank would send something large and explosive towards me. The house we were occupying would crumble, all of us here would die and be buried at the same time. Perhaps when it was all over, clergymen from the various Christian denominations would come together and bless the site where we had perished. It would be interesting to see if the stern Calvinists would thaw enough to carry out their ritual alongside Roman Catholic clergy. Soon there would be an end to pain.

The Dutch army had caved on the fifth day in 1940. We had held out for longer, for three days longer. Surrendering saved the Dutch army, but our surrender was not wanted. The battle to the death went on within Oosterbeek. German troops had moved west from Arnhem. We were totally surrounded now, with no chance of escape. Civilians with flags of surrender were shot on sight. The Tommies were fighting for personal survival. The Germans couldn't permit a defeat this close to their frontier. Survival was the prize and the most basic instinct. The winner gets to live longer. For the loser perhaps this was the decisive battle of the war in Europe. Why did it have to be in Oosterbeek? Why? We wanted to live but we couldn't fight. We had nothing to fight with.

"Mam wants water," Gerrit repeated.

I rose to search for water I knew was not there. Jan came to me.

"Your aunt wants you upstairs immediately," he said.

The opinionated man was still hitting the wall with his cap. I made my way through a phalanx of bodies to get to the first floor. It had to be about Oom Paul. I hoped he was still alive, but if he was dead, well, what could I do? If he was dead, he was one of the lucky ones.

I entered a room packed with people, many bloody and covered in bandages. Tante Catherine rushed towards me, very serious.

"It's Antje. I'm very afraid for her, Nelis. She's terribly distressed."

I felt panic in my guts. I saw Antje lying on the floor, her frail body in spasm.

"The medics don't know. They reckon it's an air blockage. Someone must get her to the Tafelberg. They may be able to operate or do something up there. It's her only chance."

In moments of intense crisis, life and death decisions have to be made, and you don't know which the right one is. I picked up Antje and ran downstairs to the cellar door exit, suddenly wide-awake. I had something to do. I had to give my beloved sister a chance to survive. Mam screamed at me. "Be careful, Nelis."

Her instructions were as relevant as Monty's Second Army.

I began a frenzied sprint to reach the Tafelberg, my sprint of madness. Antje was as light as a feather, her condition was desperate.

It was so unfair. Why did someone so harmless have to suffer so much? I ran from the house through the basement door. Her body felt limp. Silently I begged her to shiver, tremble, to do something to let me know she was alive. I ran like the wind, not minding bullets raining around me, if they cut me down they cut me down. I kept my head low, and continued my silent entreaty to my sister, 'I'm on my way Antje, I'm taking you to the Tafelberg. Stay alive, Antje, I'll get you there, I know the short cuts.' Sudden balls of yellow flame blazed out, followed by black smoke, a tank exploded. Men gave out strangled screams before dying.

Bodies were flying through the air, thudding to the ground. I heard more bangs, saw more bodies, I heard more screams. Where did that bang come from? I remember yellow flames and more black smoke, the earth trembling, the tanks fighting with rifles and machineguns, a long tongue of glowing flame homed in on a Tommy's head and neck, he screamed in terrible agony. I retched but my stomach was empty. I was thankful Antje couldn't see. No one should have to look at another human being frying to death in a ball of flame. The smell of burning flesh was horrific. I hoped that the Tommy was dead, death could only be better for him.

The British were paying a terrible price. A Tiger tank came round the corner, the street too narrow for such a monster. I couldn't get through that way, the barrel was pointing straight at me. Just in time I realised the driver was going to fire and dived and rolled over. He missed. Antje wasn't crying, she must have been unconscious. I cut between two houses. There were several explosions behind me but I kept going. I had to, I didn't dare stop. I ran through the yellow flames and black smoke, around me walls were crumbling. I stumbled over rubble and corpses but kept going when another house fell. Soon there would be nothing left. I continued pleading to Antje to stay with me, to hold on. I was getting her to help. Here was the Pieterbergseweg, we were nearly there. A frightened dog scurried across the road to shelter in a hedge. The battle was fiercest here. I wondered how they could keep it up. There were bodies everywhere, behind bushes and beside machine-guns. Dead men lay behind anti-tank guns and live ones piled on each other in gun pits and trenches. A severed leg lay a few meters from a body, which was still moving. A burst of machine-gun fire, the body jerked in death and then it laid still. German corpses were strewn with British, the living fought on. I hardly recognised this as the Pieterbergseweg in Oosterbeek.

"Alive or dead?" asked a Tommy outside the Tafelberg.

"Alive," I answered.

Inside was a scene from hell, of the wounded, the dying and the dead. I passed a row of corpses, some civilian. I ignored them, kept going. I picked my way past them.

"Where the fuck do you think..." someone started to say.

"He's a kid, let him on."

The place was dark, there was no electricity. I realised the consequences of this with dismay. I saw a tall man dressed in a green apron, with a stethoscope round his neck, standing beside what looked like a billiard table. He had to be a doctor. He nodded as a body was pulled away. I jumped the queue, and placed Antje on the wide table. The doctor looked exhausted.

"Please doctor," I said, "please save her."

He examined her, checked her pulse while I watched his face. He pried open her left eyelid, then her right, took her pulse again, put his hand to her neck under her right ear, then turned to me and shook his head.

"She's dead, son." The doctor was English.

"She can't be. She's alive, she's my sister."

The doctor nodded to someone beside him. A young aide put Antje's body in my arms, then ushered me back to the door. I kept protesting. "She's not dead. She can't be. This is our Antje." They gently contradicted me, "she's dead son, he's a doctor, he should know." Dead, Antje, my dear sister, was dead, dead and gone straight to heaven, in a state of grace, Antje, who knew about Dad's secret hiding place before I did. Dad would cry when learned of this. I would too cry when I saw him crying. We would all grieve, including Jan. I recognise now that my initial grief was manifested in anger. Why did she have to suffer? I snarled at God, "you make it up to her, you have to God, do you hear me, are you listening to me, I'm talking to you. Let our Antje be welcomed to where she belongs, with other angels in heaven."

For one long moment there was no noise in my head, but the quiet I had longed for brought no joy with it as I stumbled forward aimlessly with my sister's body. Tears fell from my eyes and I wiped her face clean with them. Then the noise started again. I was back in the thick of relentless fighting. One second I saw British forces, a second later I saw Germans. The soldiers were fighting to live, killing each other to survive with no choice. German and British bodies lay beside each other in the mud. I stepped over them, carrying Antje's body. I don't know how it occurred to me, but I realised, that even if I made it back to Mam and the rest of them, there was no point in bringing Antje back to have her buried in rubble. I should bury her here while I was still alive. I couldn't understand why no bullets had cut me down. Was Antje protecting me? I saw a slit trench and I jumped into it. I felt safer there, although no place in Oosterbeek was safe. How the battle could have raged for so long I had no idea. How can those paratroopers survive against tanks? Men with machine-guns had no chance against tanks. Machine-guns shuddered when continually fired, tanks never shudder. Would the world ever know of the courage and heroism of these men? In death or capture, there would be no relief, I felt so sad for them. I couldn't bring Antje back to the cellar, not with Mam in her present state. I had no choice. I had to bury her when the fighting stopped, if it would ever stop. There was a bend in the slit trench, a British soldier was lying there, badly injured, his whole chin gone, shot off, he was still alive, his appearance grotesque. His tongue lolled down towards his chest, he seemed puzzled as blood squirted from several parts of him. He could not survive, he was better off dead, what could surgeons do for a man with no lower part to his face? His body shuddered, he was swallowing his own blood, drowning before my eyes. All I could do was say a prayer for him, and for Antje. They would lie together, in a slit trench, without a coffin. I saw the man had a water flask. I grabbed it. It was empty, not a drop. I was so scared.

I don't know how long I lay in that slit trench, but at some stage it seemed that the battle died down briefly. I used my bare hands to pull clay over the two bodies. For the Jewish woman Hepsibah and for the German soldier Ernst Schmundt I had used a spade and had Jan Till's assistance. Now I had nothing. Tears poured down my cheeks as I covered the frail mortal remains of my dear dead sister with handfuls of pulverised earth. I prayed that the souls of Antje and the British soldier were now in heaven. I had to cover all of her body well with clay, bury her deep, dogs hadn't eaten in a week, they would be ravenous. That was why those Jews lived with the stinking body of Hepsibah for several days; they had wanted her to be buried in the ground. I understood that now. I promised that if any of us survived we would have a Mass said for her. I wondered where Mr. Brouwers was. It would be nice if one day he came back to St. Bernulphus Church and played the organ at the Requiem. I wondered if our church was still standing.

When she was fully covered over, I looked around to get my bearings so we could find the exact burial spot later. My hands were soiled and sticky, my heart full of pain. I had to tell the others. This was what happened to civilians when generals get it wrong and bring their battles into our streets and homes. Through the noise and my headache and grief, I knew there was no such thing as a just war. Why should a blind girl have to pay for the deeds of others with her life? Why should Mam and Tante Catherine have to live in mortal fear for their lives and the lives of their unborn babies?

I must have dozed. Suddenly I was awake, the lull was over, the battle had resumed. There must have been a ceasefire. Otherwise I couldn't have slept in a slit trench with explosions going on all round me. I crawled out of the trench to get out of there.

Suddenly I was hit, badly hit. Panicking, I tried to get my breath, slowly and calmly, through the nose, my ribs ached, my ears were splitting, what had happened? I focused on my breathing in, trying to ignore the dust. I was half buried, I didn't know where I was. I couldn't move my hand. I was stuck. Then I saw why, the body of the soldier with no chin was out of the ground. He had been blasted from where I had buried him. I begged Christ in heaven to take me there and then, there beside Antje, someone would bury us both and the Tommy.

Suddenly there was a hand on me. "It's okay Nelis, I'm here. I'll get you back."

It was Jan Till. "We can't leave Antje like this," I said.

"We have to, Nelis, we have to, come on."

"No Jan, we can't, we have to bury her. I'll do it."

I buried Antje again, weeping. I buried the Tommy again, weeping. I prayed for them both, and that I would never have to live through another day or another hour like this one, never, ever, ever again.

We had to detour several times on the way back. We saw another Tiger tank, enormous, intimidating and terrifying, directly in front of us. A British soldier's severed legs protruded under the massive track to the left. Did the tank driver see us or care? He was stalled in the middle of the street. I saw an anti-tank gun in the bushes nearby, its crew dead, with three mangled bodies lying on the ground close together. If nobody stopped it, that Tiger would destroy the street and every remaining house. Behind me two Tommies ran out from bushes across the street, hurling themselves the last few paces to the gun. The Tiger fired at them. They ignored the danger and immediately began to line up their gun sights. One hunched down behind the gun, the other helped him operate it. The noise of explosion was shocking. I shuddered. So did Jan. For a moment it was all flame, and then cloud. Jeez. Incredibly, the Tommies had hit the Tiger. The big tank was in flames, its ammunition exploding. The noise was indescribable. We watched the Germans bale out and run low alongside the cover of a hedge. Dad should have been there, he should have seen this. Machine-gun fire cut down the tank crew as they ran for cover. The two Tommies turned to each other, touched hands. They were unbelievable. Let no one ever dare tell me about courage, I can tell you all about it, I've seen it close up.

Somehow we made it back to the house. As soon as she saw me, Mam covered her face with her hands. She knew. A greying, bearded man alongside her put his arm round her shoulders. I wanted her to lower her hands from her face but she wouldn't. I wished I had water to give her, or food, but I didn't. Gerrit's eyes went moist when he heard. Nana blessed herself twice and looked at me gently.

"God lent us Antje. Now He has called her home. Thank you God for your angel."

We all loved Antje. She and I had had a special bond. I was her big brother, her protector and her faith in me was total. In return she had given me of herself, of her amazing intellect, of her capacity to reason and think faster than anyone I've ever known. She had asked questions beyond her years. One night, perhaps it was at the time of the heavy bombings in The Ruhr, we were both in bed, the light off, with bomber squadrons flying over Oosterbeek. She had whispered a question to me. "When the Allies bomb Germany, what do you feel when some bombs fall on people's houses and kill German children? Does this have to happen so that we can be free?" I remembered answering evasively that I hadn't given the matter much thought. She went silent and I assumed she had gone to sleep. "It's a hard choice, isn't it," she'd finally said. "What is?" I asked. "Whether Hitler and those around him are so wicked, that killing innocent children to get rid of him is justified." Only my dear dead sister Antje could have posed such a question.

I was still in the cellar with the thirsty, the bandaged and the dead. I felt I was queuing for my own Day of Judgement. I was in the Valley of Jehoshavat. I wanted to die and join Antje in heaven. I was sure I wouldn't sleep that night if I lived on. I was right, I didn't, I nodded, I drifted off, I jerked wide-awake again. Night merged into day, the thirst was no more bearable. Some wanted to walk out and end it quickly, better to go out in a spray of bullets than this endless pain and hurt and. One man, desperate and weary, went out to the street, saying he couldn't bear to listen to his children crying for water any longer. He died fifty meters from the house, his body twitching as bullets ripped into it. The bread he was carrying lay under his left arm, the neck of a broken bottle in his right hand. His children were still crying.

It was Tuesday morning and everything was silent. There was neither birdsong nor any bombardment. There was no noise from machine-guns.

"There hasn't been a shell or machine-gun fired for hours," I heard a man say.

"I wondered what was different. It's the silence."

"For several hours?"

"Yes."

"It looks like the fighting is over. I'm still alive."

"Thank you God."

The Battle for Arnhem was over. The enemy had held Arnhem and Oosterbeek. They had won the battle, they still controlled the bridge over the Rhine, and now were everywhere, shouting orders. The Allies had lost the battle, while we Dutch had lost too- our town and our city, we had lost citizens and loved ones. But the immediate threat of death and burial alive was over. We would live if we got water. Let it be soon.

"At least we're alive. Things might get better," someone said.

How many times before had that been said? But this was Holland in the fall of 1944. We were the same people who had cheered and welcomed in the British airborne troops as our liberators. The Nazis hadn't liked that at all and there would be a price to pay for this display of ingratitude and partisanship after four years and four months of Nazi occupation. We shouldn't have forgotten who were dealing with.

It was reprisal time for Arnhem and Oosterbeek. By the Nazis.

Chapter Nineteen

"Raus, raus, raus," German troops shouted.

After what we had endured, their shouting didn't fully register with us, but we were certain the battle was over. We were now on the street, many of us in bare feet, heads and limbs covered in dark red bandages stained with congealed blood.

There was water to drink and an end to dehydration. After the first three or four days, going without food is easy. But not having any water is real pain. Mam's eyes were bloodshot as I handed her a saucepan of cold water. She blinked as she gulped. She hadn't spoken a word since Antje died.

We watched in silence as British medics and injured were led away as prisoners of war. All the wounded, soldiers and civilians were tended under frightful conditions. Many of the injured were in a dreadful state, some were without limbs, others blinded and many deranged. The worst were men whose limbs had been blown off, with raw, infected stumps and jagged pieces of bone exposed. During the teeming rain of that night, many of their comrades had escaped across the Rhine to the south. The injured and the medics had provided cover for their escape by staying behind and made as much noise and mayhem as they could. In time we would learn that just over two thousand from the ten thousand of the airborne invasion sent into Arnhem had been able to escape, the others were taken prisoner, injured or killed. For those captured, the war was over. They were rounded up for dispatch to a German prisoner-of-war camp.

Being a prisoner-of-war in Hitler's Germany was never going to be picnic, not for one moment but the captured soldiers were the lucky ones. For us the order of 'raus' was more than an order to leave our cellars and places of shelter during the bombardment. Over the morning our orders became more explicit, it was raus, raus, raus, out, out, out. We had to get out of our homes, our village and our city. Oosterbeek was to be vacated.

The expulsion order had been posted days earlier in Arnhem, when the Nazis retook the bridge and regained their iron grip of the city. The notices said inhabitants had a short time to collect whatever they could carry with them. Within thirty-six hours, Arnhem had become a ghost town with not a citizen left, except for the battle-wounded at St. Elizabeth Hospital, and medical staff. Within weeks, the Nazis were to clear the hospital of patients and staff, and lock the doors, despite the fact that the need for medical services had never been greater. It was another low for the New Order.

"Only rats and Nazi looters left now. They should get on well together," someone said.

Many of those expelled from Arnhem arrived in Oosterbeek, with handcarts and prams, on their way west. We joined the tide of misery without shelter, food or hope.

"Collect only what you can carry and move out."

The houses and cellars were now empty. An aid group distributed water and bread. The queue was endless. Jan, Gerrit and I returned to our house to see what remained, Tante Catherine told me what things I should try to get for Mam who made no effort to come with us.

"I'm glad our Mam can't see this," said Gerrit.

"It could be worse. Look at the others."

The house was still standing, but there was a large hole in the front of the roof. None of the windows were intact. The broken water pipes were strewn across the front door. Everywhere was rubble and dust. We collected what we needed, clothing and blankets mostly and brought it with us with no idea where we were going to or how long we would be gone for.

"We could be away for weeks."

"How can we carry everything we need in a few suitcases?" Gerrit asked.

"We have Mr. Heemskerk's handcart in the back."

Mr. Heemskerk? How was he? Had he survived? I decided to find out and headed towards his house.

"Verboten. Verboten," a beefy, truculent Nazi sentry shouted at me.

Why couldn't he say it without shouting? There were Germans everywhere now. I turned back. We went only to where the Nazis allowed us and any refusal to obey an order meant an instant bullet.

Gerrit and Jan were arguing loudly when I returned. The row was about what we should carry or leave behind. Gerrit wanted to bring cooking pots and a kettle, while Jan wanted clothing. I became the referee.

"We bring one cooking pot and the kettle. We've got to have plenty of clothing." The two backed down.

We piled too much on to the handcart. We packed as much clothing and footwear as we could, but we couldn't stay for very long. There was no food in the house except one bottle of meat sauce and some ripening onions and lettuces from the back garden.

"We'll need food coupons. The Germans allow one helping of soup and bread only to those with coupons." Gerrit said. He was still thinking clearly at least when it came to his stomach.

We took one last look. The Van Gaals' house and others were gone. Koeman's house and the de Groots' were still standing, but there was no one around. We turned the handcart towards to the Weverstraat from where we were directed to the Utrechts Road. Mam was amazed we were able to pile the handcart so high. The wheels of other handcarts were falling off or buckling under excess loads. Fortunately for us, Mr. Heemskerk's handcart was robust with four sturdy wheels.

"Did you bring my sewing machine?" asked my mother.

"It's too bulky."

"I have to have my Singer. We could be gone for weeks."

I was about to argue against bringing it when I saw Mam's eyes. So I made the return journey to collect the Singer, and saw that the damage was mainly to one corner and the roof. There was nothing to stop the rain from getting in.

Very soon after starting with the handcart, we hit trouble. Nana was in distress.

"It's your mother, Nelis. Take a look at her leg."

"What is it?"

"See for yourself."

I looked, and my stomach lurched. The toes on Mam's right foot were like someone had taken a blowtorch to them. They were red, raw and ghastly. Puss was showing on her three middle toes, and her lower legs were badly swollen. There was no way she could walk. That had to be why she hadn't gone back to the house with us.

"It's the stress from the bombardment," Nana explained.

Jan tossed off bedclothes and other garments from the load. Incredibly, a woman produced a half tube of ointment and gave it to Mam. When we tried to thank her she was already helping others. We loaded Mam in to the top of the laden handcart while Jan and I strapped the cast-off baggage onto the handlebars and carrier of the bicycle, the one I had helped myself to from a Green policeman the day before the landings. We wore our topcoats rather than carry them, thinking we might need them. We were ready to move off.

"You okay, Mam?"

"I'm fine. Where are Tante Catherine and Oom Paul?" she asked.

They appeared, Tante Catherine happy that she had managed to procure milk for Cora. Oom Paul was a sight, his beard was gingery, his appearance desperate. Dried blood had settled on his head bandage, He walked like an old man. He let Tante Catherine, seven months pregnant, carry Cora. He said nothing. He just looked into space, an unsettling smile on his face.

"What's wrong with him?" Gerrit asked.

"Shut up, Gerrit."

I inspected the wheels under the handcart and prayed they would hold the added weight of Mam and her Singer. I pushed the handcart at first and then Jan helped. Tante Catherine walked behind us, holding baby Cora. Oom Paul walked alongside. Gerrit and Nana walked ahead. He was crying. I shouldn't have shouted at him.

We walked up Weverstraat, silently witnessing the detritus and the scars of the battle. We saw mounds of rubble, burnt out tanks and jeeps, flattened houses and more rubble. Landmark trees were damaged or gone, fallen branches now part of the deep carpet of rubble that lay beneath our feet. The chimney of a once large house stood alone, while the walls formed yet another shapeless mound of debris at its base. Was this really Oosterbeek, the neat and once beautiful suburb of Arnhem?

Others joined the exodus. From the corner of my eye, I saw every shop around Huizen's Ladies Wear flattened. Nana Nellie was now homeless with all of her personal things, the things from her marriage and family buried beneath a pile of rubble. I hoped she wouldn't look left. She looked, she saw, she walked on.

We arrived on Utrecht Road, where days earlier we had waved and cheered and cried tears of joy as the airborne troops arrived among us. Now we were part of a parade of the dispirited and dispossessed moving west by Nazi orders, our few surviving worldly goods piled on handcarts and perambulators. I was shocked when I saw the damage to St. Bernulphus, its tall front tower blown off, and rubble piled high. The battle here must have been fierce. It would be a long time before the church bells would ring again. For me, that church was special because it was where Antje had received her First Communion over four years before, the day Mr. Brouwers played *Wilhelmus* on the organ, the day our world caved in. I saw a man in a cassock, with another, surveying the damage. I saw only their backs. It looked like Father Bruggeman. I wasn't sure.

Our circumstances were desperate. We had no home, no food and no money. Dad was on the Gestapo's wanted list. I prayed hard that he was alive and far away from Oosterbeek. Antje was buried without a coffin in an unmarked grave. I had to concentrate on the living, on the here and now. Oom Paul had lost his grip. The laughing carefree man of other days was now a physical wreck. I was unable to feel sorry for him, I saw him in one light only that we had to care for him. We carried on.

We saw the British soldiers, the ones who had stayed behind to ensure their colleagues crossed the Rhine. We saw their injured, their crippled and their dying. Many of them had gone mad. They jerked and twitched and laughed hideous laughs as the bravest of the brave were led away by heavily armed Germans. Strangely, the Germans were not gloating, rather they were businesslike and proper and showed the defeated men respect. Respect from Hitler's fanatical SS soldiers is respect earned the hard way. The British had fought as few ever had to fight and had held out for over eight days without relief. An unbreakable bond had formed between us. They were our heroes, real men who had put their lives on the line for us and had shared our darkest hours. We were proud then to call them friends. But they couldn't help us now, nor we them. It was very hard.

I felt bitter about the generals who had let them down. Their intelligence people must have rejected the information so many of us had risked our lives to send. The young men who had parachuted in were thrown into a witch's cauldron of battle, despite being given a precise list of the number of Tiger Tanks and heavy guns and the locations. Had those men not known that a ferry operated across the Rhine from Driel? Had they not known they would have to fight their way over twelve kilometres to reach Arnhem? They hadn't known enough, in fact they seemed to know almost nothing. Those in charge had ignored the information supplied, and gallant men, our friends, paid the price, as did we.

"Is your mother okay?" asked Jan a second time.

"I think so."

The Hartenstein was back in German hands. There would be no more guests there for a long time. German tanks and jeeps were all over the place. Germans were also driving British jeeps that had missed the target drop-zones. Corpses were laid out in two lines, with German soldiers running to collect more. From the road it looked as if one line was of German soldiers, the other of British. Corpses were being pulled from gun pits and craters, I wondered if they would be buried in a mass grave. Perhaps they would use bomb craters, without coffins, and I had done with Antje. Silently I swore I would never eat in the Hartenstein again if they polluted its hallowed grounds with dead Nazis. We carried on.

After eight days of battle and bombardment, the silence was disturbed by the slow and muted shuffle of thousands of feet and the creaking of wheels. I had not known there were so many handcarts in the world. At first they were easy to push, but as time went on, without exception those pushing changed their posture and leaned into the carts to relieve arm and back strain. The pullers leaned forward with the same stoop. Jan and myself developed a system of changing sides with each other so that we stayed fresher than those doing the job on their own. The stream of refugees moved at a snail's pace. After hours of walking, friendly people from villages emerged from their homes with offers of help. Their intentions were the best but they had no idea of the scale of the exodus. Not all of Arnhem's evacuees of headed west, many had gone to Appeldoorn and Zwolle first, spending nights in Hoge Veluwe National Park and were now linking up with the flow. The numbers heading west continued to grow. The villagers would be swamped.

"Is your mother all right?" Jan asked again.

I looked at her and saw she was facing forward. She must have been hungry and exhausted but otherwise she looked fine.

"She's fine," I said.

"Where are Oom Paul and Tante Catherine?" Gerrit asked.

"Behind."

"They're not."

"We'll stop and wait for them," said Nana Nellie.

"It's getting dark," I said. "It's not time to stop yet."

"I'll wait," Nana Nellie said.

"They'll catch up. We're going very slowly as it is," I said.

Something was flitting through my head but I couldn't put my finger on what it was. I was too tired for words. We carried on, caught in the flow. Mam turned her head suddenly, looking anxiously at Jan and me, then immediately faced forward again. A woman came from a house and offered her a glass of water. Mam refused it. I thought it was strange that she would refuse water at such a time.

We had to find food and shelter for the night. I felt we should keep going while we still could and try to reach a larger town, someplace like Wageningen. That's it, I thought, Wageningen. That was where Armin Kessel's daughter, Marlene, lived with her husband, what was his name, yes, van Beek, Dirk van Beek. If anyone would take us in, Marlene van Beek would. She would not have been born were it not for my grandfather. Suddenly I was delighted that I had approved the burial of her father with my Grandfather. I stopped to tell the others. As I did, Mam turned and gave me a worrying look.

"Are you out of breath, son?" asked Nana.

"No. But I know a place where we can stay the night."

"Oh God, Nelis, where?"

"Wageningen. At Armin Kessel's daughter's house."

"Marlene van Beek? Nelis, you're a genius!"

"We have to stop," said Mam abruptly.

"Is something wrong?"

"My baby is coming."

"I thought something was wrong. Please God it will be okay." Jan said. It was the first time I ever heard him refer to God.

Nana pushed me aside. She took charge, and I was relieved to let her take over.

"Will she be all right?" Jan asked.

"Women have babies all the time," said Gerrit. Up to this stage I hadn't even been sure that Gerrit knew how babies were made, but suddenly he was an expert on childbirth.

Before I could say or do a thing two women of massive proportions had grabbed the handcart and propelled it to a small, old house on our right. At least Mam would not have to give birth on the roadside.

"We'll go back and look for Oom Paul and Tante Catherine," I said.

"Will your mother be all right?" Jan asked again.

Gerrit winked at me.

"You two go back and look for the others. I'll stay here," he said.

Jan and I trudged back the way we had come, against the flow of people. The flow of refugees was so unlike an ordinary movement of crowds on a street. This was a flow of the unwilling, the elderly, the lame and crippled, the shocked and weary, the injured and seriously ill, children and tearful mothers, old men and women with skinned heels and swollen feet. It was an obscenity, a vast cavalcade of the bewildered, the vulnerable and uncomprehending. Many had no idea what was happening or where they were going, when would they eat next, where they would sleep. It was a frightened and aimless crawl into the unknown.

There was no sign of Oom Paul, Tante Catherine or Baby Cora. Jan wanted to go further but I pressed that we return to my mother. We turned round.

I couldn't keep up with Jan on the way back as we dodged in and out through other refugees. He was obviously as anxious as I was to return to my mother. My father would expect me to be there. Oom Paul and Tante Catherine would have to look after themselves. Tante Catherine was one to cope in a crisis.

Dark had set in by the time we arrived back. Gerrit stood outside the door of the house, eating a sandwich. Naturally he would have stayed close to food.

"I've got some for you, too," he said, nodding towards two ladies.

Soon we were wolfing our way through solid lettuce and cheese sandwiches and drinking hot tea for the first time in almost a week. Another fresh tray of sandwiches arrived, and more tea, the two women vying with each other to react to Gerrit's gestures quickly. As Jan and I were eating, Gerrit drifted away.

"That poor boy, he told us all about it. Only one carrot each for five whole days," one of the women said. Our stunned silence confirmed it.

"A little boy of his age crawling around tanks and big guns just to get carrots to feed thirty-four of you. That boy, he is amazing," the other woman said.

"As soon as I set eyes on him I knew."

"Me too. He just has it."

Jan's mouth opened wide. My own was full so I could say nothing. But getting solid food into our starved bodies was more important. Nana came out from the house, her face giving nothing away.

"Will she be all right?" Jan asked.

"She's in good hands."

"She will be all right?"

"Say a prayer to St. Thérèse, Jan," Nana said, leaving us alone.

"Who's St. Thérèse?"

"A saint. My Nana prays to her."

"How do you pray to a saint?"

"Think of the request. Then ask the saint to ask God."

"The request?"

"You ask the saint for whatever you want."

"I want Mam to be all right," he said.

He called her Mam. His own mother was dead. My mother was now his. We looked at each other, saying nothing. Gerrit returned, still eating. Jan and I looked at each other. Suddenly and together we burst out laughing. Jan bent over, his hands to his side. I laughed until my sides hurt. Gerrit looked at us solemnly, his incomprehension only making Jan and me laugh louder. It felt good to laugh again. Of late we hadn't had much to laugh about. Now we were giddy. Gerrit drifted back to the door of the house.

We shivered in the falling darkness. A faint light shone in the house and we saw occasional figures glide by. Eventually Nana came through the front door.

"If you lie on the kitchen floor you'll be in from the cold."

"That's all right Nana but...,"

"First go to that other room to see your mother and your new sister."

A lump came to my throat. I had a sister again.

"She's very small, but she's hardy. We have to get her into a nursing home tomorrow. She's fine for tonight. So is your Mam. Be proud of your mother, boys." Nana broke off into tears.

Mam looked drawn and tired, but managed a weak smile when we entered the room. My heart was pounding as we approached her bed. Nana and two other women were there. A flood of tears hit me, Jan and Gerrit were dumbstruck.

"Antje told me it would be a girl," I said to Mam.

"Antje was right."

"Where's the baby?" asked Gerrit.

"By the cot, but you're not to disturb her," Nana said.

"Let them look, Nana," Mam urged.

"None of you is to touch the baby."

We couldn't have even if we'd wanted to. I'd have much preferred to take on a Tiger tank than those women present. I gulped when I saw how small the baby was.

"What do you think?" said Mam.

"Why is she so small?" Gerrit asked.

"I wish Dad was here," I said.

Tears came to Mam's eyes.

"He'll be surprised, that's for sure," Mam said. She smiled.

"Is your leg better?" asked Jan.

"It's better."

"It's getting better, but no walking on it until I say so," Nana said. "We'll get your mother to a nursing home tomorrow, so you boys have plenty more pushing to do."

"That's no problem," Gerrit said.

Jan and I exchanged glances and once again we laughed.

"What name do you want for your new sister?" asked Mam

"Antje," we three said as one.

"At first I thought Antje was so special that no one else should..." Nana began to cry.

"It's all right Nana. Antje it's going to be. This Antje is going to be special too." Mam cried as she spoke.

I awoke to the cry of a newborn baby. It was good to know that there was another Antje Baumann in the world. We had ourselves a full night's sleep without bombs or bullets or death, our first in over a week, even though we had had to lie on the hard-flagged floor of a small room. Nana told us that Mam and the baby both had had a good night but that we had to get both of them to a nursing home as soon as possible.

"Is something wrong?"

"Nothing's wrong. It's what we would do if we were at home," Nana said. "Your mother has come through terrible times. Her baby has come almost two months early."

For Nana, the new baby was a fresh lease of life. There were baby bottles and smelly nappies and washing, but Nana had a new purpose.

Jan and I set out for Wageningen shortly after eight. Breakfast was a cup of coffee and a slice of dry toast in the tiny kitchen of the cottage. Gerrit remained behind. We weren't the first on the move. Many, including the elderly, had slept on the roadside and were now shivering in the chill air of this late September morning.

My main concern was to find Marlene van Beek's house. She would know where to locate a nursing home. It took us several hours to reach the outskirts of Wageningen. Nana had been right, refugees on the move travel very slowly. It took us so long to get to Wageningen we knew could not get back out to where my mother and the baby were and then get them to a nursing home the same day. The best I could hope for was to meet up with Marlene van Beek and arrange something for the following day.

Others entered the town with us where we were met by groups of citizens helping those on the march. Their task was huge, the tide of misery was crawling like a flow of lava, but the number of helpers was amazing. A long line of refugees waited in line for food and assistance. From behind the reception hut, dozens of helpers brought out supplies. Others kept hot vegetable soup ready, warming it in two large pots kept on the boil in the open. The volunteer helpers were bringing organisation and order into a chaotic situation, which was an extraordinary challenge.

Jan and I pushed through the others, intent on finding what we were looking for.

"Get in line," a very stout man with a florid face ordered.

"We know where we're going."

"Get in line like everyone else. Get in the queue please."

"Let them pass, the more that move on the better. If you boys are going to Utrecht, carry on."

"We're looking for a particular family here. We want to find a nursing home."

"Get in the queue like everyone else," the stout man said. "We'll have order here."

"Why do you want a nursing home?"

"For my Mam. She's had a baby on the way."

"Where is she now?"

"Back three or four hours' walk."

The stout man was impatient with us disturbing his routine.

"If you want to stay in Wageningen you'll be dealt with when your turn comes. If you are going to Utrecht, then get out of my way."

After the ordeal we had survived, I was in no humour to tolerate the conceit of one little fat man with a bad attitude. Jan grabbed my hand and pulled me away.

"Leave him be, Nelis."

"Let us decide how long we spend looking before one of us goes back."

We walked ourselves to exhaustion over too many streets around Wageningen, before deciding that Jan should return while I continued the search.

Getting a nursing home was easy. Getting one with a bed to spare was a different matter. It took me hours to realise that I was wasting my time. I reverted to my original idea to find Marlene van Beek. When I enquired, I was guided instantly to her house.

"We've been worried sick about all of you, Cornelis," cried Marlene, when I finally arrived on her doorstep.

I filled her in on events since the airborne landings. She and her husband listened intently.

"Nobody talks about anything but Arnhem. It must have been awful."

"I'm looking for a nursing home for Mam and the new baby."

"What new baby?"

"Mam's. She was born last night."

"Bless her. Not on the roadside I hope?"

"In a house."

"Dirk, do what you can. I'm sorry, but we can't offer you accommodation. We've refugees stuffed into every room of the house."

"Is there any place in Wageningen?"

"Every house is packed solid."

"First, Cornelis, have a hot bath. You're covered in blood."

"My ear is cut but otherwise…."

"Otherwise you need a bath. Dirk will see about a nursing home."

I cannot describe the effect of a warm bath on a body totally fatigued and hungry after several days and nights of danger. That hot bath in the van Beek home was for me the ultimate luxury. I felt completely reinvigorated. Marlene van Beek knew a thing or two.

I spent a frustrating day hanging around Wageningen before I finally secured a room in a nursing home from the following day onwards. As soon as Dirk told me, I returned to immediately to my mother.

The walk back against the flow of refugees was hard. The plight of those on the road had worsened considerably. Everyone was utterly worn out. There was pain on every face. Elderly people wept openly. I felt guilty walking into such sadness. Every so often I encountered clusters of people, formed when there was a crisis, someone dying or already dead. I watched two young men dig a grave for a woman whose shoes and stockings and much of her clothing had been removed from her body before she was laid in the ground. Two women shared these items through bucketfuls of tears. A solemn, bearded man read prayers from a bible over a crudely dug roadside grave. This was yet another burial without a coffin. Of all the burials I had seen or participated in, only Granddad and Armin Kessel had had the dignity of a coffin.

"I'm so glad to see you both," Mam said, on my return.

She looked tired and drawn, but managed a smile. She was sitting up in a clean bed with plenty of bedclothes with the baby alongside. One of stout women was still there, attentive as ever. I could see that Jan had something to tell me, but whatever it was, it would have to wait. There was no sign of Oom Paul and Tante Catherine and Baby Cora. We could only hope and pray that they would be all right.

Once Jan and I were alone he had a surprise for me.

"From now on we stick close to Gerrit at all times," he said.

"Why?"

"Because of all the things he can do."

"What do you mean?"

"He's amazing, Nelis. You'll have to see him in action"

It was late afternoon the following day that we reloaded Mam on to the handcart, this time with the new baby. After more than a half-day's walking, we moved both of them into the nursing home in Wageningen. Seeing order and cleanliness again greatly lifted her spirits. The fact that Antje was born on the way from Oosterbeek caused the matron and nurses to gather around, and I was in no doubt but that my mother and baby sister were in the best of hands.

"I will do my best for your mother and your baby sister" said a young nurse with an open smile. "Before God, that is my promise to you."

Mam was at ease and recovering some of her sparkle. She had only one concern.

"I'm very concerned about Oom Paul and the others."

"I don't know what I can do, Mam. I'll try to find them."

"Talk to Mr. van Beek or Marlene. They may know something."

Dirk van Beek was heavily involved in refugee aid work, mainly in organising and sourcing food, while his wife was involved in making soup in a tent specially set up for the purpose. They could not get accommodation for us in Wageningen that day, so Jan, Gerrit and I slept on the ground in the soup tent with many others, while Nana managed to persuade the nursing home to allow her to sleep temporarily in a makeshift bed alongside Mam and the baby. We knew we'd be on the march soon again.

The van Beeks got us clothes. When Nana appeared in a white blouse and black skirt, I was shocked to see how thin she was. I knew events in Arnhem and Oosterbeek had hit her hard. Now she had Oom Paul and Tante Catherine and Cora to worry about as well.

On our first Sunday in Wageningen the heavens opened and the rain poured down. There was mud and water everywhere. The wet soaked through worn out shoes and threadbare socks. Meanwhile, refugees kept coming but now they were different. Those now arriving into Wageningen were the very old and the least capable who had been on the road for five days, some for longer. They were drenched and shivering. The aid workers did their best, but they too were exhausted. It was an utterly miserable day.

"You'd want a heart of stone up there," said Dirk van Beek, "I'm so weary I could lie down and never wake up. How those others must feel."

"I never want to live through another day like it, those old people crying, that old couple with the little blonde girl clinging on to them. She must have been separated from her parents. It's all so sad," said Marlene van Beek.

I saw Jan's jaw tense up. He and I were both thinking the same thing.

"Where do they hold children that are separated?"

"At the school near here," said Marlene.

Jan, Gerrit and I were soon after running to keep up with a young man in oilskins to a local school. There was no let up in the rain. "We have ten children here, and some adults, all are in terrible shape," the young man said.

Local women were looking after the smallest of the children. In the faces of those infants was the all-pervading sadness of the time. Those sitting at tables were cleaned up and neat. The others were waiting for attention, their hair dusty and untidy, their clothes filthy, their sad eyes looking around in silent pleading. The only noises were of the women moving about.

"The adults are in another classroom," said the young man who had led us to the school. Just as we were turning to go, my right leg was grabbed from behind. I turned to see what was happening. A little boy had grabbed me tightly. He didn't want to let go.

"Do you know this boy?" asked one of the women.

"No, Mevrouw." I replied.

A woman prized the boy's hands loose. He never looked at me but just wanted to hold on to my leg. His podgy hands gave way to stronger arms. I heard his sobs as we moved to the other room.

"It was worth a try," said the young man.

More children were being brought into the school as we were leaving, two being carried, then two walking with adults, umbrellas pulled low to cover the children. As we were passing them, a small girl, her blond hair matted with dust and grime, grabbed my other leg. She gripped harder than the boy.

"It's Cora," Gerrit shouted, "Cora!"

It was Cora. I bent down and lifted her up, she grabbed me round the neck and buried her head into my shoulder.

"You know this child?" a woman in rimless glasses asked.

"She's my first cousin, Cora Baumann."

We knew Cora could talk, but now she would say nothing, not a word. Jan, Gerrit and I asked her where her Dad and Mam were but she wouldn't say. Cora was like her Dad, she would talk when she wanted to, not a moment sooner.

"Come to reception, see if we can find out who brought her in," said the woman. A man at reception remembered Cora's arrival.

"She came in with an old couple. Some lady from Ede came with them. She was more concerned about the old couple. They were very distressed."

"What had them distressed?"

"They were old and frail. We'll see if we have their names."

After a check through lists he found that an unnamed female child of about three had arrived with Willem and Juliana Geer, who had been escorted by Mrs. Eleanor Reyden of Ede. Now we had to find Mr. and Mrs. Geer or Mrs. Reyden.

"You'll do no such thing. Sit right there and stay with your cousin until she is warmed up at least. No one leaves her side until I say so," said one short motherly type.

She was right, we would find Tante Catherine and Oom Paul too, they had to be somewhere in Wageningen. We sat in the school for hours while the rain continued. Cora said nothing all that time.

The search for Mr. and Mrs. Geer took two days, Jan and Gerrit taking turns with me. Other refugees had already occupied the house to which the Geer couple had initially been directed. On the Tuesday we finally located them at a place with lots of goats and children. Between the goats and the children, it was the most crowded and untidy house I had ever seen but the host family was not lacking in heart.

Deeply traumatised, Mrs. Geer could only give us snatches of information between sobs. The woman of the house signalled me to desist. I turned to Mr. Geer, who was frail and old and furious at what was happening to him and his wife. I had to press him for answers, let him bark all he wanted.

"Where did you pick up the little girl, Mr. Geer?"

"I told them all that below."

"But where?"

"Like I told them, on the road."

"Was anyone with her?"

"The woman."

"What woman?"

"The woman crying? I'm certain the child was with that woman."

"Do you know why the woman was crying?"

"Know? Of course I know."

"Why was she crying?"

"Because of what happened. That's why. I told them all that below at the tent."

"What happened, Mr. Geer?"

"The fool of a man with her went chasing after two old goats tied together, he wouldn't stop when the Germans ordered him. He wouldn't listen to anybody, not even to the woman. He kept on saying that the goats were his mother's."

"What happened, Mr. Geer?"

"What happened? The Germans aimed. Then this huge German stopped the soldiers from firing. He looked Gestapo. He was the tallest man I ever saw. Two soldiers grabbed the crazy man and hauled him back to this tall fellow. Like that, like the blink of an eyelid, the tall fellow grabbed the crazy fellow's head in his huge hands and swung him over his shoulders. We heard his neck crack. The crazy fellow was dead in a second. That's why the woman was crying."

"Did the big fellow have any marks on his face?"

"From here to here," Mr. Geer said, dragging his finger from beside his left eye to his mouth. "I've never seen anyone with bigger hands."

"What happened to the woman?"

"I told them all this below. She got hit on the head with a rifle butt!"

Laurence Power

"Is she alive?"

"I don't know? People ran to help her but she was unconscious when we left. We kept moving. The child wouldn't leave our side."

I had one last question. I was sure that Oom Paul had been murdered, I also knew his murderer.

"Was the woman pregnant?"

"That didn't stop her from getting a rifle on the head."

"She was pregnant?"

"I already told them all that below."

More bad news for Mam and Nana. Jan said I should leave it until Mam was back on her feet. But Mam and Nana kept asking the same question over and over, for them not knowing was as bad as knowing the worst.

Mam had a sixth sense for bad news. When I entered the room of the nursing home her smile of happiness for Baby Antje faded immediately. She raised her right hand to her face. As with Antje's death, I didn't have to say a word.

"Tell your Nana gently, Nelis."

I envied Nana her deep religious faith. She had told me that God honoured the person on whose shoulders he placed a cross to carry. Within a week she had lost her granddaughter, her son and her home. Telling her of her latest cross was the hardest thing, and she held me tightly, holding back her own tears.

"The Lord has his reasons, Nelis," she said, "we'll pray for your uncle's soul. We will find his body and bury him as a Catholic, with a requiem Mass. We'll say a prayer that Catherine is alive and well. St. Thérèse won't let me down."

Marlene and Dirk van Beek looked on in silence. They offered to take Cora, now an orphan, into their overcrowded home until Mam was ready to leave the nursing home. Dirk's demeanour grew darker with each passing day as he was having no luck finding a place for all of us together.

"Not in Wageningen, Nelis. You'll have to go on to Utrecht or Amersfoort."

"We've no money to rent a house."

"Money is a small problem. I don't know how much you know, Nelis. I'm not sure how much I should tell you."

"Tell me, Mr. van Beek?"

"Holland is on the verge of collapse. We're in the wrong place with five million others. We're facing into winter with no food, no fuel, no supplies, nothing. Electricity generation will end within weeks. Half of the country is below sea level. Canals and waterworks have to be pumped round the clock! We'll have flooding and no fresh water. I work with the Ministry of Agriculture. On quarter rations we won't make it to Christmas. Our country is spinning out of control and we're powerless to do anything. The Nazis don't care. We're trapped."

Dirk van Beek didn't need to go on. For several days now, comments made years earlier by Mr. Heemskerk had been flashing across my mind. He had said back then that famine was a possibility. Now I watched lines of people queuing in the cold and rain for a bowl of thin vegetable soup. Long soup lines were now normal. This was not what I wanted for Mam and my baby sister when they were discharged from the nursing home. They needed a proper place to stay and enough to eat.

On that chilly Friday morning, October 6th 1944, I knew for certain that a new battle was about to begin. This time it was not a battle fought by soldiers, with tanks and rifles and artillery. This battle was to be fought by every citizen to stay alive over the months ahead. All of the privations and shortages we had grumbled about were nothing compared to what faced us now.

The hunger winter was about to begin. Grim days lay ahead for Holland.

Chapter Twenty

"Leave the handcart here, Nelis. Say nothing. Carry Cora on your back," Gerrit said.

"Okay."

We walked boldly from the side road into a farmyard, where milk cans were sitting on a low platform. The front door of the house opened. A lanky middle-aged man emerged, suspicion chiselled on his rugged face. A dog followed close behind him. Both the man and the dog stayed silent. At least he wasn't running off like other farmers we had called on. Bringing Cora along had been Gerrit's idea. She was part of our routine. A woman was unlikely to refuse a request for a bottle of milk for a child. That was the theory. But farmers' wives were proving to be harder and more ruthless than their menfolk.

"Good day, sir," said Gerrit politely. "We're from Arnhem. May I ask you for some milk for the little girl's bottle?"

By now an equally suspicious woman stood close behind the man. He turned and they looked at each other in silence. Not a bad sign at all.

"Arnhem, did you say?" the man asked.

"Yes sir. The Germans forced us out of our home when the fighting finished."

"You saw it?"

"From the moment the British arrived, we saw it all."

The man and woman exchanged uncertain glances.

"You were with the refugees?"

"We are refugees. Mam's new baby was born the first day on the road."

"Come in," said the woman.

They didn't need to ask twice. Gerrit had got in his key words, Arnhem, the British and refugees. The woman moved quickly, setting her kettle of water on her iron stove.

"Was it bad? You saw the fighting?"

Gerrit could have replied, but he was well past that now. He swung his eyes towards me, hesitated for a moment and then turned back to the man. The man and woman cast me a sympathetic look.

"The battle?" enquired the man.

"Our sister Antje died in his arms during the fighting. He buried her and then he had to bury her all over again because a shell hit the spot where he had buried her. He hasn't said a single word since then. His hearing is damaged. He carries Cora. She's our cousin, my Oom Paul's child. He was…, I don't want to talk too loudly, Gestapo…, you understand?"

He now was on a one-to-one understanding with our hosts. Over the next hour they gave us thick vegetable soup, followed by fried eggs and toasted bread. In return we gave them the fully embroidered story of Gerrit Baumann's experiences during the Battle of Arnhem. We ate as they listened. At the end of it they gave each of us a slice of cheese.

"You don't mind if I don't eat the cheese now, my Nana loves a hard cheese like this. You don't mind if I take what you've given to me back to her?"

The woman retrieved the main lump of cheese and cut another slice from it.

"You eat that piece. Take this fresh piece for your granny."

"My granny is an expert cheese-maker. She says nothing beats a firm farm cheese."

Words like that was music to the ears of a dairy farmer.

"How's your mother since the baby was born?"

"Thank you for asking, sir. The baby came before time because of the fighting. She's fine now, all things considered."

"Was there a problem?"

"The stress of the bombardment caused her feet to swell up. The swelling is coming down slowly, though she can't wear shoes. She had two spare pairs when we were expelled from Arnhem. She needs a size six for now but hopefully the swelling will come down all the way eventually."

"Size six? She needs a size six? Would she wear a six with a little wear on them?"

"She can go nowhere unless she gets bigger shoes, or the swelling comes down."

"I can give her size six. She's lucky to have a son like you looking out for her."

I wanted to scream at him to say thank you to the good woman, but I was under strict instructions. Gerrit refrained from any instant or effusive outburst of gratitude. Instead he turned to Cora, sitting on my lap.

"Cora, what do you do for Nana when she feeds you?"

On cue Cora jumped from off my lap and ran with outstretched hands into the woman's arms. She nestled her face in the woman's neck.

"Aren't you the friendly one?" the woman said. "I'd love to have a little girl like you."

She was surprised and delighted at Cora's warmth.

"Don't I get a hug?" asked the lanky man, all caution now vanished.

He was given the same treatment as his wife, and was as smitten with her outgoing show of affection.

We were into the process of leaving the farmhouse when Gerrit switched his attention from the woman to the man.

"You've been so kind to us. May I ask one last favour, sir?"

"Name it."

"Have you baby calves? Cora loves to see baby calves"

"Only two are babies, one born just last night. Come on, I'll show you."

He led us into a barn. Near it was a line of cows tied with chains round their necks, noisily eating hay from which a nice fresh smell wafted. At the end of the barn was a sectioned-off pen where two baby calves were lying on a bed of straw. One of the calves rose and moved unsteadily on its feet towards us. On cue Cora became excited.

"Look, look," she gurgled.

"That one born was last night," the farmer said.

The farmer looked more closely at the second calf. "Is that other calf all right sir?" Gerrit asked.

"Why do you ask?"

"Not too happy in himself, sir, is he?"

This was what Jan had meant earlier on about Gerrit. From knowing absolutely nothing about animals and farming a few weeks earlier, Gerrit's sharp ear had picked up on farmers' language where an animal never looked well or sick but was either happy or unhappy in itself.

"You could be right. How come you're so sharp?"

"Actually it was me that wanted to see the calves, sir. I plan to be a veterinary surgeon."

"You'll be a good one. Right now I had better look after that sick calf."

"Is it a chill?"

"It could be. I'm glad we came to look."

We left that farm with four eggs, a few kilos of potatoes, a turnip and a slice of hard cheese for Nana. We had a fine pair of size six shoes for Mam. We also had a much better knowledge of the different treatments for calves according to the degree of sickness. I had been a bit player in the performance, Gerrit the star. Gerrit had realised something important and much faster than I had. This was that the Battle of Arnhem had acquired a mythic status among the rural population. Arnhem was not just another Dutch city, it was a symbol for the ultimate kind of heroism, for epic endurance, it had become the unquenchable spirit of Holland. For Gerrit, Arnhem was food in our bellies.

I was happy to play the silent role assigned to me. It worked. Cora also had a silent role and her performances to date were flawless. There was only one drawback. Cora expected to ride on my shoulders all the time. Actresses can be so demanding. When we returned each evening I would be exhausted.

It was pitch dark when we got back to a gloomy Utrecht, where we now had accommodation for the whole family on the second floor of an old world house close to the railway station. The house was in run-down condition but no one complained. Jews had been the previous occupants and the frigid apartment had been vacant for over two years. Nana claimed credit for finding it through what she insisted was a casual encounter with a man she met in Wageningen. Privately Mam told me the encounter had not been casual. Mr. van Beek had arranged for the man to meet up with Nana. He was a co-ordinator between the Dutch Reformed Church and other church groups, including Roman Catholics for people with special needs. As evacuees with children, we had been considered suitable, being homeless and without income. The man had said rent was not to be discussed until the last Hun was out of Holland. Ironically, the consequences of the defeat at Arnhem achieved what had not been possible for centuries; it made different church groups put survival and the common good ahead of their historic differences.

"That's the fifth pair of shoes you've brought back since we arrived, Gerrit. What am I to do with all these big shoes?" Mam asked.

"Exchange them for food or bedding."

"He's right, Mam. Exchange them for something you really need."

We had two small bedrooms, and a living room with a tiny kitchen, but that didn't matter because there was so little to cook. Electricity blackouts grew longer with each passing week. By mid-November we had neither gas nor electricity. The apartment was icy cold, even during the daytime. My mother stayed indoors, mostly to look after the baby and to be in from the incessant rain. Coaxing heat from an iron stove was hard work, there was so little to burn in it. I watched her grow sadder by the day and her growing state of apathy worried me.

In that awful winter, it seemed as if the elements were in a conspiracy against the Dutch people to add to the feeling of despair and hopelessness. Most days Gerrit, Cora and I left the apartment to go on trips to farms, scrounging for food. Jan wanted to come too, but Gerrit had no place for gestures of comradeship.

"It's either you or Jan, not two of you," he said firmly.

Jan and Nana Nellie worked Utrecht every day. They burned more calories walking the streets than they were able to collect in food. Some days they failed to get a single morsel, other than soup in the public kitchens. What they did collect on the streets was information, little of it good, most of it truly shocking. During my daily trips to the countryside, I was largely unaware of much of what was going on in North Holland. It was Jan and Nana kept us informed on happenings in towns and cities. Broadcasts from *Radio Orange* from the liberated southern provinces were picked up by those with radios. The information in these broadcasts was discussed on soup lines. The main thrust was not news to us. Nazis were still Nazis.

Arnhem and Oosterbeek had not been the only places singled out for reprisals. When the landings began, the exiled Dutch government requested a national rail strike, which was obeyed in most areas. When the battle ended, the strike continued, and the Nazis used it to crush the Resistance. No rail transport meant that there was no movement of goods. No food went westwards to supply large cities there. Warehouses were emptying and stocks were running out. Not one highly-placed German was seen to make a humanitarian move to avert the looming catastrophe.

The news from Amsterdam and Rotterdam was more than disturbing. There the Nazis began the systematic destruction of our major ports, the lifeline of our nation. Day after day, the people of these cities watched, as kilometre after kilometre of the great harbours was blown apart. Port workers saw dynamited cranes toppling into the sea and were forced at gunpoint to participate in the scorched-earth policy. Dock installations and warehouses were dynamited. The once mighty ports would be needed when hostilities ended and trade could flow again. There was no indication of Nazi concern for the fate of millions of their 'blood brothers' now poised on the edge of starvation. Their actions in blowing the ports set in motion an irreversible process that propelled our country to grievous starvation.

Nazi terror intensified. Near Putten, a botched ambush by a small group of Resistance fighters on a group of Germans led to frightful reprisals. As well as the execution of several people, all the able-bodied men from the town were arrested and sent to Germany, hundreds of new slaves to be brutalised and abused in a bizarre effort to prolong the war. Civilians were executed and eighty-eight houses were torched. As in Arnhem and Oosterbeek, they forced the remaining citizens onto the road and into the ever-swelling ranks of refugees. This had taken place on the same miserable Sunday that Cora arrived in Wageningen with Mr. and Mrs. Geer.

The razzias were stepped up. Tens of thousands of fresh slaves were needed to work in the ruined cities and battered defences of Germany. Boys and men as young as seventeen either stayed indoors or dived deeper, when possible. It was a repeat of what had been done to the Jews of Holland in 1942 and 1943, only then we didn't know the final fate of the Jews. It would take time to realize that there was no bestiality beyond the capacity of the Nazis.

The Rotterdam razzia of early November was more intense and bloodier than everything the Nazis had done before. The spectre of slavery that had been hanging over Holland already now circled ominously, before finally swooping in on the port city in its most chilling form. Before it ended 50,000 citizens, all male, were taken from their homes and driven to the soccer stadium. After twenty-four hours of waiting in the cold November weather, the special trains, rail strike notwithstanding, were loaded up with their human cargo and shipped to Germany without food or blankets as unpaid labour to fulfil Speer's production quotas. Rotterdam, its mighty port already demolished, was now without most of its working population. Thousand of families that needed breadwinners now more than ever, were suddenly without any source of income. Overnight and without warning thousands of Rotterdammers became destitute.

Conversations grew fewer and more solemn, stony silences longer. Only two topics came up now, the latest German atrocity or razzia, and food, always food. Slowly, through low and ever-darkening clouds, an awful truth was dawning. It was that all the rumours of food stocks being dangerously low were now a fact. No fact is more frightening for the human mind to come to terms with than famine. When you contemplate the probability of death from imminent starvation, you do not have the luxury of confining your thoughts to your own death, because those close to you must also figure in the macabre equation. Who dies first? Do I bury more members of my own family? Will my own body be left on the street for the dogs to eat? Is there anything I can do? Is there anything anyone can do?

Millions thought there was. Up to now only small numbers had been scouring the countryside in the scramble for food. Suddenly tens and hundreds of thousands of people left their towns and cities and descended on the farms like a plague of locusts. The hunger-trippers burst like a dam on Dutch farmers as the dreary daylight hours of winter grew shorter and the situation more desperate. Gerrit, Cora and I had competition, and it wasn't a question of numbers alone. Many of those who trooped out from urban areas brought money and goods to pay for what they wanted. As child refugees from Oosterbeek, we had no money and no bargaining position.

Hunger moved in and stayed. Our battle to stay alive had entered a critical phase.

"Forget it," I said.
"We've nothing to lose, Nelis."
"You've said the same thing all morning. We're soaking wet. My right shoe is in tatters. Cora is utterly exhausted. It'll take us fifteen minutes to reach the house. They'll throw us out."

"We can't go home again empty-handed."

"Let Cora decide," I said. "Cora, do we go all the way to that farmhouse up there in the fields in this rain or do we head back to the others?"

Cora looked at each of us, then she pointed at the house. Hunger had won.

She rode in the handcart that I pulled with a piece of rope and Gerrit pushed from behind for balance on the rutted road. On our journey we encountered a woman with three children. One of them, a girl of about twelve, was crying as she walked past in her bare feet. The woman looked in our direction and shook her head. Her trip had been a waste. Then we met a middle-aged couple, very citified and out-of-place in the soggy December countryside.

"She's worse than he is," said the man.

It made no difference. We were close to the house. As we made the final turn for the farmhouse, we met an old couple coming out. Both were shabbily dressed, the woman trying to console the man, who swept past us in tears.

"One by one," she said as they passed us.

This was the worst sign of all. 'One by one' was an expression we hunger-trippers had coined for farmers so greedy that they sold items on a one-by-one basis only. It was never a kilo of carrots or potatoes, it was carrot by carrot, potato by potato. We had nothing to barter, every pocket was empty. My socks were soaking, my right shoe had fallen apart and my bones ached. I wanted to avoid the humiliation of being sent away once again. I wanted it to be over with and on our way. If Gerrit's spirits were as low as mine on that dark December day, it never showed.

A gaunt middle-aged man with a long narrow face stood outside the farmhouse door. His big lipped, weather-beaten face hadn't threatened a smile in years. He wore a knitted beret and an ancient blue boiler suit. Suddenly a woman emerged from the house. She gave the man a hard look, as if to ask why he hadn't run us off already.

She had a hard wide face, her features were more weather-beaten than the man's. She wore a wraparound apron that went below her knees. Expect no favours from that unsmiling face, I thought.

"Do you have a small amount of dry hay or straw, sir?" asked Gerrit.

The question threw the farmer. He switched his gaze from Gerrit to the woman beside him. She returned his look of amazement. There was silence.

"It's for the child. We can't find a dry place to let her have a lie-down in this weather."

As he spoke Gerrit shifted his gaze to the woman, his eyes beseeching. The couple looked at each other, neither wanting to be the one to refuse. There was a long silence.

The man blinked first. "Hay?"

"Or straw, sir, as long as its dry."

"In the barn." The man pointed.

So far, so good, Gerrit, that's the toe inside the door. The farmer led the way, followed by the woman. I read her expression. It was as if she didn't trust the man to keep his distance from this filth oozing from the towns and cities. I laid Cora on the low part of a bench of bone-dry, fresh-smelling hay, and in minutes she was cuddled up in the deep sleep of the innocent. Gerrit walked close to her and lay alongside her, then he too was asleep. I assumed he was, though with Gerrit you couldn't be sure.

The light was fading fast, though it was just two o'clock in the afternoon. In the dimly lit barn the couple watched us closely. I sat and removed my tattered shoes, then my socks and squeezed them out. I dried my feet with hay. The woman left. After a while the farmer went to a beet-pulping machine and began to throw beets into the hopper.

"Can I help, sir?"

"You throw, I'll pulp."

I threw beets into the hopper while he turned a handle, cutting the beets into long narrow slices for his animals. By now, townspeople knew the value of beet as an energy source. However, few knew the difference between beet for sugar and beet for cattle. Beet for cattle made everyone feel nauseous. Soon a pile of pulped slices built up under the machine. When the pile reached the discharge point the farmer fetched a fork and filled a tub.

"We're from Arnhem."

Silence. He continued to pulp while I fed the machine.

"The Germans made us leave our home in Oosterbeek."

More silence. Maybe he was hard of hearing.

"Have you calves, sir?"

"Calves? One maybe, but he's on the way out."

"I'll get my brother to take a look. He's gifted with animals."

"It's too late. This one's got the death rattle."

The farmer was talking. Progress, I thought. He was still dour and unsmiling, but at least he had spoken to me. Gerrit and Cora were still fast asleep.

The woman returned as Cora was waking up. She watched Cora stretch, and I thought I saw a faint show of womanly interest and sympathy, perhaps the tiniest crack in that hard exterior. Gerrit woke up soon after.

"Thank you sir, thank you, Madam. That was so kind of you."

They showed no reaction.

"Gerrit, take a look at a dying calf," I said.

The calf was stretched out on damp straw, its legs rigid. A reddish dribble oozed its mouth. The animal was close to death. Gerrit climbed over the gate. The couple watched but said nothing. Gerrit searched for a pulse and then looked up at the farmer.

"Badly dehydrated. Have you any brandy?"

"No."

"Rum?"

"Yes."

"Get me brewed tea and rum and dry straw, to warm him. Can you get a hot-water bottle, Mevrouw?"

We were moving into phase two, Gerrit taking control.

Laurence Power

You're on a loser here brother, I thought. This calf is as good as dead and you know it.

The woman returned with a hot-water bottle. Gerrit put it close to the calf's body, then wrapped it in dry straw, and stayed in the pen. He looked to be in charge. In the dim light I watched the farmer trying to fathom whether this boy could work miracles or was playing games. He wasn't the only one mystified as the woman was looking at Gerrit suspiciously when she returned with brewed tea and rum.

"The correct dose is everything," Gerrit said, adding rum to tea, and shaking the mixture.

"You give it to him, sir," he suggested to the farmer.

The farmer dosed the calf. For him the calf was already dead, otherwise why bother with dry straw under it. All he had to lose was the rum and tea.

"We wait an hour, maybe less," said Gerrit. "If he survives, feed him little and often. Make sure the milk is warm and diluted. After that, it's all in God's hands."

Leaving things in God's hands was a touch Gerrit had developed because it shifted any possible for blame to a supreme being in which country people had an unshakeable belief. I said a silent prayer to God to make the calf well, if only for an hour.

The potion worked faster than we could have imagined. The calf moaned feebly. Cora giggled. I saw a slight change in the woman's face. It wasn't a smile, more a faint recognition that Cora's giggling was justified.

"We'll give it a little more time, and some more milk," said Gerrit.

His use of the 'we' was to reassure the farmer that he wasn't alone, that help was at hand with no strings attached. The calf moved his head a little, a distinct, if feeble, sign of life.

"We mustn't send the milk down the wrong way."

Soon the calf was drinking the warmed milk.

"Getting fluids in is important," instructed Gerrit.

"How do you know about calves?"

"My Nana was the best vet in Arnhem until the Germans forced us out."

"Your grandmother is a vet?"

Gerrit's performance was so good that Cora's big serious eyes sought mine. Gerrit looked at me. It was time for the kill.

"Could I ask you for milk for the little girl's bottle, madam?" he asked. He casually spread a fistful of straw under the calf's head as he spoke.

"Five guilders," she said, cutting the man off.

"We've no money since the Germans took our home."

"Five guilders."

"We don't have five guilders."

"Come back when you have."

"This child hasn't eaten since yesterday. Just one glass of milk please," I pleaded.

"Five guilders."

Cora knew there was a crisis. She stood in front of the woman and looked up at her, but there was only hardness in that bony face. Cora shifted her gaze to the man, as did I. They couldn't refuse us. Then I remembered the elderly woman trying to comfort the old man as we were nearing these people's home. They couldn't refuse! Yes, they could. They had.

Gerrit had developed a talent beyond his years, and learned to play situations with matchless timing. He was a one-trick lad but what a trick. Now everything had changed. Here was one couple, one more in the growing number of farmers who were ready to say no without blinking. A glazed look crossed his face as he put his arm round Cora and buried his head in her shoulder. He emitted a high, lonesome sound. He had filled our bellies so many times against all odds. Now he was sobbing, his body shaking like that of the old man we had met on the way in.

I lifted Cora and turned to leave. Gerrit followed us out of the farmyard in silence, back to the handcart and the muddy road, back to the miserable homeward trudge in darkness and drizzle and mud, to a blacked-out and silent Utrecht. My right shoe was shredded. Shoes were useless in the countryside, especially in this harsh winter weather. You would never see a farmer wearing shoes, they wore either wooden klompen or heavy studded boots. By the time we reached the road into Utrecht the shoe had disintegrated totally and I was barefoot. We weren't the only ones walking in bare feet and without food. Silently we linked up with others on the way back, bands of hunger-trippers, the handcart people, the footsloggers, the beet-eaters, the ooze and scavengers from the city.

There was a delay as we were entering Utrecht.

"It's the Landwacht," said an angry man walking alongside us.

"Don't' lose your temper with that scum, let me do all the talking," said his wife.

The Landwacht was the Nazi Home Guard, as thuggish and as widely feared as the Green Police.

"We've nothing," I said.

"We decide that," said a voice in the darkness.

He flashed a torch in my face and then searched the handcart, waking Cora. She cried out in distress, before trying to settle down again.

"Open your coats."

Gerrit and I did as he ordered. Nothing. He searched our pockets. Empty.

"Lift her up."

I lifted Cora. He shone a torch on the base of the handcart.

"Next."

Beside us a bony-faced woman with a headscarf and a pronounced stoop was made to empty her collection of carrots and potatoes on to the road. She looked at the men. She was in terror. She implored them to be allowed keep them, that her children at home were hungry and starving. She went down on her knees and begged.

"Move on or I'll arrest you," another Landwacht man said.

The woman jumped in fright and moved as ordered. She followed us, her bounty from her day's scavenging gone. Her shoes squelched as she walked, otherwise the silence of Utrecht was as total as the darkness.

When we got back to the apartment Nana's face told me that something new and serious was amiss. I laid the sleeping Cora on a bed without waking her. Gerrit lay down beside her, past the point of consolation. My mother moved silently in to the bedroom as I came out to the kitchen. In the faint light of a paraffin lamp I saw a strange look on her face. She averted her gaze.

"Anything?" asked Nana.

"Nothing."

"Not even a head of cabbage?

"Nothing."

"Things can't go on, Nelis. The baby cried the whole day. Your mother is worn out."

"I know."

"Do you know why the baby is crying?"

"Babies cry."

"Hungry babies cry all the time. We're going to lose this baby. Do you understand what I'm saying to you, Nelis? Your mother wants a living baby with her if we ever meet up with your father again."

I didn't respond. I was too numb, too hungry, too worn out. I dried my wet feet with a towel.

"Where's Jan?"

"He's with that undertaker he works for. Nelis, you have to do something."

"What can I do Nana? Tell me."

"Your mother needs milk. She's lost one child. We can't lose this one."

"Can't we take her to a hospital?"

"Every hospital is full. They have electricity for a few hours only, some days none. Doctors and nurses are run off their feet. They work with candles and oil lamps. Nelis, we can't cope. We need food. We need milk."

"Don't cry. We're not going on any more hunger trips. It's a total waste of time."

"That is farmers for you. Who would have thought?"

"Can I see the baby?"

Antje was in a cot in Mam and Nana's room. I smelled vomit as soon as I entered. Nana lit a candle. The baby's breathing was bad, her entire body trembling. Nana was not exaggerating. The baby's life was on a knife edge. Her lips were swollen blue and she had a bad skin rash. I had to snap out of my weariness and think fast. What did I know about sick babies?

"Are you sure we can't get a doctor, Nana?"

"We've tried everything."

"If I take the baby to a nursing home, they can't refuse to accept her?"

"Why do you think your mother is so upset? She tried three separate nursing homes today. Not one of them would take the baby. They have no beds, no medicines."

"Was she given milk?"

"She vomits it back up again. She was premature. We're going to lose her in one of these spells. I'm scared, Nelis."

"I'll call Gerrit."

There was a faint hope that Gerrit might be able to think rationally, something that was totally beyond me in my numbed state.

"Yes. Gerrit should see his sister before she passes away."

Gerrit didn't take very kindly to being roused from sleep to have a final look at his baby sister, but he realised it was serious when I explained it to him. Nana, Mam and another woman who in the darkness I hadn't seen up till now, were sitting close to the cot. The other woman was from downstairs. When Gerrit was wide awake, Nana turned the oil lamp higher, as if she expected Gerrit to see or say something that might help.

He sat on the bed. He reached for Antje's tiny hand. He worked her little fingers round the small finger of his left hand. He put his right hand on her forehead. Mam was afraid she would wake up. Once awake the baby could cry for hours, maybe die in the process.

"Her skin," he whispered.

Nana and Mam exchanged puzzled glances. Gerrit put his hand on the baby's forehead again and then sat back, pondering. He put his ear close to her, listening to her breathing. He touched the skin on her face and forehead once more. He held her limp arm in his right hand and rubbed the skin on her arm with his thumb. He turned around and looked at us.

"Her skin," he repeated.

"What about it?"

He ignored me, and continued touching her.

"It's terrible." He was speaking to himself.

"She's got eczema," said Nana.

"On her forehead. Her arms. It's not right. It's all flaky. It's not right."

Suddenly Nana let out a shout of excitement.

"Oh Holy Jesus and Saint Thérèse."

"What is it Nana?" I asked.

I was startled at Nana's reaction.

"It's the milk. Gerrit you're a genius."

"What are you talking about, Nana?" asked Mam.

"Tell them Gerrit. Tell them. I should have known. You're one treasure of a boy."

"The milk is wrong. It's not the hunger, it's the milk."

I too was mystified. I had no idea why Nana and Gerrit were so excited.

"What are you talking about?"

"She's allergic to cow's milk and she's premature. She can't keep it down. That why her skin is like that. Gerrit, I love you," Nana cried.

The gloom lifted.

"What does this mean?" I asked.

"We need a wet nurse, or goat's milk, or both, to keep her alive," Nana said.

Laurence Power

I had no idea what a wet nurse was, but a precious life depended on finding this new entity. Antje needed a wet nurse and she needed one now.

How to find a wet nurse on a winter's night, in an occupied city under curfew with trigger-happy Nazi thugs on street patrol? We were strangers here, thrown up as the debris of war. Nana had got to know a few people through her church activities, but where did they live? She met them at church or in the queue at the public kitchen, but not at their houses. In the end I would have to go from house to house, knocking on doors in the darkness and hoping I would stumble across a wet nurse. Ringing doorbells was a waste of time as there was no power and no batteries. I had another problem, I had no shoes. Jan was not coming back tonight, not with curfew in force.

"I'll have to go barefoot."

"No, you don't," said the woman sitting in the room with Mam and Nana. It was the first time she spoke.

She pulled off her boots and handed them to me. They were too small but I had little choice, it was either tight-fitting boots or no boots.

Knock, knock.

"Who's there?"

"I'm looking for a wet nurse."

"You what?" "Jeez. Get lost kid." "Get to hell. You'll wake the kids." "Stop that racket or I'll rip you in two."

More knocking. 'Get lost, clear off, get off the street. Are you stone mad?'

I was apologised to, asked did I have any bread and did I know about the curfew, and ultimately, I was reminded I could be shot on sight.

But I kept on walking and kept on trying. I worked my way through the next two rows of houses without any luck. I crossed the second canal bridge. I carried on, ignoring the curt answers and the abuse. I had been in tough situations before. I had been in Oosterbeek during the battle. I hadn't given up then, I wouldn't give up now. Knock, knock.

"Who's there?"

"We need a wet nurse for a small baby that's dying."

"Hold on a moment," a woman's voice came from an upstairs room. I wondered if she had understood what I was looking for. I stood outside, shivering in the damp air. I heard a noise from inside the hallway, then the door opened and I saw the faint outline of a figure in the darkness.

"What's the problem?" It was the woman from the upstairs room.

I explained. My voice was hoarse and weary.

"Bring the baby here."

"Yes, Mevrouw."

I had found the needle in the haystack. The relief stretched all the way to my squashed toes. Now I had to make my way back without being pulled in or shot at by sentries or Greens. I kept my nerve and held calm as I tiptoed my way back. I made it without being stopped. My mother didn't want to let Antje out of her sight, but Nana pleaded with her that this was the only chance the baby had. Mam wanted to come with me. Nana refused to let her, it was too risky.

"Let Cornelis go on his own, Corrie."

Antje woke up and cried. My mother wrapped her for the trip, but her crying would alert every trigger-happy thug on night patrol. Machine-gun fire was not uncommon on the streets at night. The Greens and the Landwacht would shoot first, because frightened people ask no questions. Mam was worried for more than Antje. So was I.

I was stopped by a night sentry. By now Antje was crying steadily. I was an easy target and I knew several rifles were pointing at me. But Antje's crying made my story more credible. She didn't let up. "Carry on," a voice in the dark said. I walked over the second canal. Suddenly I panicked. I had no idea which house I was trying to get to. Was I in the right street? I wasn't sure. Antje was crying in my arms. Those moments in the darkness trying to get my bearings were among the loneliest I have ever experienced.

"Over here," came the woman's voice in the darkness. God bless you, woman. God bless you for every day of your life, I thought.

She took the crying baby from me. I followed her into a completely dark hallway. She led me upstairs, holding my hand to show me the way. She sat me on a couch. Almost immediately the crying stopped. I listened, and after a while heard the soft murmur of a contented baby drifting to sleep.

"The spasms have stopped."

"Will she be okay?"

"Lie back on the couch and get some sleep, son," she said. "Don't go till morning."

As I drifted off to sleep, I thought of the different people I had encountered in the previous twenty-four hours. That night I had met a woman who was the best that a human being can be; during the day I had encountered others who had abandoned their humanity. I finally slept.

Jan and I arrived back to the apartment at the same time. He was astonished when he saw that I had the sleeping Antje in my arms.

"She's not crying? How did you manage that?" he asked.

He handed me a pair of man's leather boots which were in good order.

"For you."

"Thanks."

"I got them off a dead man. They are way too big but they'll do you."

That winter footwear was crucial. Nothing crushes the spirit more rapidly than leaking, tattered footwear. The fact the boots were from a dead man meant nothing. I asked no questions. I was glad that Jan was working with an undertaker and that I was shod again.

My mother cried with delight when she saw that Antje's immediate crisis was over. The woman, her name was Mrs. Van Gelderen, had also sent her a message, I was to take my mother to see her as soon as possible. Mrs. Van Gelderen came directly to the point when I returned with Mam.

"I'll do what I can for your baby, Mrs. Baumann, but you must procure goat's milk as well. I will not deny my own baby if yours is going to die anyway. Get a steady supply of goat's milk and I promise we'll keep little Antje alive."

"Do you know any place?"

"No, Mrs. Baumann. My friends had goats but someone stole them. Everything not tied down is stolen."

Mrs. Van Gelderen had several children of her own, including Janni, a boy my own age. Her husband, who was a tailor, had been picked up in a razzia. She had no idea where he was, probably somewhere in Germany, but she had the gift of universal optimism, that her husband would return safely and that her good friends would supply her with potatoes and milk. She would survive and she saw her job as helping others. In a time of ubiquitous bad news, Mrs. Van Gelderen was a breath of fresh air. She was neither pretty nor well turned-out, but to me she was the most beautiful person in the world. She was heart and hope.

"Find goat's milk. I'll have a potato roasted for you when you return."

I could have spent all the daylight hours in the queue for the public kitchen. Motivated by the promise of a cooked potato, I began searching immediately.

"If you want goat's milk, steal a goat," Jan suggested.

Since Jan had begun with Mr. Henner in the undertaking business, he had become more focused and quite ruthless. Mr. Henner did not pay him anything but instead he brought Jan to his home each day for a hot meal with his aging wife. Mr. Henner allowed Jan to take whatever boots or clothing was available from the corpses if the relatives had not already laid claim. I joined Jan in helping Mr. Henner in his business, and as the hunger and cold took its toll, business increased to at least one burial a day, sometimes two.

There were no goats to be had, stolen or otherwise. However, against all odds we did manage to procure a supply of goat's milk, thanks to Nana Nellie. She played a card I had overlooked, the Dutch

Résistance. She persuaded underground members that her son was one of the Gestapo's most wanted men in Holland. When she revealed she was the mother of Wim Baumann, she hit the jackpot.

"You should have seen the man's face. He stood very erect and saluted me. He and your father carried out raids together. Both were hold-up men for ration cards. The Gestapo and the Greens are hunting your father. He's still at large. I pray to God that he's safely across the Rhine by now. God acts in funny ways."

"How's that, Nana?"

"He has never seen his new daughter, yet his reputation helps save her life. Goat's milk will be set aside for us at a Nursing Home."

And so the second part of the miracle we needed was delivered. Antje's subsequent improvement amazed us. Within a week the texture of her skin went back to normal, the flakes and rash disappeared, her face filled out and the incessant crying stopped. She was making progress, and smiled often. Her remarkable improvement was enough to restore Mam's spirits. She smiled too, which was welcome, because now a new crisis was about to hit us.

The elements conspired against us. Two days before Christmas the temperature dropped dramatically. This was no ordinary three or four-day cold spell but was one of the fiercest in living memory. It was as if the North Pole and Siberia had come to Holland to take up a position in Utrecht. The cold was shocking even the river froze over. Windows panes were thick with ice every morning, even in bed we shivered in our apartment, which was like a cold store all the time. I thought I would never feel warm again. We stayed in bed until it was time to go to the public kitchen. On the streets things were infinitely worse, as famished individuals queued with heads bent into a freezing wind blowing relentlessly from the northeast, from Siberia. Young and old, we were chilled to the marrow of our bones. We sought the shelter of each other's bodies from the cutting blow. Hands and feet were never warm. Most of us were too weary to try skating. Without food, we hadn't the energy for exercise of any form. The cold created new problems, as people who were too sick to queue were not entitled to anything if they could not put in an appearance. The arguments about the sick and their ration cards were endless. Hundreds collapsed from hunger, many died in the queues. Arguments faded, spirits sank even further. The body count climbed as the ground became too hard to dig for graves. Our attitudes became as hard as the frozen ground. We spread the word along the shivering line, don't notify deaths and keep the food coupons from the corpses for as long as possible.

"Corpses will never decay in this cold," said Mr. Henner.

Gerrit said we would have no problems with fruit for a Christmas cake, there was no fruit and there would be no Christmas cake. Neither would we have any problems with stuffing for a goose. There was no stuffing and there would be no goose. We had soggy potatoes moistened with a few drops of goat's milk and a leaf of raw cabbage for Christmas dinner of 1944, thanks to Jan.

The weather grew colder. Each new day was an ordeal. I came to dread leaving the shelter of the apartment to queue, but the alternative was starvation. I carried Cora and she held me round the neck in a stranglehold. She was losing weight. I could tell as her legs were becoming spindly and her body was lighter. Someone told us that our daily ration was down to below five hundred calories per day. Calorie numbers meant nothing to me, but I knew that soon I would be too weak to carry Cora and that she would be too weak to stand. She spent most of her days in bed. My mother and Nana queued at separate times so that they could wear each other's clothes. Both developed skin discoloration around the eyes. My mother looked as old as my grandmother, whose hair had turned snow white since Arnhem.

The daily body count increased. Mr. Henner grew alarmed that he would be unable to cope when burials became possible again. He looked gaunt, with bags under his eyes that got larger by the day. His cheeks became lined with blue veins and a tear flowed continuously from his left eye. He had abandoned hope of petrol or gas for his hearse, using instead an old horse-drawn vehicle with a tired old horse called Van Dijk. He fed the animal on hay stolen by Jan. Jan's motto was 'if you need it, take it, if you take it, share it'. He wasn't alone. The daily sights on the streets of Utrecht were enough to concentrate every mind on the scale of the crisis.

Stark faces painted pictures that told of thousands of small stories and of one big story. The faces of the old etched the big story more clearly, the furrowed brows that had seen so much from other times and from another century, but now proclaimed nothing they had seen before could match this hell, old people shivering to death in threadbare shoes on bleak and frozen streets, the sight of women bent over and crying after hunger trips with the bodies of their dead babies lying at the bottom of their handcarts. The faces of the old were so tired, they could not comprehend that things could come to this. They didn't have answers nor could they understand why all of this was happening in Holland. Neither could they explain where the Nazis' humanity had gone. The old could not help themselves let alone anyone else. But there was also a flicker of hope and defiance in those old, worn faces, a sense that there had to be a world after Hitler and Nazism, where every single human life had a value.

The young and middle-aged told another story. Their faces expressed knowledge of serious things, the awareness of the scale of what was happening to between four and five million people, the resigned horror that we civilians no longer figured in the plans or concerns of the Allied generals, the knowledge of what would happen to the country and the farmlands when the pumps could no longer pump water because there was not enough power from the windmills, the totality of the collapse of the economy, and of farming and businesses in the occupied area. The country was looted of its raw materials and capital, the scorched-earth policy of the Germans had destroyed the ports and docks in Amsterdam and Rotterdam, the only movement of goods was via the trains headed for Germany, with their cargo of slaves and prisoners. The Ijsselmeer and the canals were frozen over and the Nazis had commandeered all waterway vessels. The lined and grim faces showed awareness and resignation at the horror of the situation and the unthinkable consequences for everyone if the Allies didn't get to us soon. It was a battle for survival and not everyone would make it. Time was of the essence but all would have to try. It was try or die. There was nothing in-between.

The children's faces were the saddest. How could my cousin Cora comprehend that there was no bread in the house today or that my mother had no money to buy bread even if there was some in the shops, which there wasn't? How could she comprehend what had happened to her father before her eyes? Cora could play a serious game, her smiles and hugs could coax bread from an unwilling giver, but she was still a child. Every time we returned she would say nothing, she just cast those big brown eyes at us in the hope that someone of us might have something that she could put in her mouth.

We dreaded returning empty-handed. A week is an eternity in famine, and Jan, Gerrit and I shed our remaining scruples and joined the hundreds of others prepared to cheat and steal and hurt others in the battle to keep our own near and dear alive.

Chapter Twenty-One

"You scout ahead, Gerrit."

"Okay."

"Tell us how many. Then keep walking."

"Couldn't I...?"

"Do as you're told or we'll go without you. Make up your mind."

"I'll do as you say."

"Nelis, grab the tow bar of the three-wheeler. Haul it. Leave the rest to Janni and me."

"Okay."

This was Jan Till giving orders. We had moved from small-time pilfering into bigger stuff. Mistakes were fatal, looters were shot on sight. Strong nerves were crucial and there were no second chances.

Janni van Gelderen was the fourth member of our group whose common purpose was to hold up a Landwacht sentry group on the way from its canal bridge control point back to base. The Landwacht three-wheeler would be piled high after they had shaken down the day's batch of returning hunger-trippers. Janni, Jan and I made a good team. Janni was so street smart that he was a real bonus. He knew every twist and turn as well as every sidestreet and back street of Utrecht. He had the ability to get lost faster than any one I've ever known and arrive back again from the opposite direction two minutes later. He wore a peaked cap a few sizes too large for him that hid the upper part of his face. Without that cap he looked a different person. The size of his cap was important, it was in his cap that he carried his revolver.

The very desperate still made hunger trips to the frozen countryside. Most returned empty-handed, but each day brought some successes, especially now that flower bulbs had been added to the list of edible foods. Some sugar beet was still out there, though the hard January frost left most beets prone to rapid decay when thawed. Getting food from farmers was tough, but getting the day's haul past the Landwacht rabble, or one of the other Food Control Groups at stop-points into Utrecht was tougher again. Our plan was simple, hold up the Landwacht on their way back to base with their day's loot.

We needed poor visibility. This was better in case of things going wrong and having to run for it. We satisfied urselves that out food situation was so desperate that we were left without a choice. Two days before, Nana had fainted and lain prone on the ice until others helped her home. Cora had spent two days vomiting after eating yet another plate of sugar beet mush. We needed food urgently. Jan and I had had no funerals for several days, so there had been no roast potatoes from Mrs. Henner.

There was serious confusion about funerals when the thaw came. With no timber available to make coffins, the municipal authorities considered the heavy death rates as a public health issue and indicated to Mr. Henner that they would take over all of the burials. Mr. Henner had no choice. He sent us home each day with empty bellies.

The notorious reputation of the Landwacht was richly deserved. They copied the Nazis by leaving their victims' bodies lying where shot as a warning to others. The more desperate the situation, the more ruthless the Landwacht became. Their grey uniforms allowed them free rein and the Nazis encouraged their excesses. We knew what we were up against. In the end it makes no difference who it is that shoots you. If the choice is to die from hunger or be shot trying to get food, you are dead anyway and the great pain is over. Death was a form of freedom, and we would live or die by our actions. We had two revolvers, Jan carrying the second. Another pair of boots from another dead man was the price.

We discussed our plan over and over. We were anxious about this particular action, but it was nothing out of the ordinary for that time. Our main worry was what to do if the Landwacht members refused to raise their hands when ordered. Jan was in no doubt.

"Don't piss about. Don't give them time to think. If they make any move, fire."

I didn't have a gun. Janni had witnessed two incidents reprisal shootings at the beginning of December, one of two youths, the other of four adults and had been so shocked that he didn't want to fire unless the Landwacht attempted to first.

"We have to give them time to put up their hands," I said.

Jan was ruthless. "The first seconds are vital. They'll put their hands up once they know we mean business."

Gerrit and I were without weapons, so our opinions counted for less. We didn't tell my mother or Nana, there was no point. Law and order was breaking down, and trees on streets and in parks were disappearing and empty houses were being stripped of their doors and timbers from floor to roof overnight. Every one knew how things were.

In the darkness we wore floppy caps so that they would find it difficult to identify any one of us later. We hid in an alley. I was wearing a pair of rubber-soled shoes I had found when I had ventured into the open front door of a house. The shoes were too large but I could run in them and make little noise. We waited.

Janni was as cool as Jan, a welcome bonus. The city was largely in darkness, except for flickering lights showing in some apartments where wind generators had been rigged up on roofs. There was a frayed silence, with no trains, no trams, with few going to work, few bread vans, no vegetable deliveries, no children going to school, no street markets. Handcarts and three-wheelers made up most of the daytime traffic. Anything that moved at night was not legitimate.

"Four," Gerrit's voice told us in the darkness. He melted away suddenly, his job done.

"More than we expected," Jan whispered. "Let them pass. We shout 'hands up' at the same time."

I put my hands to my mouth to blow warm air on them. Jan shushed me to be quiet. We waited. In the darkness there was the noise of wheels on cobbles. They're getting closer. One was out front. He had a torch. The light was poor, but good enough to show he also had a rifle. We were in it now and it's too late to turn back. The noise of the three-wheeler grew closer. They drew level. I held my breath. There was a problem, the one with the torch was ten paces ahead of the others. We needed the three-wheeler and its contents, not prisoners. I hoped Jan and Janni were thinking the same. The one carrying the torch passed, I could see only his silhouette. The others were coming behind. Then they were level. They were on us.

"Hands up," we shouted in unison. I ran in close behind the men.

"Who the fuck?" came a rough voice from the dark. I saw two pairs of hands being raised.

Bang. Bang. Two shots. A man shouted.

"Don't shoot, don't shoot," two voices cried together. The one with the torch made a run for it, perhaps also a second one.

"Take off your jackets," Jan barked.

"Now," Janni joined in. "And shoes."

I heard the clang of rifles on the pavement.

"Don't shoot. Please. Don't shoot."

"Put the shoes on the cart."

"Go. Run."

In the darkness, which was our friend for a change, Jan sounded clinical.

"In five seconds I'll spray the street with bullets. Five, four..."

They bolted into the darkness. I grabbed the three-wheeler and turned it in the opposite direction. Soon Janni joined me in the front, pulling with Jan to the rear. We pulled as hard as we could though puffing and sweating. Soon there would be Greens everywhere, shouting with sirens blazing. Janni led us across the canal and down several alleys and a narrow lane to Mr. Henner's stable, where we had planned to store the captured loot. Jan had a key and let us in. In the darkness we transferred food and clothing from the cart. We emptied the pockets of the uniform jackets and threw them back on to the vehicle. Pulling and pushing like madmen, we headed back to the canal and pushed the three-wheeler into the murky water, then listened as the vehicle gurgled its way to the bottom, carrying with it the jackets of Landwacht uniforms. The canal was a cesspool and so filthy that it could be days, if not weeks, before the three-wheeler was discovered. We kept to the shadows as we made our respective ways home.

Mam wondered why we had risked curfew.

"You're sweating," she said.

"Stay alive, boys," said Nana.

We kept silent.

"Who fired the shots?" I asked Jan later.

"I wanted them to panic. We succeeded."

"Go to sleep," Gerrit said.

I slept, eventually, after listening intently for hours for the two-tone siren of the Greens on the streets, but there was no noise, nothing. It had been just another stick-up. In normal circumstances, robbery under arms is and should be regarded as an extreme act, but under the conditions that prevailed in Holland then, we were trying to survive from one day to the next. Watching those you love sink slowly into a painful starvation and death drives one to committing desperate acts. If there had been another way to get food each of us would have jumped at the chance.

Jan and I went to Mr. Henner's stable early the following morning, not knowing there were surprises ahead.

"Shotguns," said Jan.

"What are you talking about?"

"We took shotguns, Nelis, not rifles."

"Dump them in the canal."

"No, Nelis. We'll hide them in the roof. We'll exchange them for something."

Money had no value, but things did. Things could be exchanged for clothes or a morsel to eat, something else that could make life more bearable for a few more hours. Anyone seeking medicine for a sick child would fight to exchange something which in normal circumstances they would not consider selling for any money to meet that need. Anyone with a bag of potatoes to sell was king with a choice of offers, an Old Dutch painting in a gilt frame, perhaps, or an ornate set of dining room chairs. Barter was the new business. Everything was available except food, that which mattered most.

Our haul could have been bigger, but we got four large cabbages, turnips and beets, a sock full of onions, the matching sock full of apples. We also got a supply of tulip bulbs. We collected one packet of cigarettes and several rounds of cartridges. Janni's idea of going for the Landwacht footwear also paid off, because we had something valuable to trade. Janni arrived and grabbed both pairs of boots.

"I've customers for these. See you," he said and vanished.

I brought home one head of cabbage, along with onions and apples. Mam and Nana exchanged glances but asked no questions.

"If we can get the stove going, I'd love boiled cabbage," Nana said.

"That stove is worse than a baby. You can forget the baby for an hour but keeping this thing going is a full-time job," my mother said.

"Any cigarettes?" Gerrit asked.

"One packet," I told him.

"I'll have them," he said, reaching for them.

"You'll do no such thing," my mother said. The head of cabbage and onions had cheered her up.

"Not for myself, Mam. I can exchange them. We'll have a decent meal today."

Gerrit had a nose for things, for food, or for anything that could raise spirits. The black market operated at different street corners, according to the whereabouts of the Greens, and it made sense to go to it if you had something to trade. Respectable women in good coats peddled skinned cats as rabbits, while elderly men kept straight faces as they offered chunks of dog meat as cuts of lamb or beef. It was a place where no one told the truth and nobody expected anyone else to. If anyone was at home in such a place it was Gerrit.

He was back in an hour, with a few kilos of potatoes and a recently killed plucked hen, which looked like it had reached extreme old age.

"This will keep us in chicken soup for days if we boil it," Mam said.

"We'll need to arrange more timber," said Nana.

Her use of the word 'arrange' showed that Nana knew our game. The way to get timber was to arrange it. It was over to Jan and me.

"You got this bird and these potatoes for a packet of cigarettes?" asked Mam.

"No. For two cigarettes. I have eight left," Gerrit replied.

Gerrit knew much better than I did the price some were prepared to pay for one cigarette. He functioned best in chaos and uncertainty. He was in his element. Gerrit operated on the 'one-by-one' basis and had not allowed his bad experience with that miserly farming couple who had asked five guilders for a glass of milk to go to waste. With eight cigarettes in his pocket there was every prospect we would eat for days to come.

"What about the people downstairs? Couldn't we give them a few mashed potatoes and chicken soup?" Jan suggested.

"Yes, Jan. They need a lift so badly," Mam said.

Parting with food when everything was so scarce was hard, but to receive a surprise helping, even a small one, meant so much. The woman from downstairs, Mrs. Mulder, had loaned me her boots the night I searched for the wet nurse. She was very quiet and I assumed her silence was, like Mam's, the result of hunger and depression. If anything, her situation was worse than ours in that her husband was a semi-invalid and her twin daughters of twelve were not capable of holding up the Landwacht or anyone else for food. Jan's commandment applied, if you need it, take it, if you take it, share it.

In return the Mulders provided a supply of short wooden blocks for burning. Gerrit caught my eye. By now all the wooden blocks between the tramlines over the city had disappeared and been sold door-to-door to those who could pay. The plucked hen was old and needed a lot of boiling. The tramline blocks helped in the stove.

Mr. Henner called on Jan and me abruptly, with the message I had dreaded. I had a bad feeling of what we might see and have to do in the days ahead.

"It's back to funerals," he said wearily.

He was looking more haggard than ever and insisted on wearing a black top hat, long black smock and white gloves. He didn't need these accoutrements to enhance his undertaker's gravitas, his stark pinched face and furrowed brow evoked every graveyard image.

"We've some catching up to do. We'll have to handle several funerals at a time,"

"What about coffins?" Jan said.

"No coffins. The authorities know that. We use whatever the families come up with, a cardboard box or a bed sheet. You boys will to have to get used to a lot of bad smells."

The smells were horrific. Some corpses had been kept hidden by their families during the freeze-up to get extra use from the dead person's food cards. We collected bodies from houses, morgues, churches. Sometimes we recovered them with our noses. Without exception, the corpses were emaciated and shrunken. Death from hunger is the ultimate violence. But there are worse sights than the dead.

One day Jan and I climbed four flights of stairs of an old house just off the Nieuwegracht, with instructions from Mr. Henner to prepare the corpse of a woman for collection. When we entered the building the stench of poverty hit us. The remains were skeletal. A rigid bony hand lay across her chest as if making one final plea for food and help. In the bed beside the corpse were three children, one lying down, the others sitting. The one lying was a girl of about ten, with long black hair. Her sorrowful eyes fixed on Jan and me as we stood in horror at the end of the bed. The two sitting up were boys, perhaps six and eight years of age, their hands across their chests. One of them was almost bald. His ears stuck out and his eyes were wide open, as if he were waiting for an explanation from someone about what was going on. The neck of the other boy was so thin it seemed it could not hold his large head upright on his skinny body. Their faces were of skin and bone, it could only be a matter of time before all three would die. Jan left the room in silence. I was rooted to the ground. The children returned my awed gaze. In a moment Jan returned.

"Next door," he said quietly.

I followed him to another room. There the stench was overpowering. There were two more corpses, one of an old woman, the other a young girl of about twelve. Two live children were sitting there, no hair, no flesh, no sparkle, no hope. On a dressing table beside the bed was a picture of a brawny smiling man with his blonde wife and six children, like the steps of a stairs. I surmised this family had been left without a man after a razzia.

Jan bolted downstairs, I followed. He pounded on a door. A woman opened and peered out.

"Upstairs," Jan shouted angrily.

The woman closed the door immediately. Jan pounded louder. This time she opened the door wider. She was holding an undernourished child. The flesh on her cheeks lay flush with the contours of the bone. She too was starving.

"I know," she said, then closed the door again.

I had never seen Jan in such a rage. I pulled him away. He pounded on a door at the next level. A gaunt man wrapped in nightwear and a week's beard answered.

"Upstairs," Jan repeated.

The man shrugged his shoulders, indicating there was nothing he could do. Jan struck him on the face. The man gaped in astonishment.

"Come on, Jan," I said.

I pulled him away. We descended to the street. Jan was still seething. As we blinked in the bright light an unusual sight greeted us.

Coming in our direction were three very austere elderly men dressed entirely in black. They looked like preachers from one of the Reformed Churches. Jan walked straight to them.

"Come with me," he said. "You go back to Mr. Henner, Nelis."

The men went with Jan. They would know what to do. As it transpired they did, to Jan's satisfaction they organised aid for the children still alive. The following day we brought the two dead women and the dead girl to the cemetery and got in line with other undertakers. Rows of shrunken bodies lay on the ground, waiting for burial. Undertakers, who before had always fought and argued, now co-operated with each other to lift the bodies. Sometimes the sheet wrapping a body came loose, exposing a stiff white leg. One undertaker carried short pieces of cord to tie the sheets round the ankles. Every corpse was light, the bodies of children were like feathers. They reminded me of my dead sister Antje, buried in a slit trench in Oosterbeek. Tears rolled down my face as we laid the little remains of the blonde-haired girl on one side of her mother and the old woman on the other, three bed sheets tied at the ankles, three bodies, three generations.

Mr. Henner was crying, I wasn't sure if his tears were for the dead, or from the cold. He never said a word during the funeral or on the drive back to his house. Jan and I became concerned.

"What I'm doing is not right," he said to us when we were back at his home.

Jan and I had no idea what was coming next.

"From now on we use a three-wheeler. I'm going to take Van Dijk for slaughter. There's not much meat on those old bones of his but enough to save a few lives. We'll harness a bicycle to a three-wheeler. If we can't manage it, you two will have to pull it. I'm too old. I'll walk ahead."

"We'll do it, Mr. Henner" Jan said right away.

I also agreed. Never again did I want to witness a scene such as I had in that apartment the previous day. Mr. Henner was true to his promise. He gave up his old horse for slaughter and harnessed a bicycle to a three-wheeler, but without success. On those eerily silent walks to the cemetery he shuffled stiffly. There was little dignity in death for those who had succumbed to famine or tuberculosis. Mr. Henner, by his formal dress and stoic behaviour, accorded each of the dead a minuscule patina of value as we hauled their mortal remains through the silent streets of Utrecht to their coffinless graves. This very ordinary man became my hero. What of it if his face was lined and sad and he couldn't smile to save his life? He was a good man, the best that a person could be.

As winter gave way to spring, our teeth were chattering, our bodies shrunken from hunger and our spirits in despair from the gloom and chaos all round us. In all the millennia of man's history in Europe, the spring of 1945 was like no other. Vast armies from all the powerful nations of the world pushed towards Germany to bring an end to the destructive rule of Adolf Hitler and the armies that sustained him. At the same time, these once all-conquering armies of the Third Reich fought frantically to defend their homeland as they were bombed and pounded from both east and west.

I heard of the full scale of the horror in the years after the war. Civilians in the paths of those vast armies had to survive the chaos, for chaos it was, on a scale not previously experienced. To the east, millions of Red Army soldiers crossed the Oder with Berlin in their sights, bound for vengeance for their murdered fellow citizens. The Baltic ports and the roads of Eastern Germany were clogged with refugees fleeing the Red terror while the freezing cold still held sway over the land.

The terrified millions from the east weren't the only ones on the move. There were also concentration camp inmates, slave labourers, political prisoners and millions of others. The bizarre and predatory world of the Third Reich was yielding up its ghastly secrets, the skeletons and corpses of the non-brothers, of those who had no place in the Nazi fantasy world other than as slaves.

Nothing exemplified Nazism as much as its death throes. The base and ignoble acts of the generals and top brass of the Wehrmacht and SS persisted to the bitter end. Loyalty to their demonic leader took precedence over the lives of millions, and humanity itself. Millions died needlessly that spring. The bizarre military codes that held Hitler's Germany together until the all of the earth was scorched persisted. The generals stayed obedient to the end.

It was the spring of refugees. What began as thousands grew to hundreds of thousands, then to millions of the homeless, the dispossessed and traumatised. They were all refugees now, Germans fleeing westward ahead of the Communists, Jews trying frantically to get out of Europe and into Palestine, the hungry fleeing to wherever there might be food, the homeless to places of shelter.

The refugees moved through millions of square miles of the rubble, the rubble of big cities, of centuries-old fine buildings, the remains of towns and of lands laid to waste, the end result of a botched civilization and the havoc wreaked by just one man.

Our position in Holland was unique. We weren't concerned about what was going on in Prussia or Kurland or Poland or in any part of Germany. Events elsewhere, whether historic, shocking or squalid, were of no interest. We could only focus on what was personal and all-consuming, and that extended to what might happen to us over the next few hours. Hunger was the master to which everyone danced. We dared not ignore it, not for a moment. We stopped fearing the Greens and the Nazis, death from hunger was now the great enemy and the greatest certainty.

With no flour to make bread, no potatoes nor vegetables nor other energy foods to eat, save frost-damaged beets and tulip bulbs, fear was never far away. Few dogs and no cats were to be seen. Baker's carts and even carthorses needing armed guards to protect them. Daffodil, and hyacinth and other flower bulbs became a daily food staple. Sad and weary-faced doctors and medical staff were forced to turn away the dying against every principle of their calling. Fear acquired a smell when filth and faeces bubbled from the cesspools of sewers and canals and the stench hung constantly in the air, clinging to clothes. Gaping holes appeared on skylines because houses were reduced to rubble overnight by famished people foraging for coal or timber. There was no gas and no electricity, forcing families to burn their furniture and floorboards to make heat. Corpses were abandoned without coffins in groves and laneways and gnawed on by rats and stank to high heaven because undertakers couldn't cope. No one went to work and there was no transport and no power for machines to function. Haggard women scavenged the same piles of waste over and over, while their children with swollen bellies limped barefoot behind them on spindly legs. Everyone's nose looked extra large because there was no soft flesh surrounding it and every blemish and contour stood out on bony cheeks. Every woman, even young women, looked old and dirty and seemed never to have been young or clean. People passed each other on the street in silence, absorbed in their own personal sadness and tragedy, struggling to survive each new day. Gaunt, starving children looked at adults in silence for food or some word of hope, but there was no food and no hope, there was only fear. Grown men cried and averted their gazes from their fellow men, knowing that the battle to keep their womenfolk and children alive was being lost before their eyes. The daily existence of every person was lived through one the darkest ages of man's time on earth. Normality had broken down and there was unspeakable fear in the wake.

It was a time of silence. Either the very best or very worst of people was brought out. Some, ordinary men and ordinary women, people like Mr. Henner and Mrs. Van Gelderen, stood apart as heroes. Every day they and thousands of others ran the gauntlet and were prepared to pay the ultimate price in the service of others. Some fell apart, pitiful victims of their own timidity and fear and of the bizarre conditions of the time. Some allowed their links with their own humanity to sunder and became predators and destroyers of the weak and vulnerable, inheritors to the logic and practice of Hitler.

For the most part, the church groups were outstanding, showing Christian concern and commitment, and acting tirelessly and their efforts to help retain a modicum of calm. They asked no questions, their members were as overwhelmed as everyone else and they tried to cope in a situation where no guidelines or previous experiences existed. While there were the inevitable few who were narrow-minded, the vast majority was quite magnificent. They saved many lives and helped keep morale from crumbling when food stocks ran out. Many of the church people were active in the Resistance. While for some there was a contradiction in being a church person and a member of the Resistance, for me there never was a conflict. Survival with dignity had long since passed. Now it was survival, nothing more.

Jan, Gerrit, Janni van Gelderen and I did what we could to stay alive and to help others do the same. This included carrying out a total of five robberies. We took only from the Landwacht when unrest and lawlessness was the order of the day. Nobody was injured in any of our actions, though others attempting the same ended up as prisoners or as corpses. We shared our loot with Mrs. Mulder and other families.

By late March our biggest worry was Cora. She had developed the ugly bloating of the abdomen associated with starvation. Her legs were like matchsticks. Mam was in a state of panic and begged Gerrit and me to go on fresh hunger-trips out to the farming areas. Cora needed protein, and urgently. Despite our bad experiences, we could no longer refuse to go on hunger-trips, we knew how quickly little children of Cora's age went under.

However, these fresh hunger trips were better experiences, and this was largely due to our timing. On many farms it was the main calving season and milk supplies were increasing daily. Farmers now expressed their genuine shock at the severity of starvation in Utrecht. They showed a level of generosity that had not existed when the fist serious waves of hunger-trippers had hit them in November and December. Some were openly opportunistic because they wanted to get back into some sort of easier relationship with city people. It didn't matter. A glass of milk for Cora was the same as a gift from heaven, irrespective of who gave it. One day we got soup and roast potatoes from a generous and willing couple with several small children of their own. They too were called Baumann, and they insisted that we bring Nana, Mam and Antje with us for another meal of fried eggs and boiled potatoes. Fried eggs and boiled potatoes was a banquet. Mam and the farmer's wife discussed children's ailments and for the first time in ages I saw Mam come alive again. Her baby was alive and doing well. Cora after only a few good meals was also beginning to look healthy. It looked like we could make it after all.

Chapter Twenty-Two

The air was thick with rumours. It was just a matter of time, American troops were reported to be covering incredible distances every day, they were at the Rhine, they were all over the south of Germany, soon they would cross the Rhine and head for Berlin to meet up with the Russian troops coming from the east. Berlin was under attack. The British were said to be in Enschede. One of our own cities north of the Rhine so close to the German border and being under allied control could only mean liberation from the long nightmare of Nazism. It could only be a matter of time. The days dragged, the hunger dragged and the misery, but now there was one new element. There was hope!

We dared to dream. I dreamt of returning to Oosterbeek, of meeting with my Dad again if he was still alive, of reuniting Cora with Tante Catherine, of meeting with Mr. Heemskerk and other friends, of walking through the woods with Jan and Gerrit. Fresh rumours filled the air that Canadian troops had arrived into North Holland. Canadians? That couldn't be true. It was true, people had seen them, they had jeeps and soon they would be in Utrecht. The Canadians were there, but so were the Germans. So were the roadblocks, and the Greens. Something big was happening, but what? We wondered if we could do anything to help, anything at all.

As it turned out that there was. In the heady atmosphere that prevailed, I, along with Gerrit and Jan Till, engaged in one final act of brazen daylight deceit that put us on the road back to Oosterbeek sooner that we could have imagined. It included Gerrit displaying new levels of brass neck and Jan showing unknown depths of street smart.

"I've seen Canadians, in a jeep."

Gerrit was breathless with excitement that April morning. True to form, he was the first to see real live Canadians.

"What do they look like?" asked Mam.

"Well-fed. They looked well-fed, Mam."

Magic words. All of us wanted to see Canadian soldiers, to see for ourselves what well-fed people looked like. The sight of healthy young men in uniforms other than those of SS or Wehrmacht or Greens on our streets sent spirits soaring. If there were well-fed men who were not Germans here, then freedom and food could not be far behind. Later that day Jan and I saw four Canadians in a jeep. The driver looked a mountain of a man and a large cigar dangled from his mouth.

"Smell those cigars. The Canadians have cigarettes," said Gerrit.

He was thinking ahead. The new currency would be Canadian cigars and cigarettes, or anything we could get from our liberators. The arrival of the Canadians, though heartily welcome, was nothing like the airborne landings the previous September. We were a different people now, we had seen too much, suffered and starved and lost too much to let our emotions run riot. Our response was subdued, this time we had to be sure. We bade them welcome but asked them what had kept them. We were confused, there were still Germans and Greens around, and wherever they were was danger.

"Mr. Henner wants us," said Jan.

"Can I come too?" Gerrit asked.

"Why not?" said Jan, before I could say anything.

"Good."

Mr. Henner had a surprise for us when we met up with him, a hearse with a motor.

"Mr. Louis Jansen has given me his hearse in return for all the favours I've done for him over the last few months. You remember Mr. Jansen? You boys deserve a lot of the credit for that."

"The man whose wife we helped to bury?" said Jan.

"That's the man. He thinks the world of you boys. I'll never be able to repay you for all your work and all the help you have given me. I buried a lot of poor people. I don't expect to get paid for many of them."

"How about bringing all of us back to Oosterbeek?" asked Gerrit.

Jan and I blushed at this outrageous request to a man of honour. I wanted to hit Gerrit. When it came to asking for the impossible, he was still shameless. Mr. Henner gave us a solemn, almost emotionless, look.

"I don't know if the road to Arnhem is open, or how far we might get with roadblocks but you boys have done so much for me I'm prepared to try. If any vehicle can get through it will be a hearse. When do you want to go?"

"Now," said Gerrit.

I gulped. Jan looked at me. We both looked at Mr. Henner. I held my breath.

"I've a funeral first."

"Have you enough petrol?"

"Last night Canadian soldiers gave me a jerry can with twenty-five litres. Can you imagine twenty-five litres of petrol? It's enough for the journey and back."

"Have you a coffin, Mr Henner?" asked Jan.

"No coffins."

"We need a coffin. And a corpse."

"Why?"

"To get past all the roadblocks."

"We can take the corpse we have with us."

"To Arnhem?"

"You said Oosterbeek."

"Oosterbeek is fine," I said. "But we want my Mam and Nana to come."

"They can ride in the front if you boys ride in the back with the corpse."

Jan and I exchanged glances. I would have lain between corpses at the prospect of returning to Oosterbeek and, hopefully, meeting with my father once again.

Within half an hour we were on the road, with Mam, Nana, Cora and Baby Antje in the front with Mr. Henner. Packing was easy. After seven months of wear, tear and hunger, we had nothing to bring. Mam brushed her hair for the first time in weeks and put on lipstick. She carried Antje, now over six months old and still alive. She looked at Nana. Nana smiled back at her. We left Mr. Heemskerk's handcart behind for Janni van Gelderen who waved us a smiling farewell.

On the Doorn road out of Utrecht, disaster struck. A Canadian army truck came round a bend too fast and ploughed straight into us. Mr. Henner was driving slowly, so the impact was modest, but significant enough to damage the front of the hearse. Several Canadians were riding on the lorry, but to their credit none of them got excited or upset. We got out of the hearse to survey the damage. It didn't look good.

"Looks like this hearse won't travel any further today," said Mr. Henner, with his air of pained resignation.

"How can we help you folks?" a tall man in uniform asked him. When we looked at him blankly he switched to French, testing for a common language and Jan who had passable French was then able to converse with the soldier. There was a brief silence, long enough for Jan Till to think.

"We have a very important citizen here for burial. We have twenty kilometres to go."

"Twenty kilometres, eh?"

"It's not the distance sir. This is not just any corpse." Jan's face was deadly serious.

"Zat right?"

"Yes sir. This man was the Mayor of Arnhem. This was the man who had to accept the Nazi order for every citizen to quit the city. We have to take Mr. van den Berg back to Arnhem, to his own city, sir."

"This is the mayor? We took Arnhem over the weekend. Jeez the damage. Twenty kilometres, you say?"

"Yes, sir."

He spoke in fast English with his comrades.

"Okay, you guys, you Kelly and you Ortiz, you two look after this gentleman's hearse. Load the remains of Mr. Mayor and these folks on to the lorry. Pierre, drive carefully for a change. One corpse on our hands is enough. Move it."

Instant disaster was followed by instant recovery. We were on the way back to Oosterbeek, going home with army wheels underneath us. Mr. Henner would have a major problem with a corpse in the wrong place with the wrong name but that was something he would have to deal with. With each passing minute we were getting nearer to Oosterbeek. I saw Gerrit looking at me. Jan's faint traces of a smile said 'Nelis, follow the Mayor of Arnhem for a bit of fast thinking'.

Soon these Canadians would realise that twenty kilometres wouldn't get us to Wageningen, let alone Oosterbeek. By unspoken consent we said nothing.

Pierre's driving didn't improve but we weren't complaining. The faster he drove, the sooner we would be home. I dreaded meeting roadblocks or big groups of troops on the move. Pierre slowed for each roadblock but kept going forward. Every kilometre covered was one kilometre closer to Oosterbeek. I breathed deeply, not knowing what to expect. Would Dad be there? Would anyone know where he was? Were Mr. Heemskerk and his wife still alive? Would there be anything of our house left? My heart pounded. I kept my eyes on the floor of the lorry. I couldn't look anyone in the face. Most of all I didn't want to make eye contact with Mr. Henner. He would have to face his problem sometime soon.

We passed through Wageningen. If Pierre was counting kilometres, he gave no sign. Now we were headed for Renkum, and passed the place where Antje was born. Mam returned my look. We were getting closer. My hands were sweaty. I couldn't look up. A young Canadian offered Mr. Henner a cigarette.

"Thank you, but if you don't mind I'll put it in my pocket. These ladies haven't eaten much in a long time. The smoke could make them sick."

Others rushed to stub their lighted cigarettes.

"Whatever you like, Pops. Keep the packet."

"Thank you so much, sir."

"We go right down here," said Jan Till.

"Why?" asked another Canadian.

"The fastest way into Arnhem is via Bendorpseweg. It's by the Rhine."

"You're the pilot, son," he said to Jan, "and a fine job you're doing. Tell me, where exactly are we going?"

Jan paused for a moment and looked at Mr. Henner. Suddenly the Canadian laughed out loud.

"What is it, Mike?" asked one of the other soldiers.

"We've been snowed, Ken. Snowed by a bunch of kids. And Old Pops here"

"What do you mean snowed, Mike?"

"Right now we should be taking over from the Krauts in Utrecht but because Pierre is such a bad driver we have been snowed, we are now providing a taxi service for these folks. There was no way they could have made it from Utrecht to here by hearse with all that's happening on the roads. Not a chance. What's your name, son?"

"Jan."

"Good on you, Jan. You fucking snowed us. Sorry ladies, sorry but this kid…he's good."

The atmosphere changed. The Canadians muttered to each other and laughed. We laughed with them. I swung my eyes in Mr. Henner's direction. He hadn't had much to cheer about in recent months, but now he allowed himself the luxury of a subdued smile. It was like the sun breaking out from behind the darkest of clouds to proclaim the dawn. More than anything else, for me Mr. Henner's feeble smile that morning heralded the end of the war. It was as good as over.

"How d'ya know?" I asked the man called Mike.

"Jeez son, that was easy. No tears, not one single tear for the dead man. We're giving you guys a lift home. You fucking snowed us. Sorry again, ladies about my language."

"Problem ahead, Mike," Pierre shouted from the front.

"What is it, Pierre?"

"There is some kind of demonstration ahead."

"Another food riot?"

"Could be. Stay going."

"We won't be able to pass."

We were on Benedorpseweg. The Rhine. Oosterbeek. The woods. We were so close to home. Mr. Heemskerk's house was a stone's throw away.

"You can let us off here. We'll walk the rest of the way if you want to turn," I said.

"Jeez kid, you don't say. Looks like a riot or a mob of some kind ahead."

"How about you Pops? You wanna get off?"

"No, sir. I just want to get back to my hearse," Mr. Henner said.

"With or without Mr. Mayor?"

"I have to take the corpse back to Utrecht with us."

"I thought so."

"This is gonna cost you, Mike. Snowed by a bunch of kids who wanted a lift home, and you bought it. The Mayor of Arnhem! Jeez, Mike but that means free cigars for me for a long time to come."

"Pity the Titanic is already sunk. Otherwise you would have swallowed it, Mike."

"Cut the guff, boys. Stop the jeep, Pierre. Back up to that gateway and turn back."

In a moment we were out of the lorry and on to the ground. The Canadians soldiers helped Nana and Mam down. I took Antje from Mike and he smiled. Jan took Cora. We shook hands with Mr. Henner.

"Call to see me again, boys. I'll miss you."

Tears welled in his eyes. Full marks to Canadians, they knew the parting was emotional. One of the soldiers handed him a small packet.

"You can smoke now, Pops."

"I hope your home is still standing," another of them said to me as the lorry revved and pulled away. When I turned round I saw concern in my mother's face.

"That's Frau Erica's house," she said.

"Becker's House. You're right."

"Oh Holy God and Saint Thérèse," said Nana.

"What is it, Nana?"

"That's Mrs. Koeman with a hatchet in her hand."

"And Mrs. Boom," said Gerrit.

"She's got a hatchet too."

"Look there, that man's got a rope."

"Oh my God," Mam said.

"What?"

"It's a lynching mob."

We came right up to the crowd. Mrs. Koeman's arms were no longer fat and massive, she was now much thinner. So was everyone else. Did we look like scarecrows too?

"We can't let this happen, Nelis," my mother said.

"They mean business."

"I detest Frau Erica but Holland has too many corpses already."

"Your mother is right. Your father would not want this." Nana was in tears.

"What can I do? It's very dangerous."

"Come on, Nelis," Jan said. "We'll try something."

"Let's push our way to the front, up to the gates."

"Ten seconds to open the gates," a skinny man with a knife said.

"Hear, hear. Start counting."

"Or we tear down the gates. Ten, nine, eight...."

Jan and I exchanged frantic glances. There was nothing we could do. Mobs listen only to calls for further action.

"The Greens are still about," I shouted. It was the best I could come up with.

"Not for much longer. Seven, six…"

"Frau Erica is not worth getting shot for. She should be brought to trial."

"Fuck the trial…five, four…"

Others joined in the counting. Everyone was shouting. I saw my mother pushing her way to my side, Antje in her arms. What the hell is she thinking of in front of this mob? I waved at her to stay back, but she kept coming.

"Put her on trial with her Nazi husband. I'll tell you plenty about the two of them." "We know all about her Corrie. Three, two, one…, tear down the gates."

I looked to see who it was that knew my mother's name. It was Mr. Boom of the bicycle shop, Ursula Boom's father. The bad feeling in my stomach grew worse. When a man like Mr. Boom was shouting for blood, the situation was serious indeed. My immediate concern now was to get my mother and Antje away to safety.

"Oh my God."

"What?"

"The gates are open. They've been open all the time," someone shouted.

"The gates are open. Let us go." It was a battle cry.

"Let's call on these good friends of Herr Von Ribbontrop."

Mam and I were swept along in the mad rush through the gates. I saw Jan trying to reach us. The crowd spread out as dozens of people ran on to the freshly mowed lawns on either side of the entrance avenue. A massive chestnut tree stood tall to the right as the avenue turned to the house. No one spoke, the only noise was that of badly worn shoes on the hard surface of the avenue. I experienced an emotional rush. I could soon be a witness to bodies hanging from one of the big branches of the chestnut tree. I didn't want that but I understood the feeling. Mam raised her right arm. She was so thin.

"We're Dutch. We're not Nazis," she shouted, over and over.

Nobody was listening. After the chestnut tree we saw the house, almost blindingly white in the April sunlight. I needed a moment to adjust to the glare as we were looking almost directly into the sun. It had survived the Battle for Arnhem without a hit. Fate had given a break to people like the Beckers. We saw that there were people sitting on the steps to the front of the house, perhaps twelve, maybe more. We tried to slow the mob as it advanced on the house. It looked as if the people on the steps were waiting for us. Right in the middle and surrounded by men sat Frau Erica. The mob halted.

"There she is, there's the bitch," a man said.

"My God, will you look at her," a woman's voice said.

I could scarcely take in what I saw. To the right of 'Frau Erica' sat Mr. Heemskerk with his grey wavy hair and imperturbable smile.

"Holy God and Saint Thérèse." Nana's voice came from behind. "It's Mr. Heemskerk. He'll know about my son Wim."

I searched among the faces. There was no sign of Dad. Before anyone could do anything, Mr. Heemskerk stood up and held up his hand for silence. Everyone fell quiet.

"The SS are gone. We weren't sure whether you or the Greens would get here first. Welcome to the home of Mrs. Beatrice Becker. Every man and woman on these steps owes his or her life to this great lady. She hid us in her basement while she entertained the SS upstairs. She fed us on SS food after they left. She saved our lives and the lives of many others over and over. She supplied me and our Resistance group here in Oosterbeek with vital information for over three years. She saved Mr. Brouwers, who sits here beside me. She saved Luc Gauthier, our dear friend from France. She provided the information that rescued Wim Baumann from the Gestapo while being switched from one prison to another. She saved the life of Mr. Mussel, the jeweller from Arnhem. He's here with us too. Every day for over three years this lady risked her own life to help Holland. To those of you with ropes and hatchets I say put them away, put them down. You don't need them. The days of killing are over."

"Her? She collaborated with them, Mr. Heemskerk," a woman shouted.

"Where do you think my wife and I have been hiding for the last seven months?"

My spirits soared. There would be no lynching, not today or any other day. Those with weapons backed away.

"There's a lot to tell. Right now I see Nelis Baumann and his grandmother out there. I want to speak with them in private."

Nana and I walked forward. From the corner of my eye I saw Mam with Antje holding her tightly. My heart was pounding. We were about to find out the truth.

"Is he here, Mr. Heemskerk?" I said as I approached him.

"He is, Nelis. He's in the cellar. He'll need time. He'll need a lot of time."

"What's the matter?"

"The Gestapo had him for four days before the Resistance rescued him. Four days in the hands of the Gestapo is a long time, son. Follow me."

I walked into the Becker mansion, the White House as we called it, for the first time. We followed Mr. Heemskerk in silence over the panelled floor down a wide hallway. Gerrit and Cora were also with us.

"You'll have a lot to talk about, but for now the fact that you're here is enough. You will have to have plenty of patience."

The basement corridor was over two metres wide, with several doors off it. We walked to the far end and entered a darkened room. I could make out a bed in the corner. I held Mam's right hand as we approached the bed. None of us made a sound. There was a man in the bed, unshaven and asleep.

"Wim? Wim? Wim Baumann? They're here, Wim. I told you they'd come back. Corrie is here and Nellie and Nelis and Gerrit and your new son."

"Daughter," said Nana quickly.

"Wim? Your family is back. Wake up, Wim. You have a lot to talk about!"

The man in the bed blinked. My mouth hung open as I waited for him to say something. His eyes swung slowly from one to the other. Slowly he recognised us, and as he did big tears welled in his eyes. He smiled.

Mr. Heemskerk was right. We had a lot to talk about.

The End

Printed in the United Kingdom
by Lightning Source UK Ltd.
112146UKS00001B/35